Leaving Oxford

Southern Hearts Series

Book 1

Janet W. Ferguson

This book is a work of fiction and any resemblance to
persons, living or dead, or places, events or locales is purely
coincidental. The characters are the product of the author's
imagination and used fictitiously.

Acknowledgments

I've felt like the village idiot since I decided to write this first book. I've asked random questions to friends, family, acquaintances—total strangers. I've emailed people about everything from football to medical issues to mission trip experiences. I've asked dozens of people to read and offer opinions on various versions of this story and to sign up for my blog. If I thanked everyone individually, the acknowledgment would be a novella. But…I have to thank:

God for loving and searching out prodigals like me

My husband, Bruce, for supporting me. My daughter, Mary Kristen, for reading my manuscripts twice. My son, Luke, for putting up with my hours on the computer

My sister, Betty Lister, and my niece, Heather Simoneau, English teacher and technical writer who've edited manuscripts and blogs

My cousin, Brian Hudspeth, who recruits for Tampa Bay and answered many questions

Coach Pete Hurt who allowed me to interview him about the life of a coach

First readers and cheerleaders Melissa Thompson (veterinary medicine advisor), Lisa Cantrell (nurse & medical missionary for Health Talents International, Guatemala), Dixie Livingston, Neddie Joye Tolleson, Kimberly Berry, Beth Hansen, Callie Martin, and all of the Meadowbrook Book Club

Youth minister, Scott Kopf, who offered insight on how men think and was one of the only guys I could talk into reading the early manuscript

People at Ole Miss who answered emails: Matthew T. Vincent, H Freeze, Ev Barrett, Tom Eppes

My fabulous ACFW critique partners

ACFW & RWA Mississippi groups, especially Lorraine Beatty who forced me to write better and Angela Young and Jaqueline Wheelock who tried to help me find my many typos

Mentor author Misty Beller (a saint for answering so many emails), Editor Robin Patchen (Thank the Lord, you made this better!), Cover artist Paper and Sage for a lovely cover

My dog and four cats who sit on or beside me while I write, the reason pets end up in all my stories.

…to bestow on them a crown of beauty instead of ashes…

Chapter 1

Baby steps. Sarah Beth LeClair forced one foot in front of the other and willed herself to soak in the new life bursting around her on the University of Mississippi campus. Dean Latham had been right. Teaching had renewed her…had given her purpose. But this April day, the anniversary of the events that occurred exactly a year earlier haunted her. The day her world came together and then fell apart in a matter of hours.

Only a few more steps to her classroom. She could do this. Cool air blasted as she entered the school of business. Inside the full room, she stood at the lectern and booted up her laptop. She'd barely made it on time, but at least her advertising lecture was ready to go.

The university's quarterback, Cole Sanders, lingered in the doorway with another student.

"Okay, guys, in or out, but close the door. It's time to start class."

The guy beside Cole turned to face her and offered a shrewd smile.

Oops. Not a student.

Riveting brown eyes locked onto her own, launching her heart into her throat. "Oh, sorry, Coach McCoy. From your backside, you looked like a student. I mean, from the rear you looked like…not to say the front doesn't…" She cringed. Not what she'd meant to say at all.

The class let out a snicker. "Hey, Coach McCoy," two girls on the second row spoke in unison and waved.

The former Florida star quarterback, now Ole Miss offensive coordinator, smiled wider, which only accentuated his rugged good looks. And he appeared far too young for his own good.

Despite the air conditioning blowing from the ceiling, heat crept up Sarah Beth's neck into her cheeks. "Oh, my stars." A nervous chuckle escaped as she ran her fingers through the ends of her long hair. "I have no idea what I'm trying to say, but I need to start class. Coach McCoy, you're welcome to stay. Or if you need to meet with me, I'll be in my office in an hour."

His broad shoulders lifted in a shrug. "Since you invited." He slipped into a seat on the second row.

Really? Why would he stay? Cole hadn't turned in the last couple of assignments, but he could still pass. Straightening her posture, she plowed into her advertising lecture, refusing to glance in Coach McCoy's direction until she finished explaining the year-end project. When she paused, the sun had shifted to the perfect angle through the skylight to rest on his hair. Shimmering golden hair.

She needed to focus. On the class.

"This assignment is your opportunity to bring up your average if you're behind." She eyed Cole. "Which you shouldn't be. Your groups are designed to be diverse, so you'll have to deal with a variety of opinions. Soon you'll be out of school, hopefully employed. No matter what field you choose, you'll do a lot of tongue-biting, so get used to it."

Coach McCoy smiled again and nodded, causing the tips of her ears to sting as if fire ants covered them. As if she needed another cocky former football player around, today of all days.

She hurried to hand out the assignment. "If you don't have any questions, you're dismissed." *All of you.*

The coach approached the lectern as students filed out of

the room. "I enjoyed your class and even came up with a few ideas for the football team."

A scent, something like mandarin oranges and spice, drifted to her nose as he moved closer. Too close. Was that luscious smell coming from his hair? Her stomach growled. She did love oranges.

After taking two steps away from the orange aroma, she stuffed her papers and laptop into her tote. If he wanted to talk about his quarterback's grade, he'd have to do it elsewhere. She wouldn't talk about a student where anyone could hear. "We can meet in my office."

He closed the distance she'd put between them and slipped her bag from her hand. "I'll carry this for you, Professor." He curled the bag up and down like a dumbbell. "What's in here? Fifty-pound weights?"

Was he flexing his bicep? Did he think she'd be manipulated into changing Cole's grade? Her jaw tightened as the phrase *Do unto others…*ran through her mind. She sighed and extended her hand. "I recognize you, but I don't think we've officially met. I'm Sarah Beth LeClair."

His grip was firm. "You can call me Jess."

Not changing any grades. No matter how nice his hair smelled. She pasted on a smile and led him toward the exit.

Stifling humidity and heat charged in as he opened the door for her. Summer temperatures had arrived early in Oxford, Mississippi, and took hold, transforming the landscape almost overnight from gray to a bright green. They crossed the grassy lawn shaded with massive oaks, the sweet smell of the town's rampant wild wisteria heavy in the air.

"I love hot weather." They both spoke in unison.

Jess grinned. "That was strange. Are you a mind reader or something?"

"Maybe so. I have a good idea what we're about to discuss."

His brown eyes studied her. "You do?"

Something in his tone caught her attention. She should at least be polite. "But my brain could use coffee first. Hopefully there's a cup or two still left from this morning."

Impossibly, Jess's grin grew wider. "You're definitely reading my mind. I live on it during the season. Good thing the latest research claims it's healthy. A lot less guilt."

"At least until the next study proves that study wrong. But, hey, I'm addicted. I admit it."

At Ventress Hall, the quaint, hundred-year-old building that housed her office, Jess opened one of the tall, white double doors, then waited for her to enter first. "This building has character. Especially the Victorian Romanesque turret."

A jock fluent in architecture? "I love the turret. We called it The Castle when I was in school here."

At the top of the stairs, her assistant, Cassie Brooks, stood behind her desk to greet them. The petite redhead, dressed in the usual business suit, looked over her small glasses and smiled. "Hi. There's a fresh pot already brewing in there."

"Perfect, Cassie. Thank you."

As they entered, Jess scanned her large office, ran his fingers along the mahogany conference table, and whistled. "How did you score this nice piece of real estate?"

"I host Foundation meetings here. Do you take your coffee black, or do you need cream or sugar?"

"Normally black, but today, I'll have sugar." He gave her another grin and moved close to take the coffee from her. Too close. His long, tan fingers brushed hers as she passed the cup to him.

Sarah Beth stepped sideways. Just because most women

fell all over themselves to meet the man didn't mean he could be so familiar. Especially not *today*. "Coach McCoy, have you ever heard of personal space?"

He arched one eyebrow. "Maybe."

"You're in mine." Was that obvious enough for him?

A smile creased the corners of his brown eyes as he stepped away and sipped his coffee. "Wow, this is unrivaled brew. Love it."

"I know. Smooth and silky, but at the same time, bold and rich. The company is a fair trade roastery right here in Mississippi. I'm working on a name and logo." She pushed a wayward strand of hair behind her ear. "Usually branding comes to me so easily."

"Why are you naming coffee? Are you growing it in your backyard?"

A smile slipped past her defenses. "I'm an advertising specialist for the Parker Morgan Agency."

"Thought you were a professor."

"I'm just handling a few classes for Dean Latham. It's been—a blessing. I'm glad he talked me into teaching."

He took in a deep whiff and rubbed the blond stubble covering his chiseled chin. "What about exceptional, unforgettable coffee? Or unrivaled?"

At least he'd paid attention in class. "Brainstorming like I asked the students to do?"

Jess neared again. "You're a good teacher."

She backed out of his proximity and sighed.

"Personal space. Got it." He glanced up and seemed to catch sight of something. A second later, he crossed the room and studied a group of photos on the credenza.

Why'd she let Mark bring those heartbreaking pictures here anyway? "You wanted to talk about Cole, right?" After a minute with no answer, she cleared her throat.

"Sure. But what's up with you and these celebrities? And these doctors?"

A familiar pain crushed her chest and imprisoned the air in her lungs. She struggled to force out words. "Long story."

Jess pointed at one. "This guy was the Ole Miss kicker with the record-breaking field goal, went pro for a couple of years. I can't think of his name right now, but you have a lot of pictures with him. Boyfriend?"

The smiling face in the photo helped to loosen a bit of the chokehold. "His name is Mark LeClair. My brother."

"Oh. Your brother." His shoulders lowered. "I played against him my first year at Florida. Very cool."

Jess dawdled, perusing more photos she'd scattered around the room.

As he peered at her pictures, Sarah Beth studied his profile. Tall. A strong bone structure, square jaw. Didn't look like he'd taken any licks to his nose. Oddly perfect for a quarterback. He would be great in a commercial.

Was she crazy? The last thing she wanted to do was get to know another former football player. Wasn't he here to talk about his quarterback? "What about Cole?"

"He claims his professors don't get the life of a college athlete. I'm guessing because of your brother, you do."

"I do. I was on an athletic scholarship as well. Cole's problem is more ego and being l-a-z-y."

Still inspecting her office, his mouth fell open. "Whoa, are those water skis and wakeboard behind the door available? Why are they in your office? Do you ski?"

Of course, the Florida guy liked to ski. "I'm developing a branding strategy and logos for them, too. I'd like to try them out, but I haven't made it to the lake."

"I have the boat, and if you're available on Saturday, we'll go out to Sardis Lake and get those wet."

Perspiration coated her palms while a boulder seemed to lodge in her throat. Could she go all the way to the lake? With this guy? A tremor rippled through her arms and hands. "I don't know. Where…?" Her ribs clamped down around her chest. She needed to breathe. "Where do you put the boat in?"

"My friends and I put in at Hurricane Landing."

Forcing air in and out of her lungs, she sat and gripped the arms of her chair. Hurricane Landing wasn't far. She'd been there when Mark visited. "I'll meet you there. If I can make it." She needed to think of something else. "About Cole. If he completes this project, he should pass. I have a student, Audrey Vaughn, who tutors. You know her brother Grant." Her fingers shook as she wrote Audrey's contact information on the back of her business card and passed it to him. Maybe he could read the writing.

Jess looked at the name. "Too funny. Her brother Grant's on the offensive line. That should keep Cole from hitting on her, at least, if he doesn't want to *get* hit." He hesitated. "So, what sport did you play?"

"Soccer, but I wasn't a star like Mark."

A knock sounded on the white-paneled doors, then Cassie peeked in. "You have visitors."

"Okay, thanks." Yes, thank goodness. Maybe now this man would leave, and she could return to normal. Or at least this *new normal*. "Sorry, Coach, I mean, Jess. I, um, need to get back to work." Between her stupid anxiety and his good looks, she needed to retake speech class. She escorted him to the door.

"I'll see you Saturday. Is this how I reach you?" He flipped her card over.

She nodded. Once he left, she released a long exhale.

Going to the lake should be easy, right?

Tears pressed at the back of her eyelids. If only her world and her mind hadn't fallen apart a year ago in L.A.

~~~

Jess McCoy sent Cole a text and then fought the urge to sprint back to his office. He'd spent almost two hours on what should've been a ten-minute errand. No time for lunch out before his conference call. It wasn't as if he had a shortage of women interested in him, but he'd followed this one like a puppy to her office—carrying her bag, no less. He'd surprised himself with a couple of audible calls. Not very good ones at that.

Back at his office, his laptop stared at him. Instead of words on the screen, he pictured those dark eyes outlined in long black lashes. He spun her card between his fingers. He'd seen her at a meeting a couple of months ago but hadn't paid much attention. Today, she'd fascinated him—able to laugh at herself when she misspoke, confident when she taught. The way she blushed when he looked at her.

Getting the boat ready for Saturday hadn't been on his agenda, but it was about time for some relaxation. College coaches didn't get much, just the little window between the season, the bowl games, recruiting, spring practice, and summer camps. If he bumped up to pro like he hoped, his life would only get busier. He needed to dive through that window while he could.

The knock on the door signaled Cole's arrival. "I got your message. What's up, Coach?"

Jess handed him a note with Audrey Vaughn's information. "Here's your new tutor. They'll set it up in the academics office."

"Since when did you start going to classes? A sudden

interest in advertising?" His voice held an edge of sarcasm. "Or maybe Professor LeClair?"

"Your business is my business, and my business is my business. Comprende?"

Cole laughed and scanned the paper. "Why the change in tutors?"

"Your professor suggested it. You know, Cole, you're a lot like I was ten years ago. Wanting to go pro. Next season's your senior year, and I don't want anything to stand in your way. Show the scouts you have what it takes."

Jess hoped Cole wouldn't suffer an injury his senior year. Like his own shoulder tear. By habit, Jess stretched his right arm. One freak hit, and the dream of playing professional football evaporated as quickly as a sudden rain shower on a Florida afternoon. His dreams for professional football had turned to coaching, and like he had as a player, he dreamed of going pro. With the latest chatter out of Nashville and New Orleans, that reality was so close he could almost taste it. And he wouldn't be disappointed again.

Cole scoffed. "Wait a minute. This isn't Grant's sister, is it? The guy's a beast."

"So watch yourself. Keep it on the up and up."

"But I like the other tutor. She's hot."

Jess gave him a hard look. "That might be the problem." Another issue he'd dealt with at that age—one more thing he and Cole had in common.

"Okay. I thought you told me something about having a conference call in Coach Black's office?"

"Oh, shoot." Jess hurdled his desk and sprinted down the hall. How had one quirky professor drawn him off course and reversed his whole morning?

Chapter 2

A fashionably dressed, middle-aged couple stood in the reception area chatting with Cassie. The weight sinking Sarah Beth's spirit lightened at the sight. "Bill and Carol? You're here from L.A.?" She threw her arms around her boss and then his wife.

"In the flesh." Bill grinned while Carol cupped her hands on Sarah Beth's cheeks. "You look fantastic. So much better than a year ago."

"Let's get out of here." Her lip quivering, Sarah Beth turned to Cassie. "An early lunch celebration is in order. Would you like to join us?"

"You go ahead. Y'all have catching up to do."

Ten minutes later, they entered a rustic café in the Oxford town square. The smell of fried okra and turnip greens competed for prominence above the blue-and-white-clad tables. Bill scooted out a yellow wooden chair for his wife, and then pulled out another for Sarah Beth.

Carol patted Sarah Beth's hand. "You couldn't come see us, so we came to you. The town's grown since we graduated. We drove around a bit before coming to your office."

The waitress delivered sweet tea and a basket of warm biscuits. Bill passed the bread to Sarah Beth. "Greg Latham says you're doing a great job giving his advertising and promotions lectures."

"I enjoy teaching a few classes for him." Sarah Beth took two biscuits and slathered them with honey butter. Her mouth watered at the yeasty scent. "But don't worry, boss, I'm still keeping up with all the work you're sending me. How are things back at the office?"

"Los Angeles is a nightmare, especially without my advertising prodigy down the hall."

Cutting her eyes toward Bill, Carol stopped stirring the slice of lemon around her tea.

Tension fell down around Sarah Beth's chest like a steel gate. She set aside the biscuit. "What's so nightmarish?"

"Your favorite actor doesn't like the movie promo. And you know his contract gives him control over pretty much everything."

Squeezing her eyes shut, Sarah Beth leaned her head on one hand. "Maybe we could fly him down here? I could talk to him."

"You think Dylan Conner is going to fly to Mississippi? I know we love the place, but seriously?"

Memories washed over her. Like a drowning woman, she gasped in a deep gulp of air. A groan escaped her throat as her eyes flickered open. "I can't go to L.A." She took a deep breath and forced a subject change. "Um… I'm finishing up the ski and coffee campaigns."

"Those aren't in the same league, and you know it." He shook his head. "I can ask Dylan Conner to come to Oxford, but he may laugh me out of a job."

Carol rested her hand on Bill's shoulder. "I insist you stop talking about business. Let's enjoy our lunch."

The waitress took their orders and refreshed their tea.

"So, how have y'all been?" Sarah Beth leaned forward in her chair.

Bill lowered his voice. "We're still seeing a counselor. Before you ask, yes, we are meeting with that friend of yours and studying the Christianity thing."

"I'm excited about the 'Christianity thing.' You know I love you both."

Carol flashed a grateful smile. "We have such fond memories of the business trip to Paris with you. That was a turning point for us. What about you? Are you working on your—issues?"

Sarah Beth massaged the knots pinching the back of her neck. "I'm sort of at an impasse with my doctors. They want me to take anti-anxiety medicines, but I don't want to."

"People take medicine." Carol waved off the excuse. "There's nothing shameful about it."

Then why did she feel like such a failure? "It just seems like if I had more faith, then I would be cured. I feel so stupid and crazy. I should be able to get better without medicine."

"If you had diabetes or high blood pressure, would you take medicine?"

"I've heard that argument, Carol, but this issue is in my mind."

"Your brain is an organ operated by chemicals and electric impulses and a bunch of other stuff I don't understand, but I do know those chemicals can get out of whack sometimes, and medicine can help. Think about it." Carol patted Sarah Beth's arm. "Better yet, pray about it."

"Okay, you got me. I've been praying for a cure but…"

Removing his glasses, Bill focused his attention on Sarah Beth. "Maybe you haven't been listening to the answer."

"You're right." Sarah Beth propped her chin on her hands. "And I can give Dylan a call. Ask him about coming here."

"I'll take you up on that offer. He likes you more than he likes me." One of Bill's brows lifted. "Quite a bit more as I recall."

"Don't worry. I got this." At least, a year ago she would've, anyway. Now, she only talked a good game.

~~~

On the brief drive back to her office, the view of her town and campus relaxed the knots that had formed in Sarah Beth's neck muscles. She passed through the legendary tailgating lawn, The Grove. College students studied under the shade of sprawling oaks and magnolias.

Memories of fall football seasons summoned a smile. Days when luxurious red and blue canopies with flower arrangements and meals served on fine china, even candelabra and chandeliers, crowded every open spot of turf. Fraternity pledges wearing suits and ties along with Southern debutantes in dresses visited the tents set up by parents and friends for socializing, home-cooking, and sweet tea.

Oxford had been a balm for her wounds before, when she was a teen. Her safety net. Warmth and pain mingled and coexisted in her mind here, but the feelings of safety and home and comfort prevailed.

Her grandmother had walked these sidewalks with her. Mark had taught her to drive on these narrow streets.

And then there was Adam.

He'd held her hand under one of the massive oaks. They'd giggled and staggered down fraternity row during the spring parties, talked about their future on the steps of the Union before graduation.

There was no escaping the memories of Adam here. In fact, there was no escaping the memories anywhere. But in Oxford she could function.

~~~

Jess charged up the wooden staircase in Ventress Hall. He paused halfway to the top beside the wall of stained glass and ran his fingers through his hair. What was he doing here? It had been three days. Maybe he should've called instead. At least ten times, he'd picked up her card and his phone but set them both aside.

"Hey, I'm Cassie." The petite redhead behind the desk spotted him and waved him up. "You were here the other day. Are you looking for Sarah Beth?"

Caught. "Yeah, but she isn't expecting me."

"Go on in. It'll be fine."

He climbed the last few stairs, then peeked in the office as he tapped on the open door. "Still good for skiing tomorrow?"

Sarah Beth glanced up from her computer. "Oh, hi."

Those brown eyes. They'd been on his mind all week. "You want to try out that equipment with me and a couple of friends?"

She stared at him and bit her bottom lip.

Nice. He held back a sigh. She doesn't remember or she's changed her mind? "Tomorrow is Saturday. Not supposed to rain and I have a ski boat. You have skis you need to promote." A cautious step brought him further onto the red and blue Persian rug, and he flashed his best grin. "Sounding familiar at all?"

"Are you still putting the boat in at Hurricane Landing?"

She did remember. "Yep. We can shove off about nine. We'll head back when we're bored, tired, or sunburned."

"Let me check my calendar." She stared at the screen without speaking further, tapping her fingers against the wooden grain of the desk.

He studied her silhouette, her straight brown hair falling down past her shoulders. What was going on in that beautiful head? And why did he care so much? "Schedule that full?"

"Uh, no, actually, nothing till about seven tomorrow

evening. Skiing sounds good. I guess."

"Don't sound so excited."

"I'm sorry." She closed her laptop and leaned back in her chair. "I'm distracted, and a bit of a workaholic." Her eyes met his, igniting a spark in the vicinity of his chest.

"All the more reason to get out and enjoy a day on the lake." He held up his phone. "Text me your address. I'll pick you up around nine."

Both of her hands flew up. "No." She breathed deep then lowered her hands and voice. "I mean, I'll meet you there."

A strangely intense reaction, but interesting. And challenging. "I wouldn't want you to get lost."

She stood, came alongside him, and placed soft fingers on the back of his elbow. "Don't worry, I've been there many times." Her hand pressed forward. "See you at the dock. I'll call you if for some reason I can't make it. Thanks for coming by."

Was that a nudge? Was she actually breaking her personal space bubble to shoo him out? Not that quick, she wasn't. He stopped in the doorway and locked eyes with her. "See you tomorrow, Sarah Beth."

"Um, uh, goodbye, Jess."

Was she shy? Or just quirky and standoffish? Either way, really cute. He bounded back down the stairs two at a time, an old habit he'd never bothered to break. Across campus in his office, he kicked his feet up on the desk and began conquering a long list of phone calls he needed to make.

Nick Russo poked his head in. "Hey, man. You rang earlier?"

While ending the conversation on the line, Jess motioned for his best friend to enter.

Nick stood and waited in the doorway, wearing his usual

uniform, a blue university polo and khaki work pants. "Wish I had time to kick my feet up on a desk. I've been outside doing manly work in the Mississippi heat."

"You're management now, out telling other people to do the manly work in the heat."

"Right. It's a bed of roses." A smirk twisted Nick's lips.

"Speaking of getting outside. You up for skiing tomorrow? No practice this weekend, and we're supposed to have good weather."

"Hard to pass that up." Nick bobbed his head. "I'll double-check with my sitter. Is Sam coming as the third man?"

"Yeah." Jess let his feet fall and sat up in his chair. "I'll call Sam just in case, but I invited another person, too."

"Would this other person have a name?" Arms crossed, Nick's eyebrows arched as he leaned against the door frame.

Jess lifted one shoulder. "Sarah Beth LeClair."

"You're bringing a date?"

"No. I don't know. Maybe." The leather upholstery of Jess's chair creaked as he shifted his weight. "She has some cool ski equipment she needs to try out."

"Oh, she has cool equipment. Of course, it's all making sense now." One side of Nick's mouth cocked up. "What is she? Super model? Sports anchor? Actress in town?"

Maybe bringing Sarah Beth out with the guys wasn't the best idea. But she might've said no to any other invitations. "Professor."

"Hmm…tell me more about this professor. Sounds different from your usual outings with women."

True. And the woman was unusual, too. Why did his best friend have to know him so well? "Aren't you supposed to be outside pretending to work?"

"Yeah. I'll leave so you can finish your nap." He turned to

leave, then paused and looked back. "Any word from New Orleans?"

A good kick in the gut would've felt better than the answer to that question. "That's a no go for the fall. But I've got a couple of other options in the works." No way was he giving up on coaching professional football yet.

Chapter 3

Bag crammed to overflowing, Sarah Beth prepared to meet Coach McCoy. Memories of sunny summer days spent at the lake pulled at the corners of her mouth—bare feet, church camp, her baptism, and family picnics with a juicy ripe watermelon for dessert. Sardis Lake—like holy ground—held a special place in her heart.

Water had always called to her and her brother, Mark. Like a second home, both in Oxford and back in the coastal town of Pass Christian, Mississippi, with Mom and Dad. Her mom used to joke that neither of her kids could pass a puddle or pond without getting wet.

Sitting in her dining room at her antique mahogany dining table with her bowl of organic cereal, Sarah Beth imagined herself gliding across the lake. She missed the water, but since the accident...

No negative thoughts. She needed to be able to do normal things like normal people. She pushed back her chair and stood.

Her footsteps echoed on the polished pine through her empty house as she grabbed her bag and a cup of coffee and headed out. The screen door screeched and banged shut behind her.

Situated on the leather seat of her SUV, she stared at the keys in her perspiring hand. A flood of ice water seemed to flow through her veins. Her throat tightened.

Stop. Knuckles white, she gripped the wheel. "I can get to

Hurricane Landing. I went with Mark when he was here. Lord, please help me do this."

Keys in the ignition, she rubbed her palms together and then started the car. *Breathe in.* She sucked in a deep breath. *Breathe out.* She let it go, backed out the driveway, and drove toward the outskirts of Oxford. Stunning sunlight burst through the windshield. All she had to do was watch the road in front. Press the pedal and steer. *And don't think.*

Was her whole body going to shake the entire way? At least she'd made it to the edge of town without turning back.

The tag on the truck in front of her read Lafayette County. Pronounced like the name of the French explorer in other parts of the country, locals pronounced it "La Fay' et" with a distinct long *A,* just another of the many Southern charms she loved about the area. Her chest loosened as she observed the familiar farmland and alternating pine forests on the road to the boat dock.

She hated being late and had left early in case of an unforeseen tractor blocking traffic, which should be the only problem along these country roads. Other than the incessant urge to turn around and break a speed record back to the house.

Almost there.

Sardis Lake came into view—ninety-eight thousand acres of planned flood control. The deluge of 1927 prompted the passage of the Flood Control Act which had been passed with the goal of protecting the precious Delta farmland. The tree-lined shores set against blue sky and water radiated beauty and serenity, and Sarah Beth breathed the sunshine into her soul. A deep impression of love filled her, as though the sun became a kiss from the One who made it. Maybe going to the lake today was the right decision.

The parking lot. Finally. She pushed the gear to park and rested her head on the steering wheel. *Inhale.*

Once her heart slowed to normal, she searched the area for Coach McCoy. No sign of him, so she dug through her oversize bag. Better to keep occupied. Sunscreen, floating key ring, floating sunglass holder, ski vest, and plenty of water. Oh, first aid kit and Bible. She plucked out the Bible. Underneath it, she hit gold. A forgotten bag of sour gummy worms. Mmm. She popped one in her mouth.

The Bible was marked where she'd been studying the book of John, so she opened and read through the passage again.

Reading the Bible had once been drudgery, but after she returned to the Lord while in California, the Word became alive, like a refreshing pool on a hot day. Messages stood out that had never occurred to her during a lifetime of church attendance.

A rap on her window made her jump, a squeal escaping her throat. Brown eyes blazed from under the bill of a baseball cap. It was him. His blond hair peeked out from the bottom of the hat, his five o'clock shadow a little scruffier.

Her face tingled. What was that about? She pressed the button to roll down her window. "Coach McCoy, you scared me to death."

"I heard you scream through the glass."

"I don't think I screamed." Maybe. A little shriek.

"It's Jess." A smile played on his lips.

"Jess."

"And you jumped so high I thought you might hit your head on the roof." He raised his hands. "I didn't mean to startle you."

"It's okay. When I read, I lose all track of time and space."

"Looks like you're reading a good book, or rather *the* Good

Book. Hope you're not planning to preach to me."

"Could be. Or maybe I'm afraid of your boating skills."

He rested his tanned arm on the window and fixed his gaze on her. "Don't worry about my skills."

Face burning. Again. *Oh my stars.* "I'm rolling up the window now." Sarah Beth hit the power button.

"Watch out. I need my arm to demonstrate all my skills." He struck a pose with his biceps curled like muscle-man. His goofy face made her smile.

Not going to admit that was funny. She opened the door and hopped out with her bag.

A sports car and an older black truck zipped into the lot. "Here come my amigos."

A tall blond man who looked to be in his late twenties exited the sporty Mazda. "What's up? Cooler's full and I'm ready to hit it."

"Hey, Sam. Hoping it's not too cold."

The truck parked by the sports car. A dark-haired man lingered on the phone before getting out.

Jess waved him over. "Hey, Nick, come on. I want to introduce y'all to my guest."

Sarah Beth joined the guys and offered her hand to the blond. "Hi, I'm Sarah Beth."

A scowl ran across the man's face. "Sam."

What was his deal? The other one extended his hand. His hazel eyes radiated kindness as he smiled. He stood shorter than the other two, but solid. "I'm Nick Russo. Good to meet you, Sarah Beth. That's a fine Southern double name you got there."

She returned a smile. "My parents couldn't agree on Sarah or Elizabeth, so I got both."

Sam turned to Jess. "You brought a date our first time out

21

this spring?"

Her mouth went dry as she shook her head. "It's not a date."

Jess and Nick exchanged glances.

Jess pointed toward her SUV. "Sarah Beth and I are colleagues, and she brought the goods." He moved to open the hatch. "Help load everything on board." He shot Sam a hard look. "And stop complaining."

Sam grumbled under his breath. "I hope she can ski. I'm not teaching anyone today."

Fire flickered in Sarah Beth's belly. *We'll see who schools whom.*

The polite one, Nick, unloaded the equipment. "Nice wakeboard, Sarah Beth."

Sam picked up the slalom. "This might be worth a try. Let's go." He turned to Sarah Beth. "You don't need that ski vest, you know. We have one."

"I like my bright pink vest, and it may protect me from drunken boaters when I'm in the water."

While Jess got in his truck to back the trailer toward the ramp, Sarah Beth and the other guys stood on the dock ready to help keep what looked to be an old twenty-foot Nautique ski boat lined up or catch a rope.

Sam cut his eyes at her. "Missy, you should stand back. You might get hurt."

"I'll take my chances. I could even be useful." She forced a smile and glanced at the back of the vessel. *Uh-oh. That's not gonna work.* "Wait up a sec." She waved at Jess to stop.

Jess leaned out his open window. "Yes?"

"Sorry to be a bother, but you don't have the plug in."

Jess slapped the side of his truck. "You're kidding. Sam, I thought you were doing that."

"Good eye." Nick went down the ramp to put in the plug.

"Wouldn't have gotten far if the boat was sinking."

The sun shimmered on the water as the boat released from the hitch and floated, sending small ripples in all directions. Had coming out here been the right choice? She bent down on the dock and dipped her fingers in. "Still cold. Hope this boat pulls me up quickly."

The truck parked, Jess jogged back, hopped in, and cranked up the engine. He yelled over the roar. "Don't worry. This may not have a primo exterior, but the motor's top notch. It'll pull up a two hundred and fifty pound man on a dime." His eyes ran over her as he grinned. "Not that you're two hundred and fifty pounds or anything."

The open bow looked inviting—and far from Sam—so she headed to the front and settled in for the ride. The boat took off with a jerk, and the love of the water coursed through her. The wind ran its fingers through her hair. The sun and the scent of spring chased away her fear. No anxiety, no worries. *Thank You, God, that I still have this.*

The water was smooth, perfect for skiing.

Once they reached a quiet spot, Jess cut the motor. "Who's up?"

Nick waved toward Sarah Beth. "Guests first."

"Y'all go ahead."

"No need to be polite," Nick said. "Ignore Sam. If you need lessons, we'll be delighted to assist."

She studied Nick's kind hazel eyes. "To be honest, I'm cold natured. You guys can test the water. I'm soaking in the sunshine first."

"In that case, I'm up." Nick stood and pulled on a vest. "I need to leave after lunch to relieve the babysitter. Mind if I try your slalom?"

"That's why I brought it."

The guys all took their turns with the equipment, Jess last. Once he boarded, he grabbed his T-shirt, made his way to the captain's chair but stopped before he took a seat. Several scars ran across his muscular shoulder, front and back. He leaned around the windshield. "Sarah Beth, man up and hop in."

"You sound like my brother." She laughed, walked to the stern, and jumped over the edge into the water.

Cold. Her skin tightened, and chill bumps popped up. "I'll take the slalom." She hustled to slide her feet in the bindings, then grabbed the rope.

"You good?" Jess called.

She gave him a thumbs up. The boat yanked her out in seconds. The handle felt right in her palms. Curling her fingers tighter, she skimmed the surface of the lake. *As close as I'll get to walking on water.* The cold spray from her ski tickled her calves. Bliss.

Time to jump the wake. For Sam. She angled her ski and giggled as she came down on the outside of the rippled water. Holding on, she continued the jumps until her arms and legs shook. Finally, she signaled for Jess to cut it. He circled the boat to pick her up.

Sam gave her a hand up the ladder and glared. "You were waiting for the water to warm? I think someone was waiting to see what we had, so she could make us look like idiots."

Nick punched Sam in the bicep. "Doesn't take much to make some of us look like idiots."

"Very funny." Sam slurred as he popped open what was probably his sixth beer. "Isn't anyone gonna help me drink this?"

Nick shook his head. "I have a four-year-old to watch when I get home, and Jess doesn't need a DUI in his position."

"You know he could get out of it. And you need to find a

woman to help you take care of the kid."

Nick shot Sam a dark look. "The kid's name is Katie, and do not, I repeat, do not try to fix me up again."

Jess laughed and eyed Sarah Beth. "Why'd you stop the show?"

Her muscles still wobbly, she squeezed the water from her hair and dried off. "I'm so out of shape."

"Your shape looked good to me." Jess's eyes wandered her form.

Rolling her eyes seemed the best way to handle the comment and the gaze.

"Sorry." Jess's lips mashed together before he focused his attention on the steering wheel.

She remained on the bow, but listened to the guys rib each other. Their quips reminded her of days on the water with her brother. But their conversations turned to football and Ole Miss's chances the following season, which dredged up painful memories of Adam. She closed her eyes and tried to block out everything but the feel of the sun on her skin.

Some time later, Nick cleared his throat. "I need you guys to drop me back at the dock. Daddy-duty calls." When they neared the pier, he turned to Sarah Beth. "I'm glad you came. You made a sunny day a little bit brighter."

At least she'd made one friend today. With Jess and his *appreciative* glances, and Sam's enormous chip on his shoulder, she wasn't sure about the other two.

~~~

Jess still held the rope by the dock as Nick drove off. If he didn't deal with Sam's drinking now, someone could get hurt. How long would his friend carry the bitterness from the broken engagement? Of course, Sam's controlling father didn't help matters. "Sam, clean out your cooler at the trash can or put it in your car."

"I'm fine." Sam scoffed. "I have a high tolerance for alcohol."

"That's not how I play, and you know it."

"You're not so perfect yourself."

"Made plenty of mistakes. Will make plenty more." He squeezed Sam's shoulder and glanced back where Sarah Beth still reclined on the bow. "Let's have some fun, man."

"Fine." Sam lugged his cooler up to his Mazda, came back, and plopped down, his lips mashed tight.

Jess motioned to the driver's seat. "Sarah Beth, you've driven a boat. Go ahead and take over to get used to how she handles."

"Sure."

Once she was seated, Jess knelt next to her to demonstrate the controls. A strand of coffee-colored hair fell from her ponytail and blew across her face. He couldn't resist reaching out and brushing it back from her cheek.

Stiffening, she gave him a side glance. "I'm good. Let me know when to hold up for someone to ski."

He could take a hint. She piloted the boat, her dark hair and eyes so brown they were almost ebony. Although taller than most women, about five-ten, she was feminine. Muscular, but delicate.

After a few rounds, Sam's bellow interrupted his thoughts. "I'm ready. I'm going with the wakeboard this time. But, Jess, you're driving me."

Slowing, Sarah Beth cut the motor, moved from the driver's seat. "Not a problem. I'll watch for you, and Jess can drive."

Letting out a sigh, Jess took the captain's seat and accelerated at her signal. He hadn't planned to put up with a drunk. His football players put him in that position often enough. Now he had to babysit a grown man when all he'd wanted was to have a fun day with a pretty woman.

Shadows fell across the edge of the lake. Maybe he should've called it when Nick left. But the sun, the spray of the water, the wind against his skin always brought him back to his days growing up in Florida. If only Oxford had a few orange trees...and a professional football team.

"He keeps jumping the wake and spinning pretty high." Sarah Beth's tone grew urgent. "Are you worried about him? He has to be tiring, plus all that beer."

Worried and ticked off. "Yeah. Signal for him to stop at this next bend." Jess glanced back over his shoulder.

Sam spun up in the air before Jess had the chance to slow. The board flipped to the side, Sam lost it, and hit the water with a slap.

"He's down." Sarah Beth pointed as they came back around. "And he's bleeding!"

Adrenaline took over. "I'll get him." Jess traded places with Sarah Beth and dove in. A shiver ran across his midsection as he skimmed through the chilly water to grab his friend.

Sputtering, Sam struggled against Jess's grip. "I'm fine, man. I just got off balance and took some board across the lip."

Staying close until they reached the ladder, Jess pushed Sam up first and then followed.

"Here." Sarah Beth held out a towel to Jess. "Press this against the cut to stop the bleeding."

Once Sam took a seat, Jess took his chin and examined him. "You've got a busted lip and a nice goose egg on your forehead. We should get you checked out at the ER."

"No way." Knocking away Jess's hand, Sam scowled. "I

used to get harder knocks every week in football."

"We'll see when we get back on land. The team doctor could take a look at least."

Sarah Beth piloted back to the dock and helped Jess hitch the boat to his truck. She knew what she was doing. He had to respect that. Too bad the day was ending like this.

Sam ambled toward his car while they finished up.

"Not happening." Jess sprinted to block his path. "Give me your keys. You can ride home with me, and I'll have someone come get your car later."

"I can drive."

"Not an option, man."

Sam stood motionless. The man could be stubborn. Finally, his mouth drooped, and he gave in with a sigh. "I'm not leaving my car out here. It's my baby. You bring it." He tossed his keys toward Sarah Beth. "Now."

The keys fell through her hands to the ground. She stared at them like they were a water moccasin, paralyzed with her eyes wide and mouth clenched shut.

"Are you okay?" Jess studied her expression.

She bent down to pick up the keys. "Yeah."

Were her hands shaking? What was that about? He wanted to question her, but now wasn't the time. Jess opened his truck door for Sam. "Let's go, buddy. I'm calling the team doctor to meet us at your house if you won't go to the ER." He got in the truck, shut the door, and waited for her to follow. He took another look in his rearview mirror. Maybe Sam's wipeout— maybe the sight of blood... But something was wrong with Sarah Beth.

Chapter 4

Sarah Beth's face went numb. Another road. Another little sports car.

No. This was Sardis Lake. Not L.A. Only a few miles to the center of Oxford. *God, please help me.* She turned the key to the Mazda. Earsplitting rap music blared. She cringed and scrambled to find the volume.

Jess waited in the parking lot. Sam was hurt. She had to drive this little car.

"Lord, I know it was selfish to pray for myself first. I ask for Sam to be okay physically, and for him to find You. Let me shine Your light to him and Jess and Nick and anyone in my path. Help me to see them with Your eyes, hear them with Your ears, speak to them with Your words. Lord, I feel so clueless about the right things to say."

The drumming in her chest subsided, and she pressed the gas and followed the taillights of Jess's truck. The tree-lined country roads looked like home, and they arrived back in Oxford in minutes.

Sam's house stood in one of Oxford's newer upscale neighborhoods a mile or two farther out than the historic homes near the Square. She parked his car in the driveway beside the truck, released a long breath, and got out.

Near one of the tall white columns of the home, the doctor waited under the shade of the porch for Sam and Jess. Once they disappeared inside, Sarah Beth leaned against the hood of Jess's truck. The band of tension around her midsection released bit by bit.

Minutes later, Jess came out. "Sam's going to be okay, but I'll keep his keys for a while. Just throw them in the glove box." He opened the door of the truck for her and waited until she got in.

Once he took the driver's seat, he cranked the engine and turned to face her. "Sorry about ruining a perfectly good day. I promise to make it up to you."

"You didn't do anything wrong. Sam needed to show better judgment." She glanced in his direction, her voice soft. "And thanks for opening my door."

"You're welcome." His lips lifted. "Doc used some of that super glue on Sam's cut. He didn't think Sam had a concussion but told him to take it easy for a few days. Sam will want to strangle me when he feels better, because I called his mother to let her know what happened. She'll check in on him later." Jess massaged his right shoulder.

"Did you hurt yourself?" The scars she'd noticed earlier came to mind.

"Just an old injury."

"I heard about that. You were predicted to be the top draft pick your senior year at Florida. Sorry."

Jess shrugged. "Water under the bridge. Playing pro football may've been what I thought I wanted at the time, but I've loved every minute of coaching. And there's a chance I could coach on the pro level."

Sarah Beth studied Jess as he drove. Watching him handle Sam, he seemed strong and competent, not so superficial like she'd thought that first day in her office. "Are Sam's parents nearby?"

His head bobbed. "His father manages the New South Bank where Sam works."

"Is Sam's father Teddy Conrad?"

"None other."

"Oh." She let that sink in. Teddy served on the Foundation committee with her, and she had a meeting coming up with his wealth management department. "How did you guys become friends?"

"Sam was a backup quarterback for the team my first year as a coaching assistant here. His family and bank are big supporters of the school. He'd been a high school hero in Oxford. I know you might find this hard to believe, but he had a bit of an ego. A few of the guys weren't too fond of him."

"What a shocker." She should kick herself. "That wasn't nice. I don't know Sam, and I've made an idiot out of myself more than once."

"He's not a terrible guy. Bitter about...a couple of things in his life, but he grows on you. Sort of. I can't imagine you making an idiot of yourself, though." Jess's mouth curved upward as he shot her a quick look.

His deep brown eyes only made his finely textured blond hair stand out. Her eyes drifted across the stubble shadowing his jaw. With glints of gold, it didn't look unkempt, but instead looked...roughly attractive. She'd never cared for facial hair, but somehow, he pulled it off. He could hold his own with the movie stars in Hollywood.

Los Angeles. Adam's sky blue eyes.

A shiver worked its way through her core.

"Are you cold? I can turn the air down."

Words choked in her throat.

"Sarah Beth?"

Blinking, she turned and focused on him. "Sorry."

"I'm so captivating that you fell asleep? I said, I can't imagine you acting like an idiot. And, are you cold?"

She needed to speak. "No to the cold, no to the sleeping, and yes to the idiot behavior. I used to live my life very differently. I've changed."

He stole another glance. "What happened?"

"It's such a long story. One I'm not sure you'd care to hear." Not one she was dying to tell. "The simple answer is that I gave my life back to God."

The words hung in the air.

"Are you going to tell me the long story?" His voice softened.

This was unexpected. God had opened a door, but could she make herself walk through it? A lump formed in her throat. Sarah Beth tapped her fingers on the armrest. "I can condense it, I guess."

"Why don't you just tell me in pieces? That is, if you're willing to ski with me—or us again?"

"I had a good time, right up until the end." She gave a shaky laugh. "I'm not sure where to start. I was a prodigal, if you know what I mean."

"I've been to church. So, you took your parents' money and wasted it?"

One side of her mouth lifted. "I was a prodigal child in the spiritual sense. I took all the love God gave me, all the values and wisdom my parents gave me, and walked away from it to do what I wanted to do."

"And what was that?"

Sarah Beth looked out the window at the passing landscape, but memories filled her vision. "I guess, at first, it was going to parties that were pretty wild, that I knew weren't God-honoring. Eventually, I joined in on the drinking, the language, the irreverence. The parties where anything goes, drinking games, people in the back rooms doing who knows what."

"We had those in Florida, too."

"It was sad, though, because my family believed in having good, clean fun. My parents taught us to work hard, but they liked to play hard, too. That's how I learned to ski and kick a soccer ball. Mom and Dad loved to have a house full of family and friends.

"Somehow I made my good grades, and then I met a guy. We got involved and moved to Los Angeles together, where we both pursued our professions. It took some years, some heartbreak, and some soul searching—and I know it's overused, but it really fits to say that I had a God-sized hole in my heart. I begged God to take me back and asked if He couldn't forgive me, to let a tree fall on me or a satellite land on me. I'd made a mess of my life and my heart, and I didn't know how to fix it. I asked Him to put me somewhere I was needed."

This was harder than she thought. Tears filled her eyes and blurred her vision, blurred her world.

They pulled into the parking lot at the dock. Jess put the truck in park, then fixed his gaze on hers. He took her hand as she unlatched her seatbelt, his expression intense. He seemed to peer into her past. "That was honest and deep, and I appreciate how open you are." He offered a gentle smile. "I also appreciate the fact that no trees or satellites fell on us today."

The comfort of his hand both warmed and ripped at her emotions. Emotions she couldn't handle. Forcing a smile, she pulled her hand back and opened the door. "Thanks. I think."

Jess helped gather her equipment and walked her to the SUV. "So, is the guy still in the picture?"

She blinked at his question.

"The one you went to L.A. with?"

That familiar ache wrenched around her heart and twisted. "He's not. And I'm not getting involved with anyone for—let's just say, a long, long time."

"Once bitten, twice shy?"

"Something like that." The ache sharpened. More like a cleated shoe to the chest. Words squeezed from her throat. "I should go."

Jess rubbed his stubbly chin. "That's right, you have plans this evening. Could you, or rather would you, be willing to come skiing with us again next weekend? I won't let you get thrown under the bus rescuing drunken skiers. And it's not a date."

"Same place, same crew?"

He shook his head. "Me and Nick, but Sam may be in the penalty box for at least a week."

"What are y'all, like the three musketeers?"

"More like the three amigos…or three stooges."

She managed a chuckle. "I appreciate your honesty, too. And I do love the water. Maybe I could be the extra amigo."

"Since you love the water." His focus flew somewhere into the distance. "Hmm, I've never had a girl amigo."

"I'm probably more of a stooge."

He flashed his now familiar confident grin. "See you next time, Sarah Beth."

As she drove back down the tree-lined country road, a dam burst inside. Everything rushed back up to the surface. *I miss Adam so much. God help me. How long will it hurt this badly, Lord?*

She wept all the way home, and continued to cry while she showered and dressed. Her body shook with the sobs that overwhelmed her.

She applied Chapstick with shaking hands. No mascara tonight. Then she straightened her shoulders and headed back out the door on her way to help at the Christian Student Union.

Chapter 5

Eight years earlier

Fraternity guys, sorority girls, and jocks all packed into the crowded bar. Sarah Beth endured the mob to catch a glimpse of the popular band. Sweaty elbows bumped her forearm. She moved to the bar and ordered a beer. A soccer game filled the soundless monitor on the screen above her head. Sipping her drink, she swayed as the band began their signature song. A tap on her shoulder turned her head toward a guy wearing a starched shirt and khakis standing maybe two inches away.

"You wanna dance?"

From his breath and his posture, he'd obviously had too much to drink. But she did like this song. Why not? "Sure."

He grabbed her hand and navigated to the front of the packed dance floor. She laughed at his wobbly moves but enjoyed bouncing and dancing around. When the song ended, she stepped back. "Thanks for the dance."

His fingers latched onto her arm. "You can't leave after just one song."

Heat coursed through her, and she planted her feet. *I most certainly can.* His grip tightened as he tried to jerk her toward him.

Another muscular arm wrapped around her waist in a side-hug, pulling her in the opposite direction of the drunk. She whipped around, and her gaze traveled up this new man, who stood at least six-five, his sleek light brown hair pulled back in a ponytail.

"Hey, baby sister. Didn't you know your big brother would be looking for you?" He winked as he drew her close and lowered his voice. "I know Mark."

After she sized up the stranger who'd come to her assistance, she answered the hug. "There you are!" Not one ounce of body fat on this guy and the lightest blue eyes she'd ever seen.

Her would-be dance partner took a step back, then edged away. She and her *brother* made their way back to the bar.

"Thank goodness you came when you did. I was ticked at that guy." She smirked. "I'm Sarah Beth LeClair, but it seems you already know that."

"Adam Lancaster. I was a freshman when your brother was a senior. He's a great athlete, a nice guy. Gave me some good advice."

"Something like 'study and stay out of the bars?'"

"Part of it. He had a word of wisdom for those who cared to listen." Adam chuckled. "He talked a lot about you, too. I saw that guy grab you and figured I'd better intervene before you hurt him."

"Growing up with an older brother and playing sports, my blood boils when I get mad."

"Adrenaline. Athletes thrive on it." He paused and mashed his lips together. "I saw you play soccer."

Her jaw fell. "You did?" She lifted one shoulder. "Then you know I was mediocre."

His eyes traveled down her. "I mean this in a totally non-brotherly way—you had the best legs of any girl out there. That's what stood out in my mind."

For all she knew, this guy was full of it. But he was smoking hot, so she played along. "So you were really into the games?"

A smile moved across his cheeks revealing deep dimples.

"Coach requires us to support other university athletic teams, so I picked girls' soccer. Didn't want to look at more sweaty guys."

She met his gaze straight on. "You have the most stunning eyes. So blue."

"Glad you like." He inched closer.

"Not sure about the ponytail thing though. I don't know if I can feel comfortable with a guy having better hair than me." She reached around his shoulder and ran her fingers through a few strands. "How's it so shiny and silky?"

Adam held her gaze. "I'd have to know you better to share my shiny hair secrets. Want to go outside and get some fresh air?"

"I think I do." She followed him, but hesitated at the door. "I'll text my *real* big brother first to make sure you're a nice guy." She narrowed her eyes. "He's an agent with the FBI now, you know?"

"Go ahead."

Her cell rang after she sent Mark the text. She stepped out the door and walked toward her SUV. Mark spoke on the other end of the line. "Sarah Beth, I'm on a case, so I only have a couple minutes. Adam's not an ax murderer or a rapist, but that doesn't mean I think you should go out with him. We had some good conversations when I was on the team with him, and he was open to me sharing my faith, but he never wanted to commit to it. I hope you'll take things slow. That's my spiel."

"Got it."

"And take your pepper spray, since you're probably not going to listen to me."

She smiled. "Love you, miss you."

"Love you, miss you, but God loves you more. I'll call you tomorrow."

Adam stood an inch away, almost touching her. A breeze drifted over her, and he brushed his lips against hers. "Am I safe enough?"

Sarah Beth inhaled the woodsy scent of his skin. "I have the feeling we're not safe together in so many ways."

Her words proved more prophetic than she could have ever imagined.

They lay in Adam's backyard hammock, talking and kissing all night. Adam asked Sarah Beth about her family, and he was moved to tears when she told him about the fire that had taken her parents.

He shared about his wealthy parents' loveless marriage and his life at boarding schools and summer camps. Adam's saving grace had been his live-in housekeeper, Alma, and her son, Miguel. Alma filled Adam's heart with the motherly love that he so desperately craved, and Miguel was like a brother to him. His dream of medical school and funding a clinic in Honduras were tied directly to Miguel's death from dengue fever. The dream had become his passion and reason to live after he lost his little piece of family and happiness.

"I guess the prep school thing explains this." Sarah Beth loosened his ponytail and let his sandy brown hair fall down to his shoulders.

"You're not just a pretty face." He stroked her cheek. "You're right. I was so tired of prep school uniforms and the mandatory haircuts above the ears. I figured college was my chance to let my hair down before med school. Literally."

The evening turned into morning. The night ended innocently enough, though she knew it hadn't been the best idea to go home with him. It was no big deal. Right?

Chapter 6

He should check on Sam. Jess grabbed a six-pack of sports drinks and a bowl of leftover pasta from the fridge, threw them in the truck, and headed out. Too bad his friend didn't still live right down the street. Sam's ex-fiancée ruined that setup. Along with Sam's dad. At the thought of Teddy Conrad, Jess's muscles flinched. The man was a tyrant and a bully. He hoped Sam's parents had come and gone already.

On the way over, Jess pushed back thoughts of Sarah Beth and their talk. But there she was again. Front and center. The way the words sounded when she'd spoken of her life, the way she'd laughed at herself instead of becoming defensive, her patience with Sam despite his arrogance. *And about that smile.*

In the driveway of Sam's two-story house, Jess parked and slapped his steering wheel. *Time out.* Obviously, Sarah Beth wasn't interested in anything beyond friendship. She'd said as much. After collecting the drinks and food, he pounded down the sidewalk.

No need to knock, so he entered the spacious front entryway. He travelled through the formal living area toward the hall. The TV blared from the back room. "Hey, it's me. I brought dinner," Jess called as he neared.

"I hope you brought enough for dear old Dad."

Jess's muscles stiffened again. *Crud.* Teddy Conrad greeted Jess as he rounded the corner into Sam's room. The old man's Mercedes wasn't outside. So much for getting in and out without running into Sam's father. The man sent him into combat mode. And it wasn't just the fact that Teddy wore designer everything and flaunted his wealth. Teddy defined pushy and controlling. No wonder Sam was grumpy after working for his father at the bank for so long.

"Thanks for calling us, Jess. He does have a pretty good goose egg."

Sam sat up and gave Jess a dark look. "Yeah. Thanks for calling them." His voice dripped with sarcasm. "What's for supper?"

Jess smirked. "Pasta, if you're nice." He turned to Teddy. "I didn't see your car."

"Rita ran to the store to get a few things. She'll be right back."

"I guess Sam won't be needing this food then. I'll see ya later."

"Wait. Sorry." Sam pointed at Jess. "I was just messing with you. Thanks for looking out for me."

"Right. Here's pasta with your favorite alfredo sauce I had left over." He passed the dish to Sam and turned to leave.

Teddy caught Jess's arm. "I want you and Sam to come to the Foundation meeting Monday. I have ideas that could impact the team, and you'll want to be there. I've cleared it with Coach Black."

Jess gave a single nod. "Send me an email with the details."

"And one more thing. I told you about that quarterback in Memphis. His father's a distant cousin of mine and will be in town next week. I'm having lunch with him. Maybe you could happen to be at the same restaurant?"

Was he kidding? There were only certain times coaches could meet with recruits and their parents. And this wasn't one of them. A fire burned in Jess's stomach. "You know I can't do that. Recruiting violations can blow a whole season."

Teddy's hand still held to Jess's bicep, and his tone lowered. "This is a small town. It's easy to run into people on the Square at lunch."

Jess pulled his arm from the grip. "See you later, Teddy. Sam, call me if you need something." His gut simmered. If he'd known Teddy was here… He scoffed. This day started so well. The boat, the sun…that smile.

~~~

Sarah Beth eased into the Christian Student Union parking lot alongside Chris and Kim Hardy, the student minister and his wife.

Chris hoisted a case of sodas toward Sarah Beth. "Look, Kim. We timed it perfectly. Our favorite CSU volunteer can help me carry the heavy ones."

She took the drinks from the lanky thirty-year-old. "You're lucky I love your wife and daughter so much."

As they walked into the old converted warehouse near the Square, Chris nudged her with his elbow. "You know you come for the free food and music."

Auburn curls bounced as Kim shook her head. "Ignore my husband."

"I usually do."

Kim laughed. "How are things?"

"It's been an interesting week."

Chris opened the door, and Sarah Beth blinked as her eyes adjusted to the lower lights inside the old warehouse.

"Hello, beautiful lady. Have you missed me?" With a swift side hug, Bryan Freeman, a university student, appeared from behind her. His guitar case hung on his other shoulder and he flashed a huge smile. "Let me take that heavy load from you."

She paused as she gauged her response. "I'm fine, and it's been like three days since I saw you on campus."

His blue eyes looked out from under the wispy brown hair hanging down his forehead. "That's what I'm talkin' about, Professor."

"That's Ms. Professor to you."

Feigning injury, Bryan laid his hand over his heart. "I see how it is. Now I'm recruiting you to sing with me."

Having an anxiety attack on stage was the last thing she needed. "Don't put me on the spot like last month. I haven't practiced, and I don't do impromptu."

"You know you can do it." He smiled as he plugged in an amp.

Sarah Beth cupped one hand to her ear and headed to the bar with the sodas. "I think I hear Chris calling me to carry more snacks."

"You can't hide. I'll find you."

Though she chuckled at their banter, her throat tightened at the thought of singing before the crowd. Her family had loved to sing, but it had been too long, and with the panic attacks she'd suffered the past year, she couldn't handle the pressure. She was still working on just being normal. She'd better straighten this out now.

She strode back to the stage. "Bryan, please don't call me up. I'd have to practice. I was uncomfortable last time."

His fresh young face lit up. "Great idea. We can practice at Chris and Kim's for next Saturday."

Chris carried an ice chest across the room. Maybe he could help plead her case. "Chris, you want to defend your favorite volunteer?"

Dropping the chest on the counter, he grinned. "Practice at our house Tuesday after family night."

"I thought you'd help me get out of this."

"Maybe God's calling you to share your talents, Sarah

Beth." Chris broke into an off-key rendition of "This Little Light of Mine" with hand motions. "Hide it under a bushel. No. I'm gonna let it shine."

"Stop, stop, Chris." She sighed. "I'll try to sing, but not tonight, and only if we practice to a level of professionalism. In case I feel like I'm gonna lose my lunch or suffocate, I'll only sing backup to your lead, Bryan." She paused. "Oh, and one more requirement."

"Anything for you, Ms. Professor."

"That CSU student minister must not sing. His joyful noise can only be appreciated by the Lord Himself."

"Very nice, Sarah Beth." Chris laughed. "God had to save some talents for the rest of the world. That's what I like to tell myself, anyway."

Now she had another event to fret about all next week. Singing in public and sharing more of her story with her *new friend*, Jess McCoy. Maybe she'd handle things better than she had with the last football player she'd hung out with.

Chapter 7

Eight Years Earlier

As Sarah Beth left Adam's house that morning, still damp from the dew that had gathered while they'd slept on the hammock in his backyard, the cell in her purse chimed.

Mark greeted her with a sigh. "I'm sure you didn't listen to my advice, right?"

As usual, she spilled every detail of the night to her brother, gushing about Adam.

Mark cleared his throat. "I know you don't have another family member to tell this to, but even a sister might think that was too much information."

"Shut up. I think I could really care for this guy."

"Um, sounds like you're twitter-pated, as they say in the Bambi movie."

"Oh, Mark, you kill me with your Disney lingo. Don't you guys watch anything but kids' movies anymore?"

"There's not much on television we can watch without being corrupted."

"I know. I know. Garbage in, garbage out. But, are you saying I'm in love?"

"I'm saying you're 'in like.' You have a big crush, which is usually how being in love begins."

"I want the kind of relationship you and Holly have. How do you know when you find the right person?"

He paused, but Sarah Beth could hear him breathing on the other end of the phone. After another sigh, he said, "I've told you this before. Put God first. Don't confuse passion for love. Love includes the work that happens after the passion. Love becomes a choice."

She'd anticipated Adam's call two days later, but still her breath hitched when she saw his name pop up. There was something between them—something all-absorbing, all-encompassing. Her mind went hazy reliving the soft feel of his lips on hers, the strength of his biceps as he lifted her into the hammock beside him, and those sky blue eyes that riveted her to the marrow.

"This is Adam, your-brother-from-another-mother."

A small laugh escaped her throat. "I'm sorry, but it seems creepy now to think of you in any way familial."

"That was just my catchy opening joke to begin light conversation."

"You plan these things out?" She smiled as she spoke.

"I don't do 'these things.'"

Sarah Beth could practically hear the air quotes around the last two words.

"I stay focused and on-course with my life plan."

"I'm throwing you off course?"

"Yes, Sarah Beth LeClair, you've thrown me off course. Thrown me for a loop. You've thrown me in general."

Her heart swelled, and warmth filled her as she listened to his deep voice. There was a tenderness in his tone.

"I can't eat or sleep or run or study. I keep seeing those dark chocolate brown eyes of yours. I want to dive in and swim. Hold you like the other night. This isn't me. I hadn't planned to get involved with anyone for a long time, maybe never." He laughed, and she marveled at the fact that she already knew the tone—slightly embarrassed, very tentative. "Now that I've scared you off, I wanted to ask if you'd like to hang out. I don't know how to play the games I'm supposed to play. This is all I've got. What do you think?"

He was deep. And hot. Heart-melting. "I'd like that."

Adam let out a deep breath. "So you want to email your schedule for this week, I'll email mine, and we can figure out what works?"

"That's different." She laughed. "But okay."

"Great. What do you like to do? Eat, bike, run, hike? Go to movies or concerts?"

"All of the above." As Sarah Beth hung up the phone, she stifled a sigh. Adam's honesty was so refreshing. When was the last time she'd had a relationship like that? No game playing.

~ ~ ~

The computer screen glowed in front of Sarah Beth as she sat on Adam's couch. She tried to concentrate, no easy feat with Adam at her side. The past month, they'd studied, run, and biked, but never ended up having time for activities like movies or concerts. Their studies were among their highest priorities, but their one other priority had taken her by surprise. *Battling lust.* Why was controlling herself so tough? Never a problem for her. Until now.

Adam took her laptop and slid it to the coffee table. He kissed her again. And again. She drank in the scent of him, ran her fingers through his hair. This was impossible. Wonderful. Scary.

He broke away breathless. "I can't take this anymore. I'm drunk on you, addicted to you. You need to get on birth control, or we're going to have to stop seeing each other."

Searing grief pierced her heart. Stop seeing each other? She opened her mouth, but no words came out.

He wrapped his arms around her and pulled her into his chest, his breath ragged. "I'm sorry. I told you I wasn't good at this. I don't know how… I love you, and I want to be with you, but things are so heated, and I absolutely do not want to have children."

Blinking back the shock, she studied his face.

"I don't want to have children any time in the near future, at least."

Those blue eyes crashed through her defenses. "You love me?"

Adam held her closer. "More than anyone I've ever known."

His strong arms around her felt so perfect. She'd been lonely since Mark and Holly moved away three years ago. She banished thoughts of right or wrong. "I was anemic at my soccer physicals. I've used the pill to control the problem for years."

His muscles tensed, and he pushed back and held her at arm's length. "I don't want you to do something you don't feel comfortable with, but the good, the bad, and the ugly is that I've been disciplined out of fear of pregnancy. There've been times when you've stopped things, and other times when I have, but now I'm going to leave that up to you."

"Gee. Thanks. No pressure."

"I won't pressure you, and I promise you if we are physically intimate, I won't be with anyone else. Studies show that intimacy outside of a monogamous relationship is not only unhealthy because of STDs, but it's also mentally unhealthy."

Her head cocked as she frowned at him. "That's so romantic, Dr. Lancaster."

He cupped her face in his hands. "No games. Just me putting my heart in your hands." With his thumbs, he traced her cheekbones and then her lips, and she gradually forgot everything but his touch.

~~~

Sarah Beth woke to the scent of coffee. In Adam's bed. Guilt and happiness mingled together. It was nice to be close to someone, to feel loved by someone. There was nothing wrong with that, was there?

On the night stand, Adam placed a tray with omelets and coffee for two. His blue eyes twinkled. "Scoot over, and let's eat."

"Wow, food. You'll never get rid of me." Pushing aside the sheets and pillow, she leaned against the head of the bed. She took the steaming mug he offered and sipped.

"Why don't you bring your clothes over and stay?"

The coffee went down wrong, choking her. She grabbed a napkin and covered her mouth as she coughed.

"Sorry." Adam patted her back. "I didn't mean to freak you out."

"You took me by surprise. I have a cooked breakfast, hot coffee, and an offer to move in all before eight o'clock."

"Your day's shaping up quite nicely." He took the cup and set it aside, then slipped his arms around her. "I know you've made my day."

She brought her clothes, toiletries, and a few family photos over that same day.

Chapter 8

Mondays always came too soon. This one was no exception. Sarah Beth reached her office early and set up her projector for the lunch meeting with the University Foundation and New South Bank. Her participation in the previous marketing meetings hadn't been so bad, but she knew little of procuring endowments. Was Sam Conrad going to be there? And if so, how would she manage any awkwardness that might arise? Back in her partying days, she would've joined his revelry at the lake, dipping into his cooler more than she needed to, probably thinking she was cute and witty.

But that was then.

Stomach already growling, she dug through her bag in search of her emergency stash of sour gummy worms. She crammed three in her mouth to ease the rumble. Financial and marketing team members trickled in. No sign of the dean or Teddy Conrad yet. She and Cassie set out the white cardboard boxes that contained deli lunches for everyone expected to attend, plus a few more.

Men and women in suits filed through the door. A bruised but clean-shaven version of Sam materialized among the bank reps with Teddy Conrad, the dean right behind them.

Dean Latham motioned. "Sarah Beth, you've met Teddy. This is his son, Sam."

Slapping on a polite smile, Sarah Beth extended her hand. "It's interesting to make that connection."

Sam's face reddened. He shook her hand and gave a quick

nod.

Teddy gave Sarah Beth a hug. "Sam, this woman is known as a miracle-worker in the marketing industry. She's the creative genius behind some of the most well-known ads in the country, maybe even the world."

She squirmed at his flattery. "I wouldn't go that far."

"My favorite is that dancing frog." Teddy laughed. "I crack up every time it plays. How do you think of that stuff?"

"Well, obviously I'm a little bit weird to come up with that one."

"Wait." Sam pushed his palm out in front of him. "Are you talking about the Super Bowl commercial?"

"That's the one, son. Didn't that crack you up?"

A partial smile formed on Sam's lips. "Actually, it did."

Sarah Beth shrugged. "See? Weird. I go around the house writing down peculiar ideas. You wouldn't believe the ones I've tossed out." She put her hands on her empty stomach. "I don't know about y'all, but I'm starving."

"Me, too." The dean grabbed a lunch box and opened it. "Let's eat."

The meeting and eating at the long conference table in her office commenced. Sarah Beth threw a couple of concepts on the screen while they ate.

Teddy glanced at the door a few times, then pulled his phone out to make a call. He scowled as he whispered into his cell. "Where are you?"

A familiar voice answered in the doorway. "I'm right here. Sorry I'm late."

All eyes turned to the entry as Jess strolled in wearing a blue linen suit. At the sight of him, Sarah Beth swallowed a partially chewed potato chip, which sent her into a coughing fit. She tried to stifle the whooping sound coming from her throat. "Let's continue."

He took an empty seat, and the dean passed him a boxed lunch and tea.

"I'm glad you're finally here, Jess." Teddy pointed across the table at Jess. "I want to put a face on our marketing campaign, and for obvious reasons, I think Coach Jess McCoy is *the face.*"

A small bit of tea spewed from Jess's lips. He covered his mouth as he sputtered. "What?"

Teddy ignored the outburst. "We can put him on billboards, the website, and in print. As offensive coordinator, he already pulls in recruits for the team. Why not use him to pull in benefactors, endowments, prospective students?"

Sarah Beth passed Jess a stack of napkins and attempted to hold back a smile. Nice to know she wasn't the only one being thrown for a loop today.

Dean Latham rubbed his chin and looked at her. "You're the advertising genius. What do you think?"

"I don't want to be a wet bucket or anything, but I don't think we should use Jess's face. Not that his face isn't good enough. I mean it's perfect, but—"

With a napkin covering his mouth, Jess turned her way. His eyes flashed.

Was he trying not to laugh? "Let's think this through. What if Jess gets a great job offer somewhere else?" Would he get a job somewhere else? He'd said he wanted to coach in the pros. "All our apples would be in one basket." Another reason not to get too close to Jess McCoy.

He lowered his napkin, eyes still twinkling. "I think you mean wet blanket and eggs."

"What? Anyway, he might leave, he might not, so maybe use him as one of a number of people. I'm sure we can come up with a few more marketable faces."

"I think she's right." Jess bobbed his head, his fingers running across his scruffy chin. "Not everyone likes the same face. Use some of the other coaches, players, students, professors. A diverse collection." He motioned toward her. "Professor LeClair's face is nice."

Sarah Beth managed a weak laugh and avoided Jess's gaze. "Other than suggesting me, great ideas, Coach McCoy. I'll get to work on that right away."

She went on to lay out her marketing campaign for the group. An hour later, she leaned back in her chair and folded her hands. "We've made a lot of progress today. I know you all have business to attend to, so—"

"Wait." Teddy cleared his throat. "Before we disperse, I suggest Sarah Beth bring the faces we choose to Memphis for a shoot. A top-notch photographer in the area handles the bank's business."

The tingling started in her hands and climbed up her arms. Her ribs tightened around the half breath she managed to suck in. "I can't go to Memphis. I…"

"Sarah Beth's plate is full." Dean Latham made a broad gesture. "Besides her own busy career and the foundation work, she's teaching Advertising and Promotions classes for me."

She found her voice. "Send your photographer here, and I'll direct the shoot."

Another nod of approval from Jess. "The photos should be set in Oxford, anyway."

The backup helped, but it sent another rush of steam to her cheeks.

At the close of the meeting, Dean Latham gave her a hug. "All fantastic comments and ideas, as usual."

She whispered, "Thanks for saving me from the Memphis trip."

Jess excused himself and hustled out the door. The last person mulling around was Sam. He approached her when the office emptied. "I appreciate how you handled our introduction. Sorry about Saturday. I could buy you lunch or something this week as an apology?"

Not in a million years. She bristled but controlled her expression. "That's not necessary." The phone on her desk interrupted. Thank goodness. "Sorry, need to take this."

She hurried to pick it up. "Hey, Dylan. Thanks for returning my call." She slipped a glance toward the door. *Yes.* Sam was leaving.

"Los Angeles isn't the same without you, gorgeous." Dylan Conner answered in his velvet voice.

Her relief diminished at his words. One hot mess walked out the door, but she'd dropped into another. "So how about you come visit my hometown, and we'll hammer out the promo details away from L.A. and its distractions?"

"Sounds inviting." Dylan's tone held a smooth and flirtatious air as usual.

"My assistant in L.A., Jill, can handle the arrangements for you."

"I can make a flight reservation all by myself."

"I can expense your trip."

"Not a chance. I'll pop in as soon as my schedule opens. I always look forward to seeing you."

Pop in? "Text me if you want me to make hotel reservations. They stay full here with all the events in town."

"Will do."

"Oh, I can't wait for you to taste some famous Southern cooking."

Dylan coughed. "Whose Southern cooking? Not yours, I hope."

"I didn't say I was cooking."

"Thank goodness. I value my health."

"I *did not* make everyone sick that time." She gave a little huff. "It was a coincidence. Let me know when you make your travel plans, and be careful, okay?"

"I can't promise to be careful, but I'll try not to get hurt. I look forward to spending time with you."

Such a flirt. "Bye, Dylan."

Now to plow back through the specs for Dylan's latest movie before the so-called "Hottest Man Alive" descended on north Mississippi, hopefully incognito.

Hours later, she shut her laptop and closed her eyes. Talking to Dylan brought back so many memories. Painful memories, she couldn't deal with.

In Oxford, she'd tried to forget her past, leaving her feeling like little more than a warm body most days. Some hurts left too big a scar.

What do I do, Lord? I keep going through the motions of living, but I'm so lonely.

Blinded by tears, she grappled to find her phone and make a call. She needed to talk to family.

"Hey, Aunt Sarah Beth." A happy young voice answered on the second ring. "Guess what? I'm teaching my dog a new trick. He's learning to roll over."

His simple words lifted her spirits. "That's great, Drew. You should bring Winnie next time you come to Oxford."

"When are you coming to Atlanta? You could get a dog, and they could play."

Biting into her lip, she sighed. "Wouldn't that be fun?" Her words at least sounded sincere. "Is your dad helping you train

Winnie?"

"Nope. He's out of town for work. He's gonna bring me a surprise from Washington, D.C."

"How sweet. You know, I can't wait for y'all to come over and visit soon. I'm getting the pool cleaned this week. Start bugging your mom and dad to bring you when school lets out, and I'll clean up the pool house, too."

"Okay, Aunt Sarah Beth."

"Love you, miss you, Drew."

"Love you, miss you, but God loves you more."

He already talks like Mark. I wish I could go see him.

Chapter 9

The scent of coffee and something fried sent a growl through Jess's stomach. His best friend could always be counted on for a good cup of brew before work. From the smell of it, maybe breakfast. He slipped in the door of Nick's small, two-bedroom townhouse. "You have some grub? I'm starving."

Nick stuck his head around the half wall that separated the kitchen from the minuscule foyer. "Got coffee, and frying eggs. You want some?"

"That'll work." Jess helped himself to a mug, filled it with steaming black coffee, and plopped into a seat at the small oak table. "Where's little bit?"

"The carpool picked her up early. The preschool's taking a field trip to the Memphis Zoo this morning." A heavy sigh followed his words. "Too many irons in the fire at work for me to go. I'm sick about not being with her."

If only Nick could find another good woman, like Paige had been. "You're doing the best you can. You're a great dad."

Nick flipped the eggs onto plates and joined him at the table. "Thanks."

"I'm disappointed I missed seeing the princess today, but she'll have fun. And it's the best preschool in Oxford." Jess smirked. "I'm sure some of the moms are disappointed the single dad's not there."

"Speaking of single, that's a nice girl you brought skiing. I know you *only* invited her because of the *great ski equipment*, but she was the first girl I've seen you with who wasn't—how can

I put this nicely? Snooty or shallow. Of course, I rarely see them more than a time or two, so how would I know?" A puff of air whooshed through Nick's lips. "Oh, except for that Sophia. And you know what I think about her." He cut his eyes at Jess and shook his head.

"Is the monologue over?" Jess wiped his mouth. "You're ruining the eggs."

Nick looked at Jess's empty plate and cocked an eyebrow. "Doesn't look like I ruined them too much."

Laughing, Jess rinsed his dish and put it in the dishwasher. "Can you get off Saturday and bring Katie on the boat? I was thinking of taking it out again, and I promised her she could ride soon." He slung back the rest of his coffee.

"Any other ladies going?"

With any luck, but he wouldn't give Nick more ammunition. Jess turned and walked to the door. "I'll let you know."

As he headed back to campus, Nick's ribbing trailed him. Or maybe it was thoughts of Sarah Beth. There she was again. The fact that he was pleased with Nick's approval only unnerved him more. He needed to clear his head. The woman only wanted to be friends.

At the practice field, Jess sprinted between the white lines, dropping and pushing up in intervals. He ran until his sole focus became breathing and forcing his muscles the next inch. Sweat dripped from his forehead as he rested his hands on his knees and panted.

Cole jogged onto the field. "What's up, Coach? Thinking up a new torture drill?"

Maybe torture was the only thing that would take his mind off this woman.

~~~

Early as usual and prepared for her babysitting duties, Sarah Beth let herself into Chris and Kim's yellow cottage on the north side of the Square. Her bag pulled hard against her shoulder with the items she'd packed for a tea party and painting with watercolors. Contemporary black frames lined the light blue walls of the quaint home, holding photos of family and students. The smiling faces exuded warmth as she walked through the den.

"Camilla's waiting in her room wearing an old Furby costume she found at a garage sale." Chris whisked by, carrying a tray of hamburger patties. "She plans to decorate you, too." Turning back, he grinned. "But seriously, thanks for helping out with our CSU family night."

"I enjoy it." She waved him off. "And I get off easy on Tuesdays. You have to deal with students' deeper issues."

Flapping the spatula at her, Chris furrowed his forehead. "And the grilling. No one would come if I let you grill the burgers again."

"I only burned them once." And she'd never live that down.

Chris shook his head. "We had to call the fire department."

"That was a fluke. Something must have fallen in the grill." She left the kitchen and walked down the little hall to Camilla's room. "Hello. Is Furby here? I hear we're playing dress up."

"Hey, Ms. Sarah Beth. I have a costume for you, too." Camilla picked up a spotted headband with large pink and black ears glued on it. "You put this on your head. I have pink and black face paint to make the cow face."

"I can't wait."

They played through the evening. She loved this time hanging out with Camilla, but her heart pinched a little, too. Once, she'd imagined having a home with children. A family.

With her problem, that dream seemed unlikely.

Near bedtime, Kim came to take Camilla for a bath. Sarah Beth sat on the fuchsia-colored rug, putting doll furniture back in a large plastic container. With the costumes stored away, the mess cleaned up, she was ready to leave. Maybe Bryan would go home and forget about the singing. One could hope.

As she pushed up from the floor of Camilla's bedroom, he appeared at the door. "Time to practice, Ms. Professor."

Oh, shoot. He didn't forget.

His head stretched forward, his eyes glued to her face. "What are you?"

Her hands went to her cheeks, dotted with makeup for that perfect bovine look. "New trend."

"I hadn't heard."

"I'm starting it."

"Whatever you say."

"I'll wipe this off and be right out." Maybe.

The paint required a good bit of scrubbing over the guest bathroom sink. Not quite as washable as the label suggested. After five minutes, most of her skin had returned to a near normal color. *On to face the music.*

Outside on the deck, the spring humidity held on, but a gentle breeze carried the scent of Confederate jasmine. Sarah Beth eyed her instrument of torture. Bryan Freeman. At least the rest of the students were gone. But the kid did have a voice as good as or better than any she'd met in show business. The pitch and quality were dead-on. Not to mention his range and resonance. One of her connections might speed up his career. Plus, if he made it big and moved to Nashville, he couldn't put her on the spot at the CSU anymore. She'd have to make that call soon.

As she neared, he grabbed his guitar and patted the patio

chair next to him. "Now, Ms. Professor, I think you will sound super-terrific singing a duet version that I created with a Third Day song. After that, I came up with another older song from Chris Tomlin that I think would be perfect for you. Are you sure you won't solo?"

Sarah Beth crossed her arms. "Hmm, let me think about that. No."

"Fine. No solo." With a smile, he slid some sheet music in front of her and strummed his guitar. "Jump in when the Spirit leads."

After putting Camilla to bed, Chris and Kim dropped into patio lounge chairs and kicked their feet up.

Her chest tightened. At first she tried not to look at Chris and Kim, who were watching them, smiling. But as the music took over, she let herself go. The duet Bryan worked out was lyrical and smooth and passionate.

"I feel like I'm on holy ground," Chris said as the song ended. "That was unearthly. Thank you. I hope you sing for the group. Sarah Beth, I know you don't feel comfortable doing it right now. So practice whenever you need to here at our house. I could listen to that all week."

"Me, too," Kim added. "I feel truly uplifted, even after such a long day. That's the power of song."

Bryan gave Sarah Beth a little push on the arm, lifting and lowering his eyebrows. "What'd I tell you?"

Maybe there was hope for her to overcome at least some of her anxiety. She sighed. "I give. Let's practice some more. You never know who might show up to hear it."

Chapter 10

Friday arrived in what seemed like an instant and an eternity. Sarah Beth had barely looked up from her work other than to pop sour gummy worms in her mouth. Another huge project deadline loomed, but she did her best work under pressure. A knock on her office door startled her. She jumped and the last gummy worm lodged in her throat.

Her gaze ran across Jess McCoy's broad shoulders when she looked up. This was unexpected.

"I'm sorry to scare you—again." Jess gave his usual self-assured smile. "You have to admit, you're a pretty jumpy person." He made himself at home, perusing the spacious room. "Are you going to offer me coffee, or skis—or some other little treasure you have stashed in here?"

The lump of candy slid down her throat after a hard swallow. She held out a handful of her treats. "Gummy worms?"

Jess did a double take. "Junk food? I pictured you a free-range chicken, organic milk type."

"This is my emergency stash for stress relief. Everyone has their vice."

Jess moved closer and looked down his faultless nose at her. "Any other vices you want to let me in on?"

Not going to blush. "So what brings you by?" She popped a piece of candy in her mouth.

He sat on the edge of her desk, maintaining eye contact. "Ready to ski tomorrow?"

Breaking from his stare, she chewed and fiddled with a stack of papers, pretending his proximity didn't make the tops of her ears feel sunburned. "What time?"

"Turns out I have to work in the morning, so after lunch?"

Not going to look at those brown eyes. "I have a few hours free."

"That should work. I need to text Nick and see if that works for him and his daughter."

"What's his story?"

Jess stood and looked toward the window. His shoulders sagged, and his expression softened.

Something was wrong or her question had been too personal. She held up one hand. "None of my business."

"It's fine. His wife died in childbirth. Her blood pressure."

Small needles of pain jabbed at her heart. "That must have been so difficult."

"It's been tough." His chin dipped in a slow nod. "Nick and I have been friends since we were kids back in Orlando. He went through a rough patch when we were in high school, started going down the wrong path. He and Paige met around that time. He was crazy about her. She told him to shape up or ship out. He shaped up and never looked back."

"She must've been a great lady."

"They married when they were only twenty. Were good together. They finally decided they could afford to have a baby." His voice took on a hushed quality, and a shadow passed through his gaze. "Paige had been perfectly healthy, but her blood pressure went through the roof the entire pregnancy. The doctors put her on bed rest, but when she went to deliver, she had a seizure. They lost her."

Jess studied his hands. "It devastated Nick, but he had an infant to care for. His mother was useless. Her mother just wanted to take the baby. He has a landscape management degree, so I found him a job here. We checked around with some of the coaches' wives for recommendations on babysitters and preschools."

A surge of admiration washed over her, bringing moisture to her eyes. "You're a really great friend to him."

The confident expression he normally wore transformed to something more humble. "Yeah, well, I never had a brother. He's as close as it comes." Then his jaw dropped, and he slapped his hand across his chest. "What? You didn't think I could be a good friend? You barely know me."

"You're right. I don't know you—I guess."

His eyes bore into hers. "So get to know me."

The challenge both burned and muddled her thinking. She picked up her stack of papers and straightened them a few times before speaking. "Uh, so, let me know for sure about the time tomorrow." Could he hear her heart galloping?

Jess grinned. "See you tomorrow, Sarah Beth."

"Goodbye, Jess."

~~~

Jess stifled a fist pump on his way down the stairs. Adrenaline coursed through him like he'd thrown a touchdown pass. His feet stopped midstride. *Whoa.* Why did she affect him that way?

His phone chirped. He checked the caller ID and switched off the sound. A bitter taste filled his mouth, replacing the sweetness from a moment before. Not *her.* Not now. He picked up his pace across the grassy lawn. Forget the sidewalks. He needed to go for a run.

His phone vibrated. Sophia again. She was one warhead of tenacity. Nick was right. He should've put an end to this years ago. They rarely saw each other anymore, and being together meant little to either of them. Mostly just a habit. A really bad habit.

Chapter 11

Six Years Earlier

As graduation neared, Sarah Beth ran scenarios through her mind. Over and over.

Mark begged her to come to Atlanta and find a job there—live with him and Holly as long as she wanted. But how would her relationship with Adam continue? If they couldn't be in the same city, would he still want to be with her?

With a recommendation from Dean Latham, Sarah Beth received an offer in L.A., the same city Adam was accepted into medical school. She took the position and planned a celebration dinner at his favorite Mexican restaurant.

Once they'd placed their orders, she caught his hand as it hovered over a bowl of salsa. "Adam?"

"Si?" He'd drifted to Spanish to speak with the wait staff, a skill he learned from his childhood friend, Miguel.

"Should I be looking for my own apartment in L.A.?"

After rising to his feet, he came around to her side of the booth. "Scoot over." He slid in beside her. "Sarah Beth, I'm sorry."

A hollow ache filled her heart, and she brought both hands to her quaking stomach. "It's okay."

"I assumed that you knew I meant for you to live with me. Will you?" He pulled one of her hands over his heart.

"Will I what?"

"Stay with me, like we are, sharing my home?"

Shrugging sagging shoulders, Sarah Beth scrunched her

nose as she spoke. "I guess."

"That was not quite the reaction I was expecting, but I'll take it." He wrapped her in his massive arms. "I love you, Ms. LeClair."

As happy as she was, those last few words lifted a bubble of apprehension.

Ms. Sarah Beth LeClair, not Mrs. Adam Lancaster.

~~~

They found an older studio apartment with a living room and kitchen combination. Wood floors covered the small space, but a high ceiling gave the area a larger feel. A brick wall on one side added character, as did the wrought iron spiral staircase that led to the bathroom and bedroom loft. With a broad sweep of her arms, Sarah Beth motioned towards the tall wall by the staircase. "I think we need a colossal painting here."

Adam clucked his tongue. "We can't go buy a huge piece of art for a while."

His tone ruffled her. He'd never asked her about her finances, so why did he assume she couldn't afford it? "I'll find a bargain, or maybe a big canvas to paint an abstract myself."

"Let me know the cost first."

Anger ignited in her gut and steamed up to her ears. "Adam, I have a job. I'll buy it after I give you half the rent and utilities."

He stepped back and studied her. "Sorry. I see I've hit a nerve, but I don't feel like you should pay to live with me. You didn't before."

"Because I already had the house in Oxford. I was staying with you in a place where you already lived. This is our home, not just yours, right?"

"Of course."

"Then I'll pay half of everything and buy things I feel like

I need or want."

"Fine, but be careful. People rack up debt quickly with credit cards."

Was the steam firing from her ears? She thrust her hands to her hips. "I wasn't expecting a lecture because I want to buy something to hang on the wall. If you must know, I won't be going into debt."

"Why's that?" He crossed his arms and stared.

"Because." This wasn't the time to go into the amount of her inheritance. Not like this. "I follow the Dave Ramsey plan."

"Who's Dave Ramsey?"

"Really, Adam?" She blew out a long breath. "Never mind. What's for supper? Want me to cook, or do you want to make something?"

Adam pursed his lips. "Hmm, let me think. I'm hungry so...definitely do not want you to cook. I'll do it."

"What does that mean?"

With one long step, he reached her and pulled her to him, covering her mouth with his own.

His kisses still left her breathless. When he released her, she found her voice. "You cook. I'll do the dishes."

~~~

The thrill of working in a high-rise in downtown Los Angeles with walls of windows overlooking the city still hadn't grown old. Every day Sarah Beth glided into the posh building, a rush of adrenaline pulsed through her veins. Her brain churned, whipping out ideas. A major food company had chosen her pitch for a Super Bowl commercial. Would Adam be as excited about her promotion?

After work, she fumbled for the keys in her bag and unlocked the door. She gasped when she saw a well-dressed middle-aged couple sitting on her couch.

"Are you a friend of Adam's?" The tall, thin woman's left eyebrow rose with her voice. "We're his parents. We were in the area and came to see where he settled."

She needed her business face. *Smile*. Like this was normal. "It's so nice to finally meet you. I'm Sarah Beth." She set her bag near the door. "Where's Adam?"

"He's in the shower. Would you like us to tell him you came by?"

Numbness clung to her extremities. His mother obviously had no idea that she lived here. Now what? Not the way she'd hoped to meet the Lancasters. Adam's father sat reading the *Wall Street Journal*, not even looking at her.

Sarah Beth leaned against the bar that divided the kitchen and living room, wringing her hands. "Did he know you were coming?"

"We surprised him."

Struggling to come up with what to say next, she pulled out her laptop and laid it on the counter. "That's nice."

Adam's bare feet clomped down the stairs, his hair wet, still buttoning his shirt. "Sarah Beth, you're early." He pulled her close and kissed her, like always. The knot forming in her shoulders loosened a bit.

"Mom and Dad, this is Sarah Beth—the girl I emailed you about."

Adam's father finally looked up from his paper. "The one from Oxford? Are you visiting too?"

"She lives here. I told you a long time ago we were living together."

His mother's face screwed into a frown. Her designer pumps slapped against the wood floor as she stood and paced. "You didn't say you were bringing her to L.A. I hope you don't think we're supporting both of you." She stopped in front of Adam and squared off with him. "Remember your trust fund can't be touched until you're twenty-five."

Sarah Beth's vision blurred. This was so awkward and humiliating. She needed to leave.

Adam squeezed her close and kissed the top of her head. He lifted her chin and looked at her. "Sarah Beth has a job and pays half of everything. I never mentioned her moving out, so I thought you knew we were still together." His gaze returned to his parents. "Most of the time you don't respond to my emails, anyway."

His parents only called Adam a few times a year, and now they'd shown up holding money over his head. Infuriating. She couldn't be in this room one more second. "I'm going to change clothes." She broke from Adam's grip.

Upstairs, she leaned against the wall and slid down to the floor. Her hands covered her eyes as if she could block out the image, but the conversation downstairs was still audible.

"You need to be careful." Mr. Lancaster's voice carried through the apartment. "You don't want to be tied down to a wife or baby."

"I'm in medical school. I think I'm smart enough to figure out how that works."

"You're smart, good-looking, and you come from money." Mrs. Lancaster's tone became a whine. "You're going to have gold-diggers after you."

"Tell me about it." Clearly, Mr. Lancaster's dig had been intended for his wife.

"Don't start with me," she fired back. "Adam, we can't support you as long as this girl is shacking up with you."

"Really, Mother? After the example of fidelity you and Dad set, you're going to lecture me on morality? I want nothing to do with marriage if it's anything like what you two have."

Sarah Beth's stomach twisted. *Nothing to do with marriage?*

"Your mother's right." Mr. Lancaster's voice grew cold. "You can pay your own bills until you receive your trust fund. A good dose of reality's an excellent idea. Let's go back to the hotel and leave Adam to figure out his new budget."

The slamming door left a thundering silence in the small apartment. Her heart ached for Adam. His parents never had time for him—only their money and social life. She stood and came down from the loft to go to him. He looked like an orphaned little boy. In so many ways, he was and always had been.

~~~

The next morning, Adam left much earlier than usual. On the way home from work, Sarah Beth picked up his favorite Mexican takeout and taped a note on the box that read, *Te quiero siempre*, I love you always. She hadn't called him or pressured him to talk about what had happened but waited up for him on the couch, struggling to concentrate on the work she'd brought home.

Her mouth fell open when he finally walked in. "Wow, you cut your hair." She darted over and ran her fingers through the short strands. "You look so handsome. Not that I didn't love it long before, but now you look…professional."

"So you still dig me?"

She clamped her arms around him. "I still dig you. And I have your favorite takeout in the fridge."

After pulling away, he flung himself across the couch. "I'm not very hungry. I ate at work."

"Work?"

"I got my new look so I could find a job. Gotta pay the rent, you know." He rolled his eyes and sighed. "It's for the best. I found a part-time position in the research lab with Dr. Rodriguez. I spent some time with him there tonight. This could even help me match up with a residency here. The bad news is I'll be gone more."

"I understand." She retrieved his meal from the refrigerator and sat on the edge of the couch. "At least read the note, even if you don't want the food. It's part of my surprise."

Sliding her hair away from her neck, he barraged her with light kisses. "I do like surprises."

"Not that kind of surprise." She pulled the note off the box. "Here."

He read the note aloud. *"Te quiero siempre.* You love me always—in Spanish?"

"No, silly. I'm learning Spanish. When it's time, I'll tell every bigwig I meet that they could, and should, be a part of supporting your research mission. And I want to go with you to Honduras…learn to help at your clinic. My career is based on sales and making money, and it seems so frivolous compared to what you're planning. I want to use my talents to do something important. I want to be a part of changing the world, too—with you."

Adam kissed her neck once more. "Thanks for the surprise. Maybe I'll eat the food. It is my favorite."

Chapter 12

Morning sunlight streamed through a slit in the curtains dispersing light around the silent bedroom. Another lonely Friday night in Oxford had ended. Sarah Beth slid from under the covers, pulled on gym shorts and a T-shirt, and trudged toward the kitchen. After starting a pot of coffee, she stepped through the front door onto the wide, wooden porch that wrapped around three sides of the house. Melancholy thoughts dogged at her spirits, but she shoved her feet forward and scanned the sidewalk for the paper.

A piercing squeal ripped the tranquil morning air. What in the world? She tiptoed down the stairs. From the left, in the bushes, emerged a rustling noise. Maybe she should find some kind of weapon.

Another howl threatened to shatter her ear drums. Then she caught a glimpse of something out of place. A brown cardboard box lay partially hidden behind the bushes.

"Oh my stars, that better not be what I think it is." She bent down and touched the box. Holding her breath, she pulled open the lid. A pitiful baby animal looked up at her. "Yep, that's what I was afraid of. But what are you?" She scooped up the tiny thing which was barely the size of her hand. "Really, Lord? I did tell you I was lonely, but..." The animal shivered despite the warm weather. "Let's go find a vet."

Back in the house, she sank onto the couch with the animal on her lap, and sent a text to Chris.

You up?

Maybe there was a vet at church.

He phoned back. "Little kids get up early on Saturday. They don't know about sleeping in. I'm letting Camilla paint my toenails so Kim can get some rest."

Sarah Beth laughed at his monotone voice. "That's sweet of you."

"Not really. It's Kim's turn." Chris yawned in the phone. "What are you doing this morning?"

"I need a vet."

"Why do you need a veteran?"

"Not a veteran. A veterinarian."

"You got a pet?"

"It was a gift, sort of."

Chris chuckled. "Drive-by cattin'?"

"It was a drive-by, but I think it's a weird-looking dog. I don't know. It's brown, gray, and some black around the eyes—with a squished face."

"So you're keeping it?"

"I think I have to." If God sent her a companion, she couldn't get rid of it.

"I'll text you the number of a vet who goes to our church, but if you call this early on a Saturday, don't tell her who gave you her cell number."

~~~

Dr. Ross turned the animal over. "She looks like maybe a Basset Hound-Chow mix, probably one of the most bizarre looking puppies I've seen."

Sarah Beth bobbed her head. "The Basset Hound part explains the horrendous sound it made. How something so small could make a noise like that is beyond belief. I literally had chills running down my spine."

"They do have a distinctive howl. This one looks to be about five weeks old, so you'll need to bottle-feed her about every four or five hours. In another few days, you can give her canned food mixed with water."

Sarah Beth tapped her fingernails on the counter. "Every *four* hours?"

"I'll show you what to do." Dr. Ross handed Sarah Beth the animal. "We'll give her a feeding now. Let me get the formula from the other room. I'll be right back."

"Oh, my stars." Sarah Beth nuzzled the puppy's head. "Every four or five hours? A bottle?" Would she have to take it to work?

The puppy let out a little squeak.

"I'll do my best."

With both hands full of supplies, Doctor Ross returned to Sarah Beth's side. She showed Sarah Beth how to mix the formula with water, then held out the bottle. "Here." She guided Sarah Beth's arm. "Hold the bottle like this and let her get used to it. It's a shame someone dumped her so early, but luckily a kind-hearted person found her."

"Lucky me." The perkiness she'd intended didn't quite make it to her voice. Her words sounded bleak in her own ears.

"You're doing fine. But feedings can be a little messy. Here's a towel."

"Thanks." Sarah Beth wiped the milky substance from her shirt and arm. "When do I need to come back to make sure she doesn't reproduce?"

"Not for about six months, but we'll need to do deworming and shots in a few weeks."

Sarah Beth's eyes popped open wide. "Deworming? Does it have worms?"

Dr. Ross patted Sarah Beth's arm and smiled. "Just a

precaution. If you see any, let me know, and we'll get you some medicine."

"For me?" This could be way more than she'd bargained for.

"No. If you see any when the puppy goes to the bathroom."

"Whew. Got it. I'll be right back down here if I see anything looking like a worm."

Dr. Ross gave Sarah Beth a sideways glance. "I'm sure you will. I'll loan you one of my crates until you get your own."

"Um, I kind of have plans today to go water skiing."

"That sounds fun."

"Should I cancel?" It would be a good excuse.

"She'll be fine in the crate for several hours."

"Thanks again for seeing me on a Saturday." She shot the vet a mischievous smile. "Chris said not to tell you he gave me your cell number."

"Oh, he did?" With a chuckle, Dr. Ross followed her to the door. "I didn't mind coming in. I appreciate your charity, caring for this little animal. Would you mind if I take a couple of pictures? I've never seen a puppy that looked quite like this one."

"Sure." Holding up the dog, Sarah Beth shook her head. "I should probably put a video on the Internet next time she makes that noise."

Dr. Ross pulled out her phone and snapped a few times. "That would go viral, no doubt." Dr. Ross gave her a little wave. "It was nice meeting you, Sarah Beth."

"You, too." But what adventure had she stepped into now that God had answered her prayers.

~~~

With the puppy fed and tucked into the crate, Sarah Beth

put on her bathing suit and scrambled around gathering ski equipment. What had she forgotten? She glanced at her bag. A towel. That could be important. She grabbed one from the bathroom, checked the puppy again, and then loaded the gear into her SUV. Now where was her phone?

Good grief. If she was having difficulty managing with a puppy, maybe it was best that she'd probably never have children.

Death and loss seemed to follow her. Why would it be any different with a child? Not to mention the fact that she didn't plan on dating anyone. And her mind was a mess.

She should cancel skiing today. Or at least make sure she'd get back on time. She tracked down her phone by the coffee pot and dialed Jess. His voicemail picked up. "Hi, Jess. I have to be back in four hours. Make that three and a half? I should take a separate vehicle. Or I can just skip out this time."

The doorbell rang. *No way.* It was too early to be him. She peeked out the window and blinked at the sight of Jess's strong profile as he leaned against one of the white columns of her front porch.

His gaze shifted toward the window, a grin spreading across his face.

Caught. So embarrassing. Her pulse throbbed in her throat as she disconnected the call and opened the door. "Jess, I just left you a message. I was going to meet you."

"I only live four blocks from here. It seemed silly to take three vehicles when we all live so close." He tried to take a step around her into the house.

Nudging him back, Sarah Beth slipped out the door and closed it behind her. "We'll have to get the gear out of my SUV, and I have to be back early. Are Nick and Sam with you?"

"Sam's in the penalty box, remember?"

"You could've invited him." Not that she enjoyed his company. A yelp echoed from inside the house.

Jess cocked his head. "Did you hear something?"

"Nothing out of the ordinary." Not since this morning, anyway.

"Nick's here, plus another rider taking Sam's place." Sunlight filtered through the lofty oaks that shaded her yard, and she slipped on her sunglasses. Memories surfaced of Mark pushing her in an old tire swing that used to hang from one of the big limbs. She helped Jess swap the ski equipment into the blue and white ski boat hitched to his truck. Too bad her brother wasn't here. He and Jess would probably get along well.

Jess opened the back truck door for her. "We have another pretty lady hanging with us today." Leaning in, he tickled a giggling little girl in the back seat. "Got your sunscreen on, missy?" A teasing quality seasoned his words as he mussed her hair, and the child beamed back at him.

"Yes, sir, Uncle Jess."

"Good girl." He gave her a massive smile and let Sarah Beth in. "This is my friend Sarah Beth."

"Hi, Ms. Sarah Beth. My name is Katherine Marie Russo, and it's nice to meet you." Hazel eyes that matched Nick's looked out from under a flock of strawberry blond curls. Katherine extended her small hand to Sarah Beth.

"It's nice to meet you, Katherine Marie Russo. That's a pretty name."

"Katherine Marie is a family name, and Russo is Italian, but you can call me Katie."

As they took off, Nick waved and shook his head, smiling. "That's my princess."

As they passed rows of newly planted soybean fields

alternating with forests of green trees on the way to the lake, Katie gave a dissertation of all she'd absorbed the past week at preschool and then threw out random facts about Nick.

How cute. It was clear no baby talk was spoken in the Russo home.

And obviously, Nick adored his daughter. He glowed as he glanced back at them. "Now you know everything about me. Katie, maybe you can ask Sarah Beth a few personal questions."

"I can do that, Daddy."

They parked near the dock. Katie unlatched her seatbelt, tucked her head, and hopped out of the truck clutching her bright red purse and matching flip-flops. "I love your pink ski vest, Ms. Sarah Beth. You could get some flip-flops like these to match it."

Maybe she should. The sandals were cute. "Katie, how old are you?"

With four fingers held up, Katie grinned. "I'm four. And a half."

"You're smart for your age. You should meet my friend, Camilla. She's four, like you."

Katie clapped her hands in front of her. "When can I?"

"I'll work something out with your dad and get back to you."

A hundred shades of blue reflected off the still lake, and a smattering of puffy white clouds dotted the natural canvas. Cypress trees straddled the sandy bank with long knees jutting into the water. Two of the stubborn plants grew in the lake near the dock and stood proudly with scrawny branches reaching toward the sun. How she loved this place. The slight breeze cooled the beads of perspiration already forming on her nose in the typical Mississippi humidity.

They loaded the boat and took off. Katie giggled with the acceleration, finally seeming like the four-year-old she was. Sarah Beth let the guys ski first. She was in no hurry. The water couldn't be much warmer than it had been last week. And that was chilly.

The scars on Jess's shoulder brought back thoughts of their unexpected conversation the week before. How much did Jess actually want to know? A better question might be how much did she want to tell? Was she ready to reopen those wounds? She shouldn't keep staring at him. Her eyes closed, and she filled her lungs with the warm spring air.

A little voice broke into her deliberations. "I want Sarah Beth to take me on the tube this time, Daddy."

Shaking herself back to the present, Sarah Beth opened her eyes. "I'd love to. Tubing is a favorite of mine."

Nick laughed, smile lines crinkling his temples. "You've made a friend."

After a final check of Katie's life vest, Sarah Beth jumped in. Katie followed her into the cool water, and they swam to the tube. The lake was a tad warmer than before, but not much. A tiny ladylike hand wrapped around Sarah Beth's once they'd pulled themselves onto the huge inflated ring. What an adorable little girl.

The boat yanked the slack from the line, and they sailed across the glittering surface, Sarah Beth giggling as much as Katie. Their laughter opened up something she'd locked away a year ago. Something earnest and settling. Something she'd missed.

Five good runs, and Jess slowed the boat for them to take a rest. Sarah Beth gave Katie a hug before slipping back into the water. "I feel like a kid again. Thanks, Katie."

"You're welcome, Ms. Sarah Beth."

Nick helped them into the boat while Jess dropped the anchor. Sarah Beth and Katie kicked back on the benches of the open bow, facing the guys as they floated under the cerulean spring sky.

"Katie, do you like to look up and imagine animals in the clouds?" Sarah Beth pointed above them.

"That's me and Uncle Jess's favorite."

Sarah Beth cast a glance at Jess. He smiled without looking her way.

"Ms. Sarah Beth, where were you born?"

"I was born on the Mississippi Gulf Coast in a pretty little town called Pass Christian."

"I was born in Florida by Disney World. Is that near where you were born?"

"Not so near, but the weather is sunny and hot, like Florida."

"I moved to Oxford because my mommy went to heaven, and Uncle Jess got Daddy a job here. Why did you move to Oxford?"

How to explain that one? She swallowed back the lump forming in her throat. "My parents went to heaven, too, so I came to Oxford to live with my grandmother."

Jess turned his head toward her, his brown eyes searching hers.

Katie pushed up on one elbow. "Maybe your parents are playing with my mommy, and they're riding a boat and looking at clouds, too."

The lump dissolved at the vision Katie created. "That could be. My mom and dad loved to ride boats."

A peaceful lull found them as they rocked with the breeze.

Minutes later, Katie broke the hush with a squeal. "It's Minnie Mouse in the cloud, just like we saw at Disney World.

Can you see it, Daddy?"

"I see it, baby. Just like Disney World." Nick gazed at his little girl.

Sarah Beth's defenses fell away like water droplets, and she savored the blissful afternoon. If only this feeling could last.

~~~

Jess studied Sarah Beth with Katie. For the first time since he met this curious woman, she looked relaxed, unguarded. She'd lost both of her parents. That had to be tough. Maybe that explained why she became a prodigal. His heart wrenched. What would it be like to lose his parents?

He tried not to stare at the way her tan skin glistened with the water dripping from it. Or at her lips and how she bit the lower one when she concentrated. It took every ounce of self-discipline he could muster to force his eyes away. He held his arm up and glanced at his waterproof watch. "Uh-oh. Sarah Beth's gonna turn into a pumpkin. We better go."

Sarah Beth jerked up, her elbow smacking the side of the boat. "Oh my stars, I already forgot the puppy and singing tonight. What a terrible mother I'll make."

"Singing?" Jess and Nick spoke in unison.

"Puppy? I want to see it." Katie squealed and jumped up. "And you'll make a great mother."

Did she want to be a mother? Jess let the question bounce around his mind as he hauled the anchor into the boat. "We'll get you back, Sarah Beth, but only if you tell me when and where."

"When and where for what?"

The motor roared to life, and he set a course toward the dock. "Singing tonight."

She blew out a long puff of air. "That's what I was afraid of."

Back at the dock, they hitched the boat, then took off in the truck. She explained a mysterious animal drop and a case of forced public singing.

Turning to face Katie in the back seat, Nick gave his daughter a serious look. "We can see the puppy, but the singing is past bedtime."

"I know." Sarah Beth gasped. "You can come to family night at Chris and Kim's on Tuesday. Katie and Camilla could meet then."

"That might work," Nick said. "I'll check my schedule. Then you can perform an encore for Katie and me."

Jess couldn't stop the smirk from forming on his lips as he glanced in the rearview mirror. "I'm going to the concert tonight. I'll give you the critique tomorrow."

A groan came from Sarah Beth's side of the back seat. "It's not a concert."

Once they reached her house, Jess and Nick unloaded the equipment while Sarah Beth and Katie went inside to get the puppy and its bottle. A horrendous howl came from the open front door.

"What is that hideous screeching?" Nick asked, holding his ears.

Sarah Beth stepped out and sighed. "That would be my new dog."

Jess moved to Sarah Beth's side and nudged her. "At least you have to sing better than that."

"Ha-ha, very funny. You should be a comedian."

"Whoa, touchy."

Sarah Beth and Katie took a seat on the porch swing with the puppy latched onto a bottle, while Jess and Nick pulled over two white wicker rocking chairs.

"Ms. Sarah Beth?"

Refocusing her attention from the puppy to Katie, Sarah Beth smiled. "Yes?"

"Are you sure that's a dog?"

A muffled laugh came from Sarah Beth's throat. "That's what I asked the vet, and she assured me it is a canine."

"What's a canine?"

"That's the proper name for a dog."

"Are you going to call it Canine?"

Jess hooted. "Maybe you should, so people will know what it is."

"I haven't named her yet, but I don't think so."

Standing, Nick stretched out his arms toward Katie. "We better go, Princess."

Jess battled to make himself leave. "Me, too. But I'll see you tonight. At the concert." With a chuckle, he took one last glance back at Sarah Beth's bewildered expression and that strange mutt in her arms. Tonight should be entertaining, at least. He could hardly wait.

Chapter 13

Five Years Earlier

Sarah Beth emptied supplies from her cubicle into boxes, rolled them on a cart to the elevator, and ascended to her new corner office. A dream come true—a real desk and windows offering a view of the city. Moving from the cubicle to an office in a company as prestigious as this one was huge. Now, rather than being one of the underlings, she'd have staff working for her. She wheeled around the corner to find a stunning blond woman already settled into the reception desk.

The woman stood and smiled, extending her hand. "Hi, I'm Jill Martin. They transferred me from upstairs."

"I'm Sarah Beth."

Rumor had it that the executive Jill had worked for had difficulty keeping his hands to himself, and this woman was stunning. Explained why she'd requested a transfer.

Returning the smile, Sarah Beth shook Jill's hand. "You probably know your job better than I do, so instruct me."

Jill breathed a sigh. "I'm happy to be working for you, and I've heard good things. The main thing I'll need to know is whose calls get through no matter what. Give me the names of your parents, husband, kids, that kind of thing."

A familiar pang clawed at Sarah Beth's ribcage. "No parents or husband or kids, but I have a brother, Mark, a boyfriend, Adam, and a former professor, Dean Latham. They have my cell number, so you'll probably never talk to them." She forced a hollow laugh. "I'm not sure my boyfriend even remembers what company I work for."

"I hear you. Been there, done that, bought the T-shirt." Jill's expression and tone became more serious. "That's why I needed to keep this job. I finally got the nerve to leave the rich boyfriend and try to make it on my own."

Relief settled over Sarah Beth as she situated files and equipment into their new home. She and Jill seemed to get each other. "You will not fail. I won't let you. I think we're going to get along fine."

Other staff would handle logistics, implementation, and documentation. She only needed to hire someone to be her right-hand man. Or woman. Everyone she interviewed seemed to be actor or actress wannabes. She needed someone looking to have a career with the company, someone who wouldn't leave as soon as she'd trained them.

At four-thirty, Sarah Beth rested her head on her hands. How could finding the right person be so hard?

A short, wiry Hispanic man knocked on her door. "I'm sorry, but your receptionist must have stepped down the hall. I'm here to interview for the marketing assistant position." He extended his hand to shake hers. "My name is Juan Moreira."

"I'm Sarah Beth LeClair, and I'm really tired of trying to find an assistant." She let out a deep sigh. "Tell me why I should hire you."

"Ms. LeClair, I have been working as a parking attendant at the Ritz. I can talk to the very wealthy, but I can also talk to the average guy. I am completing a marketing degree in the evenings and online. I have a wife and three kids. I am loyal and hardworking. I'm hoping for the chance to grow and learn with this company."

She eyed the small man in the gray suit. "I have three questions. Can you use a computer? Can you take orders from a woman? Oh, and by any chance, can you teach me Spanish?"

"I enjoy learning new uses for the computer, my wife sent me to this interview, and sí."

Chapter 14

Sarah Beth stood by Bryan as he addressed the crowd of CSU students. "We're singing 'King of Glory.' Join us if you know the words."

Please do. Sarah Beth captured a huge breath as the song began, shaking off the nervousness that had her heart pumping hard. Tremors coursed through her and filled her soul as the students joined in fervent praise to the Father. Again she lost herself in the music and the praise.

Why would I ever have wanted to miss this? Sorry, Lord, for letting my fear hold me back. Again. Thank You for not giving up on me.

They closed with a Chris Tomlin worship song. Peace, tranquility—even joy enveloped her. Bryan's warm eyes smiled as he harmonized with her. When the last note left her tongue, a face came into view.

Jess.

He leaned against a pole in the back corner of the old building. Her heart rate quickened. Good thing she hadn't seen him before she'd started. She might've never gotten a word out. An expression she couldn't place crossed Jess's face. Then he smiled and gave her a thumbs-up. The look vanished.

Bryan caught Sarah Beth in a hug. Students swarmed to talk to her. Struggling through the crowd as fast as possible without being rude, she made her way over to where Jess seemed to be hiding in a corner. She caught him as he edged to the door.

"Jess, wait up. Where are you going?"

His eyes darted from Sarah Beth to the exit and back. "Nowhere. Home."

"Can you stay and meet Chris? He's a huge fan. I'm sure he'd love to meet you."

"I don't know." He eyed the door again.

Chris would be a much better influence than she ever could. "Please?" She gave her best puppy dog look and poked out her bottom lip.

He let out a laughing sigh. "How can I say no to that face? Lead the way."

As they crossed the room to join Chris and Bryan near the coffee bar, coeds smiled and waved at Jess. One guy asked how spring training was going, and another wanted to know if Cole Sanders was ready for the next season. A series of students requested to have their picture taken with the famous Coach McCoy.

"Okay, guys," Sarah Beth said, "let's give Coach a break. He's our guest." This was like a mild version of being around Dylan Conner. "I'm sorry. I didn't think about your semi-celebrity status."

"What do you mean, *semi*?" He gave Sarah Beth a nudge with his elbow. "Just kidding. They're fans of the team, no big deal."

She cupped her hand to the side of her mouth. "Not sure those girls waving at you are just fans of the team."

"What do you mean?"

"I mean, they think you're attractive."

His brown eyes met hers head on. "Do you?"

Warmth flooded her neck and face. She'd stepped into that one. Suddenly, he seemed to be standing very close, and her lips suffered from some sort of paralysis.

"Sarah Beth, I asked you a question."

She produced a stiff laugh, then patted his arm. "Of course, you're a very attractive man. I'd have to be brain dead not to notice, silly." Foot in mouth. Again. "Chris, hey, I've been trying to get over to introduce you to my new friend, Coach Jess McCoy."

Chris stepped out from behind the coffee bar, staring with eyes wide but quickly recovering. "Glad you joined us tonight."

Sarah Beth pointed toward the bar. "I'll go put on more coffee while you guys talk."

At the coffee pot, Bryan slipped up beside her. "Ms. Professor, you've been keeping secrets."

"I told you guys I'd gone skiing with new friends from work."

"You're hanging out with the hot football coach."

She held back a smile. "You think he's hot?"

"Shut up. *I* don't. Just all the women in the South." Bryan slapped his hand over his mouth. "Oops, sorry, Ms. Professor. I didn't mean to tell you to shut up."

"*This* is why I didn't mention it." She grabbed a cup of the fresh brew dripping through the filter. "I need this. I'm beat." She took a sip and grimaced, the bitter taste overwhelming her tongue. "Too strong." She dumped in a pile of sugar and stirred.

Jess joined them at the counter. "Can I get a cup of that?"

Her heart skittered again. "Sure. You may need to add cream and sugar. I didn't get something quite right."

He grinned. "I like sugar, remember?"

Bryan's smile dipped a fraction as he offered his hand to Jess. "How's it going, Coach? I'm Bryan."

Jess bobbed his head. "You're a gifted musician."

"Thanks." Bryan's forehead creased as he processed the compliment.

Jess took a sip of his coffee, then let out a muffled cough. "I should take this to go."

"I'll walk you out." Sarah Beth handed him a lid for his cup. "There's a back door we can slip out so you can skip the adoring fans and picture-taking, if you like."

Jess gazed at her. "I like." He glanced back at Bryan. "Nice to meet you, Bryan."

Outside, stiff humidity hung in the spring air, but a vibrant panorama of stars gleamed. As they reached his truck, Jess stopped without opening his door. "How about you tell me more of that long story?"

An uncomfortable tingling ran through her limbs, as if she stood looking off the edge of a high dive. "What story?"

"Your story." Jess answered without looking at her and took a small sip of his coffee.

"You want to let your tailgate down, and we can sit a while?"

"Sounds good." He pulled the handle, and the metal unfolded with a clank.

Sarah Beth scooted to the opposite side as far as she could to avoid his distracting presence. *Lord, help me.* "Where did I leave off?"

"You told me that you were a prodigal, but you never told me how that happened. You said you had good parents, but you told Katie they were in heaven."

"Yeah. Mom and Dad were great. They taught us to fish, ski, laugh, and more importantly, to pray. The house I live in now was left to me by my grandmother. Mom grew up here. My father grew up on the Mississippi Gulf Coast. He called it 'God's Country' and insisted they move back when he graduated. Mom said that the coast may be 'God's Country' but Oxford was the 'next best thing to heaven,' so we spent a lot of time here, too.

"Mom and Dad taught us to have good, clean fun and about living our lives for the Lord. Not only that, they modeled it." She paused. The memories pinched, but she could do this. "One summer they sent us up to Oxford to stay with Gram for a week. They joked that they were having a date week. Mark and I'd been in Oxford for only one night when we got the call. They never figured out why it happened, but our house burned to the ground with Mom and Dad in it. I was fourteen." Even now the loss twisted her stomach and sparked tears.

"Sarah Beth, I am sorry. That had to be so difficult. Who could blame you for making a few mistakes?"

A breeze stirred the damp air. "The mistakes didn't start then. Gram was our strength, like an anchor."

"So you were okay for a while?"

She managed a small nod and swallowed. "Until I was a freshman in college. Gram wasn't feeling well. The doctors here couldn't figure out what was wrong, so we took her to the hospital in Jackson. She was diagnosed with pancreatic cancer. The good and the bad of her illness was that it was quick. At least with Gram, we got to say goodbye."

"You and Mark were alone."

"Yes. But by that time, Mark was married to Holly. I felt God had taken almost everyone that I loved. I was angry with Him. It took a while for me to move past the hurt." Way too long. Her shoulders slumped forward. "Does that make sense?"

"Makes perfect sense."

She slid off the tailgate feeling exhausted on so many levels, but relieved and clean and whole in other ways she couldn't explain. Something told her to wait to tell him more. "Jess?"

"Yeah?"

"Can we finish this next time?"

He slid to his feet and faced her. "Yeah. I'm sorry I dredged this up. I shouldn't have."

"No, no. I want to—I need to share my story. It's been a long day, and my coffee's not doing the trick."

"Whatever you're comfortable with."

She should invite him for Tuesday night. Courage. She needed a shot of it instead of this horrible coffee. "Um. You and Nick could come to family night at Chris's on Tuesday for burgers. We could talk then."

"Chris invited me. I'll think about it." He edged away.

"That's great." His cup still rested on the tailgate. She picked it up and held it out. "Hey, you forgot this."

"Right." He reached for the cup.

"Too strong, wasn't it? You can be honest. I'll pour it out."

The corners of his eyes crinkled as he gave her a mischievous smile. "Worst coffee I've ever had. Nothing like the coffee in your office."

She grinned. "Yeah, I thought so, too."

"Good night, Sarah Beth."

"Goodbye, Jess."

Now she had to fret until Tuesday about how to go on with her life story. What would he think? Would it make a difference in his faith, anyone's faith? Juan seemed to think it would. He always talked about "beauty for ashes," that great scripture from Isaiah. But did that apply to her life? To her story?

~~~

Jess closed the truck door, turned the key, and squeezed the steering wheel. How could one woman suffer so much? Yet she still sang songs of praise. He followed her taillights out of the parking lot. A yearning to make sure she got home safely pulled at him.

He trailed her SUV until she parked at her house, then circled the block and came back by. Lights on. Good. He continued the few blocks to his own home.

The songs Sarah Beth and Bryan had sung replayed in his head. The music unearthed something in him. Something deeper than he'd ever been willing to dig. His relationships with women for one. He'd never allowed himself to give much thought to their feelings. Not that he ever gave any particular woman much time or a reason to think he was interested in a relationship. A few dates to functions, then he'd drift away, ask someone else the next time. Even in high school—the same thing. Probably because of Sophia.

Sophia. If only he'd said no to her the first time. If only he didn't enjoy the things—*no*. *No more*. He was putting a stop to that.

Something or Someone had pricked his soul tonight. He finally grasped how wrong he'd lived his life. Things were going to change. He wanted to be a better man.

Chapter 15

Two years earlier

Sarah Beth stared out from the wall of windows in her office over the city of Los Angeles. The setting sun reflected off the glass panes across the street, magenta painting the sky behind the towering skyscrapers. Jill and Juan's laughter floated through her open office door. They'd become so dear to her. Juan with delightful stories of his wife and children, and Jill, the leggy blue-eyed blond, with the hysterical predicaments her looks got her into, were like family. She'd ignored Juan's invitations to his community church, but he'd continued to ask.

Working countless hours on the latest blockbuster film had only brought them closer. There were dozens of "artistic" types to satisfy in the movie industry, but they'd done it. In the outer office, Juan cracked one of his jokes about being taken hostage by two Amazons. He was such a trip.

Slipping quietly to the door, Sarah Beth leaned on the frame and scrunched her face into a mock frown. "Is any work going on out here?"

Jill punched her hands to her hips. "We're finished with everything, you slave-driver."

A wide smile lifted Juan's lips, revealing what seemed like all his teeth, white against his tan skin. "I was thinking about how God has blessed you with a talent to use for His glory."

"You sound exactly like my brother."

"He is a good man." He shook a finger at her. "You should listen to him."

"He's coming out with Holly and Drew soon, and I can't wait to see my little nephew."

Jill sighed. "Why can't I find a good guy like your brother?"

Mischief flashed in Juan's eyes as he cleared his throat rather loudly.

"Oops." One of Jill's eyebrows went up. "Why can't I find a man like your brother or like Juan, only taller?"

A wadded paper flew across the room toward Jill. "That's right. Pick on the short guy."

She tossed it back. "Like Amazon is a compliment?"

Sarah Beth laughed and pointed at herself. "By the way, this Amazon has to attend that Hollywood award thing. I need wardrobe assistance. Jill, are you up for shopping?"

"Are you for real?" Jill's blue eyes twinkled as she hopped to her feet. "You're going?"

"The big boss says I have to."

"I'd kill to go." A second later, Jill slung open her desk drawer, grabbed her purse, and dragged Sarah Beth toward the door. "We have to get you fixed up. This is going to be so much fun. Juan, we'll see you tomorrow."

Juan bowed his head with a grin. "Yes, my masters."

~~~

A pathology book lay on the floor beside the couch where Adam snoozed. His chest rose and fell in slow rhythm, his breathing loud.

Sarah Beth bent and kissed his cheek. "Hey, sleepyhead. Guess what?"

He stretched and let out a little groan.

"I have to attend a big shindig with the higher-ups on Monday for this movie we're marketing. Think you could be my date?"

He rubbed his eyes and blinked. "Monday, there's no way. I can't switch shifts."

Pain snaked around her heart, squeezing tight. Was this always going to be how things were? Completely separate lives? "But you could make some great contacts at these parties. We're talking high-dollar contributors for your cause."

"There won't be anything to contribute to if I don't work these long hours."

Right. Like one night would kill his career. Things were never going to change. The truth settled over her like a pile of stones. Her breath caught in her throat as she turned away.

Moving from the couch, Adam approached from behind, solid arms encasing her. "You'll do fine without me."

The embers of disappointment she'd been burying for years ignited into fury. She pulled away and spun around. "I don't want to do without you. I'm sick and tired of doing without you. I want to do *with* you. People are starting to think I just made up *my boyfriend Adam*"—she made air quotes around the words—"And I can't remember the last time we went anywhere together. Don't even tell me you have to pay the rent. You were old enough to get your trust fund a while back, and you get two salaries from the hospital."

"Whoa." Adam held one hand up like a stop sign, and the muscles in his jaw twitched. "You had to know that my medical career would take up a lot of time. My work is important, and I happen to love it."

"Obviously you love your career more than me." She pushed past him, picked up her keys and bag, and threw open the door. "You can commit to school, the hospital, your research, but never to me." A slam rattled the wall as she left.

She ran to her SUV, got in, shut the door, and drove out of the lot. "What am I doing? I've been such an idiot." Her thoughts accused her again and again. She'd been lying to herself for so long. Why? Minutes passed in a blur of frustration and tears. The roads jumbled before her. Where was she?

Landmarks led her to Santa Monica and the beach, then she continued north toward Malibu. For miles, she drove. Soaring mountains towered along the ocean with the full moon illuminating the sky. Scanning the radio for a station, a song caught her attention. The words said something about God being a strong tower, a shelter. She pressed the volume higher to listen. An urge to look right turned her head. Pepperdine University clung to the mountains above, and she made a quick turn up to the guard gate.

"Is there a place where I could sit for a while?"

Nodding, the guard handed her a pass. "Here's a map. There's a chapel up the road."

She wound around the mountain until she found the white stone building, parked, and got out. Her heart yearned for the closeness her parents had shared with the Lord—the looks on their faces when they'd sung praise songs in church. She'd tried to replace God with all the wrong things, and the emptiness echoed through her soul. Why had she let them down? Let Gram down. And God. How could she ever make things right? How could she start over?

The sky stretched for miles out over the Pacific. Peace descended on her. In the stillness, the phrase, *I Am here*, covered over her soul. She sat on a wooden bench staring at the ocean for a long while.

The chirp of her phone broke into her thoughts. *Mark.* Adam must have called him. "Hello."

"Are you okay?"

"Yes."

"Adam was worried about you. He said that he'd never seen you that angry. You'd never stormed out before. Why didn't you call me?"

"I was wrong about everything." She let out a long sigh, holding back the storm of sorrow that threatened to spill out. "I needed to think about what a mess I've made. I pushed God away in college, and Adam's never going to marry me." Her voice broke. "I want a family—like we had growing up. I don't know how to start over."

"Where are you?"

"Malibu."

"Long way from home." Concern etched his voice. "Do you want to come back to the Lord?"

"I don't know how."

"Wanting the Lord—that's all it takes. Baby steps back to God. You take one step toward Him, and He's running back to you like you're His long lost child. Remember the story of the prodigal son?"

She remembered the story from her childhood as tears welled in her eyes. "I do."

"Good. Why don't you call one of your friends or get a motel. Let me know where you end up, or I'll be calling the FBI office in Los Angeles."

She choked out a tiny laugh and sniffed. "Okay. I'm sorry Adam worried you. Thanks for always being here for me. Love you. Miss you."

"I love you, too. And remember—"

"I know, God loves me more, and He will be with me until the end of time."

~~~

Sunday, the small congregation of inner-city residents welcomed Sarah Beth. Juan's youngest daughter sat in her lap, and as the members sang, Sarah Beth played with the girl's shiny dark hair, the way her mother had done when she was a little girl. She hadn't allowed herself to think of that for years. The memories were too painful. Even now they pricked her heart. The minister spoke about a woman at a well—and how Jesus didn't scorn the woman for her lifestyle, but rather confronted her with the truth. Jesus met her where she was—which happened to be living with a man who wasn't her husband.

Ironic.

Juan took her arm as the service ended. "What did you think? Did you feel comfortable?"

"The lesson was appropriate." As if God had met her right where she was.

Juan's eyes held tenacity and kindness. "God knew what you needed to hear."

"Maybe so." Was God speaking directly to her? Mark would say yes.

~~~

"Hair and makeup appointment at one." Jill rounded the door to Sarah Beth's office, grinning.

Sarah Beth gawked at her. "Hair and makeup? I mean, I can maybe see getting my hair styled, but makeup?"

"I refuse to let you show up like you normally do, in just mascara and Chapstick."

"Hey, I'm trying to focus on my work, not my face. Makeup isn't practical."

"Tonight we're going for glamour, not practical." Jill grabbed Sarah Beth's fingers. "I can't believe I forgot about these. Let's get your nails done, too."

When the hair, makeup, and nails were complete, Sarah Beth went into the office restroom and slipped on her new dress. The A-line with silky blue fabric fitted to the waist flowed loosely to the floor.

"Wow, you're a knockout." Circling her, Jill whistled. "I feel like I'm looking at a movie star."

Sarah Beth glanced at herself in the mirror. This wasn't her, but Jill had been right. She couldn't have gone in just lip balm and mascara. "I can't believe they're making me attend this thing."

"I'd take your place in a heartbeat. Sounds like fun, plus all those celebrities. I'm riding the elevator down with you. I can't wait to see the expressions when the other guys see."

"I can." They'd all have an escort, and she'd be alone.

Bill and his wife, Carol, along with two other executives gathered in the office lobby to travel in the limos. Bill's mouth dropped when he caught a glimpse of Sarah Beth. "I thought we were dragging along my little Mississippi prodigy. Who are you?" He grinned. "Carol, does this look like the college girl Greg Latham sent us?"

An adoring smile filled Carol's face. "You're gonna knock 'em dead."

Sarah Beth gave both of them a tight hug. "You're the closest thing I have to parents here, and I'll always be thankful you took a chance and hired me."

After the awards, the party dragged on for hours, and Sarah Beth massaged her cheeks. Who knew forcing herself to smile could hurt this much? She needed a break and caffeine.

Excusing herself, she went to the bar. "Can I get a cola, please?"

"Of course." The bartender filled a glass and handed it back on a napkin.

Eyes closed, she sipped the drink and let out a sigh. Someone sat down in the barstool next to her. She should probably open her eyes.

A man rested his elbows on the bar to her left, then lifted his drink toward her. "You look like you're having about as much fun as I am."

Famous green eyes stared at her. Was she really face-to-face with the movie star? *Oh my stars. Literally.* She wiped her mouth with a napkin.

"Hi, I'm Dylan Conner." He extended his hand.

"Sarah Beth LeClair."

He cocked an eyebrow. "*The* Sarah Beth LeClair?"

"Uh, then no. That's not my name." She took another sip of her drink.

He chuckled. "You're not the genius who designed the promo?"

"Oh, *that* Sarah Beth LeClair. I wasn't sure where you were going."

"Where would you like me to go?" The actor shot her his legendary wicked grin.

The last thing she wanted to do was flirt. Staring into her drink, she stirred the ice around with a straw. "So, are you saying you liked my work?"

"I love your work, and suddenly, I'm enthralled with the creative genius behind it. You're an impressive lady—not just a pretty face."

Not just a pretty face. *Adam's line.* She sighed. "I hate that you said that."

"Bad memory?"

"It's complicated."

"Hate when I hear that one. How can we work to uncomplicate things?"

"I'm not sure." The million-dollar question. "I want to get right with the Lord. I'm thinking of getting my own place, maybe in Malibu. I rode up and did some serious thinking and praying there not long ago. I have stuff I need to work on, and the view of the ocean and mountains relaxed and inspired me." Why did she just spill her guts to this movie star? He probably wished he never started this conversation. "I guess I overshared. Sorry."

"Don't be." His mouth quirked into a crooked grin. "Would you want to buy or lease? Because I was talking to my Realtor about selling my condo. I bought it after my first successful film and have been sentimental about letting it go. It seems kind of silly, but I love that condo. It was a symbol that I'd achieved my dream. I have a house a bit further down the coast. The condo's furnished but vacant. If you're serious, we can look into it."

"I might be interested. So you like the area?"

"Love it. I grew up in the mountains of North Carolina. One of the few things I like to remember about home. When you said you want to 'get right with the Lord,' that reminded me of home, too. I don't think I've heard that phrase since I left the South."

"In Mississippi, we don't count you as being from the South unless you have a football team in the SEC."

"In North Carolina, we wouldn't know Mississippi was anything but a river if it weren't for the SEC."

Sarah Beth pushed her drink away and fiddled with her napkin. Could she actually leave Adam?

"Whoever he is, he's a fool to let you slip away." Dylan took out his phone. "Can I get your number to call you about the condo?"

Eyes squinting, she studied him. Could she trust this guy?

"Or I can give you my number." A confident chuckle shook his chest. "Call me if you're interested in the condo—or anything else."

~~~

Sarah Beth yawned and dug around in her bag for her keys. She finally grabbed them and started to let herself in.

The lock barely turned before Adam yanked the door open. "Hey, how did it go?" His head jutted forward, eyes wide. "Whoa."

She slipped off the high heels that had been killing her feet for the last three hours. "Same old me, just wearing all this glamour Jill made me put on."

"You look— Wow, I'm speechless."

He tried to pull her into his arms, but she stiffened. "I'm tired, Adam. It was a long night. I'm going to sleep." Leaving him there gawking, she pushed away and turned to climb the stairs.

Chapter 16

The first to arrive for family night at Chris and Kim's, Sarah Beth headed to the backyard with the puppy wiggling in her arms. The dog had grown so much in a week. No more bottles, and she ate all the time. People said God answered prayers in mysterious ways. But really? She was lonely, and now she had this little dog. Not exactly what she'd expected, but the sweet pet kept her company.

Questions nibbled at her as she waited for answers to other prayers. Would Nick and Katie or Jess actually come to Chris' house tonight? What would she say to Jess if he did come?

Minutes later, Camilla jogged out into the fenced yard and joined Sarah Beth in the grass, her attention focused on the puppy. Students trickled onto the deck, and Sarah Beth's eyes drifted toward the back door. Again.

At last, Katie came running toward her, leaving Nick on the deck. *Yes.* They'd shown up. At least Nick and Katie had.

"I'm so glad you made it, Katie. This is Camilla. I've told her about you."

The girls became fast friends and ran around giggling with the dog. Before long, they decided to play in Camilla's room and lugged the puppy toward the house.

Sarah Beth caught up with them before they reached the deck. "Your mom said no dogs inside. You'll have to leave the puppy with me." Reluctant, they complied.

The back door opened, and Jess walked onto the deck. *Thank you, Lord.* Peace washed over Sarah Beth as she returned to her grassy spot in the shade of an old oak tree.

Wearing shorts, he stepped off the wooden planks heading her way. "Surprised to see me?"

She glanced at him, then back at her puppy. "Hmm, somewhere between surprised and not surprised. If that makes sense."

"No. It doesn't." He plopped down on the grass beside her and reached to rub the little dog's belly. "You still have this thing."

"Of course. When I commit, I'm all in."

"I'll keep that in mind." One side of his lips lifted as he leaned back on his elbows with his legs stretched out in front of him. He crossed his feet.

Bits of conversation drifted down from the deck. His presence felt comfortable. Except for the urge to stare at his muscular legs.

The puppy ambled onto Jess's lap. "Did you give it a name?"

"I call *her* Ewok."

Throwing back his head, Jess laughed loud and hard. "I can't wait to tell Nick."

"What? She looks like an Ewok from Star Wars."

"I can see a resemblance." The breezed shifted, floating the scent of grilled meat their way. "Those burgers smell great. Can I bring you one?"

"Sure. I normally eat with Camilla, but I think I've been replaced by Katie."

"It happens. I'll take her place if you let me." His fingers trailed across her back as he stood. Sarah Beth looked up at him. He held her gaze and smiled.

A log seemed to lodge in her throat. She squeaked out, "Thanks."

"Be right back."

Not long after he left, Chris and Nick carried lawn chairs from the porch. Chris unfolded one and patted the seat. "You don't have to sit on the ground." He bent forward. "And I've got to see this animal I've heard so much about." He picked up Ewok and inspected her. "She's…cute…in the way that all God's creatures are." Scrunching his face, he pressed his lips together as if holding back what he really wanted to say.

Nick let out a snort, and Chris laughed as he put the puppy back down. "I'm not laughing at her. Nick is making me laugh."

"Yeah, blame it on the guest." Nick gave Chris a friendly punch.

Sarah Beth nodded. "No one's a guest for long around here. They treat you like family—for better or worse."

"That's cool with me. Katie's made a friend."

The night passed quickly, and Sarah Beth said a silent prayer about finishing her testimony to Jess. It would only get harder to delve into those emotional times, but God could use her pain to redeem other prodigals like her. No matter their past.

Just after sundown, Nick pulled his keys from his pocket. "It's Katie's bedtime."

Camilla's lips formed a pout. "Can't she stay a little longer?"

As he lifted his daughter, Nick gave her a kind smile. "We'll make a playdate, but we have to get up early for daycare." He shook hands with Chris and Kim. "We had a great time. Thanks for inviting us."

Kim rubbed Katie's back before they exited. "We'll have you over to play again soon, sweetie."

Steeling herself, Sarah Beth rehearsed what she'd say to

Jess. She could do this.

The door had barely shut when Nick reappeared.

"What happened?" Jess stepped toward him.

"Truck problem. Needs a new starter, I think, but I've been putting it off." He shook his head. "A bit too long, apparently."

"I'll take you home so you can get Katie to bed." Jess rattled his keys. "We can come back tomorrow and get it to a mechanic."

"That'd be great, if you don't mind."

"Not a problem." Jess thanked everyone and put a hand on Sarah Beth's shoulder. "See you soon, Sarah Beth. Maybe we can hit the water again Saturday or Sunday." He winked as he turned and walked away.

So much for worrying about what to say—until next time anyway.

~~~

Fifteen minutes later, Jess opened the door to his uncluttered home. He toyed with the idea of going back to Chris's to talk to Sarah Beth. That might seem weird, though. Too needy. A knock at his door pulled him from his internal debate.

Through the window, he spotted Teddy Conrad's Mercedes in the driveway. *Crud.* Should've gone back. He slung the door open a bit harder than he meant to. "Hey, what brings you by?"

Teddy looked back over his shoulder. "Let's talk inside." He slithered in the house toward the living room. "Mind if I sit down?"

Jess waved his arm toward the leather couch. He knew what was coming. Teddy thought money was the answer to everything, like a lot of fans he'd met over the years. They thought they could buy this player or that player for the team.

Tell the coaches how to get more wins. The pressure always out in front of a coach like the pass no one could catch. The team had a winning season, but there'd never be enough wins for fans like Teddy. Jess sat on the edge of the brown leather chair, his elbows on his knees.

"Jess, I told you about the player from Memphis. I had lunch with his father, like I mentioned. He'd prefer his son come here when he graduates, but one of the other SEC teams is offering a pretty sweet setup—if you know what I mean. I imagine we could use a runner at the bank next summer. I could hire a young student or athlete to deliver documents for me, take the mail to the post office, you know, little stuff. Of course, we pay well—even for small jobs like that."

"You can't pay him to do nothing." Jess's fingers curled into a fist. "Teddy, if the kid wants that kind of *setup*, let him go. Even if he is 'family,' any questionable financial benefits could be a violation of NCAA recruiting rules. It'll be the team that suffers."

As he jerked to his feet, Teddy's mouth formed a menacing scowl. "His father already works for a sister bank in Memphis, so hiring his son wouldn't be suspicious. The team will suffer if we can't compete to recruit good players."

"We had a good recruiting season. A lot of talent, eager talent, headed our way. Kids who want to play ball here and aren't asking us to do anything illegal. I'll meet with the player and his parents during the permissible time frames. I've already made the allowed preliminary contacts. I'm actually pretty good at my job."

"A good team should aim to be a great team. Remember the fans and alum can turn on coaches. You might not always be the golden boy if you won't listen to the people who sign your paycheck."

A hard punch to Teddy's face might help *him* remember a few things. Jess's fists tightened, but he commanded his arms to stay stiff at his sides. "I think I've taken care of business here. Guys like your son have come to me, and I've given them all I've got. Worked to mold them into better players, better students, better men. Helped them maximize their potential both on and off the field. I play a clean game and give it my all every single time. I teach my players to do the same. This is the last I want to hear about blurring the lines of what's right. I mean it. I'll turn you in myself if I catch wind of any wrongdoing."

Teddy stormed out the door, leaving it wide open, and Jess resisted the urge to slam the thing off its hinges. With a controlled click, he closed it and then pulled out his phone. One ring and it went straight to voicemail. "Sam, I need you to do something about your dad. He's going to end up getting me and the whole university in hot water."

Chapter 17

Sarah Beth studied the message Cassie had left on her desk. Chris was on his way. Surprising, since she'd just seen the man two days ago. She saved her work and shut the laptop.

"Knock, knock." Chris poked his head in her office.

She jumped up to greet him. "This is rare. What brings you by my office?"

"I wanted to talk in person, so I got your schedule from Cassie." He gave her a sheepish grin.

"Sounds ominous."

"A little sticky, maybe a bit awkward." Shrugging, Chris crinkled his nose like a little boy.

"I'm ready as I'll ever be. Lay it on me."

"You know how you told me that I could share your story if it would help someone?"

"Yes?"

"I shared it with Nick."

Nick. Of all people, Chris told Jess's best friend about all her past screw-ups.

Had Nick told Jess? Not that she hadn't been planning to tell him herself. Still, she'd have preferred to do it in her own way, in her own timing.

Chris continued, "He's hurting so I suggested a counselor and told him you have one you like. He seemed doubtful, so I told him your story. He's a believer, Sarah Beth. He just hasn't connected with a church since he moved to Oxford. It's been hard being a single parent. His wife was his anchor. I can't help but put myself in his shoes. I don't know how I'd go on if Kim had died giving birth to Camilla."

Poor Nick. That had to be difficult. Sarah Beth put a hand on Chris's shoulder. "I'm glad you told him. You know I want God to make beauty from my ashes."

Chris checked his watch. "Good, because he'll be here at lunch to chat with you. I've gotta run. Sorry."

"I was planning to take a lunch break in, like, fifteen minutes."

"I know. I checked your schedule with Cassie while you were in class. He'll be here any minute. I'll be praying for you to say what God wants him to hear."

Sarah Beth moved her hands to her hips. "You're lucky I like you, Chris Hardy."

As the lanky minister edged toward the door, he grinned. "I know, and I offer you edible food every Tuesday and Saturday."

"There is that, too, I guess." After pulling out a sheet of paper, she wrote her counselor's name and number. Losing someone was tough. Being a single parent on top of the loss, even tougher. She didn't mind helping, but a little notice would've been nice. At least she wouldn't have time to fret about what she'd say.

Minutes later, there was a sharp rap on her door, and Nick poked his head in. "I come bearing food." His raised eyebrows exposed apprehension.

"Then you must come forth." Sarah Beth gave him a smile. "Cassie left for lunch, so we can chat here. Leave the door cracked in case someone happens to be looking for me." She pointed. "Let's sit at the conference table."

Nick eyed the spacious office. "Nice. Jess told me about this place. He's pretty jealous of your setup."

"We have Foundation meetings here." She took a deep whiff. "What is that delicious smell?"

He handed her a Styrofoam box from the brown paper sack.

After opening the container, she placed her hand over her heart. "Yum. How did you know I love a fried green tomato BLT? And zucchini fries. Be still my heart."

"Chris told me you're crazy about that little place off the Square. He gave me your standard order. Here's your half-sweet, half-unsweet tea with three lemons. I hope they got that right."

"Chris does know me pretty well."

Nick opened his box. "I went with the fried chicken blue plate."

Sarah Beth rummaged through her bag. She pulled out papers, an empty bag of gummy worms, and a box of Band-Aids. "You didn't have to buy me lunch. Let me pay for mine."

"No way. You're helping me." Smiling, Nick cleared his throat. "Chris said, hmm, how did he put it? He said you may seem a bit eccentric, but you're like a bucket of wisdom from the well of life."

"Nice. I'll need to brainstorm quirky nicknames for him and spread them throughout CSU and the student body. We'll see who's eccentric. I'm thinking Crispy Critter, Christopher Robin, Crispy Cream…"

She bit into her sandwich. "Mmm, this is delicious." Dabbing away the blob of dressing that fell from the sandwich to her shirt, she swallowed, then sighed. "Wearing my food again."

Nick smiled. An uncomfortable silence filled the space between them.

Um…" How should she start? "I know Chris told you my

story already. I have a counselor you might like. He's normal, you know. Makes you feel like you're talking to your brother or a friend. Sometimes he seems a bit insensitive, like he may say, 'Look, Sarah Beth, stop feeling sorry for yourself, and let's deal with the issue.' Reality therapy." She laughed. "He is sensitive, but he won't let you keep wallowing in the same puddle, if you know what I mean."

"Sounds like what I need." The slight amusement lifting his lips slackened, and his gaze tightened and focused on her. "You know a great deal about loss from what Chris told me. I'll keep it to myself, but I'm sorry we have that in common."

Pain, like a dull blade, knifed at her composure, and she remained silent.

"I'm glad we both have the Lord in common, too." His tone was gentle.

"Yep." If she hadn't had the Lord, she'd have been even crazier.

~~~

What was Nick doing in Sarah Beth's office? Jess's chest felt like a three-hundred-pound tackle had landed on it. He tiptoed back down the staircase and dropped the lunch he'd bought Sarah Beth in a trash can outside her building.

Nick was his best friend. Why wouldn't Nick tell him if— No. There had to be another explanation. Maybe they were talking about Katie and Camilla playing together. There could be a landscape project Sarah Beth needed done on campus. Jess ran his fingers through the front of his hair. Or maybe not. Maybe he should step out of the way, just in case. Nick deserved to be happy.

He pulled out his phone and sent a text to Nick and Sarah Beth.

Too busy with work to take the boat out this weekend.

He heaved a sigh. Not a lie. There was always work.

Back in his office, he found the head coach, Ross Black, standing by his door. "Jess, can we talk privately?"

"Sure." Jess followed his boss into his office and took a seat. "Problem?"

"Not for you. But it could be for me." He crossed his ankle over his knee and sat back. "Word is that the Tampa Bay offensive coordinator may be retiring. He's thinking of getting out to spend time with his grandkids. Probably since he didn't get much with his own kids. You know how it is in this business."

"What does that have to do with us?"

"They tell me your name's being tossed around as a contender. A top contender. They like what you've done for the program here. You've proven yourself despite your youth."

Jess straightened his posture. Maybe it was because he was having a bad day, but the news he'd been waiting for fell flat. Why didn't he feel like celebrating? This was his dream. And back in his home state, no less, nearer his family and the beach he missed. "Tampa Bay's a good team."

"Nothing's written in stone yet, but it could mean a huge opportunity for you. You know I'd hate to lose you. Plus Oxford's a great place if you ever decide to settle down and start a family." He rose, then walked to the door. "You have a lot to consider. I'll support you whatever happens. See you after lunch."

Lunch was the last thing he wanted right now. Too much to think about with Nick living here, plus his relationship with his players...and now Sarah Beth. And for a man like him to lose his appetite... He needed a time out. Maybe a hard run.

Chapter 18

Sarah Beth sat in the living room of Nick's small, two-bedroom townhouse sipping coffee. Though the condo was cheaply built, the interior appeared well-maintained and clean. Especially for a single dad. The four-year-old couldn't contain her excitement about going to Sunday school and talked nonstop as Nick combed her strawberry blond hair. What a sweet picture. The way he was so gentle with Katie. He paused when the front door opened and shut, then footsteps. A cabinet door opened and closed. Was someone else expected?

"Hey, buddy, you got a pot of coffee for your best friend?" That voice.

Sarah Beth's pulse did a little dance.

"You know I do," Nick called back.

"Uncle Jess is here." Katie struggled to pull away.

Nick caught her arm. "One second. Not quite finished." A couple more strokes with the brush and he released her.

At the same time, Jess stepped through the archway of the kitchen. Katie ran to latch her arms around Jess's legs.

"Watch out, squirt. Hot coffee." Jess placed his cup on a side table and lifted Katie up for a hug. He blinked hard as he caught sight of Sarah Beth sitting on the couch.

She gave him a little wave. "Hi, Jess, I missed our time on the water yesterday. I mean, you know, nature and camaraderie and all." Bungling words again.

Shaking his head, Jess turned to Nick. "I'm sorry to just barge in. I didn't realize you had company. Didn't notice the

SUV…"

Nick's hazel eyes rounded. "Oh. No. Sarah Beth's just picking up Katie for church because I have to work. She offered the other day when I went by her office. I was trying to figure out how to get Katie in church again with my crazy schedule, and I needed to sort through a few other—issues, you know."

Jess let Katie down, then put both hands up. "It's none of my business."

After rising to his feet, Nick crossed the small room and placed his hands on Jess's shoulders. "You are not interrupting anything. She just got here."

Not embarrassing at all. Flames licked Sarah Beth's cheeks. "Obviously, Nick is also repulsed by me."

"Also?" Jess's head swiveled back her way.

"Ms. Sarah Beth, what's repulsed?"

Sarah Beth couldn't help but adore this child. "It's like being grossed out."

"I'm not repulsed by you." Katie twisted from side to side holding the edges of her pink flowered dress.

"Thank you, Katie. Let's go, or we'll be late. I can't stand to be late."

Katie tugged Jess's shirt. "You want to go, Uncle Jess?"

His eyes large, Jess appeared paralyzed. "I'm not dressed for church. I'm wearing shorts."

Leave it to a child. Sarah Beth chuckled to herself as she picked up her bag and keys. "You don't live far. We'll swing by and you can throw on some jeans or khakis."

"I don't know." His feet shifted across the tile floor in front of him.

Finally, his turn to look uncomfortable.

"We'll go to class with Katie and sit in to help since it's her first time." She took Katie's hand and nudged Jess out the door. "I've never liked *grown up* Sunday school. I've tried to convince the church leaders to make adult classes more like the kids' classes, where you draw and sing and eat cookies. For some reason, they won't go for it. Neither would any of the other local churches I sent the idea to."

She looked Jess up and down. "And you have to change. I can't deal with girls falling all over themselves if you show up in shorts. They'll be too distracted by your legs. It's bad enough with the rest of you."

Jess gave her a sideways glance.

Did she really just say that? "Um—let's get going." Brain first, then mouth.

"How can I say no to two lovely ladies?"

Katie called back to Nick, who watched from the door. "Bye, Daddy. Be good. I love you."

"I love you, too, darling. I'll be good." His hazel eyes twinkled.

Katie was such a doll. At the SUV, Sarah Beth shuffled a batch of papers into the back. She hadn't expected to use three seats today.

She followed Jess's instructions to his house, a gray cottage-style ranch with white trim. He really did live just a few blocks away. "Hurry. We'll be late."

After disappearing inside for a few moments, Jess jogged back to the vehicle wearing khakis. "Whew. Fast enough for you?"

"Ms. Sarah Beth?" A little voice from the back seat summoned before Sarah Beth could answer.

"Yes, Katie?"

"I don't think you should name your dog Ewok. I think a sensible name like Ginger would be nice. You could call her

Gingie for cute."

Jess snickered, and Sarah Beth smothered a laugh.

This kid should be in one of her focus groups. "I think you're right. What do you mean Gingie for cute, though?"

"My daddy says people call me Katie for short, but he calls me Katie for cute."

Sarah Beth shook her head. "I am more impressed with your daddy all the time. He's a smart man."

~~~

Jess couldn't stop grinning. Who'd believe he was sitting here in this tiny chair in Sunday school with four-year-olds? Enjoying himself. In a period of a few weeks, this woman had brought about so many new emotions. He couldn't seem to control her or these feelings. It was maddening and exhilarating at the same time.

While the Sunday school teacher told the story of Daniel in the lion's den, Sarah Beth helped herself to a second handful of animal crackers. She leaned close to Jess and whispered, "You know God's always connecting the dots. I'm studying the book of Daniel at home, too."

After class, Camilla took Katie's hand. "Mr. Jess and Ms. Sarah Beth, you can go to big church. I'll take Katie with me to children's church."

"Once again, replaced." Sarah Beth laughed. "I guess we have to go to big people church."

Jess scrunched his nose. "If we have to."

As he opened the door of the auditorium, Sarah Beth caught his bicep. "I sit in the balcony. This way."

He eyed her hand on his arm. Even the simple touch of her hand on his arm radiated warmth to his heart. Another reaction he couldn't control. "I guess I should know better than to try to lead the way for you."

She caught him looking at her hand and blushed. "I'm a balcony person. When I came back to the church, it's where I felt comfortable."

Why did he like that he'd made her blush? "What if there was no balcony?"

"Back row with sleepy teenagers and crying babies. It just feels right."

"You don't think God wants you on the front row?"

As they took a seat, she put her finger to her lips and shushed him. "They're singing. Oh, look. Bryan's leading."

Bryan. The singer. Jess elbowed her. "Now there's a young man who is most definitely *not* repulsed by you." He lifted his eyebrows up and down, then nodded toward Bryan.

Her finger pressed over her lips again.

He moved in close to her ear after the first song. "You have a pretty voice."

"Oh. Thanks." The blush colored her cheeks again.

During the message, she cast a glance his way. Was it to make sure he listened? The minister shared about having courage during trials. She'd had more than her share of trials and loss. What had he ever gone through? Nothing much. So he tore up his shoulder and couldn't go pro… The loss had been disappointing—the end of a dream. Was that dream so important? Compared to her, he'd gotten off easy. Courage. She lived it.

After the service, Bryan caught them in the hall. "I'm glad you came today, Coach." He took Sarah Beth's hand when she extended it and spun her around in a little twirl.

"That's quite a greeting." Sarah Beth blinked back her surprise.

Squelching a twinge of jealousy, Jess leaned close as they walked away. "Told you so."

Church hadn't been so bad. He'd actually enjoyed it.

~~~

The sunlit afternoon held little humidity and a cool breeze, the kind of day to be savored in Mississippi. Camilla begged for Katie to come play at her house, so Sarah Beth phoned Nick for permission. A minute later Katie headed home with Kim, Chris, and Camilla.

As Sarah Beth and Jess ambled toward her SUV, Dean Latham rushed over. "Sarah Beth, I see you have a guest, and we'd love for you both to have lunch with us. It's your favorite. Pot roast."

She looked to Jess and lifted her eyebrows.

"There's nothing like a home-cooked meal." Jess shrugged.

"We'll see you in a few minutes. Sarah Beth knows how to get there." The small, yet sturdy balding man grinned and scurried away.

How precious the dean and Mrs. Latham were to her. She pointed at the couple's car before easing out of the lot. "Dean Latham and his wife sort of adopted Mark and me after Gram died. He was one of my professors and a friend of the family. He sent my graduate work to Bill Rogers, his old fraternity brother. Bill hired me that year, and he's still my boss in L.A. Basically, Dean Latham jumpstarted my career. And they're kind enough to invite me to dinner at least once a week."

"Let me get this straight." Jess counted on his fingers. "You eat with Dean Latham for Sunday lunch and maybe another evening, and then Tuesday nights and Saturday nights you eat with Chris and the CSU students? Seems like you don't worry about what's for dinner very often."

"That's a good thing. Evidently, I have a cooking impairment."

"I heard. Chris said I was lucky I survived the coffee you

made at the CSU."

"He may be right. I hired a cleaning service in December, and the woman they sent actually told me that I should never try to use the oven again."

"Was it black from smoke?"

Her jaw dropped. "Did Chris tell you everything?"

Howling, Jess slapped his leg. "I was joking, but apparently your impairment is worse than I imagined."

"I get ideas, go to work on them, and forget about the stove. Speaking of food—here we are." She pulled to a stop in front of the stately, red brick home with white columns.

The savory smell of pot roast met them halfway down the sidewalk. Inside, Mrs. Latham, wearing the blue-and-white checked apron she'd worn every Sunday for as long as Sarah Beth could remember, led them to the dining room where Dean Latham waited.

Maybe she should've bowed out before Jess could accept the offer. Would he think she was introducing him to her family? A knot caught in her throat. She sort of was, but it hadn't been her idea.

Sunday china and cloth napkins lay waiting. This table held memories. She and Mark had eaten here many times over the years. Another bittersweet memory.

After a short prayer of thanks, the bowls of homegrown vegetables circulated along with the pot roast. A few bites later, Sarah Beth's worry dissolved as the conversation flowed easily. She savored the squash casserole and lima beans. Delicious. Why couldn't she cook like this? Maybe it was a blessing she couldn't. She'd be big as a house as much as she liked to eat.

After he'd cleaned his plate, Jess leaned back in his chair and grinned. "That was spectacular, Mrs. Latham. Thank you so much."

The compliment brought a bright smile to their hostess's face. "We have cobbler for dessert. With ice cream or without?"

"With," Jess and Sarah Beth answered in unison.

After a second helping of the fruit topped with crusty pastry, Sarah Beth pulled herself away from the table. Jess shook hands with Dean Latham then hugged Mrs. Latham. "Thanks again."

"You come back any time." Mrs. Latham beamed. "And please call me Barbara."

As they drove away, Sarah Beth shot him a side glance. "You won her over."

"I have my ways." His brown eyes crinkled into a smile, and a grin filled his voice. "Want to call Sam and hit the water? The day's still young."

"We don't get many days like this. My work can wait, I guess."

"Atta girl. I noticed you have a hitch on your SUV. Do you want to pull the boat?"

The simple question jerked her breath away. The shaking hands again. She mashed the words out. "You drive."

"Good. It looks like Office Depot threw up in your back seat."

His playful insult loosened some of the fear tormenting her. "Hey. That's like my third office. I have to carry stuff back and forth all the time."

"We could call Sam and let him off the sidelines." He paused and cleared his throat. "Unless you want to wait until Nick can go."

"Sam's fine."

Thirty minutes later, they hit the lake. The water felt right. Sarah Beth sailed through the rest of the afternoon. No accidents, no worries, no anxiety. Only waves and sun.

Sam behaved himself pretty well, too. For Sam. At the end of the afternoon, they packed up and dropped him at his house first.

Sarah Beth sucked in a deep breath. *Thank you, God, for a normal day.*

Then Jess pulled up to her place, got out, and escorted her to the front door. "Can you talk a while?"

The question ricocheted around her mind. "Sure, but I need to let the dog out." *And gather my wits before I share more about my life.*

"I'll wait." He took a seat in one of the rocking chairs on the porch.

When she returned, Gingie followed on her heels to the adjacent rocker.

Jess's eyes widened. "That dog has grown. It's huge."

"I know. The vet says Gingie might have some Saint Bernard along with the Chow/Basset Hound thing. She was thrown by the growth spurt, too."

"So, we're calling her Gingie now?" A laugh bubbled from Jess.

"Yeah. Katie had a point about Ewok. I might feel weird hollering that name down the street or at the park."

He bent down to scratch around Gingie's collar. "Do you feel like starting, you know...where we left off?"

Sarah Beth leaned back in the chair. "I left off when Gram died. I began questioning my faith for the first time. Not only was I angry with God, I wondered about things. Is there really a heaven? Is this all there is? When Mom and Dad died in the fire, there was only a memorial. It was as if they just disappeared. We were with Gram when she passed. It seemed wrong to leave her with strangers and bury her in the ground.

Her body was there, but where was she?" Sarah Beth paused and raised her hand to her forehead, running her fingers through her hair. The first time she shared all of her past would be the hardest.

"I know I mentioned that I'd started partying. I was lonely. I met a guy. Adam. A month later, I basically moved in with him, although I still owned Gram's house. He was a senior pre-med major, and I was finishing my MBA.

"He was accepted to medical school in L.A, and I had a job offer with a company there, as well. Adam said he didn't think we had to get married to prove our love. His parents had lived in a loveless marriage, so for him, marriage meant nothing. They were together only because they didn't want to divide their wealth. He said he didn't want money to be what held us together.

"We were both passionate about our careers. Adam focused on his goal to get his medical degree, specialize in infectious disease, and secure sponsors for a clinic in Honduras. Since his parents spent little time with him, Alma, his housekeeper, and her son, Miguel, were more like family than his own parents. When Miguel and Alma traveled back home to Honduras one summer, Miguel contracted dengue fever. He didn't recover. Miguel's death drove Adam to study infectious disease—to look for a cure."

The rapid pounding in her pulse forced Sarah Beth to stop for a deep breath.

The rocking chair creaked under Jess's weight as he bent forward from the waist and rested his elbows on his knees. "Sounds like a productive way to deal with the loss." His gaze still locked onto hers, waiting for the rest.

"I loved his passion for his cause. I helped plan a fact-finding trip to a successful health clinic in Guatemala.

"As the years passed, Adam and I lived together, but we rarely saw each other. I felt Adam didn't love me anymore, at least not enough to commit to me. I realized I'd made a mistake."

The beginning of the end of this story. Sarah Beth swallowed at the bitter taste in her mouth and rubbed her palms together.

"I went to see Adam's chief, Dr. Rodriguez, at the hospital. We'd worked together on the fact-finding mission, and we had a good rapport. Dr. Rodriguez welcomed me into his office, and we talked about the project and plans for the upcoming visit to the medical facility in Guatemala. Before I left, I asked Dr. Rodriguez if something was wrong with Adam—I felt some underlying tension and distance I couldn't pin down. He mentioned Adam had a new research assistant.

"It had been so long since I'd visited Adam at work, I almost got lost on the way. As I neared his department, I saw him talking at a young woman's desk. His manner was carefree and charming. He smiled at her as she talked. I felt sick to my stomach looking at them, but it was too late to turn around. Adam saw me standing there."

~~~

The ringing of Jess's cell phone broke into Sarah Beth's story. Cringing, he checked the number. One of the players. "Sorry, I need to answer this." He stood and walked to the edge of the porch. "Yeah."

Loud music and voices met Jess's ear.

"Coach, Cole's drunk and about to punch out some fraternity dude."

Not again. "Where?"

"Same as last time."

"I'll be right over." Could the timing be worse? But he

couldn't let his star quarterback end up in jail. He returned to
Sarah Beth. "I'm sorry. I hate to do this, but I've got a drunk
and belligerent quarterback over on the Square causing a
commotion. I need to corral him back to his apartment to
sober up."

"Duty calls." She waved him off. "I totally understand."

Letting out a sigh, he pulled his keys from his pocket, and
jogged to his truck. It was always something. He punched the
accelerator the few blocks to town and pulled up on the
sidewalk. He never got a ticket. Police knew his truck and were
all too happy for him to take care of these things before they
got out of hand.

The crowd in the dimly-lit bar divided like the Red Sea.
Football players on one side. Everyone else on the other. Grant
Vaughn held Cole back, his massive arms caging the tall blond
quarterback. "Not happening, Cole. We'll all pay for your—"

"I got this, Grant." Jess stood beside his players, hands by
his side, feet planted. "Cole, my truck. Now. The rest of the
team, home."

He gave them an icy stare. The players filed out, Cole last,
jaw locked.

Once they cleared the door, Jess opened his hand. "Keys."

Cole complied. "Coach, I didn't—"

"We'll talk back at your place."

The smell of smoke and liquor filled the truck as Jess drove
Cole to his apartment complex. This had to stop. He got that
Cole wanted to have a good time, but things were out of hand.
The fighting and binge drinking were not okay.

Jess parked and followed Cole down the sidewalk. After
unlocking the door, Jess held onto Cole's keys. "Let's sit on the
balcony. You have anything to drink that's hydrating?"

Cole opened the refrigerator and pulled out a six-pack of

sports drinks. "This work?"

"Bring it." Jess opened the sliding glass door and sat in one of the two navy Adirondack chairs. "Are you smoking now? You reek."

Cole sank into the other chair and guzzled the liquid. "No. I was sitting in a car with a girl I met. She was smoking. We had some beer and...you know, hooked up. We went back in the bar and this guy gets in my face saying I messed with his girlfriend."

Jess studied Cole. He didn't see any sign the kid was lying. Cole was known to be a player—one girl after another.

"Coach, I wasn't looking for a fight. I was out to have a good time. Nothing wrong with that, is there?"

Jess stretched his arms in front of him then let them fall back to the armrests. He'd made his share of mistakes back in the day. Not so much with the drinking, though. "You don't have to look for trouble. It'll find you. What do you think you should do when that happens?"

"You told me last time. I should turn around and leave." Clenching his fists, he sat up and scooted to the edge of the chair. "I get so ticked with the guys out there looking to fight the quarterback. Like they want to prove themselves. Then there's the others that want to act like you're their best bud— buying you drinks and stuff. But they don't know you. Not really."

Jess nodded. "I've been there. But it's up to you to be smart. You wouldn't be a quarterback if you didn't have something up there." He flicked Cole's head. "You know that, right?"

Cole bent forward, elbows on his knees, face resting in his hands. "I'm not so sure."

Placing a hand on his back, Jess tried to assure him. "I'm

positive. I've seen you in action."

Cole's chin lifted. "Positive?"

"Positive."

"Thanks for helping me out of that mess."

Jess stood. "I'm keeping your keys. We'll get your car back to you later—after you've had time to sober up."

"Thanks."

All the drama with college players didn't bother him that much. He enjoyed getting to know the guys, counseling them. But tonight, he'd had to leave Sarah Beth in the middle of their conversation. Terrible timing.

What would it be like in the pros? Would it be about molding the players, or more about profits and bottom line? Was that what he really wanted?

Chapter 19

Two years earlier.

"I can't believe you didn't mention this." Jill threw a tabloid on Sarah Beth's desk and stared at her, hands on hips. "Talk to me."

"I have no idea what you're going on about." Sarah Beth scrutinized the paper in front of her. A notoriously underhanded tabloid headlined with a picture of Dylan Conner and a 'mystery woman in blue.' The dark-haired woman's face couldn't be seen from the photo's angle, but the image clearly displayed Dylan's famous green eyes gazing at the woman. Jill must've recognized her dress. But would anyone else? This couldn't come at a worse time. "That area was supposed to be camera-free—secure." She waved her hands around. "Nothing happened, so there's nothing to tell. We were just chatting. Oh, and he offered to sell me his condo in Malibu. I'm supposed to call him."

"He gave you his phone number?" Jill shrieked. "He's so hot."

Another reason not to call the actor about his condo—crazed women might show up thinking he still lived there. "I'm not interested in Dylan Conner. The only reason I'd call him is to discuss a possible purchase. I have no idea what I'm doing in my life right now." Slumping forward, she let her head fall into her hands and massaged her forehead. "I'm confused about...everything."

"I've been there." Jill squeezed Sarah Beth's shoulder.

"Sorry I upset you. I'm probably the only one that'll recognize you in the photo. I'll be at my desk if you want to talk."

"I appreciate it. Better throw myself into this latest project." She folded the paper shut with a slap. "And throw this in the trash."

Should she tell Adam or hope he didn't by some weird chance see the paper and recognize her? The odds of him looking at one of those covers in a grocery store were slim. And they had enough to figure out already.

An hour later, Jill called into Sarah Beth's office, her voice strained. "You have a visitor." She cleared her throat. "A Mr. Dylan Conner."

Sarah Beth's chest tightened. What now?

"Sarah Beth?"

Was Jill joking? "Send him in, thank you."

Still speculating whether Jill was teasing her, she slathered on lip balm and shuffled stacks of papers to the corner of her desk. The door opened, and the auburn-haired actor with sparkling green eyes strolled into the office.

He surveyed the myriad of ads and awards lining the back wall. "So, this is where the magic happens."

Sarah Beth stood and extended a hand. "I'd say that your office is where the magic happens. What brings me the honor of this personal visit?"

"Can we talk?" Dylan squeezed her fingers and nodded toward the sitting area near the windows. "Incredible view you have."

"Thanks. Have a seat." She plopped into the club chair to the left of him and waited.

"I want to apologize for getting you sucked into the paparazzi vortex." He reached over and placed his hand on top of hers. "I'm not sure how someone managed it, but at least your face wasn't in the picture. Did your significant other see it? What was his name?"

Her hand slipped out from under his. "It's not your fault. You must get tired of dealing with never having any privacy." She paused and looked out the window. "Maybe I should close the blinds."

"That's not necessary unless—" Raising his eyebrows, he gave her a carnal look.

"No. Not necessary." Biting back a sigh, she stood to lead him out. "Thanks for stopping by. I appreciate it, but everything's fine."

"Sarah Beth?" Confusion crinkled his brows together.

"Yes?" Why was he still sitting in the chair?

"You do like men, right?"

What an ego. "Dylan, I've been with someone, a man, for years. He's a doctor at the university. I mentioned the other night that I'm trying to come to terms with God and what that means to my relationship with Adam."

"Adam, the doctor." He smiled as if he'd won an Academy Award. "Now I have a name. You could think more clearly if you rented or bought my condo. The view alone will sell you, and I'll make you a deal you can't refuse."

Combatting the conflicting thoughts raging through her mind, she simply nodded.

"A nice property in Malibu for a good price is unheard of. I'll have the details and a price sent to you."

"I like the area, but I haven't talked to my boss or Adam. Besides, I won't buy the first condo I see. I have to research property values and all." She met his eyes straight on. "You know if I buy it, I'll change the locks. And my brother, Mark, works for the FBI."

"Once you do your research, you'll see that I have what

you need." One side of his lips lifted into a smirk. "You are quite a challenge, Ms. LeClair."

A cone of silence would be nice right about now. She fought the urge to return with a sarcastic comment. A knock sounded on her door, and Juan poked his head in. "I am sorry to disturb you, but the president of the board of directors for the Guatemala Charity Clinic wants a conference call with you and Dr. Rodriguez in ten minutes. I alerted Dr. Rodriguez, and he is available. Are you?"

Thank goodness. "Yes, thank you. And Juan, I'd like you to listen in and take notes, please."

Juan nodded and closed the door.

"You're kicking me out?" Dylan feigned injury, his hand over his heart.

She caught her lip between her teeth. *Hmmm.* Wouldn't it be great to have someone like Dylan bring attention to the clinic? "Actually, stay and listen. You could be a part of something incredible." She explained the dengue fever research and the planned clinic in Honduras. Her best pitch hit the mark. Dylan Conner, one of the so-called "hottest men alive," agreed to become a part of Clinic Miguel's Hope.

~~~

After the conference call ended and Dylan left, Sarah Beth pulled a chair to Juan's desk. "I'm interested in getting my own place, maybe in Malibu. Could you put together some places and numbers for me? I've written my price range on this card."

"Of course." His eyes searched hers. "Are you praying?"

She dropped her head into her hands. "Every time I'm alone, whether I'm in my car or the shower or jogging, I'm crying out to Him. It hurts too much to think of being without Adam, but I know I have to put space between us, and put God first. I finally realized how much I miss God's presence and how much of His time I've wasted running after things that won't satisfy." Tears spilled down her cheeks.

"Oh, how He loves you, Sarah Beth. He has a plan for you. Every mistake and every bit of pain you have been through, and will go through, God can redeem, if you will let Him. I prayed for you and was reminded of a verse in Isaiah that says He will 'give beauty for ashes, the oil of joy for mourning, the garment of praise for the spirit of heaviness; that they might be called trees of righteousness, the planting of the Lord, that He might be glorified.'"

"Beauty for ashes. That sounds comforting." She pulled a tissue from the box on Juan's desk and wiped her face. "I appreciate your prayers. I plan to continue visiting your church. When I find my own place, I'd like to find a church home nearby, so I'll have fewer excuses to skip out."

"That is an answer to my prayers and your brother's as well."

"Have you two been talking about me again?"

Juan laughed and held up his hands. "No comment." His face became serious. "There is something I want to talk to you about."

"Sounds ominous, but all right." If he was resigning or something, that might send her over the edge.

"This trip to Guatemala, I feel led to go. I am not sure if I can afford the expense, but I must."

Of course he wanted to go. She delighted in this good man. "You know, I've been practicing my Spanish, but I'm not sure I'm sufficiently fluent yet. I'll probably need to bring along my translator."

He grinned. "Thank you. You will not regret it. Now, tell me more about this dengue fever and the safety precautions I will help to organize."

"Dengue infection is a leading cause of illness and death in the tropics and subtropics. It's spread by certain mosquitoes. Last time I checked, the disease affected up to four hundred million people yearly. With no cure or vaccines to prevent infection, I'm thinking we need a ton of bug spray, mosquito netting, and those clothes that have the built-in insect repellent.

"You've no doubt heard me talk about this before, but at the hospital, we fund research and development for a vaccine and a cure. The clinic is a separate entity—Adam's way to honor his friend Miguel in his home country. We want volunteer doctors and nurses to travel down for a week at a time to see patients while we keep a nurse practitioner on-site full-time."

"Will you have a chapel?"

"I haven't thought about that. Let's see how the clinic in Guatemala works and go from there." She released a pent-up breath and stood. "Next, I need to talk to Bill about work changes I'm planning. Pray for that, too."

"You know I will."

On the way down the hall, she practiced what she'd say. Bill's door was open, and he smiled as she approached. No turning back now. "Bill, can you set aside some time to talk?"

"Now's as good as any. Come in. What's going on?"

Sarah Beth sat with her hands in her lap. *This could work. Be firm.* "Four proposals I need you to endorse. One, this would be the perfect time for me to make that trip to Paris to call on the accounts. Two, I'd like to move to Malibu and work two days a week from home on creative projects, leaving Juan in the office to manage operational issues. Three, soon after I return from Paris, I'll be going on the trip to Guatemala to work on the mission you've heard me talk endlessly about since I came here. Four, I want to have the authority to pick and choose which products or projects I represent. No more seedy commercials, R-rated movies, that kind of thing. I want to represent companies and products I consider wholesome."

Bill sat forward and tapped his fingers on his desk. "So, little Sarah Beth is finally taking control of her life."

"No, I'm finally giving up control and giving it back to God."

"You know we don't want to lose our creative genius. I'm surprised it's taken this long for you to realize you could ask for most anything as long as you stay with the company. I don't have a problem endorsing any of those requests, and I may go with you to work the Paris accounts."

"You should bring Carol. You said she wants you to spend more time with her. I could bring Jill along. I've been trying to find an opportunity to train her more extensively. She could do so much more than what she's doing now. She's a smart girl."

"I'll talk to Carol tonight. Get Juan to make the travel arrangements for us as soon as possible. I don't know how you found such a good assistant."

"Trust me, it was a God thing."

~ ~ ~

"This is amazing." Jill twirled around as she walked across the bridge over the Seine River. "It's everything I imagined."

Watching Jill's exuberance over her first trip to Paris was a hoot. Bringing her along had been a blessing.

Carol gave Sarah Beth a hug. "I'm loving this journey, too. You and Jill are great travel buddies. This must've been your idea."

"Bill said he wanted to spend more time with you."

Carol gave Bill an appreciative look and took his hand in hers as they walked.

For Sarah Beth, Paris was a welcome reprieve from the

decisions to be made back home. She rose early and strolled by the river before the others woke up each day. Taking advantage of the solitude, she prayed for clarity and wisdom. For Adam, too.

On the last night, they celebrated their successful meetings with dinner in the heart of the city. Bill looked over his empty plate. "I don't know about you ladies, but I'm going to miss the food here." He turned to Carol and gave her a longing look. "Among other things."

Carol blushed. "Bill, not in front of the children."

Snickering, Sarah Beth rubbed her stomach. "I love traveling. There must be some kind of tour where I could eat my way through Europe."

"It's great here, but—" Jill rolled her eyes. "I'll pay for it with extra spin classes to work this off my waistline."

Sarah Beth frowned. "You're thin, blond, and beautiful. You should relax a little." She turned to Bill. "On another note, sorry about that account I passed on, but her clothes were…"

Bill gave her a knowing look. "I understand. Her clothes, if you could call them that, were against the new Sarah Beth morality policy. I think I've placated her, though. Toby Ackerman will handle her account."

~~~

Sara Beth whispered, "Shh, I think I hear him coming." As Juan rounded the corner carrying a stack of papers, she pushed Jill out from behind the door and yelled. "We're back. Did you miss us?"

Papers flew up from Juan's arms then fluttered back down around them. "Leaping Amazons. You are early."

"That was hilarious." Jill plopped down at her desk, giggling. "We really scared you."

"You did." Juan laughed. "Would you like me to drive you

ladies home so you can rest? I sense jet lag."

"And delirium. Call Jill a cab. I have to stay and catch up. If I need to, I'll shut the door and rest on the couch." After Jill left, Sarah Beth went through the work on her desk and her email. "Juan, can you update me?"

"Of course. And I have a list of properties for you to consider."

Sarah Beth scanned the numbers. "These condos are so much more expensive than the one Dylan Conner is selling. I need to go see the place for myself. I wonder if they could fit me in today."

"You should rest. You will be too tired to drive all over the West Coast."

"I'll ask the agent to drive me. I have to find a place as soon as possible."

A quick call, and the agent was more than willing to pick her up. No surprise, given the commission. Dylan insisted on meeting them.

The place was modern—open and airy. Bigger than the little studio she shared with Adam. Her gut twisted as she toured the two bedrooms. The thought of being alone...

In the living area, the sunset over the Pacific provided a spectacular backdrop through the west wall of windows. The deck outside would make a great place to pray and think. Maybe this would work.

"I couldn't have timed this better." Dylan motioned toward the glass. "The sunset alone should sell you, but I told you I'm giving you a fantastic deal. I want someone to have this place who will enjoy it as much as I did."

Sarah Beth raised an eyebrow. "I'm not sure anyone could fill your shoes on that one."

"I did have some good times here."

"Your price is the best value I've found. When could I move in if I decide to take it?"

"I could give you a key tonight. I trust you. We'll work out the financing and contract later."

"I won't be financing."

"Smart, pretty, and independent—what more could a guy want?"

She held up her index finger and pointed at him. "I'm only buying the condo. We're straight on that, right?"

"A guy can dream, can't he?"

"You could win an Academy Award for all that hot air you're blowing." She motioned around the room at the neutral, California-style décor, including two sofas and a few club chairs. "What about the furniture in here?"

"You can use it. I kept it for guests."

"I may do that for a while."

Dylan took her hand. "It's a done deal then?"

Was she really doing this? Leaving Adam to live alone? She mashed her eyes together and took a deep breath. "I may live to regret this, but yes."

Chapter 20

Gingie's howl charged into Sarah Beth's thoughts and brought her back to the present. "You want me to take you for a walk, girl?" She pulled the leash from the hook by the door and clipped it to the collar on the puppy that now seemed a foot taller than she had the week before. "Remember, Gingie, I'm the leader."

Gingie forgot.

Sarah Beth sprinted down the sidewalk trying to keep up. A tap on a car horn shot her head around. Jess passed, waving and laughing. Impeccable timing, as usual.

The puppy slowed. Finally. Sarah Beth plodded back to the house. A heavy-set gray-haired woman stretched across her porch swing.

"Hi, can I help you?"

"I'd love for you to help me." A familiar man's voice emanated from the woman's mouth.

Sarah Beth blinked hard, her mind attempting to make sense of the situation.

"Is that any way to greet a friend and client from out of town?" the masculine voice asked.

Either she'd lost her mind or… "Dylan? Is that you?"

"Priceless." Dylan bent over and snickered. "The look on your face. My disguise to get here without the paparazzi—clever, right?"

"Weird." She took a seat in the rocking chair.

He brought his legs to the wood floor and tugged at his

skirt. "Aren't you going to ask me in or something?"

"I don't have men in my house alone. Even men dressed as women." What was he doing here? Unannounced. "Can I get you some tea or something, Aunt Bee?"

"Aunt Bee? I look way younger and a mite prettier if you ask me."

She would laugh, but this could be a big problem. "Didn't. Where are you staying?"

"Can't stay here?"

"Let me think about it. No."

"I like the way you handle your clients with kid gloves."

He thought he could just show up and stay in her house? "You don't have a reservation at a hotel?"

"I looked up your address on the Internet and saw that you have a pool house."

She pushed back the urges to slap his face and to laugh. He *was* funny. Like a big kid. A naughty kid. "What if it was a storage shed?"

He cocked his head and smiled. "Is it a storage shed?"

That wig. His dress all puffy with who knows what. A laugh escaped her throat. "Are you wearing that costume the whole time you're here?"

"Actually, I'm getting tired of it. Pantyhose are the worst." He wiped his brow. "Especially in this humidity."

"Hose? I don't know how long it's been since I forced a pair of those on."

A pout formed on his lips. "Not all of us can have smooth legs like yours, sister."

His voice was the perfect imitation of an old Southern woman.

She sighed. "You are quite an actor. What am I going to do with you?"

Dylan took off his wig and gazed at her. "That's what I want to know."

"Let me make a couple of calls."

Ten phone calls later, she'd given it her best shot. Every reputable hotel in the area was booked with the writers convention in town. "The pool house is small. I have friends with beautiful homes who would love to put you up for a few days." And he wouldn't be in such close proximity.

Dylan batted his eyelashes. "I bet there's plenty of room in your pool house for little old me."

"Fine. I'll be right back. Wait here." Not wise, but she wouldn't send him packing. Yet. What if the press saw him? Or crazy fans? Or Jess? She dug the keys from a drawer in the laundry room and trudged back out the door. "Here. There should be towels and everything you need to freshen up. Unless you need some makeup remover?"

"Very hospitable of you, ma'am, but I brought my own." He winked, took the keys, and then strutted down the sidewalk to his rental car. "I'll text you when I'm ready for you to take me out and show me the sights."

"Please wear a different outfit. Something casual. And male."

"Your wish is my command." Collecting a backpack, he disappeared into the backyard, and Sarah Beth composed herself for an evening entertaining one of America's most popular stars.

~~~

A guttural growl emanated from Gingie, and the dog tore out of the bedroom. A loud crash down the hall sent Sarah Beth jumping from her dressing table. She sprinted into the living room. "Whoa, what's going on, Gingie? Slow down."

Dylan stood near the back door, wearing a hippie wig and

fake mustache, the oversized puppy on her hind legs, hanging from his sleeve. Snarling, the dog showed her teeth as she held on. Dylan waved his other arm in the air. "I give up. Don't eat me."

Sarah Beth clutched her stomach as a laugh erupted. She hadn't laughed that hard in more than a year. A tear ran down her cheek as she took in the spectacle.

"So…help me already."

"I'm trying. I can't breathe." After carefully removing the growling dog, she crated Gingie, caught her breath, and returned down the hall. "Are you and your shirt okay?"

"Fine." He rolled his eyes.

"I wish I had that on video. The stunned look on your face and that fake mustache. I'm sorry. That's never happened before. Who knew she had it in her to be a guard dog?"

"I think you mean bizarro attack dog. You told me you had some rule about men in the house, but you didn't say it was dangerous. I knocked, but you didn't answer, so I stepped inside."

"You were supposed to text me." She waved him out of the house. "Let's go, or we'll be standing in line forever."

"Where are we headed? A bistro or a club with dancing?"

Her mouth twitched into a smirk. "It's a little old store out in the country that makes the best fried catfish and hush puppies you'll ever taste. If we don't get there early, the line will be down the street unless I can call in a favor."

"That sounds…different. I'll probably fit right in with this costume."

She prayed no one recognized him.

As promised, a line snaked out of the rugged old store. Hungry hopefuls sat in rocking chairs on the long wooden porch and on tailgates around the dirt parking lot. Every sort of attire could be found, from overalls to business suits.

While they waited, Dylan took a deep whiff. "It smells great out here. This place must be fantastic. There's certainly a crowd."

She breathed in the scent of fried fish and potatoes. It did smell delicious. "It's one of the many hidden jewels around Mississippi. I loved the fresh fish tacos and avocados in California, but Mississippi doesn't have one of the highest obesity rates in the country for nothing. We've got some people who know how to cook."

"You not being one of them."

"Why are people always knocking my cooking?"

"It's not edible. Or safe."

"When have you had something I made?"

"The fundraiser at my house. You brought a dip. Bill warned me not to eat it, but I didn't listen. Big mistake. We threw it out before more guests had the same experience."

"Oh, that. I think I accidently used cumin instead of chili powder. I thought it wouldn't make much difference."

"It did. Hey, I think they called for us. You must've had some pull after all. Let's go, I'm starving." Inside, he offered his arm to her as they followed the waitress past the tables covered with red and white plastic cloths.

Along the way, Sarah Beth waved and greeted Oxford acquaintances but moved at a fast pace so she wouldn't have to introduce Dylan. No one within the brick walls covered with graffiti and old pictures bothered to stare at the long-haired man wearing a cap, fake mustache, and tinted glasses.

They took their seats, and she set her menu aside without looking at it. "So, Dylan, you want to tell me about the hold-up for the movie promos?"

"It's fine. I just wanted an excuse to see you in person.

Catch up. What are you having?"

She should've guessed. "I always get catfish, hushpuppies, fried green tomatoes, and turnip greens."

"My trainer would have a heart attack, but I'll try the same."

They made small talk and ate every bite of the deep-fried food. Plate empty, Dylan leaned back and smiled. "That was everything you promised and more." He patted his midsection. "This place has its charm."

"Had enough fun for one night? Ready to head back to my place?"

"I could never have too much fun, but heading back to your place sounds promising."

"No."

Dylan chuckled. "You can't blame a guy for trying. Can you?"

~~~

The next morning, Sarah Beth sipped her watery coffee and checked her email while Gingie lounged at her feet. She'd dug out the makeup Jill insisted she buy for special occasions and applied it. The paparazzi might find Dylan, and if she was going to be on covers of gossip rags in grocery stores around the country, she may as well look her best. Even if the press didn't see Dylan, what if Jess did? What would he think?

Dylan insisted she come to the pool house when she was ready to go out, so he wouldn't upset the *attack dog*. She scanned the yard while she waited for him to answer the door. The white picket fence surrounding the pool gleamed with fresh paint, and the thick green ivy growing up the trellis had been trimmed into submission by the new landscapers Nick had suggested. Pine straw circled the pink and white azaleas. She pulled her phone from her pocket and glanced at the time.

What was taking Dylan so long?

The door swung open. Shirtless and in boxers, Dylan stood, drying his hair with a towel. "Sorry, I slept like a baby out here. Didn't even hear my alarm. Come in."

She dropped her eyes from his bare chest to the ground. "I'll wait out here."

"Have it your way." Smiling, he turned away.

Five minutes later, he reappeared dressed in jeans and polo shirt. No costume, only a pair of sunglasses and a white baseball cap.

"You're not wearing a wig or makeup? The mustache was a lady killer." And someone might recognize him.

"Apparently, not all ladies think so. What's on tap for today? Tractor pull? Tobacco spitting contest?"

She punched her fists to her hips. "Very funny. And where exactly are you from?"

"Boone, North Carolina."

"Is that where you heard of tobacco spitting contests?"

A half-smile formed on Dylan's perfect lips. "I guess I deserve that."

"How do you feel about touring Faulkner's home, the campus, antique stores, and a great bookstore? I know it's not Rodeo Drive…" As if she had time to take a day away from work. But Dylan had come all that way at her request, and *he was* the client she needed to win over.

His hand caught the back of her arm. "Sounds perfect."

They strolled to her SUV. "I called a friend and reserved the upper floor of one of the town's nicest restaurants for supper. Your trainer may be more pleased with the menu."

"My trainer's not here, so don't worry about making him happy."

"The food's fabulous, just not all fried. You'll love the

chef."

"I trust you with my palate." Dylan pivoted toward her and winked. "And everything else."

Sarah Beth ignored his relentless flirting as they enjoyed the sunny day perusing art, books, and antiques. It was nice to spend time with a friend. She hadn't been to many of these places since college.

"This is a charming town. You should come with me to visit Boone sometime. The mountains, clear creeks, and red barns are picturesque, like a painting. It's much cooler, too. The humidity here is killer." Dylan wiped his brow as they exited the SUV. "I'll have to take another shower before dinner."

He moved closer and his gaze wandered from her eyes to her lips. "You're welcome to join me."

This had to end. "We need to talk."

"Uh-oh."

"Dylan, I'm not interested in dating."

"We don't need to have anything heavy."

"You're not getting it. A professional relationship and a friendship. That's it."

Dylan reached for her and slid his hand down her back. "I know you've been through so much, but you can't close yourself off forever, Sarah Beth. In L.A. I knew that you were with…"

"Adam. You can say his name. What you're not getting is that God is my first love now. If I ever date, the person I get involved with will have God as his first love, too."

Pausing as if in thought, Dylan worked his jaw. "Can't we just enjoy each other? See what happens?" He moved a strand of hair from her shoulder.

"I thought we had a nice time today."

"That is not what I mean." His eyes glimmered.

She scooted away from him. "Dylan, as my grandpa used to say, you're barking up the wrong hill. I'm going to change for dinner. I'll text you when I'm ready."

"I think you mean tree." He sank his hands into his pockets. "But, I got it. I'll meet you outside in an hour."

The disappointed look on his face tugged at her heart. She hadn't wanted to hurt his feelings, but she needed to set things straight. They were on very different paths.

The shower washed away some of the day's heat and tension. Of course, as soon as they went back out, she'd be sweating again with the humidity. Like air you could wear.

She stared in her closet. What should she put on? Something presentable, but not flirty. Practical. Her closet was full of that.

She picked a mid-calf red cotton skirt and a collared matching blouse with low-heeled brown sandals for the walk. Nothing fancy.

She peeked out the window. Dylan waited on the sidewalk right on time. Picture perfect. He did look nice with that dark auburn hair, those green eyes, and that beautiful smile. She couldn't deny that much. For just a moment, she wondered what it felt like to be in Dylan's arms, have those perfect lips touch hers. Wouldn't it be lovely to let herself get lost in those eyes? To escape the pain for just a little while...

Jess's brown eyes took over her thoughts. She swallowed at the lump forming in her throat.

Then Adam's.

She'd made that mistake before. God would fill the void in her heart.

Outside, she met him with a smile. "Do you mind if we walk? It's not far."

"Fine with me." His eyes fell to the ground, his voice flat.

The three blocks to the Oxford Square passed in silence. The sun dropped, leaving strands of pinks and purples elongating across luminous clouds. Gardenias and magnolias delivered bursts of color and sweet scents of an early summer in the yards along the way.

"It's a lovely evening." Making small talk was a struggle after the earlier conversation with him.

"It's nice to be able to walk downtown. You don't see that much anymore. You look lovely, by the way." The flirtatious tone rematerialized. "You're stunning in red."

Music from a college bar down the road blended with the sounds of the evening crickets, frogs, and cicadas. A perfect Mississippi evening. If only Dylan could accept the friend zone. "Do you fly back tomorrow?"

"Around lunch, out of Memphis."

"You should go to Graceland if you've never been."

"I've always wanted to see Graceland. Want to follow me up there, and we can see it together?"

An image of the interstate filled her mind. She lost her footing and tripped forward.

Dylan reached out to steady her.

Ice water seemed to pump through her veins, and her palms perspired. The gate inside her brain fell down. Again. Her vision blurred. "Um, I'm booked."

Dylan kept his hand on her arm. "You're trembling. Did you hurt yourself?"

She pressed her lips into a smile. "Just my usual graceful self."

He studied her face before he released her arm. "You're still struggling, aren't you? Are the panic attacks as bad as when you left Los Angeles?"

"We're here." Sarah Beth pointed to the restaurant housed in a remodeled nineteenth-century brick cotton gin. "Put on your tinted glasses and cap, at least until we get seated upstairs."

Dylan complied then placed his hand on the small of her back.

The touch spurred her to rush through the restaurant door, plowing into a man near the entrance. "Oh, I'm so sorry, sir."

The man spun around and caught her. "No problem, ma'am." Warm brown eyes and a familiar grin.

"Hey, it's you." Her heartbeat fluttered in her throat. *Jess.* Warmth started where his fingers held her arm and traveled throughout her body. She beamed. Probably too much.

"It is me." His smile faltered as his gaze intensified. "I need to tell you something."

The hostess interrupted him. "How many in your party, ma'am?"

"I'm Sarah Beth LeClair. I have reservations for a private party upstairs."

Jess's forehead crinkled. "You're the one who's hogging the whole upstairs? Where's the party?"

"Oh, I'm with one of my clients, and we need some privacy."

"Just you and him?" Jess eyed Dylan and raised an eyebrow.

Dylan looked on without speaking.

Fidgeting, Sarah Beth kicked at the pine floor. "How many are in your party?"

Jess waved her off. "It's just an old friend and me, no big deal. We're fine sitting downstairs. I was just giving you a hard time. Sorry."

A woman appeared behind Jess. A beautiful and sensual

woman Sarah Beth had seen before.

Sophia Edmunds. Her long manicured fingernails raked across Jess's bicep. "I'm back. Did you find out why we can't sit upstairs, Jessup?"

What was she doing with Jess? In that low-cut red dress.

Dylan stepped up and gawked at Sophia. "Sarah Beth, aren't you going to introduce me to your friends?"

The hostess arrived to seat them.

"Dylan, this is Jess, a friend of mine. Would you mind if he and his companion joined us upstairs?"

Dylan's gaze remained on Sophia. "Would not mind at all."

~~~

Jess stepped out of the way for Sarah Beth and Sophia to climb the steep wooden stairs leading to the second floor.

That guy Dylan looked familiar. The man stepped in beside Sophia and offered his arm. "I'd hate for you to fall with those high heels on these old stairs."

A wicked grin spread across Sophia's ample lips. "Thank you."

The hostess led them to a table for four near the window that overlooked the town square. She lay a menu at each place. Dylan held a chair out for Sophia, his eyes traveling up and down her curves. *What a jerk.* Jess pulled another chair for Sarah Beth. He waited for her to take a seat. She didn't seem ruffled by her rude date. Or was it a date? She'd said it was business.

"Thank you, Jess." Sarah Beth's sweet voice caused him to smile.

He held her gaze. "Thanks for letting us invade your dinner."

Dylan took off his hat and tinted glasses. "Any friend of Sarah Beth's is a friend of mine. I'm Dylan Conner." He flashed a cheesy smile. "I don't think I caught your names?"

The actor? What was he doing here? "I'm Jess McCoy, and this is my old friend Sophia Edmunds." He glanced at Sarah Beth. "She dropped in unexpectedly from out of town."

Sophia pooched out her bottom lip. "Jessup, I hardly care for being called your 'old friend.' There's only six years between us." She flipped her long, jet-black hair and turned to Dylan. "I can see why your *friend* wanted you all to herself up here. Dylan Conner. The actor, right?"

"That's the reason for the glasses and hat. And I think Sarah Beth's ashamed to be seen with me for some reason." He winked at Sarah Beth, who seemed to struggle not to roll her eyes. "Tell me, Sophia, where in the world did a vision of beauty like yourself originate? I can't place your accent."

"Most recently, Paris, but I travel the world. I own and design the Sophia Fashion line."

"You should get Sarah Beth to promote your account. She's amazing. That's why I came to Oxford, to meet with her about my latest project."

Sophia turned to Sarah Beth. "Are you Sarah Beth LeClair with the Parker Morgan Agency?"

"Yes." Sarah Beth took a swallow of water and stared into her glass. "We met in Paris."

Sophia looked to Dylan, again flipping her hair. "Her agency markets my line, but Ms. LeClair was *unavailable*. Another talent has my account."

It sounded like Sarah Beth had turned down Sophia's account. Jess couldn't help but feel sorry for her, caught in this awkward position. He hated that Sophia had shown up at his doorstep. He'd told her not to come, not to call anymore. He was done with their relationship—if you could call it that.

The server arrived to relay the chef's special and take their drink orders. He had no desire to prolong this meal, so he was happy when Sarah Beth suggested they try the special.

Jess changed the subject as soon as the orders were taken. "Sarah Beth, how's your puppy? I saw you attempting to walk her."

Dylan waved one hand. "That's no puppy. It's an attack dog. I've never heard such growling, and it grabbed my arm with its teeth."

Sarah Beth laughed. "It wasn't your arm, it was your shirt. And I did tell you the rules about no men in the house."

"Yeah, some rules you have."

Jess chuckled. "She licks my face when I sit on the front porch with Sarah Beth."

A scowl lowered Dylan's brows. "So how'd you and Sophia come to be old friends?"

Jess's jaw clamped shut, and his fists tightened.

"His sister and I were friends in college." Sophia shot an evil look his way. "Jess was such a baby when I met him. So naïve."

Dylan's eyes ran up and down Sophia. "I don't think you have a naïve bone in your body, which looks very nice, by the way."

She closed the gap between herself and Dylan then whispered something in his ear.

The two continued their voracious flirting through dinner. What was with this guy flying all the way to Mississippi to see Sarah Beth?

Business, his foot. This guy wanted more. And she was still so vulnerable, though he had no idea why. Did Dylan know? The thought rankled him.

He turned his attention to Sarah Beth. She explained her latest crazy ideas for advertisements. So quirky. But in a good way. And he liked how she listened when he talked about spring training. It was nice to find a woman who understood football and the pressures that went along with it.

When the waitress brought the check, Dylan grabbed it. "I'm buying. I showed up out of the blue at Sarah Beth's. It's the least I can do." He smirked. "And I didn't want her to cook for me."

She laughed at his ribbing. Didn't seem much like a business dinner or a date for Sarah Beth. Maybe he'd wanted it to be something more, and she'd shot him down.

He hoped.

Dylan pushed back his chair and stood. "I hate for the night to end so early. There has to be somewhere to dance in this town. Let's find a place."

Of course, Sophia readily agreed.

"You guys go ahead." Sarah Beth gave a dismissive wave.

"Too many students around here for me to go dancing. I'd end up on an Internet video." Jess gave them directions across the Square and down a block to a bar with a dance floor, and they were gone.

Finally.

"Can I walk you home?"

"Thanks." Sarah Beth fell in beside him, tension melting away from her face. "I'll take you up on that."

They exited through the crowded doorway and turned left down the sidewalk toward her house.

"I've been wanting to talk to you about Sophia."

"That's not necessary."

"I want to. I need to." The sooner he got this out the better. He raked a hand across his forehead. "But it's not something I'm proud of."

"Jess, you must know I won't judge you after everything

I've told you."

"I know, but you've straightened out your life. You haven't told me the whole story, but it's obvious."

She stopped and turned to him with those ebony eyes. "I'm not all that straightened out, trust me. And we're friends."

That friend thing again. "This is hard for me to talk about." He took a cleansing breath. "Sophia came to our house with my sister, Rachel, their senior year at Florida to spend Thanksgiving, rather than fly home to New York. She flirted with me. I thought she was attractive and sophisticated. I had a crush. Everyone in the family thought it was harmless. What they didn't know was that while they all went out shopping one day, Sophia and I stayed home." How to put this delicately? "Basically, she thought it would be fun to teach me about women." There it was. Out there.

Silence weighted the air like the humidity that warmed the night. Sarah Beth put her hand on his forearm. "You were a teenager. It was not your fault."

"I could've stopped it. Part of me didn't want to. All these years, she appears unannounced. Maybe once or twice a year. I want you to know that I called her weeks ago and told her I didn't want to continue our...relationship, if you could call it that, but she showed up last night anyway. I left her at my place and stayed at Sam's. I don't know why she insisted on going to dinner before she leaves tomorrow."

"So what made you change?"

They reached her porch, and he slumped onto the swing. Something inside him urged him on. "The night you and Bryan sang, something touched my soul. I felt so ashamed. It was like I could see all my sin before me, but your song was telling me I could be forgiven."

Unshed tears glistened in her eyes as she sat beside him.

"Oh, Jess, you can. I know it's so hard to know where to start when you've been entrenched in sin so long. You just ask God to help. My brother always says "for every one of our baby steps back to him, He runs to us."' Her gaze became more intense. "I am so proud of you."

Someplace inside cracked open. Liquid built up in his own eyes. "I want to make you proud, and I want to make God proud, too. I grew up with great parents who took me to church, but it always seemed more like a social club to me. I never took it seriously. I never gave my life to the Lord. I knew Nick had become a Christian, and I witnessed the changes in him. I watched him depend on God during his tough times, but I have to admit, I never wanted to give up control—until that night at the CSU."

"I'm not good at this, but can I pray for you?"

Jess gave a quick nod then bowed his head. An ache spread up through his ribcage. He struggled to contain it.

She put her soft hand on top of his. So gentle. "Lord, I know that you are close to the brokenhearted. You've proven it to me again and again. And Jess's heart is ready to break for You and give You control. I ask You to direct him as he tries to figure out how to start a new life. We get ourselves in such messes, God, and only You can get us out of them. Please, walk with him as he takes baby steps to You. In Jesus' name I pray, Amen."

A howl echoed inside the house. Sarah Beth gave his hand a squeeze. "Jess, I know this is poor timing, but do you mind if I let Gingie out?"

A new feeling washed over him—pure and peaceful. He laughed. "Please. I can't stand that racket."

She disappeared inside the house.

How would his commitment to God change his lifestyle?

His career plans? His relationships with—

The wooly mutt barreled out the door and soared into his lap, licking his cheek.

"She unquestionably gave Dylan a different greeting than she's giving you."

"Great judge of character." Jess scooped Gingie up and set her at his feet.

Hands clasped together, Sarah Beth sat on the edge of the swing facing him. "Jess, I believe that if you give your life to the Lord you unite with Him in baptism, and it's a good idea to join a body of believers—a church. To me, being part of a church provides support and a way to give back. What do you think about those things?"

"I'm thinking about all that. I've talked to Nick some, and I'm going to meet with Chris. He's a good guy. I feel comfortable talking with him." Giving up control went against his nature, but he would do this.

"If you want to talk with me about anything, no matter what, I hope you know that I'm here."

She was so beautiful sitting there. So kind. "I know you are. I feel closer to you in a matter of weeks than all but a handful of people during my whole life. Maybe because of Sophia, maybe because I'm a selfish jerk, but I've never connected with any woman emotionally, other than my sister and my mother."

"Did your parents ever find out about you and Sophia?"

Countless times he imagined admitting this, but he'd stopped himself…until now. He pushed against his knuckles until they popped. "No. They knew we hung out some after I graduated, but she wanted to keep everything secret."

Sarah Beth frowned and stomped her foot down with a thump. "Probably to avoid jail!"

Jess bent down and scratched Gingie behind the ears. He'd

never seen Sarah Beth that mad. The crinkle between her eyes was adorable. As long as she wasn't mad at him.

She sighed. "I'm sorry, I shouldn't have said that. I feel like steam is coming from my ears when I think about her."

"I kind of like it, as long as I am on the good side of the anger."

A smile tugged at her lips. "So good, so far."

Her jumbled clichés only made him like her more. And wonder how she worked in marketing.

They sat and rocked, listening to the night sounds. The cicadas burst into a loud song, a sure sign of summer.

He broke the hush. "I don't think I'm going to be able to sleep any time soon, and I had to run out on you the other day. Do you feel like picking up where we left off?"

"I'm kind of wired myself. Where were we?"

"You were telling me about going to Adam's office to talk to him."

Shifting forward, she seemed to flinch, and her eyes fluttered. Her fingers ran across her forehead. "Right, I told him that I'd been doing some thinking and praying and that I was giving my life back to the Lord. Because of my decision, I was changing some things. One of the changes involved me moving out. He was stunned to find out I'd bought a condo in Malibu and a new car to save gas driving back and forth in the L.A. traffic."

Were her hands shaking again?

Chapter 21

Eighteen months earlier

They sat at a corner table in the hospital café, and Adam stared at his coffee. "Why are you doing this? Is there someone else?"

Her seeing someone else? Sarah Beth's blood boiled. "*I'm* not the one seeing someone else."

"I haven't broken my vow to be faithful to you." His voice was cold, impersonal, much like the sterile lab they'd just left. "Is that what this is about? Amy and I are not sleeping together."

The greasy smell of cafeteria food, combined with his attitude, turned her stomach. She pushed her cup across the laminate table and attempted to control her volume. "No one told me anything about Amy, but you haven't been faithful to me. You may not have been physically unfaithful, but you've been emotionally unfaithful. I don't know why we should even call it 'unfaithful,' since you've refused to make a commitment all these years."

He scoffed. "So that's it. You want a piece of paper?"

A direct hit. And her heart cracked in two. This was not the place they should have this discussion, but some things needed to be said. Hands fisted, she choked out the words through clenched teeth. "First, I want to give my life to the Lord. Second, I want what that piece of paper represents if I ever get involved with someone again, which, after you, seems unlikely. Third, I've put a lot of work into the Guatemala trip to visit a clinic we can use as a model for the Miguel Clinic in

Honduras. In two weeks, my assistant and I will be traveling with Dr. Rodriguez."

His expression hardened. "Why in the world are you still going, especially if you're leaving me for...God?"

She inclined her head across the table. At least the dull beige and maroon hospital cafeteria wasn't busy. "I told you years ago I wanted to be a part of this dream. At first, it was for you, but then it became about the mission. I'm going to serve the Lord while I'm there. I've already checked out how non-medical volunteers can assist."

"Really? Enlighten me."

"I'll be cleaning, counting out vitamins, helping patients take short walks, and entertaining the children of patients."

Adam jerked to his feet. "Sounds like an accident waiting to happen. I'm going back to work."

How could someone she'd loved so much...

She massaged her forehead. Even in the same room, they were miles apart.

~~~

During the long flights to Houston and Guatemala City, Sarah Beth distracted herself by talking business with Juan. She'd tried not to look at Adam and Amy, and she'd tried not to enjoy the frown on Amy's face when they boarded the old bus. Much.

The fact that Adam brought the woman on this trip wreaked more havoc with her heart. But Juan was her rock on the eight-hour bus ride that bumped and jolted along the treacherous mountain highways. He helped her practice Spanish and entertained her with stories. It didn't hurt that despite the scary traffic, the terrain was spectacular— volcanoes, mountain after mountain, and exotic flowers. But without Juan, she'd have been crazy enduring the presence of

Adam and his *friend*.

When they arrived, the accommodations reminded her of an old college dorm. Not so terrible. And during the first day's work, she couldn't help but fall in love with the people. Juan's Spanish and experience with children made him a pro at leading games and telling stories with the kids of the patients who came for medical care. Helping him entertain came easy. Most of the day she held small brown-eyed children in her arms.

Supper in the common area smelled of onions and peppers as she waited in line. Probably black beans and tortillas, but it had been a full day, and her appetite raged full force.

After the last volunteer took a seat, Dr. Rodriguez rose from his chair and tapped a spoon against a glass. "I'm encouraged by our first day here. We've learned so much already about how we want to set up our own clinic in Honduras. Is everyone comfortable with their assignments?"

At the other end of the long metal table, Amy cleared her throat. She looked...not quite right, pale even, as she spoke. "I'd like to trade with someone. I'm a lab tech, not a nurse. I'm not used to—I'd just like to trade."

Silence settled on the group. No one offered, so Sarah Beth raised her hand. "I'm not a nurse either, but I'll trade."

Adam rolled his eyes. "How are you going to handle the sights and smells of the recovery area any better?"

Her fists clenched. The same way she was controlling the urge to throw a plate of food at him right now. "When Gram was in the last stages of cancer, Mark and I had to do things for her. Things we never—"

"Sarah Beth will do fine as an assistant." Dr. Rodriguez cut his eyes toward Adam, silencing any further debate.

At least someone believed in her.

~~~

Where was Juan? Sarah Beth scanned the dining area after their second day. The table was almost full. Adam's blue eyes caught hers. She moved to the opposite side and sat, then placed her napkin in her lap.

"What a day." The metal folding chair creaked as Juan took the seat beside her. A wide grin filled his face. "This is what I was meant to do. How was your day with the patients?"

"I enjoyed it. During downtime, I found nail polish and lotion for pedicures. The patients loved it."

"And Adam?" His voice held a kind warning.

"I was careful not to be rude to him. Or Amy. Wasn't easy."

"He is watching you. Show him God's love."

Her gaze travelled down the table. Adam *was* looking. Again. *Swallow.* She reached for her bottle of water and forced her eyes away.

Juan rested his hand on her forearm. "I've been asked to preach our last night. God's hand is pressing on me. I must build a chapel for Miguel Clinic." He put his fork down and stared at her. "Then I must preach the gospel there."

No. I need him, Lord. "Juan, it's not even funded."

"I believe it will be, so I must begin to train Jill to take my place."

A groan squeezed from her throat. "I've been training you for a promotion, so you can make oodles of money for your family."

"God is giving me a different kind of promotion."

"But, it wasn't planned to be a Christian clinic. The fund raising will need to be through a completely separate entity."

"God will provide." The confidence in his tone never wavered

She let out a deep sigh and pushed away her food. "Okay. When we get back, investigate whether we can purchase or lease lands adjacent to our Miguel Clinic to build a chapel."

His dark eyes lit up. He was so precious. Who was she to argue with God? Before she left the dining area, she managed a quick smile at Adam, then hurried out the door.

~~~

Sarah Beth trudged toward the clinic. How sad it would be to leave all these beautiful faces tomorrow. Harder than she'd expected. In just a week, so many of the women and children had captured a piece of her heart.

Suddenly, the sound of blades chopped the air, increasing in volume. She spun around. A helicopter?

The whole camp gawked as it hovered then landed. Three men exited, two of them huge, and the other pulled off a baseball cap, revealing auburn hair. Dylan Conner?

She'd warned him not to come. She hadn't had time this trip to deal with arranging protection for a celebrity. Apparently he'd planned his own. Typical Dylan. The other two men must've been bodyguards.

He waltzed over like he was walking down the red carpet. "Hi, beautiful. I hope I'm not intruding. It's the last day, anyway."

She couldn't speak. Why wouldn't he listen?

"Look, I know you're upset, but I was on location in the Caribbean and thought I'd make a run down here. Take a few pictures with the children, a few patients. I'm investing in your clinic, and I could use some good publicity. For once." He twisted his face up like a little kid. "Pweese, don't be mad."

The boiling cooled. He was so childlike—even without the cute lisp. But he wasn't getting off the hook that easy. "On one condition."

He grinned. "Anything for you."

"You have to stay and listen to Juan preach tonight."

His smile drooped. "Yes, ma'am."

Chapter 22

Sarah Beth glanced at Jess. Was he still interested? The aromas of wisteria and jasmine drifted along the breeze. The neighborhood stood oddly quiet and still except for the occasional distant bark of a dog. As if the atmosphere waited along with Jess for her to continue. No turning back now.

"I'm not sure how to describe the scene any better than to say the Holy Spirit spoke through Juan that last night. He was on fire for the Lord. In both English and Spanish, he told the story of the prodigal son and of the father who ran to his wayward child when at last he turned on the road toward home.

"Juan explained that the father didn't allow the son, who had wasted everything the father had given him, to come back as only a servant. Juan said, 'No, he put a gold ring on his finger and his best coat on his back. The father caught hold and fell into a hug with his son and kissed him. God is waiting and watching for His prodigals, and is longing for us to realize what a mess we are in without Him—to turn our steps back toward home.' He said, 'Our fathers on earth may have treated us wrongly, but God will be our Father. Even if our own mother would forsake us, God will never forsake us.'

"Tears streamed down so many faces, mine included. He led a simple verse of 'Amazing Grace,' offering a time for prodigals to come home. Many came forward to restore their relationship with the Lord. It was surreal and beautiful and moving. I saw a teary-eyed Adam dart back to the dorm.

"When we packed to go home, we were all sad—except for maybe Amy. Don't get me wrong. It was arduous work, and we were exhausted, but each of us took a piece of the beauty and simplicity of Guatemala in our hearts."

Sarah Beth smiled even as a few tears slipped onto her cheeks.

"Back in the States, Dylan opened his home to a select group of wealthy friends to raise more funds. A cover story about his philanthropy hit the newsstands. He'd provided photos hoping to better his image. The magazine picked up the similarity of my profile to the mysterious 'woman in blue.' They also noted I was living in his condo. Amy saw the article and presented the tabloid to Adam.

"I didn't see Adam come in the front door of the cocktail party at Dylan's, but Juan and Dr. Rodriguez did. The look on his face must have been menacing, because they knew right away there might be trouble. Adam was six-foot-five and an imposing figure, especially angry. They headed him off. Bill joined the group huddled in a corner of Dylan's mansion.

"Juan explained to Adam that he'd helped me research the real estate, and Dylan had simply given me the best price on a condo. Bill explained I could afford it because when my parents and grandmother died, Mark and I inherited the estates. And I was making the company a lot of money, earning my own generous salary.

"Juan asked him to go for a ride so they could talk. Thank God, Adam agreed."

Sarah Beth paused to take a deep breath. Pain radiated through her—and a touch of panic. She rubbed her moist palms together. Still, she could finish this with God's help.

"Two weeks later, Adam appeared at my office and wanted to talk. We got in my car and headed around the canyons and ended up on the coast. He began by telling me that the night in Guatemala when Juan preached, he felt the message was specifically for him. When Juan spoke about God being a father to the fatherless and that even if a mother forgot her child, God never did, he knew that God wanted him to hear that message."

~~~

Sarah Beth glanced at Adam as she drove out of the city.

"I never felt loved by my parents." He raked his fingers through his hair, his blue eyes brimming with liquid. "I believed my mother only gave birth to me to ensure my father wouldn't divorce her. My dad was never interested in me. My life was painful and lonely. The only happiness I had was with Miguel and Alma. When Miguel died of dengue fever, Alma never came back. They were gone, and I literally wished I was dead. I thought about suicide. Then, out of nowhere, I got the idea of honoring them with dengue fever research and a clinic. It helped me to hang on to life through high school and college. Until I met you.

"Only, now I don't believe the idea came out of nowhere. I've been meeting with Juan since the trip to Guatemala and talking to Mark on the phone. I finally get it. God was there for me the whole time. He gave me the hope to hang on to life until I met Mark in college and then you and Juan and finally…Jesus. Not that I think I saw Jesus in the flesh or anything weird. I feel Him. I see the miracle. I get it."

Her heart fluttered. "Are you saying what I think you're saying, Adam?"

"I'm saying I believed that night in Guatemala, but then Amy showed me those pictures, and I heard about the party. I came to Dylan Conner's, fuming and thinking you'd been having a fling with him all along. I thought you left me for him, and the religious talk was just an excuse.

"Juan was able to convince me to leave—and kept me from injuring Dylan, by the way. He assured me you and Dylan weren't romantically involved. He was probably the only person who could've. Then we talked all night about my parents, my pain—my fear. I cried like a baby. Juan was the giant, and I was the small man. He told me God would forgive me and stay with me always. You know how passionate I am when I finally decide to do something, right?"

She had to chuckle though her chest already quivered. "Yes."

"I asked Juan to baptize me. Right there in the Pacific. We were both nearly swept away in the surf, but we were laughing and crying and rejoicing, sopping wet."

Countless times over the last weeks, she'd imagined these words coming from Adam, and now they were real. But... "Wait a minute. Juan didn't tell me any of this."

"I asked him not to. I didn't want you to think it was about you. And—I mean that in a nice way."

This was so much to take in. "I'm pulling over somewhere to turn around. My condo's not far. Let's go sit on my back balcony and talk."

~~~

Jess watched as Sarah Beth continued her story, her hands shaking, her voice soft.

"Adam and I sat there on that porch and talked for hours. We decided not to jump right back into a relationship and agreed that we should both take time with the Lord to grow and study for a while. Finally, he said he should get back to the apartment to sleep before his next shift. We hit the freeway."

Sarah Beth grabbed hold of the arms of her rocking chair and stiffened.

Jess stopped rocking. "Are you okay?"

Her face was ashen. Her chest shook violently. "I was driving him back, and all of a sudden, a van crossed the median and headed into our lane. I tried to angle the car so the impact would be on my side. I wanted to protect..."

When he'd asked her to share her story, he had no idea how painful it would be for her. Now he wished he could absorb the hurt for her. Shield her. "You don't have to go on." Jess got out of his chair and went to his knees in front of her, his hands on hers.

"I have to." Though her voice shook, moonlight bathed her face and showed determination in the set of her jaw. "The van somehow missed us, swerved back into the median, and came to a stop. My car was sideways on the shoulder of the road. I heard the horrifying screech of brakes. The driver of a pickup, confused by the lights of the van in the median, swerved off to the side of the road. He hit the passenger side of my little car. Where Adam sat."

A sob sliced the air. "He tried to stop when he saw us. The van, the blow from the pickup, all happened in seconds, but to me it seemed in slow motion.

"I remember Adam asking if I was hurt. I was dazed for only a second, and then I saw the blood. Metal twisted around his right leg. He reached and turned my face toward his. He said, 'Look at me, Sarah Beth. I need you to know I love you always, and you helped save me.'

"I couldn't understand why he was saying that. I needed to make a tourniquet. Blood was everywhere. When the medics arrived, I was trying to tie my sweater around his leg, hysterical. They pulled me off him. Adam was already gone. A 'partially severed artery,' they said."

So many losses. Jess put his hands on her cheeks and wiped

her tears with his thumbs. So much for one person to endure. "I don't know how you've managed."

"Mark flew out. Jill, Juan, Dr. Rodriguez, and even Dylan took turns sitting with me. Adam's parents blamed me because I'd been driving."

Her teary eyes found his. "I couldn't function. I asked Mark to bring me back here. He stayed a couple of weeks. After that Kim, Chris, and the Lathams said they would watch over me so Mark could go home to be with his family. Chris and Kim dragged me to the student ministry. Dean Latham got it in his head I should teach a few of his classes, and then he put me in charge of the Foundation marketing. Gradually, I created a new life, or I should say, God created my new life."

"How long have you been back?"

"A little over a year now." She sat back and wiped at her eyes and nose.

What should he say? Jess returned to the chair beside hers and glanced out at the evening sky. His chest squeezed. If only he could shoulder the pain. Take it away.

Stars flickered, and a slight breeze carried a night bird's song as they rocked in the quiet.

"So say something." Sarah Beth's gaze pleaded. "Anything. Funny or crazy—or even inappropriate."

"I would've loved to see that dog hanging by its teeth from Dylan's sleeve."

She chuckled, then the sound died.

"You are very courageous, Sarah Beth, and I hate that you went through all that."

Gingie stood at attention and let out a deep guttural growl.

"Whoa, what's up with her?" Sarah Beth caught the dog's collar. "That's the sound she made before she attacked Dylan."

A limo pulled over in front of the house. The door opened.

"Speak of the devil, or should I say devils?" Jess mumbled under his breath.

Dylan stepped over Sophia and staggered out. "Hey, Sarah Beth, I came to grab my backpack. We're flying to Paris. Hope you don't mind if I take off early. Someone will pick up my rental for me."

"Be careful, Dylan." Her voice held a kind, warning tone.

The guy was making a huge mistake.

In minutes, Dylan bounded out of the pool house. He tossed her the keys before heading back into the limo. "You know you'll miss me."

The dog let out a snarl, and Sarah Beth gripped tighter. Once the limo drove away, she shook her head. "That's gonna be one hot mess."

"No doubt. I don't know who to feel more sorry for." With a shrug, Jess let out a bitter chuckle. "Probably Dylan. He obviously thought he had a chance with you. Since you weren't interested, he fell right into her web."

"Dylan doesn't know what he wants. He's like a big kid."

Jess stood and stretched. "You're probably spent between Dylan and sharing such painful memories. I should leave."

Gingie scrambled over to him and stood on her hind legs, paws on Jess.

"No. Down." Sarah Beth slapped her hands together.

Jess plopped back into his seat. "Well, okay. I was just trying to be polite."

The laugh bubbling from Sarah Beth made the corny joke worthwhile.

"I was talking to Gingie. She's too big to be jumping on people."

"I think I can take it."

"You can, but Katie or Camilla would be barreled over. I'm

going to obedience school soon."

Jess nudged her arm. "You're going to obedience school? Maybe you should try a cooking school."

She smacked him, playfully. "You know what I mean."

"I'd like to be a fly on the wall at either one."

"Because you're amused by my inadequacies?"

"Very amused." He held her gaze until she looked away. Her vulnerable expression stripped away his last defenses. There was no turning back. He'd protect this woman with his life.

She stood. "You're right. It is getting kinda late."

He returned to his feet. "I should go." He took one step but turned to face her. "You're one of the strongest people I've ever met."

Her eyes looked everywhere but at him. He reached across the short distance and pulled her into a side-hug. He didn't need to freak her out. "Good night, Sarah Beth. See you soon."

"Goodbye."

Chapter 23

After knocking, Sarah Beth strolled into Chris and Kim's home for the usual Tuesday family night. Chris, Nick, and Jess huddled in the living room in an intense conversation.

"Hey, guys. Where are the ladies?"

Chris motioned to the backyard. "Sarah Beth, can you start the burgers? Kim took the girls to the playground."

"Me? Start the burgers?" She strained her neck trying to catch Jess's eye where he sat on the couch. His head rested on his hands, still talking to Nick.

"If you don't mind."

"Sure." Something must be terribly wrong. She walked out back with the beef patties she'd found in the kitchen, lit the grill, and set three timers on her phone: a timer to flip the burgers, a timer to take off the burgers, a timer to turn off the grill. She carefully placed each burger on the rack, then checked and double-checked the patties as they heated, to make sure they cooked all the way but didn't burn, then stacked them on a clean tray and turned off the grill.

The back door creaked and opened. A huge grin lit up Nick's face. "We're going to need to borrow your pool. Tonight."

Sarah Beth's heart skipped a beat, and her stomach jumped into her throat. "Does this mean...?" Setting aside the plate of food, she ran to him.

Teary-eyed, Nick came and embraced her. "You, with your fine skis and sweet heart, have finally gotten through to my best friend. Jess wants to give his life to the Lord and be baptized tonight. I've prayed for this day for years."

Sarah Beth looked to the heavens. "Thank You, Lord." She turned back to Nick. "Call Sam and have him meet us there. He needs to see this."

Squinting, he gave her a slow nod. "I'm on it."

A caravan traveled to Sarah Beth's. Chris and Nick led the way through the gate and down the sidewalk, then stepped into the pool with Jess. Ripples formed in the blue water that reflected the evening sky. Students took a seat on the edge.

Droplets fell as Chris placed a hand on Jess's shoulder. "Jess, do you believe that Jesus Christ is the Son of God?"

"I do."

Sarah Beth covered her mouth with her hand. Joy flooded her heart.

"Do you want Jesus to be the Lord of your life?"

"Yes."

With his other hand on Jess's head, Chris sent him under the clear water. Everyone broke into applause as Jess rose up, streams of liquid cascading from him. Nick let out a loud whoop and embraced Jess with a slap on the back.

Jess gave a fist pump toward the sky. Once he'd shaken hands with a few students near the ladder, he made a straight path to Sam who leaned against the gate. "I'm glad you came, man."

"I guess you'll be preaching to me now."

Jess grabbed Sam in a bear hug, slinging water over his friend. "You know it, brother."

A slight smile pulled up Sam's lips. "Come on. You're soaking me."

Back at Chris's house, the student minister carried a pitcher of tea and opened the back door. "Uh, oh. The burgers."

Sarah Beth stepped out past him. "What?"

Cats of every size and color scrambled off the patio table by the grill.

"Oh no, I can't believe it. I was so careful when I cooked, and I covered them with foil to keep them warm. Where in the world did those cats come from?"

"My neighbor's been complaining about a colony of feral cats living under his deck." Chris snickered. "We may've just eliminated them for him."

"Those burgers were perfect." She huffed. "Now no one will ever believe me."

~~~

The adorable pout on Sarah Beth's lips made Jess laugh. "I believe you. Think of it this way, you just made those cats very happy." He gave her shoulder a little squeeze. "Pizza's on me."

Bryan strummed his guitar as they waited for the delivery.

Peace washed over Jess. A cleanness. "Do you and Bryan want to sing?" He shouldn't put her on the spot. "Or just Bryan could sing."

Her long lashes were still wet with tears, but she flashed a smile. "I'll sing if everyone joins in."

"You don't want to hear what comes out of these pipes." Jess swiped his fingers across his chin. "Your puppy sounds more in tune."

"It can't be that bad, but even if it is, it's about what's in your heart."

Pointing toward his ears, Nick nodded. "It's about protecting your eardrums once you hear his attempts to *sing*. Our high school coach banned him from leading our fight song. It was that awful."

Jess punched Nick's shoulder. "Don't start telling embarrassing high school stories. I have a few of yours, too."

Bryan cut through the conversation with singing. The song brought holiness. Tears again ran down Sarah Beth's face as she joined in with all her might.

Adam. Their last day together surfaced with the emotion of the evening. Closing her eyes, she pictured him, with his sky blue eyes, singing along somewhere in another dimension with her mother, father, and Gram. A sense of peace mingled with pain and tugged at her celebration with Jess.

She was happy for Jess. He would move into a new life with the Lord at his side. Wherever that took him in his career. If his dream came true, he'd leave Oxford sooner or later.

But she'd still be here. She took a cleansing breath, opened her eyes, and wiped her cheeks. Kim handed her a couple of tissues.

Jess's gaze captured her attention. It held an expression she couldn't place, but she managed to give him a smile.

Once everyone had their fill of pizza and congratulated Jess, the crowd thinned. Bryan gathered his guitar and stood. Before the young man left, Sarah Beth caught him by the arm. "Thanks for leading the songs."

He covered her hand with his. "You know, I would so marry you and take care of you forever, if you'd consider it."

Was he joking? "Bryan, I was born too early to be lucky enough to marry you. Besides, you deserve someone as amazing as you are."

"You aren't that many years older, and you're amazing. Don't you see that?"

"I'm not sure if you're joking or serious, but I can't think about getting involved with someone yet. If I were at that point, I wouldn't get involved with a student or any man in your age group. I've got a lifetime of baggage someone who's twenty-one wouldn't know how to carry."

Still touching her hand, his eyes searched hers. "My shoulders are strong. You might be surprised at how much I can carry."

She took her hand back and clamped her mouth shut.

"Okay, okay, I give up. For now. But in a couple of years, I'm checking back in."

Sarah Beth shook her head. "You'll make some lucky girl the best husband ever."

"You're breaking my heart, Ms. Professor."

Jess materialized at her side in dry clothes. "Sorry to interrupt, but, Sarah Beth, can I trouble you for a ride? Nick needed to get Katie home. I can find another way if it's inconvenient."

"I'm ready if you are." She hustled over to gather her bag.

At her SUV, she scrambled to shuffle a stack of papers to the back seat again. "Let me make some room for you."

After she'd cleared the space, she glanced at Jess. His brows rose, and his lips held a smirk. "So, you don't date students or any men in that age group? I liked how you added that—just in case he might drop out of school to try to go out with you."

She crossed over to the driver's side and took a seat. "Were you eavesdropping?"

"Maybe I have good ears."

After starting the car, she headed toward his place, still a bit shocked by the encounter with Bryan. The couple of miles passed in silence as she pondered the whole strange and beautiful evening.

She braked at the driveway to his house and turned in. "Are you going to say you told me so?"

"Nah, I'm trying to make a change. Besides, you already

said it."

"I know you want to. Go ahead."

Jess hopped out and lingered at the door of the SUV. "I told you... Nope, not going to do it. Good night, Sarah Beth. Thank you for...everything. See you soon."

Her eyes met his, and warmth flooded her soul. "I'm so happy about your decision."

She waited for him to walk inside. A hint of something that she hadn't felt in a very long time washed over her.

She couldn't start this. Not now. Not yet. Maybe not ever. He would be leaving Oxford. And she couldn't.

Chapter 24

Two summer camps down. How many more to go? Jess organized his equipment in the locker room. Again. He enjoyed the kids, but the heat was wretched. Mississippi summers had to have the worst humidity in the western world. Plus his mind had been wandering. A couple of days had passed since he'd seen Sarah Beth. Too long. He'd held back as long as he could. Why was that so hard? She'd made it clear she didn't want to date. Yet. He tried to give her space. Were a couple of days enough?

He drove to her house and trekked down the brick sidewalk. At the door, he raised his hand to knock, but a shadow passed the window. Someone tall stood in the entrance hall. Not Sarah Beth. A man's voice echoed through the door. Jess's stomach took a dive. This was a mistake. He couldn't assume anything about her feelings. It wasn't his place.

He turned to walk back down the steps of the gray wooden porch. A howl and then a thud came from inside. *Caught.* He picked up his pace. The door creaked open, and the dog scampered behind him. Gingie hit the back of his legs with her paws.

"Hey. Sorry. Get back here, Gingie," the deep voice called.

Jess turned to face the dog and the man. "No problem. She's friendly."

"You're Jess McCoy." The tall, dark-haired man looked to be in his thirties. His smile looked familiar. "Come in. Sarah Beth told me about you."

"I don't want to interrupt. I was…in the neighborhood."

The man laughed. "Practically all of Oxford is in the neighborhood. I'm Mark, Sarah Beth's brother, here with my family for a surprise visit."

Jess let out a deep sigh. "Oh."

Mark took a firm grip on Jess's shoulder. "Actually, I've been wanting to talk with you. Privately."

"Okay."

"Hang on. I'll put the dog up." He corralled Gingie back inside the front door, then pointed down the sidewalk. "Let's walk."

Jess let Mark set the pace and waited for him to explain.

"How is our Sarah Beth? I can tell by her voice when she talks about you that y'all are close, and she was very happy about your decision to give your life to the Lord."

She talked to her brother about him? "She was a big part of my decision. And she seems to be managing. She's talented and giving and kind."

Mark stopped, his brown eyes probing. "How do you feel about her?"

The question hovered between them like a Hail Mary pass toward an end zone. "She's…special. I care for her. A lot." It was obvious Mark was sizing him up like a protective FBI-agent brother would. Maybe he should dig deep and come clean. "I know she's been through so much. I'm willing to wait until she's ready to care for someone again." He met Mark's stare. "As long as it takes."

There. He'd said it. Out loud. Everything he never dared to admit, even to himself.

The lines on Mark's forehead flattened, and one side of his mouth lifted. "I don't mean to scare you off, but I've been praying—for many, many years."

"I don't scare easy."

"I didn't know your name or anything about you, but I have a gut feeling, you're the answer."

~~~

Such an unexpected string of events. But in a good way. Sarah Beth glanced out the window. She'd been floored when Mark, Holly, and Drew arrived. Then Jess. Now, a couple of days later, Mark and Jess had invited all the CSU students to have family night at her house. They worked together to set up a net across the pool for volleyball. Strange how normal the two of them looked to her—like they'd been friends for years.

Her precious nephew, Drew, played out back, while his mother, Holly, painted on a canvas in the dining room. She'd missed them so much. If only she could visit them in Atlanta.

Around dinner time, students arrived. Mark flipped burgers. Holly pulled out baked beans and homemade potato salad while Sarah Beth swam with Drew. Everyone sat outside to eat. When they finished, Mark rose to his feet. "Let the games begin."

Jess hit his chest with one fist. "I'm captain of team one. Mark's captain of team two." He counted out every other person as one or two. Sarah Beth was a two.

Letting out a ghastly laugh, Mark elbowed Sarah Beth. "Glad you're on my team this time."

Jess shot him a puzzled look.

The teams climbed in the water on their separate ends. Nick served first on Jess's team. Gingie darted up and down the side and howled at the players in the pool until Sarah Beth called a time out. "Sorry, y'all. I'll kennel her."

The game resumed with Sarah Beth at the net facing Jess. Nick served again. Right to Sarah Beth, and instinct took over. She slammed the ball down on the other side of the net. Into

Jess's face.

He rubbed his nose. "Ouch."

"Oh, Jess, I'm sorry. I didn't mean to hit you."

Amusement crinkled his eyes, and he let out a small laugh. "You spiked the ball at me in a Christian volleyball game?"

Mark pointed at her. "You've obviously never met my sister's alter ego, the scary beast that rears her ugly head during competition of any kind. You should play cards with her. You'd really be crying for mercy."

"A wee bit competitive, are we? I can be competitive."

"Don't do it, Jess." Mark shook his head. "You'll be sorry."

Nick tossed the ball across the net. "I could play some cards tonight. But I want to be Sarah Beth's partner so we can beat the pants off my old friend Jess."

Mark served it back. "Now, he's a smart guy. I guess I could be Jess's partner. I'm used to losing spades to my baby sister."

"I'm not sure I'd admit that, man." Jess returned the serve. Sarah Beth jumped up and slammed the ball over the net.

Mark laughed. "What were you saying?"

~ ~ ~

The week with family ended too soon. Sarah Beth sank onto the guest bed and did her best to stifle tears as Holly packed their bags.

"We'll come again soon." Holly offered a small smile with her promise.

"Please. I miss you guys so much."

"I'm surprised you have time to think of us. You've got a nice bunch of friends here now. You're making progress. Maybe you don't realize it, but I can see a world of difference between where you are now and where you were last summer."

"I guess you're right." Sarah Beth blew her nose. Gingie

plopped her big head on Sarah Beth's knee.

"You've got that horse you call a dog to guard you, not to mention Jess. He's a keeper."

"What? We're just friends."

"Don't act like you don't know what I'm talking about. He's crazy about you."

"Jess?"

"Are you really that blind? Mark sees it too. He had a talk with him."

"Why in the world?" Sarah Beth's hands flew to her burning cheeks. "Oh my stars, how embarrassing."

"Mark's protective. You know that."

"I'm going to pretend this conversation never happened."

"Whatever works, girl. I love you." Holly gave her a big hug then looked down at the dog. "You take care of her too, Gingie."

Jess drove up as Mark put the last bag in their SUV, and then Mark squeezed Sarah Beth in a hug, picking her up off the ground. He gave her a little punch in the shoulder after he set her on her feet. "Remember. Baby steps. I love you, miss you, but God loves you more." He turned to Jess. "And you. Thanks. Keep in touch."

Sarah Beth couldn't stop the eye roll or the blaze searing her face even as tears threatened. "What are you thanking him for?"

Grinning, Mark got in and shut the car door.

Splinters poked her composure, and her throat tightened. She could hold off the tears until Jess left, couldn't she?

As if he could read her thoughts, Jess slipped his arm around her and pulled her to his chest. "It's all right if you cry."

She tried not to get tears on his shirt, but it was nice to have someone hold her like this. A friend with a shoulder to cry on. He was just a friend. Wasn't he? She couldn't handle more than that. Not with her issues.

He pulled back and pressed his thumb across her cheek to wipe a tear. "Maybe this will cheer you up. I'm having company, too. And I'm inviting you to dinner at my house to meet them."

That got her attention. "Who?"

"My parents and my sister."

Heart in throat. Pounding. Meet his family?

Chapter 25

Sarah Beth accepted Nick's offer to pick her up for the dinner with Jess's family. From her booster seat in the back, Katie waved at her. "Hey, Ms. Sarah Beth. I can't wait to see Pop McCoy and Sue."

In the front seat of the dusty old Dodge pickup, Sarah Beth twiddled her thumbs. "I'm nervous, Nick. It's crazy. I've met celebrities and wealthy businessmen and spoken in huge lecture halls. What's wrong with me?"

Nick smirked and shook his head. "If you don't know, I'm not gonna tell you."

"What's that supposed to mean?"

He laughed. "Don't worry. His parents are great. They practically raised me, too. You'll love them." He parked and gave her a pat on the arm. "And they'll love you."

As they walked up the sidewalk, Katie led the way singing *Tomorrow.* Her latest favorite tune after seeing the children's play in town. She ran up the five steps to the pale gray and white porch and burst through the door without knocking. "I'm here, Uncle Jess."

A tall well-dressed woman with short blond hair and big brown eyes scooped up the little girl. "Katie-bug. I've missed you." The woman turned. "Hey, Nick. And you must be Sarah Beth. I've heard so much about you."

As Jess's mother introduced herself, he strolled in from the living room.

Sarah Beth massaged her temples. "It's nice to meet you,

but I'm scared about what he's been telling you."

A wicked grin lifted Jess's lips. "Don't worry. I only told her the truth."

"And that's the deeply troubling part."

Mrs. McCoy let Katie down, gave Sarah Beth a little hug, and winked. "It was all good. But if we play any games, I want to be on your team."

"Jess McCoy." Sarah Beth shook her finger at him.

Jess's mom took Sarah Beth by the elbow, pulled her closer, and spoke barely above a whisper. "You're a woman after my own heart. Do you play tennis?"

"I've hit a few balls around." Sarah Beth gave her a knowing smile.

"We'll go for doubles tomorrow. You and me against Jess and his father."

A hearty laugh came from Jess. "I heard you, and I'll be looking forward to that."

Mr. McCoy, tall and auburn-haired, entered the room and bear-hugged Nick. "You're looking better than I've seen for a while now. Oxford's treating you pretty well, too?"

"Yes, sir. Katie and I are loving the small-town life."

Turning to Sarah Beth, Mr. McCoy greeted her with a vigorous handshake. "I'm happy to finally meet you. I'm Sean Jessup McCoy the fourth, but you can call me Sean."

"I love that name. Irish or Scottish?"

"Irish, back to the ship my great-grandfather crossed over on."

She looked at Jess. "So you're the fifth?"

"Yes, but do not try calling me Cinco."

Nick rubbed his arm. "I think I still have the scars from that one."

Sarah Beth surveyed the tasteful modern décor that was

free of clutter. "I love your house, Jess. Stylish. Very clean, too."

Mrs. McCoy turned her attention away from Katie for a moment. "You've never been here?"

"Never past the porch." Jess glanced her way. "She's got scruples."

"That's a fancy word coming from my baby brother." An attractive blond woman who looked to be in her late thirties entered, drying her hands on a dishtowel.

"Hi, I'm Rachel. Jess's favorite sister."

"Only sister." Jess eyed her. "And I went to college, too. I know a few big words."

"With a sports management degree?"

"Not everyone wants to be an ambulance chaser."

Rachel gave Jess a little push. "Don't listen to him. I'm a corporate attorney."

"Yeah, for Mom and Dad."

"I work hard. Don't make me hurt you, baby Jessie."

"Now you did it, calling me Jessie. I'm posting that video of you singing." He pulled out his cell phone.

She grabbed at the phone. "You wouldn't."

He swung away and turned to Sarah Beth. "She sings worse than I do."

Nick made a face. "One would think that would be impossible, but sadly, 'tis true."

"Et tu, Nick?" Rachel held her hand over her heart and laughed.

Mrs. McCoy signaled. "Come to the table. Sarah Beth, you and Katie-bug sit by me. I want to hear the scoop on my boys from those who know and will talk."

Jess and Nick exchanged glances. After Jess brought the food to the table, they settled into easy conversation. The tension squeezing Sarah Beth's shoulders relaxed, and the tightness in her abdomen disappeared. This felt…natural. Easy. Not to mention the Cornish game hens were delicious.

After her second helping of bread pudding with rum sauce, she raised her glass. "Mrs. McCoy, the dinner was fabulous."

Laughter spread around the table.

"What? What's so funny?"

Mrs. McCoy smiled and patted Sarah Beth's hand. "First of all, call me Sue. Second, they don't let me cook. My cooking is dreadful." She gave a grand sweep of her arm. "Jess prepared all of this."

A grin lit up Jess's face as he laid his napkin on the table. "I had to learn to cook. I like to eat good food, and until I started making the free-meal rounds with Sarah Beth, it was all up to me."

His sister nodded. "Cooking was never one of Mom's talents. Jess and I are both gourmet cooks. I'm surprised he's never cooked for you."

"Keeping it a secret, no doubt, or he'd never get rid of me."

Jess shot her a strange look.

Foot in mouth. Again. When would she ever learn? Brain first. Then mouth.

~~~

The cool bottle of water hit the spot. Sarah Beth swigged it back. The set of tennis with Jess and his parents after church had been fun. Even though she and Jess's mother lost, the game had been close.

Jess joined her on the bench. "Sorry about bruising your leg."

"For the fifth time, it's no biggie. I know you didn't mean to. Remember who you're talking to?"

He pinched his nose. "Yeah, I think my nose is still

crooked from that volleyball game."

"It wasn't that bad. No blood."

"Now you sound like Dad."

Sean laughed. "I made a man out of you."

Sarah Beth smiled and studied the older McCoy. "My dad always said that, too."

After a moment of silence, Mrs. McCoy sat on the other side of the bench and tapped her leg. "Did Jess tell you that we're opening another office in Los Angeles? We're headed out there for a couple of months."

Icy fingers wrapped around Sarah Beth's lungs causing her breath to catch. No words formed. She shook her head while the world began to spin.

"We discovered a niche in the theme park industry a number of years ago and started our own business facilitating amusement parks in going green. We've been successful because we were one of the first companies to provide that kind of service. Recently, we decided to branch out, and we landed contracts in L.A."

Her breathing was shallow, but she needed to speak. "Y'all are welcome to stay in my condo in Malibu."

Mrs. McCoy patted her back. "That's such a generous offer. We'd want to pay you rent."

"It's vacant. I'd like someone to use it. "

"Fabulous. You should come with Jess and show us the best spots to go."

A fog clouded Sarah Beth's brain. Thoughts shut down. She gripped the edge of the bench.

Jess placed his hand on her back. "Are you all right? You look pale. Do you need some more water?"

Staring at the concrete, she forced herself to speak. "I was dizzy for a second. I should go home and get something to eat."

Mr. McCoy rushed to help her to her feet and toward the truck. "Let's get some ice cream. That always makes me feel better after exercise."

Mrs. McCoy wrapped an arm around her from the other side. "That's why we never lose these extra twenty pounds, Sean."

~~~

The way his parents fawned over Sarah Beth warmed Jess's anxious heart. They'd taken to her right away, and hopefully nothing was wrong with her other than a bit of overheating.

Or was it something more?

"Feeling better, sweetie?" His mother rubbed Sarah Beth's arm.

"I'm fine now. Ice cream soothes many ailments—even losing the match."

"We have to let them win sometimes."

His father flashed a teasing grin. "I think that win was pretty clear cut with my last shot."

"We'll have a rematch next time we're in Oxford, or if you decide to visit us out West."

Without answering, Sarah Beth leaned forward and studied her ice cream as if it were a textbook.

Something wasn't right. Jess stole another glance. A piece of this puzzle was missing. "You know, Sarah Beth is a marketing whiz. Maybe she could give you some ideas."

The crease that drew Sarah Beth's forehead together relaxed. She looked up. "I'd love to create some strategies for you."

His mother tilted her head. "We're not a big corporation. I'm not sure we can afford you."

"I wouldn't charge you to play around with some ideas.

Jess is…a close friend, and I like what your company is doing for the environment. I'm not sure what that involves besides recycling. You'd have to enlighten me about the benefits your company has to offer and what kind of market strategy you currently have. I'd need your logo, mission statement, corporate vision, and those kind of things."

"I'll have everything in an email to you tonight. This is very exciting. I can't wait to see what you come up with." She turned to Jess. "I like this girl."

Sarah Beth's dark eyes met his, her cheekbones pink.

His ribs rammed into his heart, which was already sprinting down the sidelines, while his eyes memorized the curve of her lips. "I do, too."

If she only knew how much.

~~~

Jess paced the oak floors of his kitchen after his parents left. Sarah Beth had shared much of her story with him. Mark had, too. But there was something missing.

He had to call her. Now. As he found her number on his phone, he slipped outside.

"Hello." Her voice was so sweet, that one word spread sparks through him.

"My parents want to adopt you. They loved you."

"Aw. Tell them I'm available, and I liked them, too."

"So, I've been craving barbeque from Memphis. Want to go up next Sunday night?"

The line fell silent for a moment. "Get the guys and go up. I'll stay here and watch Katie and Camilla."

His feet set a fast pace down the road toward Sarah Beth's house. "That sounds fun, if you don't mind watching them."

"I'd love to stay here and entertain them."

His pace quickened. "I have another trip to run by you. We

play Alabama early September, and I can get a cheap block of rooms for the CSU if you wanted to organize a trip."

"I can organize it, but then I could still babysit for the weekend on that one, too."

"You're so generous to offer to babysit. One more thing, can you drive me to Batesville tomorrow? I need to have my truck serviced."

Nothing. No answer at all.

Just as he suspected. "Sarah Beth?" He turned toward her driveway.

"Sorry. I'm checking my schedule. I can't tomorrow."

"What about the next day. Or the next?"

Another bout of silence answered him. This had to be an anxiety disorder she'd been too embarrassed to share. His heart ached for her.

"Sarah Beth, meet me on your porch. Please."

"Are you outside?"

"I walked over while we were talking."

"Do I have to?"

"Yep."

The door opened, and he hung up. A clip held her dark hair. One small wisp hung down by her ear, and she bit her lip. He wanted to touch that hair and pull her in his arms. The way she avoided his eyes, that wasn't the right move for the moment.

"You can tell me, Sarah Beth. Maybe I can help you get through it."

She shuffled to the swing and sat, studying her fingernails. "I haven't been able to make myself leave Oxford since I came back. Over a year ago now. Every time I think about even going to Tupelo or Batesville or any place outside my little world here, I can't breathe. My palms sweat. My face tingles, and I feel like I might faint. Oh, and my heart pounds like it's going to explode through my chest."

"I thought that's what happened when my mother asked you to come to Los Angeles. I wasn't sure if it was L.A. or if it was any place that required you to ride on the interstate or what." He sat next to her on the swing. "You could have told me."

"I know. It's not that I didn't trust you. It's embarrassing. I've been seeing a therapist. I've prayed. Mark and Chris and Juan have prayed for me and with me. I feel like such a failure. I'm considering medication." She breathed out a long sigh.

Jess rested his hand on hers. "You should try the medication, and once you've been on it a few weeks, we'll go for a ride down Highway Six. We'll ride as far as you feel comfortable, then try it again every couple of days, maybe a bit farther each time. I've known a few players with anxiety disorders or post-traumatic stress. A guy I played with in Florida had been through a hurricane as a child. Every time there was a thunderstorm or tornado sirens went off, he freaked. He started taking medicine, and after a month or so, he felt much better." His thumb traced the knuckles of her soft fingers. "You have nothing to be embarrassed about."

The swing swayed, and they sat without talking, her hand still beneath his. Would she let him help her?

~~~

The electricity from Jess's hand resting on hers surged up Sarah Beth's arm to shock her heart. What did that mean? She sucked in a chest full of humid summer air. He was nice-looking after all. Perfectly normal to feel some attraction. But she needed to block that from her mind. She had to. He deserved better. Someone normal.

If only she could absorb some of his strength. Could she

really get well? How she wanted to believe she'd be able to visit her family in Atlanta, travel to her office in Los Angeles, go to Memphis. Go anywhere.

"You're a good friend. I'll give it a try. Maybe. Sometime."

"I care about you, Sarah Beth." Jess cleared his throat. "And you know I'm a quarterback at heart, and a coach. I come up with a strategy, and I execute the plan."

"Right, Coach. I'll try the medicine and let you know when I'm ready to start riding the roads."

"How about in three weeks? At that point, you should expect me to start annoying you to go a mile or two farther than you've been so far."

"What if I freak out on you?"

He turned and held her gaze. "You won't, but if you do, we can turn the car around." He caressed her hand. "I'll calm you down somehow." A smile played at the corner of his lips. "Maybe I'll throw a tennis ball at you especially hard."

Sarah Beth chuckled. "Or a volleyball."

"I could sing."

"That would freak me out for sure. You and Chris could go neck-and-neck in the joyful noise category."

He pretended to be outraged. "I thought if it came from the heart, it was good."

"That's not necessarily true for human ears."

He let go of her hand and squeezed her knee. "Uncalled for."

"That tickles. Stop."

Jess tried to grab her knee again. She held his hands away. Or was he holding hers? And why was she giggling like a little girl? "Okay, you can sing. I was just teasing you the way you guys tease me about my cooking."

His eyes focused on hers. She looked at her hands wrapped

in his and swallowed hard. Again. Did he hear the gulp? Or her heart that seemed to be banging against her chest?

Jess released her hands. "If you freak out, I have many ways to distract you."

"Sounds like punishment." She sat up straight. "Oh my stars. Gingie's not crated, and it's too quiet. Hang on, I'll be right back."

She ran into the house. A pile of items that had been on the floor of her closet now cluttered the living room. *Nice.* After shuffling through the collection of unofficial chew toys, she headed back toward the front door. "Come on, Gingie." The dog cowered the whole way. Outside, Sarah Beth found Jess kicked back on the swing. "She knows she was a bad girl."

"Going through the chewing stage?"

"Every pair of my shoes littered the living room floor. And a couple of purses. Luckily, it must have taken her a few minutes to gather them. She only had time to ruin a few pumps." She scratched between Gingie's ears. "You're a sneaky puppy, aren't you?"

"You're taking it pretty well, considering. Obviously you're not a shoe fanatic."

"No, shoes aren't my thing."

"What is your thing?" His stare probed her.

She twirled a loose piece of her hair around her finger. "I don't know. I guess because of the fire at our house in Pass Christian, I don't think of possessions as permanent. I know they're temporary. My thing might be people, God, my work, music."

"That makes sense, but I have a question about something that doesn't. How did you drive to Sardis Lake that first day if you can't leave Oxford?"

If only he knew how close she'd been to staying alone in

her house that day. "When Mark brought me here right after the accident, we drove to that part of Sardis Lake to sit and talk every day. He wanted to get me outside. If you had been planning to put the boat in somewhere else, like at Batesville, I wouldn't have gone. When you said Hurricane Landing, I just thought maybe I could make it there, like it was part of *my* Oxford."

Jess's chin lifted as he smiled. "I'm glad you did."

"Me, too." Her cheeks burned. More. If that were possible. "I should go in and do some work or something."

"Yeah, I have a long list of phone calls to make. I'll talk to you tomorrow."

"Goodbye, Jess." She led Gingie in.

"See you soon, Sarah Beth."

His voice trailed her, turning her insides out. Would he be able to help? Was she brave enough to try?

Chapter 26

A second cup of coffee did little to snap Sarah Beth's mind into action. The computer screen glowed before her, along with the anxiety prescription she'd picked up, but her thoughts drifted to the previous night's conversation. Her palms sweated just thinking about trying to leave town. And about taking the daily medicine. Sure it was okay for others, but she'd thought she could get over it on her own. Her heart warmed as she pictured Jess's eyes when he'd offered to help. And his hand holding hers. And his fingers caressing hers. Oh, goodness. Maybe a call to Jill would get her brain back on work. She stared at the prescription bottle again. She'd take the first pill after lunch. She grabbed her phone from the tabletop and pressed Jill's number.

Jill picked up on the fifth ring, her voice husky. "Hello."

"Morning, Jill. How's life?"

Jill yawned. "You know it's early in LA, and I'm kind of riding the struggle-bus this morning."

"I thought you gave up the partying."

"I did, but it was my birthday, and I was feeling sorry for myself."

Sarah Beth's hand went to her forehead. What a terrible friend she was. "Oh my stars. I knew it was your birthday yesterday, and I forgot to call you."

"It's okay. I got the gift you sent. I love the earrings, by the way."

Sarah Beth's stomach twisted. How could she forget to call

her assistant and best friend on her birthday? "Still, I meant to call you. I'm sorry I got—caught up in something. So what happened?"

"I went out to a club with a couple of old friends and had some drinks." Jill paused. "Um, you might fire me when I tell you this, but I hope you'll still be my friend."

Nothing could be that bad. "I'll always be your friend. Start talking."

"Dylan Conner came by the office to talk to Bill a while back. He came on to me a little and gave me his number. He said to call him sometime if I wanted to hang out."

"Don't tell me you called him last night."

"And I left with him, I guess."

"You guess?"

"I'm sorry." Jill's voice quivered. "I know he asked you out."

"I was never going to go out with Dylan. And I'm not firing you."

"Oh, Sarah Beth, are you sure you don't have feelings for him?"

"We're friends. But I'm worried for you."

"I am, too. I've seen the tabloid photos of him and that fashion designer, Sophia, the one you wouldn't represent in Paris because of her racy line of clothing."

Oh, what a small, creepy world. "Yeah, the tabloids and Sophia are troubling."

Jill cleared her throat. "You didn't call about this. What's on the agenda for today?"

"We can talk as long as you like about anything you want. Everything else can wait."

"There's nothing else to say about last night, other than I'm an idiot." Her voice broke. "Let's move on. I don't want to talk about it anymore, as long as you're still my friend."

"Always." Sarah Beth ran her index finger across the keyboard. "I called to clear my head and see if you can acquire some freebies." Hopefully the freebie mission would turn out better than the head-clearing. "You met the McCoys, who are staying in the Malibu condo. Jess McCoy, his friend Nick Russo, and Nick's daughter, Katie, are coming out for a visit. Katie's a precious four-year-old. Could you ask Juan what kinds of places are popular for kids? Oh, and I want Jess to meet Juan and see the architectural models of the clinic and church."

"Hmm. This Jess sounds important."

Sarah Beth cleared her throat. "Jess and Nick are both good friends."

"So, both of them, off limits?"

"What? No."

"I'm just kidding, especially after my blunder last night. Pray for me, will you?"

"Jill, I pray for you every day, but I'll say an extra prayer about this whole Dylan mess."

Once they hung up, Sarah Beth let out a long sigh. If only Jill could find a nice guy. Now that her brain was more muddled, she may as well try the new medicine. Her hands shook as she twisted the lid. She stared at the little white circle in her palm. The doctor said to try this one, and if it didn't work out, they'd try something else. What did that mean anyway? What happened if it didn't work? Would she be even crazier? She'd probably get fat. Maybe she'd get mean.

She was being ridiculous. No more thinking. She popped it in her mouth and swallowed.

~~~

Jess struggled to concentrate on the job at hand after his

conversation with Sarah Beth. On the sidelines of the university's practice facility, he tried to focus on the young quarterback who launched a ball downfield. The high school player had an arm, no doubt. Timing and velocity were dead on. And the kid seemed willing to listen. No bad attitude. They'd need a strong roll-out passer if Cole got injured. Their backup quarterback could sustain a drive, but didn't have the arm Cole or this kid did. The rapport was there, too.

If only Teddy would back off.

Teddy and the boy's dad, the so-called distant cousin, laughed together across the field. Not cool. He'd need to keep an eye on the situation. He wasn't getting drawn into something sleazy.

The quarterback jogged to the sidelines after the drills ended.

Jess slapped him on the back. "Good arm. I like the way you handled yourself out there. Your senior year is coming up. The other defenses better look out."

"Thanks, Coach." The six-foot-three-inch player grinned as if Jess had awarded him a Heisman.

Always a good sign when they called him Coach, not Coach McCoy. Teddy didn't need to worry. This one was leaning his way. He could feel it.

Since it was Tuesday, Jess cut out from the summer camps early for family night. When he arrived at the student minister's house, Chris shuffled around, frantic, while Camilla watched a cartoon on TV.

"Where are Sarah Beth and Kim?"

Chris' mouth twisted. "Sarah Beth isn't feeling well, and Kim's sitting with her."

Something was wrong. Jess's stomach lurched. "What happened?"

Chris stood, still holding paper plates, mouth half open, as if thinking how to answer. "She had an adverse reaction to a new medicine she tried."

Jess's heart rate accelerated to a sprint. "You're kidding. Is it the medicine I talked her into taking?"

Setting aside the plates, Chris placed both hands on Jess's shoulders. "Mark and Kim and I have been trying to convince her, too. This is a fluke. Absolutely not your fault."

This couldn't be happening. "Do you think it will be all right for me to go over and sit with her?"

"I don't know."

Didn't matter. He had to go. "I'll see you later, Chris. Sorry about not staying to help." Jess pulled his keys from his pocket and ran full speed to his truck.

The few miles to Sarah Beth's felt like a hundred. Once he reached her door, a loud howl greeted him.

The door opened a fraction, and Kim peeked out. "Oh, Jess. Sarah Beth's not feeling well."

"Yeah, I heard. I feel bad about encouraging her to take the medicine. I was wondering if I could come in. Do you think she'd mind, since you're here?"

Kim raised her eyebrows. "I'm not sure she'll know you're here. I gave her one of the pills the doctor called in for the nausea, and it's made her drowsy. At least she's not sick to her stomach anymore, poor thing."

His breath caught. It felt like he'd been sacked. More than once. "I feel terrible. I didn't know this could happen."

"It's not your fault. You know that, right?" She touched his shoulder. "There's always a possibility someone can have an adverse reaction to medication. Sometimes people have to try a couple of different prescriptions until they find the one to help."

Wagging her tail, Gingie pranced around Jess's legs, vying for attention.

"Gingie's happy to see you. Sarah Beth's on the sofa. I'm going to the kitchen to get a drink." Kim left him alone with Sarah Beth. He sat on the edge of the couch and stroked the hair framing her face.

Dark brown eyes flittered open. "How did you get here?"

"Kim let me in. I heard you were sick. I'm so sorry. I wanted you to feel better, not worse."

Sarah Beth sat up and blinked a few times. "Evidently I'm the one in a million who has a bad reaction to this drug. The doctor said I can try a different kind. Here." Sarah Beth patted the seat beside her. "You can lean back and share the couch with me."

Her face was so pale. "No, you lie down."

"I can sit up a while." Her head wobbled a little as she spoke. "I'm just sleepy and a little goofier than usual."

"If you're sure." As he sank back onto the couch, Gingie bounded into his lap. The weight and the surprise pulled a throaty laugh from Jess.

Sarah Beth leaned across and shook her finger at the hefty puppy. "You know you're too big to be a lap dog, Gingie."

The dog stayed put, and a second later, Sarah Beth's head sunk to Jess's shoulder. Her body relaxed, breathing slow and steady.

A quiet sigh slipped from Kim when she returned to the living room with two bottles of water. "I leave the room for a couple of minutes, and this is what happens?"

"I think I'm stuck here for a little while." The only thing better would be a long while. This felt right. Like he was home. Both his girls curled up beside him.

Kim shook her head. "Fine, but I'm ruling the remote."

~~~

. Sarah Beth's legs ached to stretch. She attempted to twist around and lay back on the couch, but fur brushed her arm, and a lump pushed into her back. "What in the world?"

She turned her head to find Jess and Gingie beside her on the couch, while Kim slept curled up on the love seat.

Jess woke as she tried to untangle herself. "Hey, how are you feeling?"

Her heart squeezed at the sound, the proximity. "Still a bit like a bus hit me, but better."

"I should go. I'll let myself out and check on you later." He attempted an awkward hug that melted into something more natural. Soothing and warm.

Before he pulled away, he kissed her forehead. "See you soon."

Sarah Beth breathed in the scent of him. Her face tingled. But in a good way. "Bye, Jess."

~~~

The sun hung low in the western sky as Jess ended the call and placed the phone on the truck console. The timing was terrible for Tampa Bay to invite him for a visit. He'd stop by Sarah Beth's as he'd done every evening after his camps to make sure she responded better to the new medication she'd started. He needed to tell her about this trip.

The invitation signaled they were indeed looking at him as a candidate when their offensive coordinator retired. Most of the staff were good guys, people he'd like to work with. But was this move what he wanted? Was now the right timing?

The short drive didn't give him time to settle anything in his mind, and Sarah Beth waved from the porch swing as he pulled up. How could one woman both paralyze and move a man with such force? He sighed, opened his door, and then climbed the stairs two at a time. "Hey. Having a good day?"

A smile lit up her face. "A great day. Got lots of work done." She narrowed her eyes as he moved closer. "What's wrong? You look sad."

Nailed. How did she read him so easily? "I hate the timing, but I have to go out of town for two weeks. I'm going to Tampa Bay to look at how they run their program, and then I promised to visit Mom and Dad out West. I'd put it off, but I'm running out of summer."

She shrugged. "I knew y'all were going. You have a life outside of trying to help a crazy friend. I'll be fine, and it's only two weeks."

Maybe to her. He joined her on the swing. "Mom wants to take Katie to all the places for kids." He watched for her reaction. "The woman is dying for grandchildren."

Her gaze fell to her feet. "Rachel never wanted to marry?"

"She was engaged in law school, but he broke it off. She's never gotten involved with anyone again."

"How sad." She let that sink in. Then her brows lifted. "Oh. You guys go by my office. I asked Jill to get you passes to fun places like amusement parks, and you can meet Juan. He'll show you the architectural models for the clinic and the church. We're close to finishing the clinic, but I need a few more big sponsors or a fundraiser to complete the chapel."

Jess pushed his feet to the ground and stopped the swing. "There's plenty of money in Oxford. We can do a fundraiser with the CSU. Have you asked our church to sponsor?"

"I told them about the project, but they never offered. I'm still a new member, and I didn't want to push fundraising on the leadership."

"When I get back, we'll work up a plan."

Hands lifted, Sarah Beth looked up to the heavens. "Thank

you, Lord. Who would've thought a few months ago that Coach Jess McCoy would be such a blessing to me and so many more?"

His turn to stare at his feet. "Thanks for the vote of confidence."

"It's true. And when you get back, I'll be ready to start our projects."

Maybe if she got better, she could go to Tampa with him. "Including leaving Oxford?"

Her teeth bit at her bottom lip. "I guess, that too."

Jess gave her his best coach scowl. "You better be, or you're running laps, lady."

She laughed. How he loved the sound. This might be the longest two weeks of his life.

Chapter 27

Still too hot outside. July temperatures soared into the upper nineties, and with the humidity, it wouldn't cool down much, even after sunset. Sarah Beth took a seat on a barstool beside Nick in the kitchen of Chris and Kim's house.

Nick lifted his glass of iced tea to his forehead. "We need to be in a pool. It's miserable."

Dabbing her neck with a napkin, Sarah Beth shook her head. "It would have to be bigger than my pool. I jumped in earlier, and it was like bath water."

"I guess we'll have to wait for Jess to get back and hit the lake to cool off." Nick bit into his burger, piled high with fresh garden tomatoes and homemade pickles.

"Sounds like his trip is going well. Oh, and I have a friend I want you to meet when you join him. Go with him to my office to pick up the passes. Her name is Jill, and she's really sweet and gorgeous. You'll love her."

A choking cough erupted from Nick, and he set down his burger. "You've talked to Jess? I haven't heard from him. *And* I thought I made clear to everyone that I don't do fix-up dates."

"I wasn't fixing you up. Juan and I are praying she'll give her life to the Lord." She shoved the rest of her cheeseburger into her mouth. Maybe that would keep her from saying the wrong thing. But Nick and Jill *would* be perfect together. He was alone, and she needed a good guy.

"As long as you're not trying to fix me up, I'll talk to her.

Who's Juan?"

She swallowed the lump of bun stuck in her throat. "Juan's my assistant who's hoping to be a missionary in Honduras. They could both go to lunch or dinner with you guys. I'd love for my friends to get to know each other." She thrashed her arms around in a little happy dance.

Nick laughed. "It would be more perfect if you joined us."

That ended the dance. "I guess Jess or Chris didn't tell you that part."

"What?"

"You see, I've had this problem since the accident…"

She described her anxiety disorder and Jess's plan to help her. Nick listened without interrupting.

When she finished, Nick put a hand on her forearm. "Jess will do what he says. He's a good man and has stood by me through some tough times."

"You know, I never would've guessed he was a good guy when he walked into my office to talk about Cole. I thought he was full of himself."

Nick let out a small laugh. "What kind of quarterback—or coach, for that matter—isn't confident?"

"I'd call it bossy, but you can call it confident if you want."

Her phone rang, and she turned it over to check who was calling. She smiled and answered. "Nick and I were just talking about you."

When the call ended, Nick lifted one shoulder. "You know, Katie and I could take you for a drive this week. We could carry you and that monstrosity you call a dog out to another part of the lake, farther away, for a walk."

"I don't know." She wasn't dying to start the process of going farther away. "I'm not sure about Gingie. I'm having trouble training her on the leash. She breaks into a run with me stumbling behind trying to control her. I'm planning to enroll her in obedience school soon, but they won't take her until she's a couple of months older."

"I can train your dog for you. Bring a harness and a bag of treats."

"Are you sure?"

"Before my father went to prison, we always had guard dogs. I had to be able to control them or get eaten."

"Your father's in prison?"

He lifted one shoulder. "Meth."

Poor Nick. One more thing he'd been through. "I'm sorry. I didn't know."

"It was tough. Mom left us to get away from him when I was thirteen. She lived with anyone who would take her and her bottle of gin."

Sarah Beth's heart hurt for him. He'd endured his share of pain, too. "Were there other children?"

"I have a brother. Also in prison. He's five years older and in the *family business*." Air quotes surrounded those words. "If I hadn't met Katie's mother, I'm sure that's where I'd be right now."

"I think she'd be proud of what a good father you are to Katie."

"Thanks." His voice was soft. "So about that drive?"

"Call me when you're brave enough to start training me and my puppy. I'll have the harness and treats ready." But would *she* be ready?

~~~

"Let me know when you want me to stop." Nick smiled at Sarah Beth in the rearview mirror. "I didn't know I'd play chauffeur for you ladies today."

Stopping two miles back down the road would've been

good. She swallowed hard at the lump in her throat that seemed to be choking her. "Katie asked me to sit with her first, so what could I say?" Plus, the back seat was safer, and she could hardly see the road. She squeezed her large tote close to her chest to comfort herself.

"So, I'm stuck up here with Cujo."

Katie huffed. "Her name is Gingie, Daddy."

"I know, sweetie. I was teasing Ms. Sarah Beth."

"Daddy?"

"Yes, dear?"

"Is Cujo what they call that green stuff that covers the trees?"

"No. That's kudzu. They call it the vine that ate the South."

"Ate what?" Katie's eyes grew large.

Despite her nerves, Sarah Beth smothered a laugh. He'd stepped into that one.

"It didn't really eat the South. It just grows all over stuff."

"Kudzu. That's a funny word. So what's Cujo?"

Shaking his head, Nick cleared his throat. "Daddy shouldn't have mentioned that. Cujo was a bad dog in a movie, nothing like Gingie. I'm not communicating very well today."

"Look, y'all." Katie's words curled with the drawl particular to northern Mississippi. "Watermelons. Can we get one? Please, please, please?" Pointing, Katie bounced in her booster seat.

Sarah Beth followed the girl's pointed finger to a truck farmer parked on the corner of two country roads. Her heart accelerated to a gallop. They were far enough. She needed to turn around and go home. "I love watermelon. Pull over now. Let's take it back to my house and eat it."

"Not home yet. We just left." The sad look on Katie's face fought against Sarah Beth's urge to go back.

"We're near an entrance to the lake. Let's take the watermelon to a picnic table."

"And how are we going to cut it?" Nick asked.

Sarah Beth dug into her bag. "I have a Swiss Army knife, and I'm ready to get out. Now."

The truck slowed to a stop. Nick glanced to the back seat. "I guess I know when I'm outnumbered. What all do you have crammed in that big bag, anyway?"

Heartbeat slowing, Sarah Beth loosened her hold on the bag. Whew. The air released from her lungs. "A lot. I like to be prepared."

After Nick purchased the melon, he drove down the gravel road to the lake. Once they'd unloaded, he worked with Gingie on two basic commands in a grassy area nearby. Sarah Beth labored with the watermelon and her small knife. Her hands still shook from the anxiety she'd suffered getting to this part of the lake.

The first command was for Gingie to look at him as he held a treat. The second was to sit. The dog responded to Nick's instructions.

"You do know what you're doing." Sarah Beth's attempts to cut nice slices weren't going well at all. She'd barely made a dent in halving the thing.

Katie stood beside her, smiling and chattering.

Nick joined them with Gingie on the leash. "You doubted me?"

"More like I doubted my dog."

"Can I help you butcher that watermelon, too?"

"I almost have it." She glanced at her progress. "Or maybe not. You'll need to sanitize your hands if you take over."

"I suppose the sanitizer is in your bag of tricks, Mary Poppins?"

"That and a spoonful of sugar. Check the bench on the other side of the table."

After he'd wiped his hands, he extended his arm. "I can't watch you mutilate a perfectly good watermelon. I'll cut while you try the commands with Gingie."

She dug out her best little kid voice. "Fine, but you're not the boss of me."

"Just what I need, another sassy little girl."

Before Sarah Beth had given the second command, he held out a slice. "Come and get it."

"That was quick." The sweet fruity scent filled the air, reminding her of summers past. Sarah Beth took a bite.

Nick smirked. "I have a few talents."

Katie grabbed a piece of watermelon. "Yummy."

"Oh, yes. Sweet and ripe." Sarah Beth spoke between mouthfuls.

"And messy." Nick nodded at the juice running down Katie's face and arms. "I hope you have some paper towels in that bag."

The phone chirped in Sarah Beth's pocket. "Great, now my phone's going to be sticky." She pulled it out with two fingers and pressed answer. "Hello?"

"This is Stacy from church. Can you help in the nursery Sunday? Everyone else has cancelled for vacations, and I see you've already completed the safety training and background check."

"Um, I guess I can help. I've never worked with babies, but I can try if you can't find anyone."

"Great. I'll email the instructions." The woman sounded relieved.

Nick picked up his own piece of melon. "Problem?"

"Yeah. The church must be desperate if they're calling me.

Their normal volunteers are all out of town. I don't even know how to change a diaper. I mean, I can play with a four-year-old, but babies—they scare me."

"I took the day off, but our flight doesn't leave until Sunday night. Do you want me to help you?"

"Would you? I'd feel so much better."

He gave her a warm smile. "I would."

"Thank you so much. You're a man of many talents—watermelon cutter, dog trainer, dad, and nursery helper. I appreciate your friendship, Nick."

"You're more than welcome. What are friends for?"

Sarah Beth turned to Katie. "So what's next? Wanna play?"

Nick and Gingie trailed behind as Sarah Beth and Katie skipped down the path to the water. They frolicked along the edge of the lake then headed for home, tired and dirty.

Katie nodded off a couple of times on the way back but woke as Sarah Beth opened the truck door to exit. "Can you play again tomorrow, Ms. Sarah Beth?"

"Sounds fun, but we can talk about that in the morning."

Katie nodded. "I'll find your number on Daddy's phone and call you."

Katie was such a great kid. Sarah Beth smiled and waved until they were out of sight. Maybe she could be a mother someday. But how could she be responsible for a child when she couldn't even manage her own anxiety?

Chapter 28

Sarah Beth twisted her hair into an elastic band and pulled on her running shoes. The phone on her night stand buzzed.

"Ms. Sarah Beth?"

That delightful little voice. "Hi, Katie."

"Would you be able to go eat ice cream with me and my daddy after work?"

"I'd love to."

"Yay. Here's Daddy."

The phone clonked around. "Hey." Nick's voice.

"She's so cute."

"You say that now, but once she memorizes your contact, you might change your mind. Jess can verify that."

"Aw, that's sweet that she calls him."

"She also calls his mother every day. Most of the time I don't even know when she does it. She loves to talk on the phone."

"So Jess's parents kind of adopted you and Katie."

"Pretty much."

"I like his parents. I told Jess they could adopt me."

"How did that come up?"

"He was joking around that they loved me."

Silence lingered on the other end of the line.

"Nick? Are you still there?"

"Sorry, I was distracted. So, do you want to drive to New Albany for ice cream, or Batesville?"

Her chest tightened at the thought. "I thought we were

staying in Oxford."

"You did so well yesterday, I thought I'd check. What if we get ice cream in Oxford and then go for a ride in the country? It doesn't get dark until about eight." His tone was soothing. "We can turn around any time you want. I promise."

He thought she'd done well? She forced herself to inhale. "I'll try."

~ ~ ~

Nick motioned toward his truck, which was parallel parked in front of Sweet Cream's pale yellow awning. Once they'd ordered and paid, he headed toward the street. "I'm going to regret this, but I'll let you girls bring the ice cream in the truck. It'll occupy you-know-who for a while." He nodded toward Katie.

Sarah Beth pointed to the pink plastic benches outside the ice cream shop. "We can eat it here. We don't have to go for a ride."

"Let's get this show on the road." He scooped up Katie then opened the front door for Sarah Beth.

Katie stopped her licking for a second. "Daddy said he'd show me a farm, but only if you got to sit up front this time." She scrunched her nose at Nick.

"We have to share our friends." Nick smiled as he chided her.

"Next time it's my turn again."

Sarah Beth laughed. "I feel so popular."

"Don't let it go to your head." Nick gave her a stern look.

Her phone buzzed. "It's Jess." She touched to answer. "Perfect timing, you can talk to Katie and me. We're just having ice cream, and Nick's taking us for a ride in the country to see a farm."

"Oh." His voice faltered. "I won't keep you if y'all are

hanging out." He paused. "I only have a second before I head into another meeting, then I'll stay pretty tied up."

Her heart sank. Already he had to go? "Oh, okay. I'll talk to you later." She tucked the phone back into her bag and stepped up into Nick's truck.

The country road cut through the north Mississippi hills. Sarah Beth squirmed in her seat as she spooned her mix of pistachio and white chocolate frozen yogurt into her mouth. *Please help me get through this drive, Lord.*

The cool flavors mingled and soothed her tight throat. The passing countryside held green fields, trees, gravel roads, and farmhouses.

After twenty minutes, though, she rubbed her palms on her legs as they began to perspire. Her breathing sped up. "I can't. I have to turn around now."

Nick glanced at her. "Sure, here's a gravel drive."

Worry sifted her nerve endings. But he was true to his word and turned the truck around.

"Daddy, is this the farm?" A puzzled look wrinkled Katie's forehead.

"We passed it. Didn't you see it?"

"No." She twisted her head around. "Can we go back?"

"That's exactly what we're doing."

Ten minutes later, Nick turned down another gravel road.

Sarah Beth's face screwed into a frown. "Do you know these people?"

"Just thought I'd show up."

"Really?"

Nick chuckled. "One of my suppliers lives out here. I told him Katie wanted to see a farm." He pulled over near a barn and turned off the truck.

"Is this the farm?" Katie bounced in her seat as Nick came

around to lift her out.

He smiled. "That's right. They grow cotton and soybeans, and they have a catfish pond."

"Can we eat cotton?"

"We don't eat cotton. We make clothes out of cotton. At the end of the season, this field will be white as snow."

"Can we come back then?"

"Sure. But today, we get to feed the catfish."

Katie clapped her hands then threw her arms around him. "You're the best daddy in the world."

Puzzled, Sarah Beth studied Nick. "What if I hadn't made it this far?"

Nick winked. "I thought you would, but if not, I could've brought her back."

"Hmm, I'm going to enjoy feeding the catfish as much as Katie. Thanks for inviting me."

"You're welcome. It's nice to have another adult along. A quasi-adult anyway."

Sarah Beth's hands punched her hips. "I hope never to lose the wonder of childhood."

With a smile, Nick nudged her elbow. "I just enjoy giving you a hard time."

"Oh, thanks a lot. It's like having another brother." And he was like a brother. Wasn't he?

~~~

Jess went over the notes he'd made on his tablet, but he couldn't concentrate. His best friend and the woman he cared about were hanging out. He should be glad that Nick was taking up the slack while he was gone—helping Sarah Beth with her anxiety. But why did his stomach churn when he'd hung up the phone? Was this jealousy? If it was, he was being petty and needed to get over it.

He'd pick up where they'd left off when he got home. The trip would be over in ten days. He touched the screen and looked at the routes he'd charted for Sarah Beth. He'd studied the roads leaving Oxford and even followed them on Google Earth to know what to expect. This was his biggest challenge. Could he use his coaching skills to help someone—an adorable someone—with something more important than football?

It would take a lot of trust on her part. And prayer. He pictured her sitting in his truck. He imagined the tone of voice, the instructions he could use. Like drills, but nicer. Then he pictured her and Nick. And Katie. He closed the cover of the tablet. Maybe a move to Florida would be a good thing.

Chapter 29

The Veggie Tales clock on the wall read ten twenty-five. Sarah Beth rocked the screaming bald baby in her arms. When would Nick get here? She'd tried everything she knew to soothe the infant, which wasn't much. Nothing helped. The baby's little lips quivered, and such a loud wail emanated from the tiny mouth. She'd arrived at the church nursery well in advance to familiarize herself, but so had this little fella's parents.

Nick poked his head around the half door. "Still need my help?"

"Whew. Am I glad to see you. This fella's mother said it was time for his bottle, and he hasn't stopped crying since I fed him."

Nick held out his arms. "I think I've got this one." He lay the crying infant over his shoulder and patted hard against the pint-sized back.

"Oh my stars. What are you doing? You're beating him." A loud belch echoed around the cinderblock walls. "Goodness. Did he make that noise?"

Nick gave her a triumphant look. "And that is how you burp a baby." He turned the little guy around and cradled the smiling infant. "Good one, buddy. You feeling better?"

Sarah Beth laughed. "You boys come out doing that, don't you?"

"I'm one hundred percent positive girls do, too."

"Does this mean you'll change all the diapers?"

His eyebrows raised. "I'll change the first one, then I'll

supervise."

"It was worth a try."

Two other babies arrived. One made himself at home in Nick's lap, the other slept in her carrier. Not so bad. She could do this again. Maybe.

Church ended, and the parents picked up the little ones. Sarah Beth turned out the light and walked with Nick to pick up Katie from children's church.

With puppy dog eyes, Katie looked up and tugged on Sarah Beth's shirt. "Will you go eat chicken nuggets with us? Please?"

"I would love to eat with you." Sarah Beth shrugged. "I love eating in general, after all."

Nick nudged her. "I'm sure you would rather eat something besides chicken nuggets, but I'll buy."

"As you may've heard, anything's better than what I cook."

"Let's head out then."

They ate and talked while Katie played on the indoor playground. After thirty minutes of Katie showing them how well she could climb and slide, Nick called her in. "It's time to pack for vacation, Katie-bug."

On the way out, Sarah Beth pressed Nick's forearm. "Don't forget about getting to know Jill and taking her to eat with you."

"I remember. I've already been praying for her. And *you* remember, I don't do fix-up dates. This is purely about sharing my faith and being a friend."

Sarah Beth saluted. "Got it." She dropped her hand to her heart. "The fact that you're praying for her already moves me. Thanks."

Once again, Katie tugged on Sarah Beth's shirt. "Will you carry me to the truck?"

"Sure." As she edged Katie into her booster seat, the small

girl put her hands on both Sarah Beth's cheeks. "Ms. Sarah Beth, can you be my new mommy?"

Nick and Sarah Beth shared an awkward glance. Sarah Beth covered the little hands with her own. "You have a mommy in heaven, so I'm more like your fun Aunt Sarah Beth."

"Okay, but I'd like a mommy who could talk to me. Out loud. I guess you can be my aunt like Uncle Jess is my uncle."

His eyes downcast, Nick's shoulders slumped.

Poor thing. Sarah Beth's heart hurt for him.

She gave Katie a hug and kiss. "I miss my mommy, too, but you have lots of people who love you. Plus, I think you have one of the best daddies in the world. Don't you?"

"Yeah." She grinned. "The best daddy in the world."

Katie moved past the moment, but Nick pressed the back of his hand against his mouth.

Sarah Beth rounded the truck and laid a hand on his shoulder. "She's fine. I meant what I said. You're a fabulous father."

"I just never thought about her wanting a mother. I thought she was happy with the way we were." His fingers pulled at the top of his hair. "I've only been thinking about myself...not wanting to have my heart torn in two again or deal with dating and all that. Maybe I've been wrong."

"It's something to pray about. Ask God to help you be open, willing, and able to love again if that's His plan."

Giving a weak smile, Nick rubbed his eyes. "Chris was right when he said that you may seem a bit eccentric, but you're like a bucket of wisdom from the well of life."

Her lips pressed into a pout. "I'm still kind of ticked at how he worded that."

He met her eyes head on. "Maybe you should follow your own advice and pray to be open, willing, and able to love again if that's His plan."

Her situation was different. A tightness rose in her throat. She needed to leave. "Have fun on your vacation, and be careful."

Chapter 30

The ring of the phone interrupted Sarah Beth's feasting on a plate of good, salty black-eyed peas and cornbread she'd picked up in town. She set aside her dinner and swallowed a sip of milk. "Hello." A bit garbled, but the ID showed it was Jill.

"Whoa, Sarah Beth. Those Southern men are smoking—all that and a bag of chips. Jess is so hot, and Nick is adorable in a deep and mysterious way. So which one are you interested in? I know you have to find one attractive."

"They're both good friends."

Jill blew out a loud sigh. "Jess is tall and picture-perfect, but he didn't have much to say. Nick and I talked a lot, but I'm not sure whether I'd be taller than he is if I wore high heels."

The conversation gnawed at Sarah Beth's gut. "So wear flats." Her voice came out sharper than she'd intended.

"Aha. So you have feelings for Jess. I was testing you."

"Testing me?"

"I did have a great time hanging out with Nick, and I love that little Katie. She's a doll."

"What did you mean by testing me?"

Jill sighed. "When I gave you an opportunity to tell me why I should or shouldn't go out with both of them, you only told me what to do about going out with Nick. You said 'wear flats.' You said nothing about Jess."

The gnawing graduated to a bite. "Since when are you Sherlock Holmes?"

"Since I found out two single, smoking hot, Christian men

are your new best friends. You've been keeping secrets. And what more can you ask for? You have to find one dateable."

"I don't want to talk about this anymore."

"I'm sorry, but I'm excited for you. You're making progress and moving on after you went through such a terrible loss. You know I love you like a sister. Now, I know you're still my boss…"

"I love you like a sister, too, but let's talk about something else."

Another sigh came from Jill's end. "Will do, but it's not going to be as much fun."

~~~

Sarah Beth checked the time on her phone. Early for family night. The last several days seemed to drag by. Strange that Jess hadn't called, considering the first week he'd been gone, he'd touched base at least once a day. It wasn't like he owed her a call. Still, what was this little ache in her chest?

Maybe something had gone wrong. Or he was mad at her? She was always blurting out stupid things. Especially with Jess.

His plane should've landed two days ago. She shut the door to the SUV and scurried up the sidewalk to Chris and Kim's. Being so early, maybe she should knock.

Kim pulled the door open with a crooked smile. "Wow, this must be the night for being super early."

"What do you mean?"

Kim pointed out to the deck. "Jess is already here, too."

Her heart skittered again. Why hadn't she noticed his truck? "Oh."

Kim shooed her toward the back door. "Go on."

"Where's Camilla? I usually play with her."

"At a friend's house."

"Can't I help you in here?"

"Absolutely not." Kim crossed her arms at her chest. "Go."

With cautious steps, Sarah Beth headed out onto the deck.

Heat rose from the grill where Chris turned and smiled. "Hello, Sarah Beth, come on out."

Jess turned, his arms limp at his sides. For a moment she held his gaze, her feet planted. Why should this be awkward? They were friends. She closed the distance between them and grabbed him in a tight hug. "I missed you. I heard from you every day and then nothing. I got worried."

After she spoke, he slid his arms around her and lifted her off the ground. "I missed you, too. Sorry I didn't call again. I... Never mind. I'm sorry."

When Jess released her, warmth remained, enveloping her, soothing and tender.

"What about me?" Chris threw open his arms. "I feel so left out."

"I just saw you Sunday. Jess has been gone two weeks."

Jess stood tall. "That's right, buddy."

Things seemed normal again. Maybe she'd imagined something was wrong.

Not a lot of students attended the gathering. So many were on vacation or home for the summer, the small group dwindled after dinner. Kim and Chris had their bags packed to head out on a trip of their own the next day, so Sarah Beth called it a night at nine o'clock.

Jess walked her out, his presence comfortable. Did the night have to end already? "Jess, you know, someone else missed you."

Stopping, he faced her. "Who's that?"

"Gingie."

He continued to stare, eyebrows raised above those

luscious brown pools of light. "Did she tell you this?"

"I could tell. Oh, and Nick taught us how to sit."

His gaze fell. "You didn't know how to sit?"

An owl hooted from the direction of the large oak across the road, and a light breeze fluttered his blond hair. She could string words together in an intelligent way. With other people. But not him. "Ha-ha, very funny. You know what I mean. I've been practicing all week."

"Maybe I should come say hello to Gingie and see you sit."

Maybe she'd never be able to string words together around him. Something about Jess McCoy kept her tongue-tied. "Maybe you should. I'm very good at sitting."

Jess flashed a smile. "I'll see you on the porch."

~~~

Jess pulled into the driveway behind Sarah Beth. He'd missed her bubbly smile and the way she sometimes misspoke or blurted things out when she talked with him. But what about Katie? That little girl needed a mother. He wouldn't be the one to deny her.

A full moon lit the porch with a whitish glow. Faint silhouettes of magnolia and pine trees shadowed the sidewalk and half the stairs. Sarah Beth ran inside to let the dog out, returned with a couple of bottles of water, and switched on the lighted ceiling fans.

Gingie barreled over to him, whining.

"Hey, girl. I think you did miss me, didn't you?" He rubbed the dog's head then sat back on the white front porch swing. The sound of the frogs and crickets echoed through the balmy night air. Jess searched Sarah Beth's expression. "So you missed me, too?"

Her cheeks flushed, and she bit her bottom lip. "You need me to say it again?"

He liked that he'd made her blush. "Come sit down." He patted the seat.

The swing rocked as she sat beside him. She fidgeted with the chain securing the bench to the ceiling. "So tell me about your trip. Is your family doing well? Did they like the ideas I sent them? Did you meet Juan and see the clinic and church plans? Oh, did Nick and Jill hit it off? I was praying they would."

He planted his feet. "Slow down. That's a barrel of questions." Did she say what he thought she had? A moment passed. "I want to start with the last one. Are you saying you want to fix Nick up with Jill?"

One shoulder lifted as she answered, "Not exactly, but Jill would love to meet a nice guy." She toed at a wood plank. "Okay. Maybe I was. Nick's a good man. Last week when you weren't here, he took me around. I think because you were gone, he was lonely. He said he liked to have another adult to talk to, and you hadn't called him."

"I didn't realize." Jess slumped. Nick lonely? Could that be all there was to Nick hanging out with Sarah Beth while he was gone? "I should've called him. You know, Katie calls me every day since she found out how to find my number on his cell. I figured Nick would get on the phone if he needed to talk."

"She's discovered my phone number now too, so I know how you feel. And he's such a good guy. I thought maybe if he and Jill hit it off, they could talk on the phone, chat online. Get to know each other. He would be a good influence on her."

This had been what he wanted, needed, to hear, but he had to be sure. No timeouts left. Push on. "Let me ask you something. Are you sure there's no possibility of, you know…you and Nick?"

Her eyes shot open. "He's a great guy and all, but I feel for him in a more brotherly way. Why would you think that? Because he took me driving?"

Jess studied his hands. "Katie told me that she wanted you to be her new mommy. You'd spent time together, and Nick's like a brother to me. Little girls need a mother." He closed his fingers over hers. "You'd be a wonderful mother."

The chains of the swing creaked as they rocked. She didn't move her hand away. It felt right beneath his.

Sarah Beth sighed. "I know Katie needs a woman in her life. I still miss having a mother. Poor Mark has been my sounding board all these years." Her head shook slowly. "But I can't date Nick so Katie can have a mother. That would be crazy. What if he met someone he was actually interested in? Then I'd be in the way."

He searched her eyes. "You're sure you couldn't come to love Nick?"

"I don't have a crystal ball, Jess, but I don't have feelings for him in that way."

He was conscious of the warmth of her breath as she spoke. Her hand still under his. Relief washed over him. "Okay." One side of his mouth turned up. "What were those other questions?"

Her lips pinched together. "Just tell me about your trip."

"Your condo in Malibu was perfect. My only hang-up was that it used to belong to that cheesy actor. But I can see how you were able to think and pray and draw closer to the Lord with the Pacific to the west and the mountains on the other side."

"Yeah. Pretty spectacular view. What about the food?"

"I tried the fish tacos at the little café you recommended. You were right." He smiled at her. "You may not be able to cook good food, but you know it when you taste it."

"I won't say I told you so."

"Touché." He chuckled, then took a more serious tone. "I found that chapel at Pepperdine. I went by myself to think and pray. I decided to tell my dad about Sophia."

Her gaze fastened onto his. "How did that go?"

Jess looked down at his feet. "We were hiking and stopped for a rest. I told him, but asked him not to tell Mom or Rachel. He was understanding and let me talk. He wondered if that was why I never connected emotionally with any of the girls I dated, why I never got serious about anyone."

He'd said more than he'd intended. Again.

"Did your talk help?"

"Enough about that."

She clucked her tongue. "You never answered about Jill and Nick."

"You should have seen Nick's eyes when we picked her up. They hit it off right from the start, and she hung out with him and Katie all week."

"I told you she's gorgeous. So different from me. Every golden strand of hair in place, impeccable makeup, manicured nails." She huffed. "Her outfits are accessorized. I never can figure out how to do that. I feel like I wear a uniform compared to her. Oh, and she's super organized."

"Some guys like that Barbie-doll look. Not me." He smirked.

Her gaze wandered as she took that in. "Did you meet Juan?"

"I did. He gave me the numbers we need to finish out the chapel. We've got work to do, lady."

Sarah Beth's brows lifted a fraction. "We?"

"I'm good at strategizing."

She slipped her hand away and clapped. "I love

strategizing. When can we start?"

So cute. But he missed her hand already. "We need to schedule people and organizations to hear Juan's presentation. First, I think I need to make a quick trip down to Honduras as soon as possible. I need to see the property for myself. "

"You just got back." Her voice fell flat. "I should go with you."

He slid his arm around her and softened his tone. "Juan will go with me. A weekend trip. And when you're ready, we'll go together."

"Why can't I move past this? I get so disappointed in myself."

How he'd love to take away her pain. "Hey, I created a system for you while I was gone." He gave her arm a squeeze. "We'll chart each road you travel and the mileage. Every time we return to that road, we'll try to go at least a mile farther. I've been doing some reading on anxiety disorders. Your medicine helps regulate serotonin. Sometimes to get past your panic attacks, you may have to take a mild sedative. For example, if you can't get past a certain point on our rides, a calming medicine could help you break through that barrier. Those drugs are habit-forming, so you only want to take them if necessary. What do you think?"

Eyes as dark as the night sky stared up at him. "Sounds like you've given this a good bit of research."

Those eyes unearthed emotions so powerful within him. "I want to help." He willed his arm back to his side and forced it down. *Don't scare her off. Look away. Now.*

"I'd better talk to my doctor and therapist and let you know what they say."

"Talk to them tomorrow, and make a list of people we can invite to a fundraiser. We'll meet for dinner, go for a drive, and talk shop while we ride."

Her eyes narrowed. "I'll check my calendar and get back with you."

"What? You have to check your calendar?"

"No." She gave him a playful shove. "But you sounded a little bossy."

"Sorry. I was in coach mode." He smiled. "Are you free tomorrow after work?"

Long lashes batted for a second. "Let me think about it. Yes."

"Great. I'm ready to get started."

"You are a man after my own heart. Once I get a plan, I'm prepared to move."

After her own heart in so many ways. He should leave while he was ahead. Jess stood and stretched. "Not bringing messy stacks of papers along, are you?"

She ignored his teasing. "That gives me an idea. I think Jill should come work in Oxford for a few weeks to help me organize. And maybe you and Nick could come to dinner."

"You are a tricky one, Sarah Beth LeClair." He stroked his chin. "I should get going. I'll see you tomorrow." Their eyes locked. "I missed you."

Her lips parted, but no words came out. He smiled to himself as he walked away. His heart had never been this full. Somehow he would help her move past her anxiety.

Chapter 31

Sarah Beth squeezed the fabric of the seatbelt crossing her chest as the truck coasted down Highway Seven with Jess at the wheel. The country road ran along the fringes of small towns and communities with names like Water Valley, Velma, and Coffeeville. She knew these roads, but the farther they drove, the more her insides turned to liquid and flowed like ice water through her veins. She gripped the door handle of the truck, knuckles white. "I'd like to turn around now."

Jess glanced at her and slowed the truck at the next gravel road. He pulled in, pushed the gear to park, then gave her hand a squeeze. "You did well. I'm proud of you."

After forcing oxygen in and out of her lungs a few times, the tightness receded. She let out the air with a long sigh.

He still held her fingers in his. "Your hand's like ice. Do I have the AC too high?"

"I think my blood stopped flowing—even though my heart was beating like a hummingbird in a hurricane."

"I don't think that's a saying."

"My daddy used to say that about a storm he got caught up in near Cat Island. If Daddy said it, it's a saying."

Chuckling, he slipped his hand back to the gear shift, then turned the truck toward the highway. "Is that near Pass Christian where you grew up?"

He pulled into the lane headed back to Oxford, and her chest released more of the tension. "Yep. I could never make myself go back there after the fire. I suppose I avoided that situation, too. The town took a beating from Hurricane Katrina. Mark went to help out after the storm. He said eighty-five percent of the town and virtually every public building was damaged or destroyed."

Jess shook his head. "That storm was a monster. Mark told me about going back afterward."

"He did? Why did y'all talk about that?"

Jess took his time answering. "He talked about growing up there. Your parents. It's still important to him. Maybe someday you'll be ready to go back for a visit. We can conquer that, too."

A town so full of memories—memories that should be good, but with her parents gone, the fire, so much pain... How many times had she planned to go but backed out? Another reason to be disappointed in herself. Why couldn't she be strong like Mark?

Quiet fell between them. The farms, country churches, and barns raced past her window.

Before long, the roadside looked like home. Were they that close to Oxford already?

"It seems so scary leaving, but we're almost back. It's ridiculous that I think the way I do."

"You went a good distance today. Focus on your progress, not the problem. Worrying about panicking heightens anxieties."

She swallowed hard. "Right, Coach. By the way, I did my homework on the fundraising. When we get to the house, I'll show you."

Fifteen minutes later, she bounced inside and grabbed her laptop and flash drive. Gingie followed her out.

Jess lounged, legs stretched out on the swing. "So what've you got there, Ms. LeClair?"

A breeze rustled through the pine trees. The sight of him

on her porch felt as natural as hot weather in the South. Like he was meant to be there.

"Scoot over so I can show you."

His feet hit the porch with a thud. She sat beside him and popped in the flash drive. "This is my list of contacts and ideas, along with presentations about the clinic and Juan's mission."

He clicked through the presentation. "You're good at what you do."

She grinned. "And no piles of papers."

"For the second time today—well done. I'm proud of you."

She grew hot under his gaze. Why did his approval mean so much? Her lip quivered and her nose stung as she tried to control the emotion bubbling up.

He closed the computer and set it on the ground. "What did I do?"

She sniffed. "I don't know why I'm teary-eyed." She rubbed her nose. "When do you leave for Honduras?"

"Friday. Juan is meeting me in Houston. Are you sure you're okay?"

She nodded. "You're such a good friend to do this."

His mouth twisted as his eyes roamed her face. Then he pulled her into a hug. "I'll see you tomorrow, Sarah Beth."

"Good bye, Jess."

Chapter 32

Horrific images of Jess and Juan crashing off a mountain road in Honduras plagued Sarah Beth. She prayed for their protection. For the tenth time—this time on her knees. *Lord, I know You're in control. Please, help me calm down.* She busied herself at home studying a telecommunications portfolio. At least she tried to.

She needed another way to distract herself. This was the perfect time for Jill to visit. The pile of papers on the desk and the others around the room were proof. She did need help. And if Nick happened to come to dinner while Jill visited…

She contacted Jill and set the plan in motion.

Then she called Nick.

"Just checking if you have to work tomorrow, and if I should pick up Katie for church."

"She's spending the night with Chris and Kim. I hardly know what to do with myself here alone. It's been a long time since I've been in my condo at night without the princess."

"I guess that would be strange. Maybe you should do something fun. Speaking of—I have good news. Jill is coming to help me get my work organized."

"If your house is anything like your SUV, then I guess I believe you."

"Are you accusing me of being messy, a liar, or both?"

A cough erupted across the line. "I'm not touching that one."

"I hope Jess is safe down in Honduras. The roads can be

treacherous, and there's crime."

"Sarah Beth, just give it over to the Lord." His tone was strong.

"I did, but I keep taking it back."

Nick laughed. "I know what you mean. I do that with Katie. I worry about all kinds of things far into the future, even pray about them. But doubt creeps back in. It's a daily process. Read something inspirational, or listen to Christian music. You know what helps me? You should try this."

"What?"

"Clean comedy. Download Christian comedy or buy a CD."

"I'm gonna try that. Thanks, Nick. I'll go online and see what I can find."

"Goodnight, Sarah Beth. I'm happy that Jill's coming. I have to admit I enjoyed her company in L.A."

"She's pretty, too. Like I said, right?"

"Bye."

Nick and Jill could be perfect together. What could go wrong?

~~~

The concrete tarmac outside the window tore by in a blur as the plane rolled into the Houston airport. Jess stretched his neck to both sides and rotated his stiff shoulder. The whirlwind trip had been hard but worth it. He couldn't wait to start working with Sarah Beth to complete the funding. Actually, he couldn't wait to work with Sarah Beth on most anything. He missed her. Even more than last time. He'd call while they waited for their connecting flights.

When the plane halted, he followed Juan down the small aisle and exited the gate. The scent of coffee hit his nose. Caffeine first, though.

His arms and legs needed a better stretch. "Juan, would you like a cup of coffee?"

"Yes. Lead the way."

Only two people waited ahead in line. The aroma alone perked him up.

He paid for the brews and handed one to Juan. "It's on me."

"Thank you. I am just turning my phone off airplane mode." Juan's phone chirped over and over. "Oh, my." He checked the texts, then chuckled and dialed. "Sarah Beth, I had no idea that you worry so much for me."

Jess had to laugh.

A smile filled Juan's tan face. "Si, we both made it back safe and sound. Jess took many pictures for you to use in one of your magical presentations. He's a good man." Juan hesitated.

Jess smiled. Funny that she'd texted Juan so many times. She'd worried about them. Maybe missed him, too. He touched Juan's arm. "Tell her I'll call her when you finish."

~ ~ ~

The phone still cradled in her hand, Sarah Beth's worry eased. Juan and Jess were safe. *Thank you, Lord.* Four minutes passed since she'd hung up with Juan. The phone buzzed, her heart followed suit. "Hello."

"I needed a jolt of caffeine. We used our mosquito repellent, as promised. No one was hurt or injured. And I took pictures of everything for you. How was your weekend?"

She sighed, treasuring the sound of Jess's voice. "Quiet. I did quite a bit of worrying about you guys, but Nick suggested that I listen to some Christian comedians. It actually helped."

"Nick usually has good advice. I'll come by as soon as I get back and show you the pictures." He paused. "If you want."

"Sounds great." Worry and guilt needled her. He had to be tired. What if he wrecked? "But maybe you need to rest."

"I'll let you know if I do."

Now he would fly back to Memphis, then drive another hour home to Oxford. She pushed back the vision of twisted metal on the side of the interstate. "Would you mind giving me a call if you get sleepy?"

"I don't mind at all." His voice was rich and smooth. "I'll see you soon."

But time moved like molasses, so she prayed and listened to more comedy shows while she huddled over a legal pad for a brainstorming session. These were going to be some original, if not bizarre ideas. She should've thought of using comedy a long time ago. It felt so good to laugh again.

A couple of hours later, she flinched at the knock on the door. Gingie bounded through the house, slid on the hardwood floors, and crashed into the entry wall. Sarah Beth jogged behind the puppy to open the door. When she did, the brown eyes firing into hers caused her breath to catch in her throat.

Gingie danced around Jess's legs until he bent down and scratched behind her ears. "Good girl, you didn't jump up—but it sounded like you almost broke through the wall."

In the low light, Jess's blond hair glinted golden, which seemed to be hypnotizing her and paralyzing her mouth. Sarah Beth swallowed hard. "I'm glad you made it back safely. I hope to hear Juan's in L.A. soon."

"His flight was leaving about an hour after mine, so it'll be a while. Poor guy had to be tired. I know I am."

She'd asked too much of him. "You need to go home and sleep. We can look at the pictures tomorrow."

"No way. I already downloaded them to my laptop. It

won't take that long to look. Besides..." His eyes smoldered. "I missed you."

Her breath hitched. Again. She swiped at her neck, turned, and shuffled toward the porch swing. The humidity raged in full force. "Let's sit down and see those pictures." Jess stood by the door, unmoving. Sarah Beth cocked her head. "Aren't you coming?"

He flashed a devastating smile. "Not until I hear if you missed me, too."

Her stomach fluttered like a swarm of wasps protecting a nest. "I worried about you and..."

He still watched, waiting.

"I missed you."

"Good."

Sitting beside her, Jess opened the computer and leaned in close to explain each picture. His shoulder touched hers.

Definitely hot out here. Focus on the pictures.

After the last slide, he closed the laptop but didn't move away. "Juan will be here in about three weeks if I can get everything lined up."

"Hmm, I'm bringing Jill here right away to help me organize my work, but I'll have to send her back to the office in time to cover when he leaves. While she's here, maybe we could have dinner, take her out on your boat—with Nick and Katie."

"Sounds good. And suspicious."

She should make herself scoot over. But the touch of his shoulder next to hers locked her there while the swing rocked with a soothing creak. She stole a glance at Jess. His eyelids looked heavy. "You should get some rest."

"If I stay much longer, you may find me curled up on this swing in the morning."

The words created a vision of him that she quickly pushed away. "It's amazing that you came by after such a long trip. Thanks." She smiled but stared out into the darkness.

"I'm happy to be a part of what God's doing." He nudged her with his elbow. "And we'll have fun working on this together, right?"

"Right, Coach."

"Good answer." He rose to his feet, taking away his warmth. "Lucky it's only a few blocks. See you tomorrow."

"Bye, Jess." She watched him walk to his car, still unable to force herself to move. She pictured him sitting next to her and warmth washed over her again.

What am I doing, Lord? We need to talk.

Chapter 33

"Hey, girl, you look wonderful." Jill pulled Sarah Beth into a tight hug. "You're tan and healthy, much better than when you left. Oxford must've been the right choice."

"I'm doing better." Sarah Beth bobbed her head. She wasn't as good as she'd liked to be, but better than when she'd left California. "And you look perfect, as always, even though you traveled hours in a plane and another in the car. How do you do it?"

"Would you try if I told you?"

"Not if it requires time and effort."

"Exactly what I thought." They strolled the brick sidewalk up to the porch. Jill swept her hand toward the large oaks and Victorian home. "Your town and house are both charming. Just like you described."

Inside, Jill admired the floral painting that filled the entry wall. "Who's the artist?"

"Mark's wife, Holly, painted the pictures. It's her hobby, but I think she could make a career of it." Sarah Beth led her to the kitchen. "Water or soda?"

"Water would be perfect." Glancing at the desk and nearby table, Jill's head dropped. "Looks like you weren't kidding when you said you needed me to help you organize your files."

Sarah Beth retrieved a cool bottle from the refrigerator and gave Jill her best puppy dog face. "You are the best organizer I've ever met, and I need you." She motioned down the hall. "Do you want to stay in my guest room or have the pool house to yourself? Either one's fine with me."

"I'd love staying with you in the house, but I'm going to be here for almost three weeks. If I stay in the pool house, we won't have to tiptoe around if one of us is sleeping."

"Pool house it is. Are you too tired to hang out with Jess and Nick tonight? I could invite them over for dinner."

"Are you cooking?"

"Ordering barbeque."

"Then sure." Jill gave her a lopsided grin. "Hmm, I slept on the plane. If I rest for an hour, I think I can manage dinner with your friends." Her eyes pinned Sarah Beth. "You're not very subtle, though. You know that, right?"

Sarah Beth snickered. "My, how I've missed you. I don't think I realized how much until just now. You know me so well."

A high-pitched howl traveled from the back of the house.

Jill covered her ears. "What in the world is that horrible sound?"

"I did tell you about my dog, right?"

~~~

Jess took a quick look in the mirror. Time for dinner at Sarah Beth's. Maybe she was right. Maybe Nick and Jill could be a good match. Nick hadn't put up much of a fight about going to dinner, and he'd actually looked nervous. But he'd agreed.

It would be a relief to find a nice girl for his best friend— and a mother for Katie. If Jill was a nice girl. He didn't know much about her.

As Jess scooped up his keys and exited the back door, a red Mazda pulled in behind his truck.

Sam stepped out. "Where you headed?"

"Sarah Beth has a friend in town and invited us to dinner."

The tall blond sank his hands into his pockets. "Us?"

"Nick and Katie. You can tag along. She's picking up barbecue. Nothing formal. She probably figured you had plans."

"I don't want to horn in." From the sour look on Sam's face, he must've been having a bad day.

Jess motioned toward his truck. "I'm inviting you. You want to drive yourself or ride with me? Or did you come by for a reason?"

"Thought you might want to shoot some hoops or something at the gym. And I wanted to tell you I've tried to get Dad to lay off with the recruit. Don't know that he'll listen. Dad seems tight with the kid's father. He's a distant cousin or something—not from the good side of the family either. I'm trying to keep a handle on him the best I can, but he's never been this bad." Sam threw his chin back and smirked. "I'll take my car in case I get a better offer later. I know where she lives." Once he'd slid back behind the wheel and shut the door, Sam punched into reverse.

Jess scoffed. "Great. Teddy out of control." He watched on as Sam sped away before getting into his truck. "And Sam needs to slow down."

~~~

Another round of giggles erupted from Sarah Beth as she played one of the comedy acts she'd downloaded. She'd picked up the food, ladled it into china serving dishes, and set the table while Jill rested. Would the night go as planned? If so, Jill and Nick would hit it off and spend the next three weeks getting to know each other better.

"Hello," Jill called from the back door.

Sarah Beth grasped her stomach, laughing. "Oh, hey, you're up."

"Are you all right? I knocked, but you didn't answer, then I heard that cackling and thought your dog was killing a chicken."

"Ha-ha. I was listening to a comedian. One of Nick's suggestions. Laughter really is great medicine—and please, you never have to knock. Come on in from now on."

Jill studied her. "I'm happy to see you laughing. We went through some dark times together."

True, and hopefully they were done with dark for a while. "Those days seem more distant now. I'm thankful I had friends like you to pull me through." Her smile faded. "Let's talk about something upbeat. How about some mood music?"

Jill gave her a suspicious look. "What kind of mood?"

"All my music is contemporary Christian now, so whatever mood that puts you in."

"Just checking—I'm keeping an eye on you and your matchmaking."

The front doorbell chimed, and Gingie tore across the floor, tripped over the new rug in the entrance hall, and smacked into the wall. Again.

Crazy dog. Sarah Beth followed and swung the door open. Nick and Jess stood with hands over their mouths, shaking. Trying not to laugh. Nice. Katie smiled up at her while holding Nick's hand.

"Hey, come in." She pointed at the floor. "I bought a rug so Gingie wouldn't crash land like she did the other night." She sighed. "But she tripped on it."

A laugh escaped Jess's throat. "And still crashed."

Sarah Beth folded her arms at her chest. "Thank you, Captain Obvious. Y'all come on in."

Gingie let out a guttural growl and arched her back, hair raised.

"What in the world?" Nick pulled Katie up to his chest.

Down the sidewalk ambled Sam.

Jess pointed with his thumb. "Oh, Gingie saw Sam. Hope you don't mind. He dropped by as I was leaving, so I invited him. You did say the dog was a good judge of character. She didn't like that Dylan Conner either."

Katie jumped out of Nick's arms and ran. "Ms. Jill."

Jill scooped Katie into her arms. "Hey, Katie-bug."

With a scowl, Nick nodded. "Dog's got good instincts. Heard the actor took off with that Sophia. Good riddance to them both."

Sarah Beth shot him a look. "We need to pray for Dylan. We're all sinners, saved by grace."

Nicks lips turned down further. "I'm commanded to love, but maybe not like. I don't know Dylan, but I can't stand Sophia."

Gingie broke into ear-piercing barks and snarls as Sam got closer to the house. Sarah Beth yelled over the barking. "I'm going to kennel her."

They all answered in unison. "Good idea."

Nick raised a hand. "I'll do it if you point me in the right direction."

Hands over his ears, Sam entered. "Sounded like a pack of beagles and a wolf. I never heard anything like it."

Jess slapped him on the back. "Sarah Beth's little pet finds you dangerous."

Sam's gaze traveled over Jill. "Her little pet might be right." He extended his hand. "I'm Sam Conrad. I don't think we've met."

No way. Why had Sam had to come? "This is my friend Jill from L.A. Let's move out of the entrance hall. I think I saw a present in the living room for Katie from Ms. Jill."

Nick rejoined them. "A present?"

"Thank you." Katie kissed Jill's cheek. "What is it, Ms. Jill?"

"Open it and find out."

Slipping down, Katie ran to the coffee table where a large silver bow adorned a package wrapped in pink. "It's so big." She took her time opening the paper, one piece of tape at a time.

What child took this long to open a gift? Sarah Beth made ripping motions. "Tear into it, Katie. I wanna see what she got you."

Jill shook her head. "You open it any way you like. Sarah Beth can wait."

Katie's eyes widened as she opened the box. She jumped up, her arms full of shiny fabric. "Look, Daddy. Princess costumes. Three of them."

Nick's eyes gleamed. "You didn't have to buy her anything."

"When you were in L.A., I saw her eying them. She's a girl after my own heart. I couldn't decide which princess she'd like best, so I bought three."

"I hope she isn't too much a girl after your own heart. Daddy may go broke."

Katie hugged her dad and gave him a pleading look. "Can I go put them on?"

"Of course, my princess, but you should put on one at a time."

"Oh, Daddy, you're so silly."

As she ran out of the room, Nick's hazel eyes met Jill's. "Thanks. I mean it. Daddies sometimes don't realize what little girls dream about."

"Almost all little girls want to be a princess. She knows

she's Daddy's princess, though. She's lucky."

Minutes later, baby blue satin and organza swished as Katie trotted back in and twirled. "Look at me."

They admired and complimented her until Sarah Beth led them to sit down to dinner in the formal dining room.

Sam stayed close to Jill, and Sarah Beth steamed. Could her blood actually boil? It sure felt like it.

After dinner, Sam moved closer and put his hand on the small of Jill's back as they cleared the table. "Jill, I grew up in Oxford, and I'd love to take you on a tour. I know this county like the back of my hand."

Sarah Beth clenched her teeth. She could give Sam the back of her hand. He wasn't getting close to her Jill. That was not the plan. "Jill and I have a ton of work to do, as you can see by the stacks of papers around the house. I don't know when she'll be free."

"Are you really such a slave driver?"

Sarah Beth gave him her best menacing look. "She's only going to be here a short time. I'm sure you and your father are busy managing my favorite bank all day. If we have time for a tour, I'll have Jess let you know."

Jess came alongside of Sarah Beth and nudged her. "If you ladies get a break, we'll go out on the boat. Do you ski, Jill?"

"I've surfed a lot, but never tried skiing."

Nick waved her off. "If you can surf, you'll be a natural at skiing."

Sam bobbed his head. "I've taught many people to ski. I'll be happy to offer my assistance."

Blood boiling over now. From the back room, the low guttural growl echoed down the hall.

"Was that thunder?" Sam looked out the window.

Sarah Beth glanced at Jess. "Maybe I should unleash the

guard dog?"

Jess smiled. "What were you saying earlier about grace?"

Sometimes grace was awesome, and sometimes it was the most difficult task in the world.

Chapter 34

Jess checked the ball and hitch once more on the back of his truck. With the boat secure, he took off toward the lake. No traffic. Surprising, considering the good weather. Sam and Nick followed in their vehicles. Now he'd head into what promised to be an interesting afternoon with those two falling all over Jill. And Sarah Beth freaking out about it.

Summer football camps in the heat this week had been grueling, but he hadn't let that stop him from visiting Sarah Beth after work every day to strategize fundraising plans for the Honduras church. He'd found Nick puttering around the backyard *training Gingie* while Jill gave swimming lessons to Katie. Every day. A likely story. Nick looked happier than Jess had seen him in years. Both he and Katie glowed.

Nick had invited Jill to church the day before, and she'd agreed. Funny, Sam kept coming up with excuses to drop by Sarah Beth's, too. He'd even attended church for the first time in a long time—obviously for the wrong reason, but at least he went.

The picture of Sarah Beth frowning when Sam dropped by the house… That was too funny. And cute. She'd had the same frown when he elbowed her in church today. The minister spoke on grace, and he couldn't resist. Even her frown was adorable though. The speedometer took a forward bounce. He needed to slow down with the boat hitched to the back. But he couldn't wait to see that sweet face again.

Ten minutes later, he unhitched the boat into the lake. The

weather cooperated nicely, and the water shone smooth as glass. A perfect day for skiing.

Sam and Nick drank in the view as Jill took off her cover-up. While Sam gawked without shame, Nick only allowed sidelong-glances. Sarah Beth rolled her eyes. Winking, Jess motioned to the water. "Sarah Beth, why don't you ski first today? You need to blow off some stress and have fun."

"You're getting to know me too well."

If only he knew what she was thinking.

They made four runs down a quiet section of the lake. Sarah Beth didn't let go of the rope. She must really be stressing over Sam hanging around so much. He took a quick glance back to see her jump the wake. What fun to watch. The girl was good.

After another run, she let go.

"She's down," Nick shouted.

Jess circled, then cut the motor.

Nearing the ladder, she extended her hand. "I'm gonna need some help getting in. I wore myself out."

After Nick pulled her up, she plodded to the open bow and sank with a sigh. Right in front of Jess's side of the windshield. Her tan hands squeezed the water from her dark hair and twisted it into a ponytail holder—her long perfect neck and shoulders in front of him. He should force his eyes away. Now.

Jill reached across from the other cushioned seat on the bow and tapped her arm. "That was impressive."

"I love the water. You want to try?" Sarah Beth's lips twisted before she spoke. "Nick can show you how."

"I'll try after I ride with Katie on the tube. I promised."

Sam and Nick jumped up, offering help as Jill slipped the ski vest over her shoulders.

A few rides on the tube, and Katie climbed back into the

boat. Jill fumbled with the skis they'd thrown her until she had them adjusted and positioned out in front. She pulled up on the first try, but signaled she was ready to stop after one run. They circled back to her.

"That was a blast. I would've kept going, but my hands are killing me."

Nick edged in front of Sam to give her a hand up. "I have gloves you can wear next time. You were fantastic—not that I expected anything less than perfection."

Sarah Beth chuckled. "You noticed that Jill's a perfectionist already?"

Jill jammed her hands to her hips. "Just because I do my makeup and nails doesn't make me a perfectionist."

"Are not the canned foods in your apartment in alphabetical order?"

She giggled and looked away. "I admit it. I have a problem."

Nick handed Jill a bottle of water. "Bring that problem to my condo anytime."

Jill gave him a wide grin. "I enjoy putting things in order. I know it's kind of weird."

"In a good way." Nick smiled at her. "You're hired."

"You'd have to get used to the new system."

Nick narrowed his eyes. "I think I can handle it."

"Hey, me, too." The first chance Sam got, he jumped into the conversation.

Sarah Beth stomped one foot. "My place first." She blew out a long sigh. "But the magnificent thing about Jill is that she works so quickly. Nick can be next in line." She turned to Jill. "How do you manage to be so organized?"

Jess dropped anchor, kicked his feet up, and savored the flawless sky. And tried not to stare at Sarah Beth. *Discipline.*

Jill dried her hair with her towel. "My parents were hippie wannabees. There weren't many rules in our house. When I started kindergarten, I fell in love with the structure and schedule. I'd never had a routine before that. At school, things made sense—felt safe. That's why I majored in elementary education.

"When I joined a sorority, you would've thought I'd stabbed my father. He said it went against everything he stood for. Kind of ironic coming from someone who said there was no right or wrong." Her cheek rested on her hand. "My parents are atheists."

Sarah Beth threw her hands in the air. "If there were no right or wrong, and we're like animals, why is it universally agreed upon that it's wrong to steal or kill?"

Nick inched closer to Jill. "I can relate. Mine wouldn't win any father-of-the-year awards. He's sitting in the Florida state penitentiary for selling methamphetamines, along with my brother. He would've pulled me into the family business if it hadn't been for God and Katie's mom."

A serious expression covered Jill's face. "She must have been one great lady. I'm so glad she found you."

Jess nodded. "She was. I'll always be indebted to Paige for saving my best friend. I tried to keep him out of that mess, but he wouldn't listen. She came along, and boom, he left that life and never looked back."

Nick fixed his gaze on Jill. "I believe God puts people in our lives to point us in the right way. Sometimes we choose to ignore His messengers. Sometimes we're wise and listen."

~~~

The large canvas bag on Sarah Beth's arm weighed more than ever. Of course, her whole body felt like it weighed a ton. She'd skied too long, but the stress of watching Sam flirt with

Jill had lessened. For a minute or two.

Nick hitched the boat to Jess's truck while Sam lingered with Jill and Katie. Why wouldn't he get the hint and leave?

Sam slid his hand behind Jill's elbow. "Jill, I would love to give you a ride home. There's another route that's more scenic than the way we came."

Whining, Katie threw her arms around Jill's legs. "I want Ms. Jill to ride home with me. I want her to come to my house and play princesses."

Yay for Katie.

Nick scooped his daughter up. "Katie, you need to say 'sorry.' That's not how we act."

Katie rubbed her eyes. "Sorry."

He brushed her hair back and kissed her forehead. "My girl's tired."

Sarah Beth nudged him from behind. He glanced at her and fumbled with his keys. "Jill, it might help if you rode with us and kept her awake so I can bathe her before bed."

Reaching out, Jill ruffled her fingers through Katie's hair. "Of course, I'd love to."

Yes. Sam can leave now. "Jill, do you have your key? I may get Jess to take me to look at the interstate before I go home."

Grunting, Sam waved them off. "I don't know what that's code for, but I'm outta here."

After opening the truck door for Sarah Beth, Jess got in the other side and shook his head. "Poor Sam. Since his broken engagement, he's floundered in the dating world. Swears off women for months, then tries again every once in a while. Has the worst luck. I kind of feel sorry for the guy."

There it was. A twinge of guilt bit at Sarah Beth. But just a small one. "I guess I do, too. But I want him away from Jill."

"You would've wanted her away from me, not too long

ago."

"You want to go out with her, too?"

"You know what I meant."

The truck picked up speed after they hit the highway. They'd made it this far last time. Her face tingled. Palms perspired.

Breathe in. Hold it. Breathe out.

Not working. "No, still can't do it, Jess. You have to turn around."

Why did this have to happen to her? So stupid. And unfair. Couldn't she just sit in this metal box like a normal person and ride down a concrete strip? What was so hard about it?

Jess slowed. "Let's go to one gas station farther than last time?"

Was it possible her own chest could squeeze her to death? She moved her bag into her lap, hugged it close, and tried to unwrap the self-induced boa constrictor. "Okay. But that's all."

"You can trust me."

This was more about trusting herself and her physical reactions. A fear of being crazy since the accident. A fear of being crazy forever and stuck in this quaint prison.

When Jess turned into a service station, she let out the breath she'd held hostage. "This is so frustrating."

He pulled over and put the truck in park. His hand moved behind her head and stroked her hair. "There's no rush. You're doing fine. Give yourself a break."

She stared out her window. Why couldn't she do this? And why did she love the fact that he was comforting her—and touching her hair? She couldn't let herself... He deserved better.

His hand moved to her chin and turned her face toward him. "Look at me, Sarah Beth."

If only she could stop her chin from quivering.

"We can keep trying as long as it takes."

Those intense brown eyes. So kind and strong. Her gaze shifted to his lips. She swallowed hard. She needed to force her eyes away.

Soon.

Or in a minute.

"Thanks, Jess, you don't know how much I appreciate your patience."

"I *am* very patient, if I do say so myself." A grin filled his face.

Radio. Now. She punched the button for the Christian music station and sang along. Trying to keep her eyes pointed anywhere but at Jess.

Back at her house, he walked her to the front door. "Are we working on clinic business tonight?"

"I'm beat from the sun and the water. Let's start fresh tomorrow."

Jess pulled her to him and kissed the top of her head. "I always start fresh."

And her face was tingling again. But in a different way. She pushed her hands to her hips. "Did the old flirty Jess just resurface?"

"See you tomorrow, Sarah Beth."

She stifled a giggle as he sauntered to his truck. Her gaze followed him until he turned down the block and her phone rang. *Jill.* She'd totally forgotten about her.

"Can you come pick me up? Katie's asleep and Nick can't leave her alone. We didn't think that one through."

Sarah Beth snickered. "Not a problem. I just need to take a shower and change." But she'd take her sweet time.

After a long hot shower, she drove to Nick's, parked in

front of his condo, and sent Jill a text. She didn't want to wake Katie.

Jill came out and dropped in the passenger seat. "It took you long enough."

"Sorry. Tell me everything."

"You are not sorry, and you know it."

"I'm a wee bit sorry."

A smile tugged at Jill's lips. "I guess I forgive you, but only because I had such a nice time. He's dreamy. Inside and out. We got Katie cleaned up and dressed in her little pink nightgown. Then we took turns reading her stories. He sang 'Jesus Loves Me.' We both gave her a kiss goodnight. Of course, she got up and needed a glass of water and another kiss. He was so patient and loving."

"Did y'all talk about anything besides Katie?"

"All kinds of things—his past, my past. I even told him about my stupid mistake on my birthday and how bad I felt about doing something so reckless."

Sarah Beth's eyes widened. "You told him about Dylan Conner?"

"I didn't tell him who it was, just that I'd made a mistake. I want him to know what he's getting into—if he is interested. You know, I hadn't been with anyone since I left my ex-boyfriend, Hunter, years ago. One weak moment. Anyway, he was very understanding. He told me that God can make me new. I can see how faith sustained you and Nick through tough times. And Juan. I'm just not sure I can make that kind of commitment. Yet. But I'm going to study a few articles he's emailing."

"I'm glad that you're giving the Lord some thought—and Nick."

Jill blinked. "What a shocker."

"I know I've pushed Nick on you, but if nothing else, he's a great influence and friend. You were right to be honest. Jess was honest with me about some things in his past, and I didn't hold it against him."

"Let's talk about you and Jess. What's with that?"

"I don't know. I don't want to get romantically involved with anyone. I'm still working on getting myself better."

"But you have feelings for him, right?"

"He's been kind. He's attractive. I…care about him. It's just not the right timing."

Jill laughed. "I know I'm not the one to say this, but I've heard it come out of your mouth. Are we talking about your timing, or God's timing?"

Chapter 35

Why did three weeks have to pass so quickly? Sarah Beth crossed the front porch and gave Jill one last hug then went inside. But she couldn't help peeking out the window, could she? On her knees with her nose on the windowsill, she found the perfect vantage point. Gingie copied her, the dog's foul breath fogging the window. *Doggie breath mints on the shopping list.*

Nick had already made such an impact on Jill. And Sarah Beth had given her a small Bible to read on the flight home. She smiled when Nick's hand rested on Jill's back as they strolled down the sidewalk, then he held her in a long embrace.

Sarah Beth stifled a squeal. Yes. This was perfect.

He lifted his hands to hold her face. Sarah Beth gasped as she watched his lips moving. What was he saying? Wait. He was leaning in. *A kiss.* And a longish kiss. That was almost too easy.

~~~

Jess threw Bryan's duffle bag on the back seat of his truck. Bryan nestled the guitar in the truck himself as if it was his baby. Jess could hardly blame him. Music for Bryan was like football for him. A part of him for as long as he could remember. What would he have been without it? Would he be the same man? And where would he be if the injury had never occurred?

Sarah Beth seemed pleased when he'd recruited Bryan to sing an opening and closing song at their fundraising presentations. And he liked pleasing her. Too much.

She'd labored to find the perfect songs, worked and reworked their presentation on her computer, made four copies in case they lost one, then emailed everything. Again. She was thorough and passionate about her work. They had that in common, too.

Jess parked in front of her house on the way to pick up Juan at the Memphis airport. He and Bryan laughed as Sarah Beth jogged down the sidewalk, papers in hand.

Beside the truck, Bryan pushed his hand up. "Halt. We have the copies of the presentation, the flyers, the music, two guitars, nice clothes and shoes. And razors."

Bits of sunlight danced off her dark hair. Those ebony eyes were thoughtful.

Jess laughed at her furrowed brows. "I studied the list you repeatedly sent each of us. We're ready." He saluted. "Thanks to you."

"If you lose anything, even a guitar, buy another one. I'll pay for it. Oh, and call or text me after each event and let me know how it went."

Jess nodded. He'd call her. Every day. Just to hear her voice.

Bryan came alongside. "Don't worry, Ms. Professor. We've got this. Now give us a hug, and we'll be off to Memphis to pick up our new friend Juan."

Jess shot Sarah Beth a look as she gave Bryan a side-hug.

She moved to give Jess a similar one.

Not happening. None of that. He folded her into his arms and gave her his routine kiss on the top of her head. He'd rather have kissed those pink lips.

Someday.

When she was ready.

Would she ever be ready?

He liked that she stood there looking dazed as they turned to leave.

She caught his arm. "Wait. We forgot the most important thing."

Jess turned back. "What in the world could we have forgotten?"

"We didn't pray. Who wants to lead?"

Bryan motioned to her. "You must have something on your heart, so why don't you?"

Sarah Beth put her hands on their backs with the lightest touch. "Lord, please protect Jess, Bryan, and Juan. Let their words and actions be pleasing in Your sight. Lord, open and move hearts for Honduras if it's part of Your plan. Not our will, but Your will be done. In Jesus' name. Amen."

Jess added, "Amen." He hated to leave her again. She worried so. But he was going where he felt God leading.

~~~

Jess called Sarah Beth after every fundraiser. So funny. She insisted each guy get on the line and provide her with their own versions of the evening.

The night of the Nashville event, Bryan called her first—on speaker. "Ms. Professor, did you forget to tell me something important? Like that you sent a talent scout to hear me?"

"Oh, I did forget. Sorry. But it sounds like it turned out well. He wouldn't have talked to you if he didn't think you were good."

Bryan glowed. "You think?"

"I wouldn't have called him if I didn't think you had what it takes. You have a God-given gift."

"He gave me his card, and he said he might even drive down to the meeting in Atlanta tomorrow night with a producer."

"See. I'll be praying for you."

Bryan's voice quivered. "Thank you so much. I don't know how I can ever thank you enough."

"Thank God. He gave you the voice. I just made a phone call."

~~~

Jess watched for his exit off Interstate Eighty-five, north of Atlanta. The fundraising had gone well in Memphis and Nashville. This last night would be with Mark's congregation in Atlanta.

Mark. Sarah Beth's brother had become a close friend. He'd be great to have as a brother. But would it ever happen? How would things turn out? Sarah Beth and her anxiety, the mission in Honduras, all of it? Nothing had weighed on his whole being like this woman. Not even football.

Juan and Bryan both had impressive faith. Two men so different from himself, now brothers in Christ. Christianity was like a team. Different strengths and abilities, called to the same purpose, watching each other's backs—all with the perfect Coach.

Late Sunday afternoon, Jess, Juan, and Bryan climbed in his truck and headed back to Oxford after three days away. A light rain pitter-pattered on the windshield as Juan and Bryan bantered about their successful trip to the rhythm of the wipers. The previous night, they'd finished up in Atlanta at Mark's church.

Sarah Beth must've been waiting on the porch because she sprinted down the sidewalk toward his truck. Maybe she had missed him. Good.

Wait. Why'd she run to Juan's side?

She threw her arms around the short man, nearly knocking

him down. "You're here."

Juan laughed. "Whoa. Remember, you are the Amazon. I am the small man."

"I'm not an Amazon, and you are not now, and never will be, a small man. It's so good to see you. Come on in, and tell me everything."

Jess joined them and gave her a sideways glance. "Where's my hug?"

Her arm slid around his back. For way too short a time. "Tell me everything."

"What else is there to tell? You've grilled us every night."

"I'm sure there's more. Let me catch Gingie first."

On cue, a crash and a howl sounded from the house.

Juan stopped. "What is Gingie?"

Jess smirked. "That's the beast she calls a dog. You think Sarah Beth's an Amazon, wait until you see this animal."

Juan didn't move. "Maybe we should stay outside."

Jess patted him on the back. "You should be safe. The creature is a good judge of character."

The door opened, and the dog struggled loose, bounding toward an ashen-faced Juan. When Gingie reached him, she lay on the ground and rolled over. He bent down to pet her belly. "You are not a beast. You are a good dog, aren't you?" At his praise, she sprung up and licked his cheek, knocking him to the sidewalk.

Jess chuckled. "They've both greeted you. It should be safe now. Let's get ready for our last presentation at the CSU. I've got home-field advantage here."

~~~

The day after the CSU fundraising presentation, Sara Beth circled the patio of the pool as Juan tallied the gifts and pledges they'd collected for the Honduras church. Would they have enough? They'd worked so hard. Surely the Lord would bless Juan with this ministry. But she had to be patient.

Juan lay his tablet on the glass table. "We are very close to our goal, but still short. We may not meet our target before the Honduran rainy season sets in." He handed her the spreadsheet.

The distant bellow of a train whistle wailed as if to signal her disappointment. A breeze rustled the leaves of the oak that hung over the fence. She bit her lip. There was one more thing she could do. It made perfect sense. She handed him back the numbers. "I could sell my condo in Malibu. It's worth more than we need to finish our goal. I could even see if Dylan wants to buy it back. He was sentimental about the place."

Juan's tan forehead wrinkled. "Give God time to answer our prayers. Giving provides the heart and soul of the giver a great blessing. Maybe it's His will that someone else provide the money."

"You're right, of course, but I may see if Dylan is interested."

"You never plan to move back?"

The thought of the place sent a sour taste to her tongue and a jittery feeling down to her toes. "I can't see myself back in that world." And maybe Dylan needed the blessing of giving.

Juan sank back into the lawn chair and folded his hands behind his head. "God knows the plans he has for you. Plans for peace and not evil."

She finished for him. "...plans for hope and a future. Jeremiah 29:11. I know you're right."

~~~

It was all Sarah Beth could do to nod at Juan as he hefted his suitcase into the car. Another goodbye. She hated them. If only he and Jill could work here.

He smiled. "I talk to you on the phone many times a day. Why are you crying?"

A hiccup escaped her lips. "I miss how the three of us worked together."

Juan laid his hands on her shoulders. "Our lives must change. We must grow. Growing hurts, but we can look back afterward and see that the change was worth the pain."

She wiped at her eyes. "I know you're right, but I'm tired of growing so much."

Chapter 36

The next morning, Sarah Beth touched the contact on her phone while she sat at her desk.

Dylan answered on the first ring. "I thought you'd never call. Are you finally ready to admit your true feelings for me?"

She let out a long sigh. "Dylan, Dylan, you know you only want what you can't have."

"Until I get it." He spoke in his usual flirtatious tone.

"Then you wouldn't want it."

"Things would be different with you."

She tapped one finger at a time on her desk, over and over. "I called to give you first shot at buying back your condo."

"Don't tell me you're never moving back."

"I don't see it happening. Besides, we need it for the Honduras church."

"Babe, I'll send you a check for your mission. I'm about to cash in on the movie you marketed."

"But I want to sell the condo anyway."

"I'll buy it back and save it for when you finally come to your senses."

Why wouldn't he listen? "Dylan, I'm not coming back."

"That's what you say today, but you don't know the future." His voice became low and sultry. "Of course, you could stay at my mansion if you come back."

"Dylan."

He sucked in a long breath. "Fine. Maybe I'll hide from Sophia there. She keeps showing up at my house. Someone should've warned me about that one."

Sarah Beth winced. "You didn't give anyone time to warn you. If you don't like her, why are you still seeing her?"

"What do you care?"

"I'd like to see you with a nice girl."

"But not you, right?" Dylan's voice cooled. "How about the hottie in your office? She's nice."

Now he was ticking her off. "Stay away from Jill."

"I think I struck a nerve. Is someone jealous?"

Her ribcage constricted. "Do you want to buy the condo or not? I'm putting it on the market tomorrow."

Dylan exhaled loudly. "I'll buy it. Is that fellow Juan still handling your business in L.A?"

"Yes."

"I'll follow up with him in the morning."

"Thanks." That settled, she fought the urge to hurl the phone against the wall. *Be nice.*

The line was silent.

Dylan spoke at last. "I'm sorry, Sarah Beth. I'm a jerk sometimes. You know it. I know it. Will you still talk to me?" He cleared his throat. "Pretty please?"

Her ribcage loosened, and the adrenaline seeped away. Poor Dylan. Everyone knew his face, but he didn't seem to have many real friends. "I forgive you." How could she not?

"You are the most complicated woman I've ever come across."

She had to laugh. "I don't believe that for a second."

~~~

Sarah Beth glanced at her chirping phone as she chewed the last sour gummy worm from her stash. Juan was up early. "Hello."

"You will not believe it. God answers prayers. There is so

much to do. But do not worry. I will get everything taken care of—"

"Slow down, Juan. What are you telling me?"

He caught his breath. "Dylan Conner gave us enough to finish the church, *and* he is buying your condo. I will fax the paperwork to you."

She smiled at his excitement. "I guess you better start packing. You'll be moving to Honduras before you know it."

"I know. I need to do so many things. I need to prepare sermons, and the kids need shots, and we must decide what to take and what to sell. I need to take care of the business here."

"One thing at a time. Jill's ready to move into your position, but you'll need to let Bill know so we can hire a replacement for her."

"I have done that already." His voice hushed. "About Jill. I am worried for her. She has been sick all week and is not eating. She looks pale."

A sense that something was wrong weighed heavy on Sarah Beth. "She hasn't mentioned feeling bad. I'll find out what's going on."

After ending the call with Juan, she dialed Jill.

"Hey." Jill's voice was barely above a whisper.

Sarah Beth's stomach took a dive. "You sound terrible. What's wrong? Juan said that you don't look well. Are you sick? Have you been to the—?"

"I'm not sick. Not like you think, at least. I may as well tell you." She gave a heavy sigh. "I haven't been to the doctor, but I went to the drugstore and bought a pregnancy test."

The air whooshed out of Sarah Beth's lungs. "No, you can't be."

"I can be."

A singular thought took over. She needed to be strong for

Jill. "It's going to be fine. We'll be together through this."

"I can't believe it." Jill's voice broke. "I was with Dylan for one night. I haven't been with a man in years." She sobbed. "What am I gonna do? I don't know if I can…"

"I'll be here for you and the baby." *Please don't let her think about ending the pregnancy.*

Between sobs, Jill sniffled. "I just found a good man, and now I'll lose him. What's Nick going to say if he finds out?"

"I know this wasn't planned, and the timing is rotten, but God knows and loves this baby. He will provide for you both. Trust Him."

"Sarah Beth, I want to believe…I don't know. Please don't tell Nick or Jess. Definitely don't tell Dylan. Promise me. I need time to think."

"It's not my news to tell."

"Oh, and one of the VPs insisted his nephew from the mailroom be transferred into my old position. The kid could care less about anything I've tried to teach him so far."

"I'll clear my schedule to take up the slack. Maybe the assistant in my University office could help out more. I haven't given her much to do besides my scheduling and the Foundation files."

"Is that Cassie? I met her. She seemed competent."

"Very. She's part-time because she wants to be home with her son. I haven't taken the time to get to know her. I've been so caught up in myself since I came back. I feel guilty, now that I think about it."

"The work isn't going to all fall back on you. I'm not dying. Women work in my condition. I just wish I didn't feel so green—and achy."

"I won't teach Dean Latham's classes in the fall, so I'll have more time. He'll understand, and it'll work out. Don't worry about anything but taking care of yourself. And the baby."

Sarah Beth paced her office. She wouldn't let Jill go through this alone.

~ ~ ~

Jess paced the hall in front of Coach Black's office. What did his boss want? He was vague on the phone when he'd called and said to come straight over.

The door clacked as it opened. Coach Black's mouth pressed into a thin line as he crossed the room. What was that expression? Good or bad?

Then he clapped his hand onto Jess's bicep. "We got an early verbal commitment from your Memphis quarterback. Hitting the newspapers as we speak. Congrats."

Jess's shoulders loosened. "Gotta love it. Not that it'll keep the other coaches from trying to change his mind before signing day, but still good news."

"I was surprised to hear it. 'Bama was after him hot and heavy."

"Maybe Teddy Conrad will get off my back. Until next time."

Coach Black frowned. "You don't think Teddy…?"

Jess's stomach sank as if he'd just thrown an interception, leaving a bitter taste in his mouth. "I warned him not to. He knows what a booster violation is."

"If there's any chance, I'll need to report it to the NCAA."

Jess rubbed his fingers across his forehead as a headache started. "I'll talk to Sam and see if he knows anything. If there's a violation and someone has to take the fall, I won't let you be the one."

~ ~ ~

Sarah Beth sat on the edge of the aqua wingback chair beside Cassie's desk. "I'm sorry I haven't tried to get to know you better, Cassie. The past year has been…"

"A tough year for you." Cassie gave her a sympathetic smile. "Dean Latham explained. I can only imagine how difficult things have been. I went through a nasty divorce a year ago, so I've had my own adjustments."

How could she have been so self-consumed? "I feel terrible I didn't know."

Cassie's smile faltered. "Don't waste time feeling bad. I'm making it. Did you have something you needed today?"

"I wanted to ask if you'd be willing to work some extra hours here for me? You know, for my real job? In L.A.?"

She nodded. "As long as I can be available for my son. Teens still need their mothers—even if they won't admit it."

"Not a problem."

"Great. I'm not sure I have the creative juices like you for marketing. They didn't teach that in law school."

"Law school? You're a lawyer?"

Cassie's blue-green eyes twinkled. "Dean Latham told you nothing about me?"

"Apparently not." The phone in her hand vibrated, and she checked the screen. "I've got to catch this."

Sarah Beth slung her bag on the conference table and answered. "Is everything okay, Jill?"

"Fine, boss lady."

"I don't love when you call me that, but I've got an idea."

"Not surprised."

"I've been thinking about this a lot, and I hope you'll agree. Why don't you move here? We'll have the lines forwarded. You could stay the rest of your pregnancy, and I'll help you, especially when the baby comes."

"You can't be serious?"

"I'm totally serious. I'm sure Nick misses you, too. He's so gloomy, I can't stand to look at him."

The line was silent.

"Jill? Are you still there?"

"Um, I told him I couldn't be involved with him anymore."

Sarah Beth let out a sigh and thought of the long-faced Nick she'd seen around campus. "I knew something was wrong with him. Did you tell him why?"

"No."

"We'll worry about that later, but think about moving here. At least for a while."

"I'll think about it."

~~~

Jess trekked up the sidewalk toward Sam's house. This would be a tough conversation. Sam was a friend. And the man was honest to a fault. But no one wants their parent accused of unethical behavior.

The wood bit into his knuckles as he knocked, the way the sick feeling bit into his gut. He brushed his fingers over the doorknob. *No.* He would wait for Sam to answer this time.

The door flung open. "Since when do you knock?" Sam studied Jess's face. "What's wrong?"

"Let's talk inside."

Sam waved him in. "I'm getting a beer. I know you don't want one, but I always offer. It's the polite thing to do."

"And I always say thanks, but no thanks." Jess followed him into the spacious designer kitchen and slid a chair out from under the dining table. He sighed as he sat. "I need to know about Teddy and Zach Garcia. Word is that Zach's committing to us. He'll sign a letter on the early signing date."

Sam shrugged. "That's great." He took a sip of his beer. "But you think Dad might have offered something to swing him your way?"

Jess ran his fingers across the cherry finish of the table. "I want to make sure he didn't. My job's on the line."

Sam sat down, his expression hard. "I'll find out. I'll turn him in myself if he violated recruiting rules." He clenched his fist. "I'm sick of his meddling in every minutiae of my life. And now he's meddling with yours, too."

"I'm sorry to ask this of you."

"No, man. It's the right thing to do." He smirked, but his blue eyes were kind. "That's the way you roll, right, Coach?"

At least Sam was okay with this. "I try. But, let me ask you. Teddy claims you're distant cousins with this Garcia kid?"

"That story could take a while."

"Save it. If we need it for the NCAA, you can write it down for me."

~~~

Sarah Beth grabbed her chiming cell. *Jill.* Maybe she'd made a decision. "Hey."

"Okay. I'm coming to stay with you."

Relief enveloped her. "Oh, Jill. You won't regret it."

"I know deep down you've been scared I'd end the pregnancy. And I know how you feel about that."

Sarah Beth traced the edge of her desk with her finger. "Are you going to raise the baby?"

"I think so."

"What made you decide to come here?"

"Honestly, it was Dylan Conner."

Sarah Beth gasped. "Did you tell him?"

"No, no, no. He came by the office today to talk with Bill. I could've died. Not only is it awkward, but he stops by my desk and says hello. Like nothing happened. I mean he's never rude—he may even be trying to act nice." Air whooshed across the connection. "What about when I start showing? He might put two and two together. And he comes and talks to Bill fairly often. I guess they're friends."

"I don't think you can keep this from him forever."

"Why not? It was one night. Can you imagine the life this baby would have if some gossip rag got hold of the news?"

Sarah Beth's own experience with those papers was bad enough. The poor child. "I hadn't thought of that. You don't have to decide everything today. Just make the reservations and come south. We'll pray that God will show us His plan."

Chapter 37

This could work. Sarah Beth hung Jill's clothes in the walk-in closet of the pool house's only bedroom, while Jill emptied the rest into a small antique dresser on the opposite wall. The pool house wasn't as small as a tiny house, but it was close. Three large windows allowed a good bit of light to flow into the combined living room and kitchenette. And at least, the bedroom was a nice size. Being in Oxford would give Jill the privacy she needed to figure things out.

And no worries about bumping into Dylan Conner.

With everything on hangers, the ample closet still had space. "Jill, do you have anything else?"

"That's all I brought."

Now that the clothes were unpacked, maybe they could talk. Really talk. Sarah Beth threw herself across the bed. "How're you doing?"

Jill zipped the empty suitcase and set it aside. "I'm getting used to the idea. Finding out that I'm pregnant…was surreal." She plopped onto the bed beside Sarah Beth. "My mother helped me pack. She was compassionate, even excited about the baby. She claims to be a deist nowadays. I was shocked. I think my little brother sent her into a panic. She needs a higher power."

"Tell me more about what's going on with your brother. I take it he didn't fall in love with structure in kindergarten like you did."

"If only." Jill shook her head. "Because of the fourteen-year age difference, we aren't close. All I know is that he's spent time in juvie, and now he's attending the alternative school."

Sarah Beth studied her friend. Between Jill's washed-out face and the way her clothes bagged off of her, the past few weeks must've been harder than she'd let on. "You're pale. Why don't you go on to bed, and we'll finish this tomorrow."

Jill rubbed her wrists. "That sounds good. My hands and feet are killing me. But I'll join you for church in the morning."

Church? God did work in mysterious ways.

~~~

Though Sarah Beth drove below the speed limit and took the curves as slow as possible, Jill's expression worried her. Thank goodness the church building wasn't far.

Jill sighed and hurried to exit the car. "Fresh air."

"I'm sorry you're so nauseated. I did some research last night. Ginger is supposed to help."

The smile Jill struggled to give didn't quite reach her eyes. "I'll have to try that."

Inside, as they neared the stairs leading to the balcony, Katie scampered up and wrapped her arms around Jill's legs.

"Ms. Jill, you're back."

A somber Nick lagged behind. Jill gave him a weak smile and picked up her four-year-old friend. Katie sprang into a discourse about every memorable event she could think of since she'd last seen Jill. Then she opened her little purse and pulled out half a sausage biscuit. "Ms. Jill, you can have the rest of my breakfast if you want."

Blanching, Jill gently set Katie down. "Thank you, sweetie, but I'm not feeling well." Jill bolted down the hall leaving Katie and Nick behind.

Nick's eyes followed her. "Is she all right? She looks thin."

Sarah Beth bit her lip. "She's been ill."

His head whipped around. "Is it serious?"

Not going to break. I'm a vault.

"You should talk to her yourself." She pointed. "Here's Jess." Saved by the handsome man in jeans.

Jess's blue polo accentuated his light hair as he glanced at his watch. "Hey, I thought you guys would be seated by now."

Nick boosted Katie into his arms. "I need to run my girl to children's church."

"I'm waiting for Jill," Sarah Beth whispered. "They all just ran into each other. She's in the ladies room."

Jess leaned close, the citrusy scent of his hair distracting her. "Why are you whispering?"

She returned to her normal voice. "Just go save our seats. I'll be there in a sec."

Two songs ended by the time Jill and Sarah Beth made it to the balcony, and Jess lowered an eyebrow and pointed at his watch.

Sarah Beth put her lips near his ear. "Jill's not feeling well, and I'm whispering because church started."

"You're not funny." He peered down his nose, but a smile played on his lips.

On the other side of Jess, Nick sat with a stoic expression. Poor guy. If only he knew the truth. Wouldn't it be easier for him to understand her rejection?

At the last amen, Jill clutched Sarah Beth's arm. "Let's go. Now."

They were halfway to the car when Jess caught up. "Why are y'all running off?"

Sarah Beth bit her lip. "Jill's still not feeling well."

He motioned toward the front of the SUV. "Can you come over here for one second? I want to ask you something."

"Okay." Swallowing a bit of anxiety, she handed Jill the

keys and moved to his side.

He shuffled his feet and ran one finger across the dusty hood. "Football's going to consume my nights and days now that the season is starting."

Sarah Beth gave a stiff nod. "I understand." Was he trying to ditch her? It wasn't like they were dating or anything. And if they weren't dating, why did the idea of him ditching her make her want to cry?

His hand moved to clasp hers. "Do you think, when I do get a break, we could go out on a date?"

Blood rushed to her face, and her heartbeat drummed in her ears. "Huh?"

His thumb inched up and down her hand, and his expression softened. "A date. Like when a man picks up a woman he likes and takes her to dinner and a movie."

Sarah Beth stared at his hand holding hers. "I...I don't know if I'm ready to date. I mean, I've been reading a book about purity, and it says that men and women should only date when they're thinking about commitment."

"Chris gave me the same book." His gaze explored her face. "You don't think you could ever consider making a commitment to me?"

Sarah Beth cleared her throat. "Yes. I mean..." She sighed. "I'm confused. I'll give it some thought. Going on a date, I mean."

Jess laced an arm around her waist. "That's all I ask."

Her world tilted, and she melted into his shoulder, brain foggy. He escorted her around the SUV and opened the door for her.

His confident grin returned. "See you soon, Sarah Beth."

After the door closed, she released a weighty breath.

Jill perked up a wee bit. "Tell me everything."

Sarah Beth's hand still tingled where Jess's had been. Between the hand-holding and the date invitation, she'd lost her ability to think. "He wants to go on a date."

Jill snickered. "You've been dating for months, silly. You just choose to pretend otherwise."

Chapter 38

The look on Sam's face as he entered the coaching offices launched Jess's stomach into a nosedive. He wouldn't stall, though. Not about this. "What did you find out?"

Sam plopped down in the chair across from Jess's desk. "We haven't hired the kid or anything, and no money has gone his way." He paused and sighed.

"But?"

"His father got a small promotion. Whether that was on the up and up, I don't know. That's all."

The sick feeling in his gut told him to notify Coach Black, just in case. Better to be up front now than in the news in a few months for a recruiting violation. Maybe it was nothing. Maybe not.

~~~

Out in the pool house, Sarah Beth took the computer from Jill's lap. "I'll make you some ginger tea. You're green again. I can tell."

"Thanks. How about a saltine and Tylenol?" Jill propped her feet on the ottoman, laid her head back, and closed her eyes.

"Knees still hurting?"

Gingie pawed at the door.

"Shoo. Get." Sarah Beth shook her finger at the dog.

Jill covered her mouth and nose with her hand. "You can let her in."

The nausea had to get better soon, or Jill would shrivel into nothing. "I remember last time I let in the smells of dog." Sarah Beth turned on the Keurig and slid a tall mug under the spout. Her friend couldn't live, much less nourish a baby, on the amount of food she kept down.

"I have to go to the doctor today, so I'll be outside anyway." The grimace on Jill's face said she was dreading it already. "I don't know why they call it morning sickness. I'm sick day and night. Last time I went, the doctor said to give up on the vitamins, keep hydrated, and eat peanut butter and crackers."

"Peanut butter?"

Jill nodded. "The thought of meat repulses me, and I need protein."

Sarah Beth handed her the cup of ginger tea and uncapped the pain reliever. "Your tea and doctor-approved pain relievers." Considering the bony hand that took the steaming mug, she should stock up on peanut butter.

"You're the best friend I've ever had."

Sarah Beth fought the anxiety that begged to show on her face. Why wasn't Jill getting better? "Need something else?"

Jill's lips formed a crooked smile. "I need you to say yes to Jess. Oh, and maybe a fat ripe watermelon."

A watermelon, she could do. Going out with Jess, another story. What would happen if her heart was ripped apart again?

But since Jill seemed to really want her to go...

~~~

Jess strode down the aisles of the grocery store. Picking up flowers had seemed like a good idea. Until he arrived. Football players on aisle one. Jess glanced down at his khakis and starched white button-down. A dead giveaway. And buying flowers. Obviously a date. *They'd rag him for weeks.*

He looked both ways before he stepped up to the floral

counter. Now, what to buy? He reached for a multicolored bouquet. No. One rose. Simple. Not too much. He picked up a red one, then turned toward the registers.

"Coach," a voice from behind hammered him. "Look at you. Struttin'."

Caught. Grant Vaughn and two other lineman.

"Hot date, huh?" Three huge guys surrounded him and snorted.

Keep the game face. "None of your business."

"Don't be ashamed. You rule, Coach."

He gave them his sternest look, pinching back a smile. "Turn and walk away. Now."

They sauntered away, chuckling.

Terrific. His pace picked up toward the checkout counter. Outside, he shut the door to his truck and lay the rose on the front seat.

When had he made this transformation? He'd spent more time with this woman than he'd spent with his friends or family the past six months. Sometimes inventing excuses to see her. Okay, a lot of times. Now she'd agreed to *one date.* He'd tried to suppress all this...gushiness, but no luck. On the field, he'd commanded hundreds of young men in a game of controlled violence, but with this girl, this woman, he couldn't control a thing.

Five minutes after leaving the parking lot, he arrived at her house. In two long strides, Jess cleared the stairs and approached Sarah Beth's door. He tapped twice and waited. The ferns by the door swayed in the breeze. Was he swaying, too? He hadn't been this nervous since the bowl game he played against Ohio State. Crazy.

The door swung open. Sarah Beth's dark hair hung below her shoulders against a peach-colored dress. She looked him up and down with that ebony gaze. "You look like a frat boy."

Was that bad or good? He brought the rose from behind his back. "For you."

Her eyes lit up. "That is so sweet. I'll put it in water. Be right back." In no time, she reappeared.

"You ready to go? I hope you don't mind I picked the restaurant and the movie."

She slipped her hand under his elbow. "What's not to like?"

He wasn't going to let the shock of her clasping his arm show on his face. But he had to admit, it did feel nice. "You can pick next time. I don't want you calling me bossy again."

"I'll let you know after our date if there will be a next time." Her eyes cut toward him. "No pressure."

He opened the passenger door and waited for her to be seated. "Very funny." Sarah Beth flashed a smile that beat any trophy he'd ever won. Maybe better than becoming a first choice draft pick would've been.

~~~

The steady chirp of tree frogs filled the night air as Sarah Beth's foot hit the top step of her porch. How had the evening passed so quickly? Naturally. In fact, the most relaxed date ever. And it was over. "What a delightful evening. Thank you."

Jess inched closer. "You're welcome."

Her breath caught as his eyes fell to her mouth. She couldn't do this. It was too soon.

Not now. Maybe not ever.

With one arm he pulled her close, the other hand lifted her chin.

Much too soon. Not yet.

His thumb traced her lips, then his lips traced her lips. And stayed. With a light hold he cupped her head, ran his fingers through her hair. Kissing her gently, but deepening with each passing moment.

Wasn't she going to stop him?

In a minute. She'd stop him in a minute.

The rest of the world faded.

Finally, he released her, but he lingered with his forehead on hers, and then brushed her lips once more. "Goodnight, Sarah Beth. I'll see you soon."

She stood motionless with a warm ache in her heart as he ran down the steps two at a time. When his taillights disappeared, she touched her lips, then fell into the rocking chair.

~~~

Jess looked down the long table in the compliance meeting room. Coach Black sat on his side, along with Sam, the compliance director and a representative from the NCAA on the other. The palpable tension in the air speared at Jess's insides, but he rested his hands on his legs and breathed normally. He'd prayed about the situation for days. Prayed this morning at home and all the way to campus. And Sam was there to back up his story. A muffled sigh escaped. Too bad this all happened.

The memory of Sarah Beth's kiss popped into his mind again. He'd never imagined emotions running that deeply for a woman. What if he lost his job here?

The NCAA representative looked up from his notes and cleared his throat. Jess straightened and met the man's gaze. He'd always played offense, and he wasn't changing that now. All he could do was tell what he knew and hope for divine coverage.

~~~

Sarah Beth walked into the pool house and held out a page

she'd printed. "Look at this logo. Do you like?"

Jill glanced up from her laptop. "I wasn't sure this was possible, Sarah Beth, but since your date, your ideas have been crazier than ever. Which makes them better than ever."

Sarah Beth set her hands on her hips. "I'm not sure if I should take that as a complement or an insult."

"I'm happy for you."

A frown pressed her lips together. The memories of Jess's kiss flooded her with a rush of delight tinged with fear.

"What are you thinking?" Jill snapped her laptop closed. "You don't regret going out with him, do you?"

Her hands moved to cover her face. "Don't you think it's too soon? I'm...I'm not ready."

"Why? Because you don't have feelings for him, or because you're scared?"

Petrified. Confused. Petrified again. Sarah Beth massaged her forehead. "Let's talk about something else. You know, a football weekend's descending upon us. Our population at least triples for the home games. The Square's a nightmare to get around."

"I think you're scared. It's obvious you have feelings for him." Jill's eyes closed, and she swallowed. "Oh, no." She sprang up and rushed into the bathroom.

Sarah Beth studied her emaciated friend staggering back to the bed. Even her blond hair seemed thinner and had lost its sheen. "I'm sorry you can't seem to get over the nausea."

"I go to the doctor again next week because of the weight loss. He'll have more options for me this time. I'm sure of it."

Was Jill putting on a brave front for her?

~~~

Skin and bones were all Sarah Beth felt as she slipped her arm around Jill to help her outside toward the SUV. Even at ten in the morning, the humidity left them both sticky. But they had to get answers at the doctor's appointment today.

On the brick sidewalk around the pool, Jill's footing faltered.

"Are you okay?" Sarah Beth caught her, and with her foot, slid a lounge chair under her.

Heart racing, she patted Jill's cheek. Though Jill's eyes fluttered, they didn't open.

"God, help me." Sarah Beth's hands shook as she punched 911 into her phone. "Send someone. My friend's passed out, and she's pregnant. Hurry." She gave them the address.

What should she do while she waited for the ambulance? She glanced around the pool. Nothing. She couldn't do anything. An image of Adam flashed before her eyes. Just like that horrible accident. She was no help at all.

Oh, God, please help Jill. She fell to her knees beside her friend slumped in the chair. *God, I'm begging. Let the ambulance get here.*

After minutes that seemed like hours, red lights flashed beside the fence. *Thank You.* She raced to open the gate. "Here she is. Be careful. She's pregnant, and she passed out. I didn't know what to do."

The paramedics rushed over with a stretcher. "Step aside, ma'am."

Sarah Beth staggered back as they examined Jill who was still unconscious.

They asked a string of questions, and Sarah Beth answered as best she could.

Once they strapped Jill on the stretcher, they wheeled her to the ambulance. Sarah Beth ran behind them, her heart banging against her chest. "Is she okay?"

One of the men glanced back. "We'll take care of her. You

can meet us in the ER."

Sarah Beth nodded, but her brain jumbled in a stupor. Meet them at the ER? She mashed her hand to her forehead. Keys. She spun around. Hadn't she just held the keys? On the ground by the chair. She bent to grab them. Her hands shook. Her legs, too.

I have to go to the ER. Now. "Help me, Lord."

She couldn't fail her friend.

She took fragile steps to the SUV and opened the door. The hospital was only a mile or two. *Just drive.*

Trembling the whole way, forcing herself to breathe, she pushed the gas. Her hands steered, but tears welled up in her eyes. Why? Why? Why did she have to feel paralyzed like this when her friend needed her? She slapped the steering wheel.

Driving the two miles drained her as if she'd run a marathon, but she made it to the parking lot, threw open the door, and raced through the ER entrance. "My friend was just brought here in an ambulance. I need to be with her."

The woman at the desk glanced her. "What's the name? I'll check." Once she found Jill's information, Sarah Beth wove through a small maze of halls, doors, and curtains. In the room where Jill lay with an IV already attached to her arm, Sarah Beth collapsed into a chair beside the hospital bed. "You're awake. Thank, God."

Jill offered a weak smile. "Sorry."

"Why are you sorry?"

"I scared you."

A doctor entered the tiny room and approached the headboard. "We're admitting you for dehydration. We need to get some fluids in you and do a sonogram to check on the baby. I want to make sure we take every precaution."

Jill put her hand over her mouth, stifling a sob.

Sarah Beth rubbed her shoulder. "I'm praying for you, and I'm not leaving your side."

~~~

The morning sun beat down on Jess's back as he ran through the parking lot. The call from Tampa Bay had finally come. The job was his for the taking. But he'd asked for time to think about the offer. At least a week. They'd given him ten days.

Ten days to decide whether he'd leave Oxford or stay and be with this woman. A woman he was in love with. A woman who couldn't leave this town.

Now another meeting with the NCAA. Maybe they'd make a decision. Across the sidewalk stood Teddy Conrad. The urge to turn around speared Jess. But that wasn't how he played. He'd face the man head-on.

It didn't take long for Teddy to see him. Once he did, he moved with speed, his face contorted. As soon as Teddy was within five feet, his finger shot out at Jess. "How dare you try to turn my own son against me? I'll do everything in my power to get you out of this town. Every alum I know will find out the kind of man you are."

Jess almost felt sorry for Teddy. Almost. "Let them know I'm an honest man who plays by the rules in football and in life. After that, do what you will."

"What a joke. See how far those naïve ideals carry you. And stay away from Sam."

Adrenaline coursed through Jess's limbs. "I'll keep my naïve ideals, but as far as Sam goes, you're doing a pretty good job of turning him against you on your own." Jess passed the madman on the sidewalk, giving a wide berth to avoid further confrontation. There was nothing more to be said while both their tempers flared this hot.

~~~

Squirming from side to side, Sarah Beth tried to find a comfortable spot on the plastic chair by Jill's bedside. Her phone rang. Again. The office would have to wait. She checked the number just in case.

Not the office. Oh no. "Jess, I totally forgot our ice cream date. Jill's in the hospital." Her hand popped her forehead. So much for not telling anyone. Sarah Beth mouthed to Jill, "Sorry."

Shaking her head, Jill mouthed back. "It's all right."

"What's wrong? Is there anything I can do?" Jess's voice held concern.

"Say a prayer for her, and I'll call you later."

"Uh…okay. I sure will."

After ending the call, she silenced the ringer, set aside the phone, and curled her legs beneath her. She settled in and allowed her mind to rest. Another episode of NCIS started— apparently, a marathon. This was the fourth one they'd watched since Jill was admitted. The IV fluids hydrating Jill perked her up, and a little color returned to her face as she stared at the TV monitor on the wall.

An hour later, a rap on the door shook Sarah Beth from her daze. Probably another round of questions from another hospital worker.

"Knock, knock." Jess cracked the door, holding a yellow balloon. He gave Jill a little wave. "Hi, ladies. Jill, I wanted to come by and tell you myself that I'm praying for you."

Jill smiled. "Is that for me?"

He gave her a sheepish look. "Yes, and I brought you something else. You and Sarah Beth may never speak to me again. But the man's been worried sick about you since he saw you at church. He knew something was wrong and keeps asking me if I know anything."

Sarah Beth breathed a sigh. This had been bound to happen eventually. And Jess was being so sweet.

A look of resignation settled on Jill's face. She motioned to the chair. "If he's out there, send him in. I may as well tell him everything and get it over with. He'll know eventually."

With red eyes and a dozen multicolored roses, Nick entered the room. "I didn't know what color you'd like."

Jill's face lit up. "Thanks. Come in. You look so worried. I'm not dying, although the way I've felt lately, I wasn't sure."

Nick set the roses on the table by her bed and sat. "I haven't been to a hospital since…"

Jill's gaze fell to her lap. "I'm so sorry. I wasn't thinking about Katie's mom. I'm such an idiot. I should tape my mouth shut." She waved off Sarah Beth and Jess. "You two go on and get your ice cream. For that matter, you probably haven't eaten. Go home, walk your dog, and eat a meal. You can tell Jess everything while you're out."

Sarah Beth did a double take. "Everything?"

Jill shrugged and looked at Jess. "I trust you. Go."

~~~

The smell of grilled meat permeated the air of the old gas station that now served as a greasy spoon. Jess studied Sarah Beth as she picked at the hamburger in front of her. Not eating. That wasn't the woman he'd gotten to know. "So what's going on?"

Sarah Beth explained the predicament, imploring him to keep the paternity of the baby confidential.

Of all the bad luck. Jess pounded his fist on the old, wooden table. "This is crazy. Just when Nick and Jill find each other… Life's so complicated." He grabbed a home-cut fry and dipped it in ketchup. "I pray the baby and Jill make it. Nick can't go through that kind of loss again. I don't know what I would do if you…or my child…you know, if I lost…you." He shoved the fry in his mouth and told himself to shut up.

Her face went slack, her dark eyes unreadable. "You want children?"

"I want to have as many children as my wife wants to have—if she wants to have them."

"But what do you want?"

Jess shrugged. "I'd like to have a child, but it's not a deal breaker. Why? Is there something I should know?"

She covered her food with a napkin and slung her bag to her shoulder. "Let's go back to the hospital."

Had he said something wrong?

On the way out the door of the cafe, Dr. Marlow, the team physician, caught Jess's arm. "Hey, I heard you got a sweet offer from Tampa Bay."

Oh, crud. How had word gotten out that fast? Jess closed his eyes and shook his head. When he reopened them, he searched Sarah Beth's face. Were those tears?

Dr. Marlow let his hand fall. "Sorry, Jess. I didn't mean…"

Jess shrugged. "I get a lot of offers. No worries."

He took her hand, and they left the restaurant and walked down the sidewalk to the truck. Her grip was light. Why hadn't he told her right away? At least about the possibility? He should have, but with her problem, he'd feared she'd close herself off from him. And he wasn't sure he could leave her.

She paused at the truck while he opened her door. "You should consider the offer. That's big-time. And back home in Florida, too."

He pulled her closer and pressed his lips to her ear. "Haven't you heard? Home is where the heart is."

"But, Jess—"

He put his finger over her mouth. "Let's deal with today's issues." *Like kissing away the fear in her expression.* His lips found hers for the slightest moment before she slipped from his grasp.

~~~

A tearful Jill greeted them in the hospital room. Nick sat on the bed holding her hand.

Sarah Beth's stomach dropped to the linoleum beneath her feet. "What happened?"

Nick spoke when Jill couldn't regain her composure. "The doctor said the baby isn't developing at the proper rate. He wants Jill to go to the University Hospital in Jackson. They have more sophisticated sonogram technology and a specialist he wants her to see."

Sarah Beth's hands perspired, and her breathing became shallow. How would she get Jill to Jackson? The room started to sway. Jess's arm wrapped around her waist.

"Katie's going to stay with Chris and Kim." Nick's voice was calm. "I've already arranged to take off work, so I can drive her."

Because he knew crazy Sarah Beth couldn't handle it. Lowering her eyes, Sarah Beth forced a weak smile. "Of course, Nick. You're such a good man. I appreciate you taking care of her. When will you be leaving?"

"Tonight." Jill smiled through her tears. "They called ahead for us. I'll be released soon, and we'll pick up a few things at the pool house. Do you think you could pack my clothes and some peanut butter and crackers?"

"Of course." Numbness travelled through her. She should go now. She couldn't do anything more for her friend.

"I'm going to be okay, Sarah Beth. Don't worry."

She couldn't meet Jill's gaze. What good was she to

anyone? Jill was trying to comfort her when she should be the one taking Jill to Jackson.

Jess took her hand. "Let me take you home. We can get your SUV later."

"No." Tears fuzzed her vision as she broke contact. What a failure she was. "I'm tired. Once Jill and Nick leave, I'll call it a night. Goodbye, Jess."

Back at home, Sarah Beth packed Jill's bag, laid it on the front porch swing, went inside, and turned off the lights. She'd disappointed herself. She'd let Jill down.

It was one thing when the anxiety affected her own life. But now...the panic attacks, the crushing anxiety, the fear of leaving Oxford, not only hurt her, they hurt the people she loved the most.

Disappointment and frustration crushed her from all sides. Shaking, she climbed in the bed and pulled a pillow over her head. Her mind felt crumpled. The bars that held her tightened. Her safe haven had become her prison.

Chapter 39

"Coach, you got a minute?" The massive offensive lineman, Grant Vaughn, filled Jess's office door.

"Just packing up for the day." Jess motioned toward a chair. "Have a seat."

Grant fingered the arm of the wingback without looking up or speaking.

"Personal or team related?" Maybe a little nudge would help.

"I heard you're a Christian. Now, at least."

Unexpected turn. "Yeah. I'd been to church some growing up, but never really took it to heart until recently. I committed my life."

Grant finally made eye contact. "Would you mind praying for me?"

"Sure." Did he mean right this minute? "About something specific?"

"You know, just temptations of college life. Partying and all. It's hard always saying no, going against the grain."

"I get it. It's tough out there. Even when you're my age."

"Even for old guys, huh?" Grant smirked. "You might add my temper to the list, too. My sister says I have anger issues."

Jess ran his fingers across his forehead. "I've noticed a time or two. Don't mind when you take it out on the field…within the game's boundaries, of course." His abs tightened. He'd never prayed with anyone other than Sarah Beth or Chris. "You want me to, you know, say it now?"

Grant scooted to the edge of the chair. "Nah, I know you'll cover me. Thanks, Coach."

"You bet." Jess rose to his feet to walk Grant out. "Hey, Grant."

"Yeah?"

"Add me to your list, too."

One side of Grant's lips lifted. "Will do."

He needed all the prayers he could get with everything on his plate. His life seemed to be coming together and falling apart at the same time. A sigh worked its way out as Jess watched his player walk away. Making a difference with these college guys had always meant something to him. Molding them into men. Once again, he wondered if he'd get the same satisfaction in the pros.

After shutting off the light, he made his way home. He tried Sarah Beth's number again. Straight to voicemail. For five days, he'd called her. Over and over. Every single call unanswered.

He'd driven over and banged on her door. Nothing. She had to be upset about Jill. Maybe she was afraid of losing her friend, but Jill had returned from the Jackson hospital two days ago with instructions to stay in bed. At least, according to Nick, who visited her daily. Maybe that was the problem. Could Sarah Beth be jealous of Nick with Jill?

No. It must have been the Tampa Bay comment from Dr. Marlow. It was his own fault for not telling her. He had to do something.

Keys in hand, he cranked the truck and peeled out of his driveway, speeding toward Sarah Beth's. The house was dark even though the SUV sat in the drive. He went to the door and knocked.

Nothing.

Nick's truck was parked near the pool house. Maybe together, he and Jill could get him some answers. He didn't have anything to lose at this point. Jess hurried down the back sidewalk and knocked.

The door swung open. Nick's serious expression warned him that trouble brewed.

"Sorry to bother y'all." Jess's chest squeezed so tight, he felt his ribs would splinter. "I can't get Sarah Beth to answer the door or my calls. Since the hospital…"

Jill waved him in from the sofa. "Come in and sit down."

He pulled over a straight wooden chair from the adjoining kitchen, though nervous energy bounced his legs like a time when he'd waited twelve hours in the airport after missing a connecting flight. Only worse.

Jill raised her phone. "I've been worried, too. She's checked on me when Nick's not here, but doesn't say much. Let me try to call her now." She pressed the number and put the phone on speaker.

Sarah Beth answered on the second ring. "Hello, Jill. Are you okay?"

"Fine. We're praying the baby will grow in time." Jill cut the phone off speaker and raised it to her ear. "Nick's convinced me that God's in control. You don't have to worry. I believe in the Lord, too." She sighed. "But, what's the matter with you, Sarah Beth?"

Jess cocked his head. He'd love to hear what she was saying.

"I don't know. Are you sure there's not something more that's troubling you?" Jill paused. "Thoughts of Adam? He'd want you to be happy. I know he would, and you know it, too."

A second later, the call ended, and Jill placed the phone on the sofa beside her. "She said she needed to be alone for a while, and didn't want to talk about it, but it wasn't about Adam or anyone else. It was about her."

Jess let his head fall to his hands. "I don't get it. Maybe she doesn't want anything to do with me. Maybe I should take the offer from Tampa Bay."

"Tampa Bay?" Shaking her head, Jill dialed another number. "No. You're not. And I can't take watching that dark house from my window another second. I'm doing something about it."

~~~

Sarah Beth had pretended not to hear Jess knocking at the door. Every day. She'd crated Gingie when she'd heard his truck.

He hadn't come by today, though. Not even a phone call. Maybe he'd finally given up. He could move on with his life in Florida. That was his dream, after all. And he could find a nice normal woman there to have a family with.

She huddled under a blanket on the couch and mashed her eyes closed. Why couldn't she take her best friend to a hospital three hours away? When Jill needed her most, she'd failed her. Why couldn't she get better? Was this some kind of punishment?

The front doorknob rattled, then opened.

"What in the world?" Sarah Beth's head popped up. Where was the key to the gun cabinet? She threw off the blanket and ran to the kitchen.

Footsteps echoed through the door and down the hall. *No time.* She pulled an iron skillet off the hook and hid behind the door, ready to swing.

A tall shadow moved through the archway toward the living room. Sarah Beth screamed and swung.

The man ducked and clutched her arms. "I see you finally

figured out a use for that skillet."

"Mark? What are you doing here? You scared me to death."

"I didn't think you'd be home. Shouldn't you be at work?" Mark pried the skillet from her fist and set it on the hall table. "Aren't you going to give me a hug?"

She fell into his arms, unleashing a torrent of tears onto his shoulder.

"What's wrong? You have your friends worried about you."

"I'm taking a vacation. I haven't taken off since..." She spoke between sobs. "Did Jill call? She didn't need to bother you."

"Jess called me, too. He says you won't answer the phone or the door. Your boss, Bill, called. Chris called. Dean Latham called. Are you getting the picture? You have a lot of people who care about you."

Weeping shook her entire body.

Mark pulled keys from his pocket. "Come on, we're riding out to Sardis Lake."

The sun set earlier now, streaming sharp reds and pinks across the western sky. They arrived at the lake and perched on the bumper of his SUV. Mark nudged her elbow with his. "Sarah Beth, you've run so hard and pushed yourself your whole life. That mindset allowed you to achieve success in athletics, academics, and your career, but there are some situations you can't push past or run through. Some trials take time and patience and faith."

"I've had time. I've tried to be patient and have faith. Nothing's changed."

"Remember when I called you in Los Angeles and counseled you about taking baby steps back to the Lord?"

She nodded.

"You're going to have to be patient with yourself and be satisfied with your baby steps with the Lord at your side. You've accomplished so much through the past months, despite your self-perceived weakness and failure. The church in Honduras is funded and being built. Your friend Nick and his daughter are involved with church again. Jess, and now Jill, have become believers. The campus ministry is growing. You've taught and influenced dozens of college students. I've heard your work for the Foundation is incredible." Mark gave her a little punch. "Hey, you even saved a weird-looking stray puppy."

"I don't know." She wiped her nose with the back of her hand. "I just want to be well again. Normal. I hate these panic attacks."

He patted her knee. "The apostle Paul had a thorn in his flesh that he begged the Lord to take away, but in the end the Lord answered Paul, 'My grace is sufficient for you, for My strength is made perfect in weakness.' We don't always get the answer we want or think we deserve. Sometimes we learn to live with the answer we didn't want—the weakness—and that requires a much larger faith, as far as I'm concerned. Now, I'm not telling you to give up on getting back to what you call *normal.* I'm saying to do your best one day at a time, and be okay with where you are that day."

"I feel like I'm an addict or something with that whole *one day at a time* thing."

"What you're going through will give you more compassion than the average person because you understand what it's like to try to get through a day carrying a burden. God can use everything you're going through to help others. You can inspire and comfort hurting people in ways that *normal* people can't."

They fell silent watching the last of the magenta sphere sink into the horizon.

The next morning, the hinges to Sarah Beth's bedroom door creaked, and footsteps padded into her room. *Mark better not—*

A pillow swatted her head. "Rise and shine."

"Too early." Her eyes cracked and then reopened to the blurry sunlight streaming through the window.

"It's time for a run, a shower—which you really need by the way—and then we're heading to campus. I brought my laptop and top-secret FBI work along. We can share your office."

She couldn't help but smile at her big brother, even though he'd always been so obnoxious in the morning. Rising with a groan, Sarah Beth fumbled around the floor for her shoes. How would she have survived life without her Mark? And how had he turned out so perfect when she was so messed up?

~ ~ ~

Crimson haze reflected on the surface of the lake. The weight on Sarah Beth's soul lightened with each step. Everything Mark had said the past few days made sense. Of course.

Life would go on, and she'd deal with it one day at a time. One moment at a time if necessary. She pointed toward the west. "The sky's been so beautiful out here all week, but the days are getting shorter." Her teeth dug into her lower lip. "I'm sorry I worried you. And everyone."

Mark blew out a long exhale. "If Mom were still here, what would she do before she left? You know, girlie stuff?" He clicked his tongue. "I got it. Tomorrow, I'll take you to get one of those mani-pedi things and a new outfit, maybe a haircut.

Isn't that what girls do to feel better?"

Laughing, she gave him a playful punch. "Please never say mani-pedi again. But, I could use your help picking out some new running shoes. And if you can stay one more night, we can go watch a soccer game."

"Yes." Mark flashed a grateful smile. "That's why I love my baby sister. Girlie, but not too girlie."

Back at the car, she leaned on the hood, laying her phone down. "It's your fault, you know? I always wanted to be just like my big brother. Except without hairy legs."

"Lucky for you, they make razors."

"Hush, or I'll take you to the nail salon."

"Just kidding." He picked up the phone and held it in front of her face. "Now call poor Jess and apologize for not answering his calls."

She stood motionless, chewing her lip. What would she say?

"He at least deserves an explanation."

"Fine." Sarah Beth touched the screen and waited four rings before voicemail picked up. "Jess, sorry I haven't answered your calls or knocks. It was about me, not you. And uh… Well, bye." She ended the call. What was she doing? She should've hung up and called back later, but that would be weird, too.

Mark furrowed his eyebrows. "What was that?"

"I left a message."

"First class, Sarah Beth."

"I didn't know what else to do." Now Jess would think she was even crazier.

Chapter 40

Jess had listened to the stupid message ten times. He tucked the phone in his pocket and started his truck. What did Sarah Beth mean? *It was about her.* At least she'd called, but nothing in her voice said she wanted to be with him—or even talk to him again. He'd put off the coaches in Tampa all week, but he had to give them an answer soon. Then there was the recruiting situation. When would that be resolved? Why had life suddenly become so complicated?

The short drive to church wasn't long enough to decide what he'd say or do when he saw her. If he saw her. He'd puzzled over the message for two sleepless nights. But his commitment to serve the Lord wasn't based on Sarah Beth, so he ignored that little tug to stay home.

Since meeting this woman, the insecurity that railed him reminded him of standing on train tracks. He heard the train but didn't know if it was about to crush him or to pick him up for a great journey.

The church came into view. He was here. Now to decide where to sit.

~ ~ ~

The temperature had fallen while they'd been in church. A cold front must've been moving through. Sarah Beth shivered as she stood beside Mark in the parking lot. He chatted with Dean Latham and his wife.

Jess walked down the sidewalk toward them, but he hadn't joined them in the balcony where they usually sat together.

Who could blame him after she'd behaved like such a nut?

Still, it pinched her heart.

She gave him a little wave. He regarded her with dark-circled eyes. A lump knotted in her throat. She crossed the parking lot in a jog. "Hey, did you get my message?"

"Yes." One shoulder lifted as he shook his head. "But I didn't know what you wanted me to do. You didn't say call back."

"I'm sorry. When I couldn't take Jill to the hospital in Jackson, I felt like such a failure as a friend and a human being. I—"

"Great game last week." Mark caught up and shook Jess's hand. "I liked how we held on through the fourth quarter. Your quarterback's got some guns on him. Too bad this was bye week. I would've liked to watch my team play."

A weak smile crossed Jess's face. "Thanks. Did you catch the New Orleans-Tampa Bay game?"

She lagged behind and took stock of the view, Jess and Mark talking sports, all the way to the SUV. They got along well, but she'd been trying to apologize.

Dean Latham cornered all three of them. "Come to lunch. We've missed the company."

Jess looked to Mark. "I don't want to intrude."

"Don't be ridiculous." Clapping Jess's shoulder, Mark pointed with his other hand and made a face at Sarah Beth. "You're in charge of this nut when I leave after lunch."

"Nice, Mark." She shot him a pointed stare.

Jess's posture straightened. "I have missed Mrs. Latham's pot roast. Since the season started, I've had to make a quick exit after church to watch film with the team. But since we were off this week..."

She'd love to end all the pain and confusion she'd seen in

Jess's eyes. But would she ever be the kind of woman he deserved?

At lunch, guilt crushed Sarah Beth's throat as she studied Jess. His eyes drooped as he made conversation, along with the corners of his mouth. Gloom covered his every movement. By dessert, she'd lost her appetite and stirred her spoon around the banana pudding on her plate.

Mark stretched and scooted his chair back from the table. "There's nothing like your cooking, Mrs. Latham. Thank you." He stood. "I'd love to stay longer, but I better get on the road. The sooner I start the drive to Atlanta, the sooner I'll get back to the family." His gaze shifted to Jess. "Would you mind giving Sarah Beth a ride home? My luggage is already in my SUV."

Likely story. That stinker planned this.

Jess crinkled his eyebrows. "No problem."

They all stood and escorted Mark down the sun-brightened entrance hall. The Lathams took turns embracing him. Jess followed with a handshake.

Mark gave Sarah Beth a stern look. "Be honest. Quit trying to be perfect. Or else I'm telling everyone about your weird childhood stunts." Then he folded her in a tight hug.

Sarah Beth grunted. "Talk about tough love."

"Love you, miss you, but God loves you more."

As usual, Jess walked Sarah Beth to his truck and opened her door. She gave him a tentative smile. "Thanks."

Once they were both in the truck with the engine started, Jess stroked his chin. "A cold front's moving in, and the temperature's supposed to drop even more tonight. I thought I'd take the boat for one last spin and then put her up for the winter. My schedule's too busy this time of year to take her out anyway. Would you consider going with me? No pressure. Not a date."

"Of course." Now she had to figure out what to say and where to start.

Jess switched on the radio while they rode to his house and hitched the boat which was fine with her.

Once they reached the dock, she helped him launch it into the water. A cold wind stirred the water under the afternoon sun. They cruised without talking until Jess cut the engine. Few boaters passed in the crisp air, so they drifted in the middle of the lake.

She tried to gather her courage and force out words to explain why she'd behaved the way she had. Why she'd hurt him. "You want to talk?"

"Do you?" Jess kept his eyes fixed ahead. If only he'd look at her.

"Yes and no."

"I'll wait, then." His voice was subdued. He closed his eyes and settled down in his seat, legs stretched toward the open bow.

The wind blew ripples and small waves across the lake, sunlight shimmering on the pinnacles. She shivered as they drifted in silence. The temperature had to be dipping into the fifties. Leaves dropped and drifted in the breeze, creating cascades of gold and amber and auburn. Mark's advice came to mind. She needed to explain her withdrawal. But how should she start?

Opening his eyes, Jess straightened in his seat. "We should head back. I've got hours of recruiting film to watch."

Oh no. She hadn't explained yet. And she had to.

The key clinked in the ignition, but the engine didn't respond. He ran his hands through his blond hair. "What's wrong now?" He moved back to check the motor and the battery, then tried again. Nothing. He clucked his tongue, and pulled out his phone. "No service. You?" He raised his phone in the air above his head.

Sarah Beth rummaged through her bag. She found her phone, no bars. "No service here, either."

"I've never had any trouble with the engine. The battery should be good. Maybe another boat will pass, and we can get a tow."

They scanned the lake. No boats. They waited long minutes and nothing.

Jess looked toward the bank. "I could get out and swim with a rope and pull us to the shore."

"No." Sarah Beth reached over and gripped his bicep. "It's too cold, and there's nothing on that shore. No dock or store. You'll be hypothermic in no time. My parents warned us about situations like this. We should drop anchor and wait for help." She dug in her bag. "Here. I have water, sour gummy worms, hot tamale candy, and peanut butter crackers. We can stave off hunger. I have one of these foil blankets, too, if we get cold. Shoot. I should have brought two."

Jess raised his eyebrows. "Can you pull a rabbit or maybe a marine mechanic out of that thing?"

"Maybe later." God had given her this opportunity to be honest and share her heart. Like Mark had said she should. "I think I'm supposed to spill my guts now."

Jess put his hand up. "You don't owe me an explanation. I pushed you. You told me you weren't ready to date the first time we came here. It's all right. We can slow down."

Sarah Beth fixed her gaze on him. "You remember what I said the first time we came out here?"

A smile tugged at Jess's lips. "I remember the first time I came into your classroom. I was tracking down Cole to return his phone. You were cute and funny."

Sarah Beth bolted upright and gasped. "You were giving him his phone?"

"He left it in my office, and I was trying to catch him before class started."

"I thought you came to convince me to change his grade."

Nose crinkling, Jess shook his head. "I'd never do that. I could get into a mountain of trouble."

"Why'd you come to my office?"

Jess grinned. "I was intrigued. You were so disinterested. I wasn't, uh…"

"You weren't used to a woman not falling all over you?"

His grin widened. "I wasn't going to put it that way."

"But when you came to Christ…that was real, right?"

His hands clasped hers. "Sarah Beth, nothing that happened after that first day on the boat was a game. You told me part of your story, and all games were off. I knew something was different about you. I had to know more, and that night at the CSU, I realized what made you different. I fell in love with you that first day, and that night at CSU, I fell in love with the Lord."

Sarah Beth's heart drummed as if she'd just swum the length of the lake.

His head lowered, his smile gone. "So, there you have it. I spilled my guts instead of you—laid it on the line. I'm sorry if that's not what you wanted."

A gust of cool air rushed across the water, rocking the boat. "Jess, I'm scared."

He squeezed her hands. "We'll be fine. Someone will find us."

"No, not of this." How to explain? She stared at his hands holding hers and rubbed her thumbs across his fingers. "How can I be a wife and mother when I can't even leave town? What if our child needs to go the hospital in Jackson—or just wants to be on a traveling soccer team? What will I do? Say, 'Sorry, baby, Mommy's crazy. She can't go with you. Good luck, feel better'? You deserve to have children, and I'm just too messed up, Jess. You deserve someone normal. You should go coach professional football. Live your dream. Find a nice girl that's the whole package."

With one quick movement, he hauled her into his lap. "Sarah Beth, I feel like I've been looking for you all my life. I don't want anyone else. If you're scared to be a mother, then we won't have children. We could build a shack on this lake and only leave for food if that would make you happy. If I lose my coaching job and have to dig ditches to stay in Oxford, that's what I'll do to be with you. I don't care about Tampa Bay. I love you, Sarah Beth. I'll wait until you're ready, but please don't shut me out again. I can't handle that. You have to talk to me when you get scared, even if it's to tell me you don't feel the same way about me."

She breathed in the citrus and spice scent of his hair and melted into his shoulder. "I do love you, Jess McCoy. But I want you to be happy."

Lifting her chin, he cupped her face. "You make me happy." His brown eyes held a passion that gripped her whole being. The wind ruffled his blond hair as his mouth inched closer. His lips mingled with the wind brushing across hers, lightly at first. His thumbs traced her cheekbones, his fingers slipped through her hair, sending a wave of warmth and washing down the fears, the guilt. The kiss deepened. Everything else dissolved away, his strength soaking into her heart.

At last he let her go. "Lord, we need this engine to start to keep me from temptation."

Sarah Beth sucked in a deep breath, opening her eyes. "Me, too. Give it another try."

Rotating toward the ignition, he turned the key. The motor roared to life. The smell of diesel fuel and oil circulated in the wind as she looked toward the sky. "Thank You."

Chapter 41

In the truck, Jess hummed along with the radio. It didn't matter if he was off key. All was right with the world. Like winning the national title...but better. Much better. Sarah Beth loved him.

When they reached her door, his lips followed the curve of her neck to her cheek, then her ear. "I never wanted my kid to be on one of those travel soccer teams."

Sarah Beth pursed her lips. "Next, you'll be calling me a nut, like Mark."

Pulling her closer still, her warmth filled him with hope. "As long as you're nuts about me."

A howl reverberated from the other side of the window. Sarah Beth moved to the door to let Gingie out. "You know, Jess, I was praying for a companion that first day that you came to my classroom, but I thought this mutt was God's answer to my prayer. Now I have to wonder why this strange creature descended upon me."

He huffed. "I can't believe you met me and still thought that brute was the answer to your prayers."

Her lips brushed his, teasing. She rubbed his nose with her own. "See, I'm nuts."

Was he blushing now? His face burned as she toyed with him. "I do like nuts." They held each other until Jess tore himself away. "Sarah Beth, please be patient with my crazy football schedule. Don't give up on me or disappear again. Promise me."

Her brown eyes softened. "I'm sorry I hurt you. I won't give up or disappear. I promise. But what about your offer? Professional football is your dream. Maybe I can keep practicing leaving Oxford, or Mark can drug me and haul me there. Do you want to go?"

The tenderness in her voice, her gaze, gave him happiness. Didn't she know by now? "Professional football *was* my dream. When I was twenty-two, the NFL seemed like the ultimate success. Besides the fact that you're enough for me now, I think success is helping these boys God brings under my influence become young men. With the skills for life, not just football." He sighed. "Unless the NCAA slaps a recruiting violation on us."

Her chin lifted. "Wait. What are you talking about?"

Had he said that out loud?

"Jess, tell me. Don't leave anything out. No more keeping things from each other."

He took her hands. She was right. No more keeping things from each other.

~~~

Sarah Beth flew through the open door of the pool house, a stack of files piled in her arms. She hurried into the bedroom. "Let's play catch up."

A smile spread across Jill's thin face as she sat up. "Bring it on." She held out her hands to take a few folders. "I'm glad Mark helped you see how important you are to us. You've been a wonderful friend to me. I can't imagine going through this pregnancy without your support. But remember, that doesn't mean you have to do everything for me."

"Thanks. I'm glad Nick's been here to take up the slack. Can I be nosey and ask where things stand between you? I saw him kiss you goodbye before you left that first time."

A pillow soared across the bed and smacked Sarah Beth in the head. "I knew you were peeking out the window."

Giggling, Sarah Beth picked up the pillow. "I couldn't stop myself."

Jill sighed. "I finally met Mr. Right, but I'm pregnant with another man's baby. Of course, not just any old Joe's baby. The father would have to be one of the most famous faces in the world."

"I shouldn't have asked."

"You can ask me anything. We both need to be more open." She rolled to her side and slid her hand across the white cotton bedspread. "Nick's stepped up as a friend. Of course, we always have our sweet chaperone, Katie. So, now it's your turn to update me about you and our favorite coach."

Sarah Beth squeezed the pillow to her chest. "He says he loves me, even if I'm a nut."

Jill's forehead wrinkled. "What? He said that?"

"Not exactly. It was more like he loves me no matter what."

"That's more like it. I'm happy for you. You deserve to be happy."

"You do too, Jill. Why can't life be easy?"

Jill tapped her fingernails on the computer in her lap. "It'd be much easier if we didn't make stupid, impulsive decisions. I'm speaking for myself, of course."

"I've made my fair share of bad choices. We all do. That's what's so remarkable about grace. Sometimes, even though we're forgiven, we still have consequences."

A bitter laugh passed Jill's lips. "I'm living with the consequences." She sat back up. "But the best thing I can do for now is figure out how to be a good mother. Nick brought me his plethora of parenting books. The man takes his parenting very seriously. He also brought Bible study books and videos. I'm learning so much. I'm talking to my mother about all of it. Would you mind if she comes for a visit next month?"

Bible study books and videos? This was fantastic. And talking to her mother about it. "Of course, I wouldn't mind. She's welcome to stay with me. You both are, if you need more space."

Sarah Beth sank back into the chair and closed her eyes. Maybe every tear she'd cried these past years had been worth it. God was redeeming all that pain. Beauty for ashes. Like Juan had said.

Chapter 42

Jess parked his truck on campus and steeled himself for the early morning meeting with compliance. No matter how many times he'd prayed, worry still nagged him about whether he'd lose his job in Oxford. What would he do for a living? Sarah Beth had made some progress, but he'd never want to push her too hard.

The ring he'd purchased came to mind. After their last few goodnight kisses, he didn't want to wait much longer to ask her to marry him. Or to get married for that matter. Leaving her at that doorstep was way too hard. But he wanted to know the outcome of this meeting first, so she'd know what she was getting into.

Lord, I know you've got only the best plans for me and Sarah Beth. Help me calm down.

A cool, light wind swept across his face as he stepped onto the sidewalk. With it came peace. No matter what the outcome, God was on his side. He hoped Sarah Beth would be, too.

~~~

Sarah Beth shivered under the gray clouds that covered the chilly November sky above the lake. What a pleasant surprise Jess's visit had been. Football season had forced them to be creative in finding time to spend together, even more so as the team readied for a bowl game. But they'd managed plenty of nice outings. And goodnight kisses.

A smile floated across her lips as she watched him still fiddling in the truck. He was so handsome. And he loved her.

Leaving him on the porch had become more difficult after every visit he made. She toed at the loose gravel on the asphalt. If not for God, it would've been impossible.

What was taking him so long to get out?

Showering leaves of gold and red covered the landing. Yellow tinged the Cyprus trees that billowed in the wind. They'd be lucky for a short walk along the lake before the predicted rain set in.

Finally, Jess rounded the truck and let down the tailgate with a clatter. He patted the end, signaling for Sarah Beth to sit. "I've got good news."

She complied, and he stood in front of her, cloaked with an anxious expression. "Aren't you going to sit with me?"

He remained where he was. "I found out today that I still have a job. No recruiting violation."

"That's fantastic."

He dropped to one knee and presented a small French porcelain box in the shape of a ship.

"What are you doing?"

He squared his broad shoulders and bit his lip. "There's an old Irish tune my Grandfather used to sing." He spoke, his voice soft. "I won't butcher the song by trying to sing it, but the words I remember are something like this. 'The water is wide. I can't cross o'er. Neither have I wings to fly. Give me a boat that can carry two, and both shall row, my love and I.' Will you try that with me, Sarah Beth? I know life can be hard, but let's row through it together. I want to come home to you every night. I don't want to squeeze in visits here and there. I'm asking if you'll marry me, Sarah Beth LeClair."

Tears blurred her vision. Had she heard him right? The lump in her throat kept her from speaking.

"Open it."

With shaking hands, she lifted the lid. A diamond solitaire on a platinum band glittered despite the cloudy day. She slid the ring over her finger. A perfect fit.

Jess's eyes probed hers. "Is that a yes?"

Didn't he know she was busy being a blubbering idiot? She jumped from the tailgate and squeezed her arms around his neck. A little too hard, maybe, because they fell into a heap in the parking lot. She swallowed back the tears. "Let me think about it. Yes."

Jess fell back, laughter rumbling from his chest. "The crazy life with Sarah Beth. I can't wait."

She propped herself on one elbow and looked down at him. "Such a beautiful proposal. Until you said that." She planted her lips on his and kissed him. The world around her faded. Only his lips, strong arms, and her.

Jess's arm nudged her away from him, and his breath hitched. "I think it's best we leave the pavement and go announce the good news to our friends and family. And maybe have a short engagement." A grin crossed his face as he took her hand in his. He helped her to her feet. "You've made me a happy man."

~~~

Sarah Beth jumped out of the truck, her heart soaring. Vehicles lined the street behind her home, and she motioned toward the pool house. "Looks like Jill and her mom have company. Let's go give them the good news."

Jess jogged behind her. "Wait. You forgot your gigantic bag."

The pool house door stood open. Kim, Chris, Nick, and Jill's mother crowded into the small living area.

Sarah Beth's stomach took a nosedive. "Has something happened?"

Kim broke into a big grin. "No. Everything's more than all right."

"Oh, good, because we have some big news."

Nick gave her a curious look. "Big news? We have news, too. Where have you guys been? We tried to call both of you."

"My fault." Jess raised his hand. "I nabbed our phones and turned them off. I didn't want any interruptions. I forgot to turn them back on in all the excitement." He pulled Sarah Beth's phone from his pocket, switched it on, and handed it to her.

Chris raised an eyebrow. "What excitement?"

Jess wrapped Sarah Beth in his arms. "I asked Sarah Beth to marry me."

"And I said yes."

The small room erupted into embraces and congratulations.

Then Nick knocked on the bedroom door. "Sarah Beth and Jess are here. Are you ready?"

The door swung open, and Jill emerged in a shimmering off-white dress, her hair styled, makeup perfectly applied. Katie stood at her side.

"What's all the ruckus out here?"

Nick winked at her. "Sarah Beth and Jess got engaged today. He turned their phones off. That's why we haven't been able to get them."

"Wonderful news." Jill crossed the room and hugged her.

Sarah Beth hugged back, then held her friend at arms' length. "Why are you out of bed? And what's with the dress?"

"Nick heard Mom was coming..." Her voice broke.

Katie hugged Jill's legs. "Daddy and I asked Jill to be my new mommy."

A glow radiated from Nick. "And she was kind enough to

say yes. I thought the best time to marry would be while her mother was here. She gave us her blessing, so we were waiting on our best friends to get here to be our witnesses. Now that you are, Chris can start the ceremony."

Jill's eyes fell to the ring on Sarah Beth's hand. "We had no idea Jess was proposing today, or we would've waited until tomorrow."

"Don't be silly. I couldn't be happier."

The short, sweet ceremony inside the pool house brought tears to everyone's eyes. Except Katie, who could hardly wait to dig into the ivory cake with pink flower petals.

Sarah Beth lifted a glass of sparkling cider. "I'm so giving y'all a huge party when you're ready."

Nick turned to Jess. "Speaking of parties, did you guys set a date?"

"We didn't get that far. I had a time frame in mind, but it's up to Sarah Beth."

Sarah Beth studied him. "What time frame were you thinking? Because on the way here, I was mulling it over."

Jess laced her fingers in his and held her hand to his face. "You first."

"No. You."

Nick rolled his eyes. "Please. One of you has to give."

"Christmas Eve." They both spoke at once.

Sarah Beth's mouth dropped open. "You were thinking Christmas Eve, too?"

"I don't want to wait, but I will if you want to plan a big wedding."

"It's perfect. Mark and Holly are coming for the holidays. They'll already be here. And I don't want to wait, either."

"Remember with the bowl game, I'll only have a couple of days off for a honeymoon. Christmas Eve and Christmas. But right after we finish up with that, recruiting starts. We can plan a second honeymoon when you're ready and I have more time off."

Her teeth dug into her bottom lip. "I'm not dying to travel a long way, after all."

"Until then, every day with you will be like a honeymoon for me."

She kissed him on the cheek. "You are so cheesy sometimes, but I love it." Her phone rang in her jacket pocket. "It's Mark. I can't wait to tell him."

"Um." Jess cleared his throat. "I asked his permission three weeks ago."

"But you didn't know I'd say yes." She grinned and touched the screen. "Hey, big brother, guess what."

"Ms. Sarah Beth LeClair?" Another deep voice spoke, but not Mark.

Sarah Beth's heart fluttered. Why did someone have Mark's phone? "Who is this?"

"This is David Ward from the Gulfport bureau. I went to college with Mark. You might remember me."

"They called you Super Dave. I remember. Did Mark lose his phone?"

"No." A sigh crackled the line. "Mark was down here helping me with a case, and he's been injured."

Sarah Beth's vision blurred. A bitter taste rose up her throat and into her mouth. What awful thing could've happened?

"You're not driving a vehicle right now, are you?"

The question kicked her in the diaphragm, expelling all the air from her lungs. She forced out her voice by sheer will. "No. I'm home. How bad?"

"He's in the ER at Memorial in Gulfport. He's been shot."

Chapter 43

"No." Sarah Beth's posture crumbled. "He's not going to die, is he?"

"Haven't heard anything from the doctor yet. I'll call you when I have an update. By the way, I couldn't get his wife on the phone. He'd told me when he got down here she and his son were on a Disney cruise with the in-laws. An early Christmas present or something."

"That's right. Please, Lord, let him be okay." Her voice broke, and she ended the call.

Jess placed his hands on her cheeks. "Tell me."

"Mark. Shot. Gulfport." Her chest quivered, and she fell into him.

"Oh, baby." He pulled her head close. "I'll make a quick trip down to check on him. Maybe go to Memphis and fly standby tonight."

"No." Sarah Beth ripped from his hold and rushed out of the pool house. "We need to pack. I'll find a pilot and charter a small plane right away."

Jess caught up to her. "What do you mean *we?*"

"I'm going with you. I don't care what kind of medicine I have to take to get there, we're going to Mark. You're not leaving Oxford without me."

Chapter 44

An hour later, Sarah Beth white-knuckled the handrail to the plane's entrance. Rain pelted the tarmac. Wind blew from the north, sending an icy chill through her veins.

Jess's hand rested on the small of her back as she willed herself to put one foot in front of the other. At last she made it inside the small aircraft and took a seat. With shaking hands, she attempted to strap herself with the unwieldy seatbelt.

Jess reached across and guided the buckle. "Let me help you. I'm right here, and we're fine."

She buried her head into his shoulder and held his arm as if bracing for the next hurricane—waiting for the next storm surge to wash through her life.

The pilot turned back. "You scared of flying in a small plane?"

"She gets anxious about traveling."

"You sure you want to go tonight? It's going to be a bumpy ride, but I'm ready for takeoff."

Sarah Beth pushed air through clenched teeth. "I'm good. Let's go." She sat motionless with her face tucked into Jess's shirt as the engines bellowed. The plane taxied down the runway, her stomach lurching the whole way.

Strong arms tightened around her as they took flight. "Tell me what you're thinking, Sarah Beth. Maybe I can help you replace bad thoughts with good ones."

Ugh. Her thoughts did need replacing. "I see myself as a little animal trapped in a flying tin can, and I want to scratch my way out, run back home, and hide."

"That wouldn't be good for any of us at this height."

"You asked."

"Kind of wish I hadn't now, but let's think about how we can replace it." He paused and rubbed her back. "Maybe picture yourself as a Canadian goose soaring in a V formation with your family, the feel of the wind beneath your wings."

"A goose bit me at a petting zoo in Florida, and I've never liked them since."

"How about this? We're on our second honeymoon. We're on the way to Ireland to where the McCoy clan originated. We can see the land beneath our plane, green with rolling hills." He shifted around and lifted her chin up. "I hold your face like this, and then I kiss you like..."

Though her eyes were shut tight, she felt his lips brush hers. Softly at first. Then deeper. Maybe this was working. A little. The sounds of the plane and the wind faded.

When at last he let her go, she opened her eyes and gave him a partial smile. "That wasn't really a visual."

"Part of it was." His mischievous brown eyes locked on her own.

The plane jolted, but she swallowed back the fear. "Do you really want to visit Ireland?"

"Definitely. We could go to France first, if you'd rather, and look up the LeClair ancestry. Any place with you." He pulled her close again.

"If only Mark..." Her brother had to be okay.

Jess pushed her hair back from her face. "He's strong. He'll make it."

~~~

While they waited for David at the Biloxi airport, Sarah Beth took deep inhales and exhales like her counselor had taught her. With each breath her chest trembled, her tight muscles refusing to release their hold.

"Let's pray while we wait." Jess took her hand and squeezed. "God, heal Mark, and please keep us covered with Your protection. Calm Sarah Beth's heart and mind." He kissed her palm before letting it go.

Sarah Beth studied him. If only she could absorb his courage.

Moments later, a hulking dark-skinned man with closely shaven hair approached. "Sarah Beth? You made good time getting down here." David's large hand grasped Sarah Beth's shoulder. "I remember Mark's kid sister who tried to go everywhere with him. Funny thing was, he let you." His deep voice lowered. "I'm sorry to see you again under these conditions, but I'm praying we'll have good news soon. I have my prayer warriors on it."

They entered the sedan. Her hands shook, and her heart drummed in her ears. As they headed out of the lot, Sarah Beth fidgeted with the handle of her bag. The air seemed stale, and her head swam. She lay back against the seat. *Not Mark, too. Please, God.*

The overcast sky and fog helped as they pulled onto the main road. The less she saw, the better.

At first she wrapped her arms around herself, then shifted and pulled her blue handbag into her lap and rummaged through it.

Though the roads were flat, her stomach twisted as if she were riding a monstrous roller coaster. Her heart rate accelerated, and she covered her eyes, turning away from the car door.

Jess squeezed her hand. "Don't jump out or anything. We're fine, and we're together. We got this."

Minutes passed as David raced through the low-lying streets. Her heart kept up the thrashing against her chest. He glanced at her. "Girl, you're shaking my whole car with your knees bouncing against the seat like that. Don't worry. We're almost there."

"Oh, right. Sorry." But it was taking forever. She felt as though she could run to the hospital faster. Or back to Oxford. Her feet refused to quit tapping, and her clenched fists shook.

At last the massive red brick hospital loomed before them. "There it is." Sarah Beth unhitched her seatbelt as David pulled near the emergency entrance. As soon as he hit the brakes, she sprang from her seat and out of the car, sprinting for the glass double doors.

~~~

Jess ran after Sarah Beth as she rushed down the sidewalk. Bits of conversation drifted from pedestrians along the dark street. Drizzle soaked the cool air while white lights created a cheery glow in contrast to the worry enveloping him. Not the way he thought the night would end. One minute he'd been ecstatic about the celebration of his engagement, and then the next, their world reversed. Somehow, no matter what, he'd protect Sarah Beth through all of this. She didn't deserve any more grief.

Chapter 45

At the window, Sarah Beth obtained Mark's location, ran in, and swept back the blue curtain dividing the area. The empty hospital bed brought her to her knees.

"He's not here."

Jess kneeled down beside her. "Probably running tests. Come sit down."

The wrenching in her midsection tightened up a notch with the antiseptic smell and the moans coming from behind another curtain.

His arm encircled her, giving her strength. "David stopped to find out Mark's status."

Forty-five of the longest minutes ever passed before David approached with a doctor beside him.

"Are you family of Mark LeClair?"

Sarah Beth scrambled to her feet. "I'm his sister. Where is he? What's happened to him?"

"We cleaned and stitched his gunshot wound. Luckily, it missed the bone. He's bruised and sore from a fall, but overall, doing exceptionally well. I'd say he's a lucky man."

"Thank you, God." Sarah Beth lifted both hands.

"We'll move him into a regular room as soon as possible. There's a waiting area down the hall to the left. I'll have the nurse at the desk let you know when he's settled in."

"Thank you, Doctor."

More waiting, but the news had been good. Sarah Beth repeated silent *thank-yous* to the Lord over and over while a television droned on about how to redecorate on a budget. Jess and David talked football and the latest news, but she couldn't concentrate on either.

An hour later, the nurse sent them down a maze of tan walls and fluorescent lighting.

David pointed. "Here's the miracle boy, now."

An orderly rolled a groggy Mark into the small room as they approached. He reached out his hand to Sarah Beth. "You're here?"

"Yes." She brushed his dark curly hair from his forehead. "Of course I'm here."

Mark's heavy eyelids closed again.

David clasped Sarah Beth's shoulder. "God's at work. Mark looks good."

The doctor appeared in the doorway. "You may be right. He should be able to go home in a couple of days."

Sarah Beth squinted her eyes and studied the long-faced doctor. "He's not going to be able to drive home, is he?"

"Not with his shoulder injury. He'll have significant pain. One of you should plan to drive him."

"Can he fly?"

"The risk of blood clots makes flying out of the question." He made a note on an electronic pad and turned back toward the door. "I'll check on him again in the morning."

A sinking feeling tore at Sarah Beth's gut, but she pushed it away. Mark would need a ride and someone to take care of him until Holly returned from the cruise. And she knew what had to happen. After the doctor left, Sarah Beth turned to Jess. "You should fly home now. You have practice in the morning, and I know how important the bowl game is to your career."

"You are more important than any career."

"I love you, too, but…" She swallowed back the boulder

in her throat. "I need to... I'll drive Mark to my house."

"What?" Mark's eyes fluttered opened, his voice scratchy. "Am I still on the coast?"

Sarah Beth let out a small laugh. "This was some big plan to get me to leave Oxford, right?"

Mark gave her a weak smile. "It worked."

His pallid complexion and the IV in his hand left him looking so frail, so human. He'd always seemed so solid and strong. Larger than life.

As Mark drifted off to sleep, Sarah Beth joined Jess on the plastic couch. "Call the pilot and see if he can take you. You've practiced with me, I've been taking the medicine the doctor prescribed. We'll make it back."

"Are you sure?"

No. Yes. Maybe. "Positive."

Jess pulled her into his arms and kissed her. "I am so proud of my girl." He held up her chin. "Beautiful and strong. You did what you had to do by coming down here. Hire a driver, phone a friend, but whatever you do, make it back up to Oxford. And to me. You hear?" He planted a kiss on Sarah Beth's forehead as he had done so many times before. "I love you."

"I miss you already, Jess McCoy."

Chapter 46

At least she'd slept a few hours. Sarah Beth lay motionless on the couch trying not to disturb Mark. His chest rose and fell under the white sheet. Strands of dark curls stuck to his forehead, and he needed a shave. Holly would have a duck when she found out he'd been shot. How did she manage the anxiety of having a husband in such a dangerous profession?

Mark shifted his weight and groaned.

After pushing to her feet, Sarah Beth stepped to his side. "How do you feel?"

"Like I took a bullet, fell at least twenty feet, and miraculously lived." His weak voice was raspy.

"I think you've earned the privilege of being called the needy sibling now."

David stepped through the door carrying two white sacks. "I see Sleeping Beauty awoke."

"Very funny, my friend." Mark smirked, but worry crinkled his forehead. "I'd shake your hand or hug you, but my shoulder hurts too much. Anyone else injured in the pursuit?"

David kinked his neck from side to side. "I have a tension headache and could use a massage."

"Advil and a gift card, on me."

David passed Sarah Beth the smaller of the two bags. "Jess told me that you might need some of these."

She looked in the sack. "Yay, sour gummy worms. Thank you."

"The other bag has a couple of shrimp po'boys. You can't

come to the coast without at least a little real food." A grin filled the big man's face.

Mark shook his head. "My little sister wouldn't want to miss the grub."

"Oh, and I had your vehicle brought up here for when you're released."

Sarah Beth's stomach plunged. The vehicle she'd have to drive six hours north to get back to Oxford. Perspiration coated her palms at the thought.

~~~

Dread filled Sarah Beth as she pulled Mark's SUV around to the hospital entrance. An orderly wheeled him to the door. Watching out for his shoulder, Sarah Beth helped him navigate the seatbelt.

Mark patted her hand. "Thanks for taking care of me."

"I owed you big-time."

Sarah Beth pulled out of the lot, listening to the drone of her electronic navigator's voice. Her pulse was normal. But how long would it last? Where would they be when panic took over? The SUV bounced forward as she hit a huge bump.

Mark let out a muffled groan.

"Sorry."

"You can't help a pothole in the road." He pointed at an empty lot. "So much was flooded or destroyed in Katrina. Some people never rebuilt."

She accelerated into the lane. Her fingers squeezed the steering wheel. Cars sped by. *Concentrate on the pickup in front of me.*

Mark punched on the radio which had Christian music primed. "You want to sing, Sarah Beth?"

Maybe singing would help. "At the top of our lungs. Dad loved to sing, didn't he? We used to sing on all our road trips."

"Oh yeah. We could've been like the Von Trapp family. The Jonas brothers." Mark tried to snap his fingers on his good side and wiggled, then groaned.

"It troubles me that you tried to dance like that."

She turned up the volume and belted out the words to worship songs as they turned onto Highway Forty-nine doing the speed limit. Two eighteen-wheelers pulled up beside her. And stayed.

"Really, guys? Can't you move on? Oh my stars." She had to get back home, and she couldn't do five hours of this.

Chest tightened. Face numb. Not good.

"You're doing fine." Mark's deep voice soothed her. A little.

Sarah Beth continued north, and a quiet snore escaped Mark's throat. Leafless trees, like skeletons pointing aimlessly, lined a swampy strip of road. The swamp turned into forests of pine trees and fields littered with cattle and old barns. But the ride was getting old fast. She sang with the radio, counting the songs.

Every song brings me closer to Jess.

As they neared the more urban area outside of Jackson, a tingly sensation traveled from her hands across her chest. The road seemed to mock her. Her abs tightened.

Oh, come on. Why can't this go away?

The traffic became heavier. Her palms perspired. Why was it so hot? She jerked the air-conditioner knob to high and adjusted the vents. Crud. She wheeled into the last gas station before they reached the interstate and parked.

Mark woke with a start. "Where are we?"

"Jackson. I need a break."

"Do you want me to drive?"

"Don't be ridiculous."

"We could get a hotel and spend the night."

She hit the steering wheel. Harder than she'd meant to. "I'm going to find a way to drive these last three hours home to Oxford and Jess." She rubbed her hand. "While you were sleeping, I passed a cross beside the road covered with red flowers. I got to thinking, would I even know the spot on the highway where Adam died? Should I go and put a marker there?"

"Sarah Beth, I can't imagine losing Holly the way that you lost Adam. I'd rather take a bullet any day. And if it were little Drew, you'd just have to lock me up in a padded room."

"Adam was such a beautiful person. If only I'd been living my faith when I met him."

"Don't you dare do that to yourself. The apostle Paul said, 'Forgetting what is behind, and striving toward what is ahead, I press on to the goal...' No one is sinless, but by the grace of God, we are saved. I know that a part of you will always mourn his loss, but let the guilt go. Adam wouldn't want you to feel that way. You don't need a marker. The clinic and the chapel are his legacy."

"You're smart—for a brother." She picked up her bag. "I'm running in the store to get a snack and a cup of coffee. You want something?"

"I'll come with you. I need to stretch my legs."

As they exited the Quick Stop, Sarah Beth motioned over her shoulder. "When we get in, set the GPS to avoid the interstate."

Mark opened his mouth, then closed it.

Sarah Beth held the door for Mark and waited until he'd climbed in. She helped him with his seatbelt, then went back to the driver's seat. "You know, today, I was thinking about the last time we saw Mom and Dad. When I think of that day, pulling out of the driveway, I see them in slow motion waving goodbye to us."

Mark popped open a drink. "That's strange. Me, too."

A sour gummy worm slid down her throat almost whole. "It was like that the day of the wreck. Slow motion. I could see it coming, but couldn't stop it."

"It's like time slows down in those big moments in our lives."

She turned the key and put the SUV in reverse. "I'd like for the world to slow down, now that I found Jess—after this drive, of course."

Mark laughed. "Wait till you have kids. Then things really accelerate."

Straightening her posture, she eased out on the highway. "I'm not sure I'm ready for that. I mean, Jess says we can have how ever many children I want, but I'm scared."

"You'll make a fantastic mom. The fun mom all the kids like. They'll be flocking to hang out at your house."

She allowed herself to imagine it, children filling her living room, pitter-pattering across her front porch. "I like the sound of that."

They rode in silence until well past Jackson. Mark drifted back to sleep. How, she couldn't imagine. Her hands ached from clenching her fingers around the steering wheel. Her insides remained shaky, even though they'd been on the road for hours.

Mark shifted with a groan. "What are you thinking about now?"

"Pulling off the road. Running and screaming."

"Little sister, you scare me."

"I know. Go back to sleep. I just need to keep my foot on the gas and steer. Not hard. Me and God." She hummed praise tunes and kept going.

Two hours later, Mark lifted his shoulders.

"We're near the home stretch." She pointed to the road sign ahead. "I've practiced driving this highway with Jess."

"Thank you, Lord."

"Hey, you know I did a good job, buster."

"Yeah, I was the one who taught you to drive."

"Mark, do you think you should try to contact Holly?"

Mark shook his head. "I'm doing fine, so I'll wait until they debark. No sense making her freak out when there's nothing she can do. Besides, I've got you to take care of me."

"Yes, you do. I get to help you for once."

"And I plan to be high maintenance." Mark snickered, then picked up his phone. "I'll call and give your fiancé our ETA."

While Mark and Jess talked, she glanced at her engagement ring. Her heart filled with warmth. *Lord, help me be thankful for every ordinary day. These chaotic ones make me long for normal. Please help me to be a loving wife to Jess. Oh, and thank You for saving Mark.*

Mark's voice interrupted her prayers. "Earth to Sarah Beth."

"Sorry. I was praying, and I thought you were still talking to Jess."

"I hope you were praying with your eyes open. Jess said he'd be waiting on your porch."

Her heart thumped hard as they crossed into the city limits. "Look! We're back to Oxford. I did it."

"You sure did. Good job."

"I'll race you to the porch when we get out."

Mark laughed. "Uh, no. Even if I weren't injured, I might be trampled to death."

Sarah Beth pulled into the driveway and put the SUV in park. Jess and Gingie stood waiting. "I'll be back to help you in a sec."

Mark smiled. "I can wait."

She threw open the door to the SUV and ran down the sidewalk. Gingie leapt toward her. "Whoa." Sarah Beth held up her hand, but there was no stopping the mutt. She braced for impact.

"Gingie, I missed you, too."

Mark heaved himself from the vehicle. "So much for beating me to the door." He gave Jess a salute. "She did it. I'm here in one piece."

"She is amazing." In an instant, Jess's arms encircled her, and his lips met hers.

She was home.

When he released her, she sighed. "I can hardly believe this is real."

Jess chuckled. "I am the real McCoy."

"That was bad. You've said that before, no doubt."

"It's funny to me every time."

"I love you, Jess."

"Hey, Sarah Beth, I love you, too, but God loves you more."

Chapter 47

Sarah Beth peeked into the sanctuary packed with football players, coaches, church members, clients, and a good many McCoy cousins who had traveled to the wedding. Bryan played acoustic Irish love songs on his guitar. Time for the bridesmaids to make their entrance.

Mark handed Sarah Beth her bouquet. "You nervous, baby sister?"

Sarah Beth looked down at her feet. "As long as I don't trip in these shoes, I'm good."

Mark took her arm in his. "That's what I wanted to hear. If you trip, you can blame it on me."

"I would've done that anyway."

~~~

Bryan sang "The Water is Wide" as Jess escorted his new wife back down the aisle. His wife. He glanced at her. Wow. She *was* stunning.

Sarah Beth pointed. "There's Bill and Carol. And Juan made it."

A horse and buggy carried them around the Square and down the street to the reception. He exited first and then offered his arms to his wife to help her from the carriage. His players, Cole Sanders and Grant Vaughn, held open the doors for them. At least those two got along when it counted. White lights, poinsettias, and greenery transformed the CSU. Sarah Beth had performed another of her miracles.

Jess laughed as they worked their way around the room full

of guests. "Here come more of my cousins. What'd I tell you?"

"I wouldn't have believed it if I hadn't seen it with my own eyes. I hope they aren't planning to stay with us...especially the one with the harmonica."

He held her gaze. "We won't be home tonight, so we don't have to worry."

"Oh my stars, I forgot."

Jess squeezed her close. "I most definitely have not forgotten."

She was blushing again. Then her eyes bore into his. "It was only a momentary slip. Trust me."

Was he blushing now? His face smoldered all the way to his ears.

~~~

"Did someone say honeymoon?" Juan embraced Sarah Beth, then Bill and Carol followed suit.

Sarah Beth wiped a tear that spilled down her cheek. "Juan, I can't believe you made it. I thought there was no way."

"I wanted to be here." His head pointed to Bill. "And you have the kind of boss that made it possible. God is good. The church has opened its doors. I can't wait for you to come and visit when you are ready."

"I look forward to that too, Juan. I will come. One day, soon."

Juan turned to Jess. "Where will you spend your honeymoon?"

"I rented a cottage on the lake, and the caterers stocked it with delicious gourmet food. I won't have to cook, and we won't have to leave the cabin for two days unless we want to go for a walk by the lake."

The photographer waved for them to come to the other side of the room.

Juan grinned. "Go on. Enjoy your celebration."

"I love you, Juan. You too, Bill and Carol."

She touched her hands to Jess's clean-shaven cheeks. "I will enjoy celebrating Christmas with my husband. I love saying that. My husband." She ran her fingers along his jawline. "So smooth. I love it, but you look really young."

"Now you see why I keep the five o'clock shadow." His eyes focused on her. "How soon can we leave our party and start our honeymoon?"

Sarah Beth held his gaze. A profound sense of home washed over her. "I'll go toss this bouquet. You tell Mark to let the limo driver know we're leaving Oxford."

Don't miss the next book in the series.

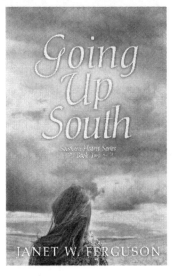

Going Up South

No one told him he had a son.

Actor Dylan Conner is furious. Not only has he been left out of his child's life, the baby boy has been given another man's last name. Determined to be a better father than the sorry guy who'd left him and his mother, Dylan fights to ensure a significant place in his son's life. Unfortunately, his bad-boy reputation overshadows his good intentions. Only one woman in this small town sees beyond his

Hollywood image. And he's falling for her. Too bad she's the custody mediator.

After her scandalous divorce in the small town of Oxford, Mississippi, attorney Cassie Brooks has no intentions of practicing law again. The humiliating experience left a bitter taste for love, marriage, and her profession.

Now friends need Cassie's help in a custody negotiation, and her role demands she remain objective. She never expected to be drawn to Dylan Conner—the actor who everyone warns is bad news. Not only is the mediation at stake, but so is her heart.

Dear Reader

Thank you for your time and resources you spent on this little book. My one desire is that you know God loves you more than you can ask or imagine. He can use you in your weakness. He can use you wherever you are, whatever you're going through.

Blessings in Him who is able!

Did you enjoy this book? I hope so!
Would you take a quick minute to leave a review online? It doesn't have to be long. Just a sentence or two telling what you liked about the book.

About the Author

Faith, Humor, Romance
Southern Style

Janet W. Ferguson grew up in Mississippi and received a degree in Banking and Finance from the University of Mississippi. She served her church as a children's minister and a youth volunteer. An avid reader, she worked as a librarian at a large public high school. She and her husband have two children, one really smart dog, and four too many cats.

https://www.facebook.com/Janet.Ferguson.author
http://www.janetfergusonauthor.com/under-the-southern-sun
https://www.pinterest.com/janetwferguson/
https://twitter.com/JanetwFerguson

Publisher's Note: This book is a work of fiction. Names,
characters, any resemblance to persons, living or dead, or
events is purely coincidental. The characters and incidents
are the product of the author's imagination and used
fictitiously. Locales and public names are sometimes used
for atmospheric purposes.

Oxford, Mississippi, is a real town, but other than the
name, the events in the location are fictional. None of the
events are based on actual people. The charming city made
the perfect backdrop for a novel and a wonderful place for
my character to run home.